THE RIDE INTO TOMORROW

WRITTEN BY

DOUGLAS R. GRAY

Order this book online at www.trafford.com
or email orders@trafford.com

Most Trafford titles are also available at major online book retailers.

Note for Librarians: A cataloguing record for this book is available from Library and Archives Canada at www.collectionscanada.ca/amicus/index-e.html

Printed in Victoria, BC, Canada.

ISBN: 978-1-4269-1646-5 (soft)
ISBN: 978-1-4269-1647-2 (hard)

Library of Congress Control Number: 2009935800

Our mission is to efficiently provide the world's finest, most comprehensive book publishing service, enabling every author to experience success. To find out how to publish your book, your way, and have it available worldwide, visit us online at www.trafford.com

Trafford rev. 10/19/2009

North America & international
toll-free: 1 888 232 4444 (USA & Canada)
phone: 250 383 6864 • fax: 812 355 4082

CHAPTER ONE

Rega had room for one more earth specimen. She was from the planet Arian of the Crygon star system and was searching for a specific creature. Two days were spent patrolling the western coast of North America. She finally found what she had been looking for, a female Bottle-nosed Dolphin preparing to give birth. Rega set the controls of the IV-208 (Interstellar Vehicle 208) to track and hover. This had to be fast. She was at the western edge of the coastal ADIZ (American Defense Identification Zone), and wanted no American aircraft coming after her. Rega'd had American airships chase her before. Going to the cryogenic room, located in the center of the ship, where specimens are encased and frozen for later resuscitation. She took one of the two remaining capsules out, readying it for its new occupant. Going to the compartment which housed duplicate consoles and panels for the tractor, radar and heat seeking beams, she could also control the ship from here in an emergency. She felt the ship dive, then level off. The ship was at approximately thirty-five thousand feet. Low enough for beaming, yet high enough to escape if needed. Rega would have liked to get closer to her prey, but safety came first.

A red triangle appeared in the center of the screen. She had lock on. The female dolphin was just giving birth. When the infant was clear of the mother, she would engage the tractor beam and bring it up.

Out of the corner of her eye she saw a red light blinking. Danger.... something was approaching the craft at a high rate of speed. No warning. Was something wrong with the defense system? Rega switched the radar, with the heat-seeking beam, in that direction. It could not be a missile, there was a life form on board. Before Rega could react, the aircraft struck the star ship on the port side, aft. With the outboard cameras on Rega could see the aircraft come apart. Pieces were flying in all directions. The heat-seeking beam had locked onto the life form. It was falling back, toward the planet. With seconds left to work with, Rega switched the tractor beam to the life form. Locking on, brought it on board.

The pilot's body had been severely damaged. Rega placed the human on the examining table and striped him. There were many broken bones. The right arm had a compound fracture. Rega turned on the scanner, checking the body for internal damage. No damage, good. She went into a storage room and reactivated a robot, which had been beamed aboard many years before. Rega connected the robot to the visual monitor. Having no knowledge of the human body, she would need the help of this robot. Not knowing the safety procedures of hospital operating rooms and really not caring, Rega set to work. While setting bones and sewing up wounds, she had nicked herself several times. Finally, the job was done. All internal organs were functioning properly. The skeletal structure was correct. He was placed in a cryogenic capsule. When the healing process was done, she would disconnect the life support systems then turn the capsule on.

CHAPTER TWO

The man awoke with a start. His eyes slowly adjusted. He was in a mist of some type. Slowly, he checked his body, moving his fingers, then his arms, toes, knees and legs. Everything is working. He wondered. Why am I doing this? He lay there trying to put this straight in his mind. Who am I? Dirk Conal MacGlashan. Call sign, Scotty. Everything fell into place, his life, Nancy, his daughter Marnie. All of these thoughts went screaming through his mind. What had taken place on the last day of his life?

Bolting to an upright position, his head struck something, knocking him back onto his elbows. He lay back down. Raising his arms he felt something similar to the canopy of a jet fighter enclosing him. What in the bloody hell is going on here? He pushed against it, trying to open it. Dirk slid his hands along the sides searching for a release handle, nothing. He struck the top and sides, trying to knock it loose. How do I get out of here? He heard a faint whirring noise, like a small fan. The mist cleared. This is a capsule. Hearing clicking sounds, the top opened upward. Sitting up, Dirk looked around with extreme interest.

This is definitely not the cockpit of an F14. Dirk saw a circular room, approximately thirty-five feet in diameter. He could see no one. Swinging his legs over the side he started to stand, he heard a metallic monotone voice ask, "How do you feel?"

Dirk looked in the direction of the voice. Only no one was there, at least, not human. He saw a robot. If that's what you could call it. It looked like a very large trash can with three legs, small rubber tires for maneuvering around on. Two arms, similar to a round two and a half-foot accordion, one finger like appendage and a pair of pincers on each.

"Well, who are you?" Dirk asked. Looks like something from TV's 'Lost in Space'.

"SCANER" was the reply.

"Big question. Where am I?"

"You are in an interstellar craft. Do you require clothing?"

Looking at himself he realized all he was wearing was a smile. "Yes"

SCANER went into a storage room, moved to a panel and pushed a button. A door opened and he retrieved a flight suit. Dirk inspected the garment. It's mine. Over the left breast pocket was a small leather patch printed with the following. MacGlashan, D. C. LCDR, U.S.N., imposed over this, a set of Naval Aviator wings in gold. After putting this on he knelt down and looked at the metal nameplate located on the top front of this small robot. It read: S.C.An.E.R., Self-contained, Analytical, Electrical, Robot. Prototype #1, N.A.S.A., Cape Canaveral, Fla. U.S.A. well thought Dirk, that explains who you are and how you got your name.

"How did you get here?" Dirk asked.

"I was taken on board 5 July 1959, then put into storage."

"You've been here for twenty-five years?"

"I have been on this spacecraft for forty of your years" replied the robot "This is 20 Sept 1999"

This is impossible, thought Dirk. Doing some fast figuring. I am now forty-six years old, no way!

"I am thirty-one years old, I was born Feb. 1, 1953 and today is Aug. 10th 1984"

"After your operations and all your bones knitted properly, you were placed in cryogenic. I started to revive you two days ago when Rega died."

"Rega, who's Rega? And what do you mean, 'You were placed in cryogenic'?"

"Rega was the operator of this craft. You were frozen."

"Whoa, frozen?"

***

Sitting down Dirk started thinking through the events of that last day or whenever he had last been on Earth. The painful remembering of that last day on earth.

He had risen at 4:30am, had breakfast with Nancy, at 5:00am kissed his daughter, Marnie, goodbye as she lay sleeping. He had a 7:00am take off scheduled at N.A.S. Merimar. The squadron would be doing A.C.M. (Aerial Combat Maneuvers) that day.

***

He had landed at 10:15 am. The plane captain relayed a message to him. Report to the Squadron Commander A.S.A.P. When he entered the CO's office and saw the Base Chaplain, he instinctively knew something devastating had happened. The C.O. informed him Nancy and Marnie had been killed in an accident at approximately 7:30am. Nancy had been taking Marnie to school when another car ran a stop sign. Nancy died instantly. Marnie died at the hospital.

***

In a state of shock, anguish and rage, he walked to the flight line and then down to the end of the ramp. Without really realizing what he had done, he had gotten back into his aircraft. Against all of the rules and regulations he had lived by for the past thirteen years. He took off for what would be considered an unauthorized flight. Dirk remembered taking off and putting the F14 Tomcat into a 35-degree climb, afterburners on the whole time. Climbing straight out, not caring or thinking, just going as fast as the aircraft could go. These were the chain of events, which would change his life forever.

***

Approaching thirty-five thousand feet somewhere out over the Pacific, the reality and enormity of what he had done struck home. Dirk, in the process of leveling off and coming about, saw a movement out of the corner of his eye. Looking to his extreme left, he saw a strange saucer shaped craft coming toward him. His natural instinct was to pull to the right and down. Before his body could react to the message his brain sent, there was a tremendous crash. His last thoughts were of Nancy and Marnie. Yet here he was alive. What had happened?

Dirk looked at Scaner. "What happened? I struck something. I was flying and I struck something."

"Rega was in the process of transporting a new born mammal from the ocean to a holding capsule, when you struck this craft. She changed the beam to you and brought you onboard. The extent of your injuries was such that I was reactivated. I have been programmed in human anatomy. I was hooked up to a video projector. She did the reconstruction to your body. You have a few scars because of the damage to your body. You were placed in a cryogenic capsule to recuperate. When you healed I activated the capsule."

"Ok, where is this Rega now?" Dirk asked.

Scaner moved over to a panel on the wall of the room, pushed another button. A panel opened, Dirk could see another capsule, like the one that he had been put in. This one was in an upright position. The mist clouded Dirk's vision. "How do you clear this mist away?"

Scaner moved to push the correct series of buttons but Dirk stopped him.

"Show me how this is done. If you and I are the only two here, I'm going to have to learn all I can about this craft."

Scaner moved to a projection screen, plugged in and the correct steps were shown on the screen. Dirk pushed the buttons and the mist cleared. What he saw was a very slender form that looked almost human. The Arian, Rega, was about five feet tall. Her head was different from ours in a couple of ways. The forehead was very much more pronounced. Her ears were much smaller than a human, and lower on her head. The hairline started at the back of the head. Where one might think she was bald. Her body, although fully clothed, was very slight, very petite, almost frail looking. She had all the curves and bumps of a human female.

Dirk wondered what type of person she had been, good-natured or what? Being cooped up in this craft alone for any length of time might tend to make anyone a little grumpy.

"How did she die? Better yet, what did she die of? Do you know?"

"She died of an acute case of Asian Flu. When brought on board you had the first stages or symptoms of the virus. Although she had inoculations for most of the diseases she would encounter on Earth, this virus was not one of them."

"It took her fifteen years to die of the flu?" Dirk asked

"At the speed we are traveling, a month and a half is almost equal to fifteen years."

Dirk stated his squadron was going on a WesPac (Western Pacific), cruise and they had just gotten their shots updated. After thinking about what Scaner said and if the time was right, his squadron had been to WesPac many, many times since he took that last flight. That is, if there's a WesPac left. It is hard to comprehend fifteen years in a capsule, literally frozen.

"Are you all right?" asked Scaner.

Startled, Dirk shook himself, "Yes, I'm okay, just a blast from the past."

"A blast from the past?" questioned Scaner.

"Just a saying from the 80's. Now, what or where are we heading at?"

"The control room is this way". Scaner moved toward an amber light on the wall of the room, he reached up and touched it. A panel opened and they went into another room. The walls of this room were completely filled with panels of dials, gauges, small print out tapes and monitor screens. A half circle desk located in the center with a high back chair. A chair made for sitting in for long periods of time. The desk had instrument panels, which stood, at a 45-degree angle on each side, leaving the front open. The desktop had levers and gauges imbedded in it.

This has to be where the pilot sits. Dirk thought.

Scaner went to a control panel and again plugged himself in. A section, at least ten feet across, opened, showing a large screen. The screen came to life.

"Wow!" exclaimed Dirk.

What he saw before him were stars, moving at a tremendous rate of speed. No, not stars moving, we're moving, at a tremendous rate of speed. Man, this mother could out drag a Chevy

Sitting in the pilot chair, he promptly got back up. Way to small. These folks must take their own chairs with them when they change craft thought Dirk. He looked at Scaner.

"This needs adjusting." Dirk mused.

"Sit down. To your left is a panel cover which slides up." Scaner said.

Dirk sat down and slid the panel open, finding eight toggle switches. He touched one and the chair moved forward. Soon he had the chair adjusted. There were two lighted finger panels on the bottom, he pushed one and the chair moved back to its original shape. He pushed the other and it went back to his shape. Not bad, a smart seat.

Dirk scanned the panels and gauges in front of him, all had very strange lettering he could not understand. These have got to be translated. thought Dirk. You can't start pushing buttons. Just to see what would happen.

"Are there any manuals on the systems for this craft?"

"In the panel directly behind you." replied Scaner.

Dirk went to the panel and touched the button, which opened it, there where six shelves of very thick manuals there. <u>This will take me the rest of my life.</u> Picking one out he opened it, no help there, it needed to be translated.

"Scaner, is there a way to translate these into English?" asked Dirk.

"Yes, take the manual to the next panel and open it. There is an automatic page finder. Also a system for translating to any dialect the Arians have come into contact with."

Dirk set the manual on the shelf and then slid the shelf back into the panel, set the machine to English and waited. Nothing happened. He looked around. A huge panel opened directly in front of the desk. There was the projection of the manual. He sat back down at the desk. To his right another section lit up. He touched the arrow right light and the manual opened to the glossary. As he started to go through systems, his stomach growled, telling him it was time to eat.

"There has got to be a galley on this ship" he mused.

"There is a galley on the other side of the cryogenic compartment." replied Scaner.

"Let's go." Dirk said, and led the way through the capsule room, as he now thought of it.

***

He went to the portside wall and touched another amber light, the door opened and he walked into the sleeping quarters for the crew. Set up for two people. Very adequate for resting in, two large beds, a desk with a computer and monitor. Probably for the ships systems and personal items. He went to another wall and touched the amber light. This time he got the galley.

"Okay, Scaner let's see the menu."

Scaner went over to the view screen and touched a switch and an array of items showed. Nothing he had ever seen.

"Translate this to English, Scaner."

The screen went blank, for a few seconds and all the items showed up in English. Even then he did not recognize anything. The items were numbered one through three, with sub titles a,b,c etc. I guess #1 is breakfast. Two must be lunch and so forth. Dirk pressed the #1 and then subtitle a. A panel opened, a cup of coffee with powdered milk and sugar on the side was there. The tray they were sitting on slid out. The panel closed but the light was still on. Dirk sat down at the table and enjoyed the first cup of coffee he had in years. I can't get over the years part. This is going to be tough to deal with. Although he felt that he had been here only a day. He had really been here for fifteen years? How come I don't feel any older? How come my beard isn't growing? He unconsciously felt his chin and cheeks. His whiskers had grown a little, like he had not shaved for a day. As he sat there thinking, a light started blinking. He went over to the wall and pressed the switch. The panel opened and there was breakfast. Two eggs sunny side up, three strips of bacon, crisp. Toast with a buttery substance along side. Everything was delicious. Dirk didn't wonder how old the eggs were until he was finished eating. Well, I don't feel like I'm going to get rid of them, so I won't even ask. Finishing his second cup of coffee he thought. Now for the rest of the ship.

He put his empty dishes on the tray a voice asked. "Did you enjoy your meal?"

Without thinking Dirk replied, "Yes, Thank you". Dirk almost jumped out of his skin when he realized he had been asked a question from someone. "Who are you?" No answer. "Who are you?" Still no answer.

"It is an automated voice. When you order breakfast again and ask for subtitle a, that will be the way you get the order of food. If you want to change how your meal is prepared, push this button. You can request how you want it prepared." Scaner said.

"Can the voice be changed to a female rather than male?" Dirk asked.

"Yes. As soon as we get back to the control room, I can do this. Why do you ask?"

"Well, back home, most of the fictitious space programs on TV have a very sexy feminine voice. All right, let's go through the ship now." stated Dirk.

Scaner led the way through another door and they were in another sleeping room. There was one large bed. Queen size, this ought to fit me. Dirk started to push buttons and panels opened up showing clothing, one held bathroom supplies. One door led to a bathroom with a shower stall. Sliding back a panel over the washstand, he found feminine articles. These have got go

"Are there any other sleeping quarters?"

"No, there are only the two." replied Scaner.

"I'm going to put these items in storage, and use this as my sleeping quarters." Dirk stated. "Let's continue through the ship." Scaner led the way out and they were back in the capsule room, Dirk motioned Scaner to follow him. Dirk went to the next door and opened it. They were back on the flight deck. Dirk now had a mental picture of how the ship was laid out.

He went over to another door. This was a control room of some type.

"What is this room used for?" Dirk asked.

Scaner went to a panel and opened it, Dirk could see into the capsule room.

"This is the transporter station, when turned on, you can pin point an item outside of the ship for over ten miles. The beam can lock on. It then can be brought onboard into the capsule room."

"If something or someone was brought on board alive, how would you be able to control it?" asked Dirk.

"There is a laser which can be used to stun whatever is brought on board." stated Scaner.

"This looks like a storage room too." Dirk said. "Look at the equipment in these compartments." One cage in particular caught his interest. In it were suits, space suits. Not the kind he had seen back on earth, they weren't as bulky and cumbersome looking. He went into the cage and took one off of a hanger looking it over, tried it on. Not quite big enough. He found a larger one. He tried this one on. It stretched a little and then settled to his size. <u>They must have three sizes small, medium and large.</u> <u>Each size molding to the size of the wearer</u> thought Dirk.

"Scaner, plug into the monitor and let's see the instruction manual on this." Dirk said

"Now that all the systems have been converted to read in English, you can do this by yourself." stated Scaner.

"When did this occur?"

"While you were at breakfast. You requested everything be translated to English. I went into the main computer banks and changed all items to English."

As Dirk studied the manual on the space suit Scaner went over to another compartment and came back with some clothing and a pair of boots. He held them out for Dirk.

"Where did these come from?"

"From that compartment." pointed Scaner.

CHAPTER THREE

Dirk went over to storage area Scaner had pointed to. Checking it out Dirk found all types of clothing there, shoes, hats, shirts, pants and suits, all looking as though they had come from earth.

"Where did all these come from?"

"According to the master log, these were taken from humans the Arians had brought up from Earth. Some were later released. But their clothing was kept here." replied Scaner.

"What do you mean some?"

"Not all of the humans survived the experiments."

"Oh my God!" exclaimed Dirk.

"There are remains enclosed in the capsule room." stated Scaner.

"I'm not up to looking at remains right now. This set of clothing did not come from Earth. Are they Arian?"

"This is an Arian interstellar flight suit. It is treated so your body temperature will remain constant."

Dirk took the suit and went back to the sleeping quarters. Trying it on, he found it was quite comfortable to wear. It felt like a second skin. The boots were a stretch type with a soft rubber sole, constructed so you wouldn't slip. Looking at himself in the mirror. I'm still in the U.S. Navy Dirk took the patches off of his flight suit and attached them to this suit, also the gold oak leaves of his rank. Looking again into the mirror he thought. Now I really look like a spaceman. Right out of a TV series. I don't know where in the hell

I'm going, so there ain't no sense in rushing. But at least I'll look the part.

"Let's get back to the flight deck and see where we are going. Where we've been and how far we have to go."

Entering the flight deck Dirk put the navigational chart on the screen.

"We'll be at the home ship in about three weeks. We don't know what to expect when we get there. These people are not overly friendly so what kind of weapons do we have?" Dirk thought aloud.

He found the proper sequence to get into the fire control systems. The laser could be directed and fired manually or automatic. There were twenty thermal torpedoes. Each having settings, which enabled you to control the amount of damage done. Dirk programmed Scaner to be able to operate either of the weapons systems. There were also hand held laser weapons. He checked the selector switch. No stun, just on and off. Dirk thought to himself, These babies are made for killing. Well, that's what my 9mm is for. He had found his original equipment and retrieved his 9mm Navy issue weapon. This was now safely stored in his quarters.

Dirk took one of the lasers to the tool room and dismantled it. The selector switch could be adjusted for stun, which he did. Dirk found six more hand lasers and did the necessary switch over. He set the weapons back in their holders. Noting they were placed for instant access. He felt the ship shudder. Quickly checking the instruments, all appeared normal. The ship shuddered again. A light flashed on the propulsion panel. While he was checking out the system, Scaner plugged himself into the main panel.

"The crystal in the reactor is failing. It needs to be changed." stated Scaner.

"Ok, let's go to the reactor room and do it." I don't know why I said that. I don't know how.

Riding the elevator down to the next deck, Dirk went into the reactor room. A transparent domed enclosure housed the crystal. It was giving off small-multicolored beams of light. According to the manual, this is not the normal pattern for it.

"How do I get into this?" thought Dirk aloud. The manual led him through a very precise routine. Finding the extra crystals, he replaced the old one.

"We're back on the road again." Dirk said

"Is this another 80's saying?" asked Scaner

Dirk laughed. "No, this one's from the 70's."

Dirk and Scaner went back to the fight deck and rechecked the instruments. All were up and running. Dirk got the manual out for the propulsion system and checked the life span out for a crystal. He found they were good for approximately six years. He only had one left in reserve. <u>Wherever that mother ship is I hope they have extras</u>

CHAPTER FOUR

Being out of cryo for five days now, Dirk had a good feeling for the ship. The ships proper name was IV-208, Interstellar Vehicle #208. He renamed her "NanMar" after Nancy and his daughter, Marnie. All of the logs now read this. He had even gone out in the space suit and attached metal placards fore and aft, reading "NANMAR" with U.S.A. printed under the name.

During one of his intelligence gathering forays around the ship, Dirk had discovered a two-man shuttlecraft. It was powered by a smaller crystal propulsion system. The guidance system looked like a yoke from a small plane. It even had a single laser weapon mounted in the nose of the ship. <u>These Arians don't trust anyone. Well, if you were going out into strange country you should carry something bigger than a slingshot.</u> <u>Teddy Roosevelt said it right. "Speak softly but carry a big stick, or something like that"</u> Dirk thought

***

Dirk went back toward the flight deck, through the capsule room. He stopped and looked around at the panels. <u>I have got to check these out. I can't ignore them any longer</u>

Going to the first one to the right of door leading to the flight deck he pushed the open switch. Inside was large ape. From what he could recall it looked like a mountain Gorilla. It had been a male. Its abdominal cavity had been opened. In containers, on shelves beside it, were the remains. Again he had nasty thoughts of these people. He remembered the experiments done on animals back on Earth. We did research for the benefit of mankind. At least that's what I'd like to think. This adds up to pure butchery. He went though the remaining capsules, almost getting physically sick a couple of times at what he saw. My God, thought Dirk what kind of people are these Arians? Why were they cutting up humans and keeping specimens for? What in the hell is going on here?

He had two to go, one was the remains of Rega so he skipped it and went to the last. He opened the panel, this capsule was full of mist. He started the exhaust fan, after the mist dissipated, he just stared.

"My God, she's beautiful." Dirk blurted aloud.

He took the numbers off of the capsule, went to computer in the transporter room. Going into the memory bank. He found the correct series of numbers. Entering them, he found the date, time and location when she had been brought on board. Kathleen Lyn Bucannan, DOB (date of birth) 2 December 1942, tractor beamed 25 August 1972, Three Forks, Montana, 4:00am.

Dirk went to the flight deck, sat in the pilot chair, opened the outer panel and sat there watching the stars go by. Thinking this latest discovery over, he decided to resuscitate her. Well, man can't live on bread alone. Once in awhile company is nice.

Dirk went back into the capsule room. Looking at her, decided.

"Okay Kat, it's time to wake up." He refilled the capsule with mist and then set the series for resuscitation. Every few hours for the next two days Dirk checked on progress of the system. While Dirk slept Scaner monitored the capsule.

***

At 3:00 PM on the second day an alarm rang and a light started to blink. Dirk came from the flight deck and checked the capsule.

Scaner was plugged into the capsule. The mist was drawn out and the lid opened.

The woman's mouth opened and produced a scream such as Dirk had never heard, and she hadn't even opened her eyes. She started to scream again. Dirk covered her mouth with his hand. Her eyes popped wide open, the pupils were slightly dilated. Nice shade of green thought Dirk. Slowly her eyes became focused. Dirk took his hand away from her mouth.

"You're okay, just lay there and do as I say. I want you to move your fingers, now your arms, now try your legs. All right, everything works. Try to sit up?" She did. Dirk had covered her with a sheet and as she sat up he handed her a robe to put on. After she had put on the robe he helped her up. He then took her to the sleeping quarters designed for two.

"This will be your quarters." Dirk said. The woman had not uttered a sound since the scream. Dirk went to the door to the bathroom opened it. Then went to the door to galley. Dirk pointed to the clothes on the bed.

"If they don't fit there are larger sizes."

She sat down on the side of bed and stared at him.

"I know this is quite a shock to you. How you got here. How long you have been here are questions you want to ask." Still the woman sat there staring. Dirk decided he would try to shock her into speaking.

"Your name is Kathleen Lyn Bucannan, DOB 2 December 1942, you were beamed up on 25 August 1972 at 4:00AM near Three Forks, Montana, and this ain't a TV show. Now what do you have to say, Kat?"

"How did you know I'm called Kat?" replied the woman.

"I didn't. I called you that when I read your profile. Tell you what. I'm going to leave so you can get dressed. There's a shower stall in the bathroom. I put all the female things I could find in storage there also. I'll be in the galley getting dinner ready. So when you get ready touch this light and the door will open, okay." Kat nodded.

Dirk was finishing his second cup of coffee when the door opened. Kat stood there looking around the room. Dirk stared at her, auburn hair, green eyes and a figure that filled the Arian space suit out. God, I hope she doesn't have a lousy disposition. Dirk closed the manual he was reading and got up.

"If you'll follow me I'll show you how this galley works." He went over to the selection panel. Offering suggestions as she worked it.

"It's nice to see you're a good eater." Dirk said

"Why do you say that?" asked Kat.

"Well, a lot of women I know don't eat a full breakfast like that, especially since its four thirty in the afternoon. But how were you to know, right?"

While Kat ate her meal, Dirk had a light supper.

"You certainly don't eat very much." stated Kat.

"I usually have a snack in the evening before I go to bed."

"Just where do you sleep, in the other bed?" asked Kat

"No, my room is through there." pointed Dirk. "I usually hit the sack around eleven o'clock in the evening. Do you like ice-cream?"

"Yes, I love it."

"Well, we make the best in the galaxy. You'll have to try some."

He showed her where to put her empty dishes. As she turned back to him a feminine voice asked. "Did you enjoy your meal?"

Kat almost jumped right over Dirk. She spun around looking for a woman. Dirk started to laugh.

"What's so funny?"

"I did the same thing the first time it happened to me, it's automated. If you have any special requests, push this button and you can order anything you'd like. Go ahead, answer her."

"It was fine, thank you." Kat said.

"We are glad you enjoyed your meal."

"Would you like to tour the ship now? Or would you like to sit here and talk for awhile?"

"I would like a tour but one question first. Who are you?"

Dirk told her who he was and how he got to be here. The memories of Nancy and Marnie came flooding back. He shook himself back to reality. Kat looked at him strangely.

"I'm alright, just something private." Dirk stated.

***

Dirk took Kat on the grand tour of the ship, explaining how things ran and what made them run. Their last stop was the exciter room. Kat just stared at the crystal glowing in its enclosure.

"That is the most beautiful diamond I have ever seen."

"How do you know it's a diamond?"

"That's one gem every woman can identify."

"This is quite a dilemma. The manual says they're good for six years. I just replaced one eight days ago and now this one doesn't look so good. Here are the pieces of the one I replaced."

Kat picked up one piece and rubbed it on her sleeve. The dark film rubbed off, Kat held it up to a light. The diamond picked up the light and a cascade of multi-colored lights danced around the room.

"This stone appears almost perfect. Are there any more?"

"Let's look around, maybe there are."

It took them about ten minutes to find a cache of stones.

"What would you guess the value of these stones are, back on Earth?" asked Kat.

"Rough guess, about two million dollars. When we get back to Earth at least we'll have some spending money."

Dirk took Kat to the flight deck. Thinking out loud Dirk said "We're going to have to put a another chair in here."

"Why?" Kat asked.

"That way two of us can run this ship if need be."

They had just finished installing the chair when a red warning light came on.

CHAPTER FIVE

The computer came on automatically, stating there was another ship approaching and would be in firing range in three minutes.

"Kat, strap yourself in and turn on the weapons systems."

Kat sat down but had a bewildered look on her face. She turned on the systems for laser and torpedoes.

"What are you going to do?"

"I'm going to get ready to defend this craft. We don't know who or what is in the other ship. I'm not taking any chances. We've both been through a tough experience and that alone makes me a little jumpy. The people out here have a tendency to act a little irrational. I believe they would rather shoot first and asked questions later." Dirk switched on the comm channel and spoke.

"This is the ship NanMar of the United States of America. Please identify yourself."

No answer. Dirk repeated the message, no answer. They could see the approaching ship on the large view screen. Dirk threw the master-arming switch for the laser weapon. A range and lock on device showed up on the screen. Something similar to the HUD (Heads Up Display) device on his old Tomcat. He told Kat to throw the warm up switch on for the thermal torpedoes.

"Just two. We don't know if it will fire one at a time or all at once."

The red warning light blinked on and off. Dirk could see the other ship firing at them. He maneuvered the ship away from the incoming shot. The other ship adjusted and fired again. This time

Dirk brought the ship around in a tight turn, inverted, and went into a dive. He inverted again and came up, toward the underside of the ship. As he righted the ship he fired. The laser struck the other ship. Literally punching a hole completely through it. As the other ship slowed down, Dirk and Kat could see articles coming out of the ship as air rushed out. The decompression took only seconds. Dirk came up low and from behind to look the ship over.

"Christ, what a rust bucket. Look at all the stuff falling out of it."

Kat spun her chair around. "Why did you do that? You didn't have to kill them. You could have done something else."

"Well, I tried to contact them. Look, I'm not going to sit here and discuss this. Hey, he shot first. That alone says he, she or it was not friendly. He wasn't even a good pilot. We outgunned him with a simple maneuver they teach in the second week of flight school."

"I'm sorry but where I come from I don't see things like this happen. I'm a veterinarian from Montana. We don't have things like this happen."

"Scaner plug in to the main computer and keep us right along side. We're going over to the other ship and check it out."

The tone of his voice said it all. I will be obeyed, and I will answer all questions later. Kat started to get up but still shaken, sat back down. Kat sat looking at Dirk. "I'm alright now, let's go."

Going to the airlock Kat thought to herself. This ain't over yet When we get back to this ship I'm going to give him a piece of my mind Who does he think he is, ordering me around like that. They stopped at the storage compartment, found a suit, which would fit Kat. Dirk showed her how to recharge a rebreather and how to work the small jet blasters so she could move about in space. He tied a line between them and told her to follow him.

***

Going into the airlock Dirk closed the inner door, depressurized and opened the outer door. He motioned her to squat down and push herself through the hatch. The momentum brought them almost half way to the other ship. Dirk gave a short blast, bringing them the rest of the way. The hole from the laser was not big enough to get through. Finding an airlock, Dirk opened the hatch and they entered. As they waited for the outer hatch to close and the inner hatch to open Dirk motioned for her to get behind him.

Dirk untied the rope and handed it to Kat. She had already untied herself. When Dirk handed her the rest of the rope she instinctively tied a loop in the end of it and coiled it. She held the rope in her hand. Stepping out of the air lock, Dirk pulled the 9mm Berretta from a pocket in his suit. He looked to his right, toward the front of the ship. Dirk heard Kat gasp and turned to the left. He saw the rope snake out toward a space suit that was holding a weapon. The space suit reacted, trying to catch the rope. Kat was more accurate. The rope settled over the hand and Kat jerked the rope back toward her. The space suit, pulled off balance, fired toward the ceiling. Dirk spun around and fired twice. The first round caught the space suit in the center of the chest and the second shattered the face covering. Dirk approached the space suit with his weapon pointed toward it. The suit did not move. Dirk reach down, picked up the weapon, handing it to Kat.

He opened the face covering. Whatever it had been was beyond recognition. The sudden exposure to a vacuum had literally exploded the form. He told Kat not to look but she was already looking over his shoulder.

"I've seen cows in worse shape get up and walk home. Well, almost."

Dirk took the weapon from Kat and looked it over. It looked like an old thirty-caliber carbine, similar to the ones used in World War II. Barreled for a smaller caliber, but the clip was bigger. He ejected one of the projectiles and looked it over. It had a small barb on the point and the bottom was hollowed out and a chemical substance was in the shaft.

He reloaded it and gave it to Kat and explained how it worked. He motioned Kat to follow him and they went over to the hole he had made with the laser. He called back to the NanMar. "Scaner, can you hear me?"

"Yes, I can hear you."

"I'm going to fire a shot through the hole the laser made, analyze the projectile and record the ballistics on it."

"I am ready"

Before Dirk could reach for the weapon, Kat stepped up to the hole and raised it her shoulder and fired. It looked like a mini rocket going off.

"Ballistics checked and recorded." replied Scaner.

"Where did you learn to shoot?"

"I used to hunt with my Dad and my brothers. You should see me shoot skeet."

Dirk looked at her and smiled. "Ok, let's check out the remainder of the ship."

They went to the flight deck and looked around. The force of decompression had dislodged about everything. Dirk went to the main computer banks and switched the emergency power on.

"Well, what do you know, it works." Dirk looked at Kat. "We'll put a disc into the main computer and record where this ship has been. Also what it's carrying for cargo. It might come in handy." He put a disc into the slot and pushed the copy switch. "Let's check out the rest of the ship while this is doing its job."

***

They went into what looked like a cargo hold. There were all kinds of machinery strapped to the deck.

"Look at this." Kat said.

Dirk went over, there were twenty-five crates of weapons. One was broken open. It held five more dart throwers. There were ten crates of loaded clips also.

"I think we have captured a gun runner of some type." Dirk said.

"More like a pirate." Kat replied.

"Scaner, are there any other craft in the area?" Dirk said.

"Checking now... No, there is not."

"Inform us if any show up."

"Understood"

Dirk looked at Kat. "Let's see what other "goodies" this baby's got."

Dirk came across a small locked compartment. He found a pry bar and opened it. There was one carton in it. Dirk opened it and sang "Diamonds are a girls best friend."

Kat came over and looked. "These have got to be at least fifteen karats apiece. My God, this is a fortune!"

Dirk counted them, there were twenty of them. "We'll take these back with us. There are foodstuffs and weapons we can use. We can pull the NanMar along side and transfer this stuff. We've got plenty of space for storage." Two hours later, they had what they wanted on the NanMar.

***

Back on the flight deck of the NanMar, Dirk studied a nav chart. "If we can find a safe place to hide that ship, we can stop back and get more or all of the stuff on our way back to Earth."

"Just what do you have in mind?" asked Kat. "Oh, by the way, when you started spouting orders before we went to the other ship I decided to give you a piece of my mind. But after what happened over there, I realized you're used to giving commands and having them obeyed instantly. And this is hostile country. All this is going to take some getting use to."

"Where did you learn to throw a rope like that?"

Kat smiled and said she'd tell him about it someday. "And now, kind Sir, what are we going to do about the ship we just shot up?"

Dirk replied. "Well, there's got to be a spot where we can hide it. I'm not planning on spending the rest of my life scooting around in space. I want to get to the mother ship and then back home to Earth."

"What if, when we get to the mother ship, these Arians don't let us? No one so far has been overly friendly."

"You noticed that too." replied Dirk. "We'll figure something out. Let's get a cup of coffee and come back to the flight deck. There's got to be a place to hide this other craft close by."

Kat blurted. "I thought ships had bridges and airplanes had flight decks?"

"Huh?"

"I thought ships had bridges and airplanes had flight decks?"

"They do. I know, this is a ship. Okay, from now on it's the bridge. Right?"

"Right."

CHAPTER SIX

Once they got to the bridge Dirk sat down, brought up the star chart on the monitor, which showed the course, they were on. Dirk engaged the enhance mode, the areas on the right and left of them showed up. Not to far away was a large asteroid. Dirk set a course for it.

"What are you planning to do with the alien in the other craft?" Kat asked.

"We can't do anything with it now. It's not going anywhere. I put it in one of the storage lockers. If it's floating around in space another ship might find it and go looking around. We don't want anyone finding that spacecraft.

Kat found a crater, which looked big enough to hold the alien craft. They eased the ship down. Using the tractor beam to push the other craft into the crater.

Dirk marked the location on the chart and set in the coordinates for their original course. Dirk told her to mark a radio frequency on the star chart and he gave the numbers. While she was doing this Dirk had put the events of the encounter into the Captain's log. Also recorded the items they brought back with them.

"What's with the radio frequency?"

"A way we can home in on it in case this asteroid moves before we come back this way." Dirk checked his watch, 12:30 am. My, my, how time flies when you're having fun thought Dirk. "I don't know about you, but I'm tired. It's been a long, fun filled, day. I'm going to bed."

"Yes it has. A lot of things have happened to me today. I feel as though I have only been away from home for one day but it's been years. It's really hard to comprehend all this. I believe I'm going to have a glass of warm milk, take two aspirin, then I'm going to bed also." Kat said.

"Scaner, the ship is on automatic pilot. Monitor the systems, and call me if anything happens."

"Aye, Aye Skipper."

"That's all we need, a bloody robot with a sense of humor." Dirk laughed. "Good night."

"Good night." said Kat

***

Dirk went to his quarters, took a shower and crawled into bed. At the point where sleep is just a moment away, he felt more than heard someone in the room with him. He opened his eyes. Kat was standing next to the bed.

"I need to be held." she said. "Just hugged and held."

Dirk flipped the sheet back and Kat got in. She slid over to him and he put his arms around her. She pushed herself against him. Dirk could feel the warmth of her body though the thin material of the robe. He felt her shudder and felt tear's on his chest. She cried very softly.

***

He couldn't remember when he fell asleep but when he awoke he was alone. At 6:30 am, he got out of bed went to the bathroom, did the usual things. Going to the galley, Dirk got a cup of coffee called Scaner on the intercom. All was well, all systems checked out. Taking the cup of coffee with him, went to Kat's door, peeked in. She was sleeping on her right side, hugging a pillow. Letting her sleep, he went to the bridge.

CHAPTER SEVEN

Dirk switched on the monitor and brought up the flight path to the mother ship. Nine days to go. He sat down at the control panel, inserted the disc from the other craft, putting the information on it into their memory banks. He then played it back on the monitor. *This has been one busy little feller* Dirk thought.

The alien had traveled to the outer edges of three galaxies and did a lot of trading on those planets. He took out the disc and placed it in the file with the other discs. *I've got to go through these other discs when I have the time.*

***

Dirk wondered how things were going to go when they reached the larger craft. How many aliens were on it? What were they like? The only other alien they had encountered had tried to kill them. All of the signs pointed out that the Arians were not very nice folks either. Dirk had decided to take the remains of the people and the other animals back to Earth for proper burial. This was the least he could do for them.

"Ok, Scaner, its time you had a P.M."

"What is a P.M.?"

"Preventative maintenance, a grease job and an oil change. We'll charge up your batteries while we're at it."

Dirk and Scaner went to the transporter room, which also served as a tool room and storage space for clothing. Dirk found the tools that he needed and went to work on Scaner. In about an hour Scaner was all set. Dirk had found a polishing rag and cleaned him up too.

"You go back and monitor the radar while I get a bite to eat." Dirk said.

Dirk went to the galley and pushed the order button.

"Good morning."

"Good morning Toots, I'd like a ham and cheese omelet, wheat toast, juice and coffee." As Dirk was drinking his juice, he heard the door open to Kat's room. He looked up and smiled at her.

"You look as though you slept good." <u>God, she even looks beautiful in the morning</u>

"I did. I'm sorry about last night. I shouldn't have come to your room like that."

"Don't ever be sorry about being human. Everyone needs a hug every so often."

She just looked at him, wondering how one minute he could be so ferociously protective and then be so calm and understanding the next. She smiled and touched the side of his face with the palm of her hand. Kat walked around him to the meal panel and ordered breakfast. As they sat there sipping their coffee, they discussed the near future.

***

They had decided they would have to place the firearms at places where they would be readily accessible. Dirk took the food stores to the back of the galley and stored them in the proper bins. Most of the meals were ready-made's. Everything was in packets, including the eggs.

"I wonder how they get eggs to stay fresh?" Dirk mused.

"I don't know, but do you really want to? You might not want to eat them if you do."

"I thought of that before."

After the trays were put away, they turned their attention to the placements of the weapons. They even put two of the dart throwers in the small shuttlecraft. Checking in on the bridge, they went back to the galley.

As they sat there Kat looked at Dirk.

"I was born and raised in Helena, Montana. Went to College in Great Falls where I studied Veterinary Medicine. I was working in a holding pasture on some cattle, which were going to be shipped that morning. Hearing a loud whirring sound, I looked up. This huge round shape was above me. Standing there mesmerized, I didn't move. There was a beam of light and then I couldn't move. I tried, but I couldn't. I could feel myself being raised upward. I don't remember going through an opening of any type. When I awoke I was lying on a table, but still couldn't move. There were no restraints on my body. I remember a woman, at least I think it was a woman looking at me. There was a tray full of surgical instruments next to my head. She had a scalpel in her hand and was getting ready to cut when something went wrong. The ship shuddered and the lights went dim. She dropped the scalpel in the tray and went off somewhere. I could hear her talking to another ship but I couldn't understand the language. She came back and started again. By this time I was furious. I knew I screamed aloud because she stopped and backed up."

"The next thing I remember is you standing over me and putting your hand over my mouth. And the rest is recent history."

"This is going to be a little hard on you, but did you leave anyone behind?" asked Dirk.

"Yes, my father and two younger brothers, Bill and Matt. No husband and no children, if that's what you want to know. I'm twenty-nine years old, I almost got married twice but backed out. Neither could accept me being a Vet or the long hours I had to put in."

Dirk and Kat looked at each other for a few minutes. Finally Dirk said. "What really pisses me off is the fact these Arians come to Earth, take what they want and then leave. Not to mention the experiments they perform on whatever or whomever they take. Your life has been cut short, mine stopped the day Nancy and my daughter were killed. I left three sisters and one brother plus my dad back on Earth. I'm probably listed as missing and presumed dead. But the worst is, I took an F14 Tomcat for an unauthorized flight. I just took off and went straight up. The last thing I remember was striking this ship. I didn't even know it was there, no warning, no nothing, just ka-bam."

"What's an F14 Tomcat?"

"It's a jet fighter plane that's carrier based. She'll do Mach one plus. They're not the fastest but they're still one hell of a fighter. You could tell the pilot in the ship we got yesterday never flew one."

They both sat there deep in their own thoughts.

"I'll tell you one thing, lady, I going to do my best to see that you and I get back to Earth in one piece. But let's take one thing at a time. A: We know we are going into a very hostile neighborhood. B: So we better get ready for it. C: We'll be there in about nine days." Dirk rose and took their dirty dishes to the tray and pushed the panel shut.

"Great meal, Toots."

"We are glad you enjoyed it."

As the days went by, Kat became more and more proficient in navigation and in how the armament worked. Dirk set up a target in the capsule room and Kat practiced with the dart thrower and with the laser. He also sent out a couple of targets and held practice drills with simulated torpedoes. They got the firing point procedures down to less than one minute.

CHAPTER EIGHT

Three days from the mother ship, the crystal started to fail. They went to the reactor room. Sure enough, this crystal was going out too. Kat suggested they use one of the crystals they found on the alien ship. Dirk went to the bridge and retrieved box.

He switched to generator power, shut down the exciter, changed the crystal and re-engaged the exciter. The generator shut off automatically and full power was restored. Dirk and Kat checked the systems gauges. This time the reactor showed a reserve of power.

"It looks like the Arians have been getting their crystals from some cut rate store. That ought to teach them not to be so cheap." Dirk said.

"I think we ought to split the crystals into two packets, leave some here, and take the rest topside and stow them somewhere where they'll be safe." Kat said

Dirk looked at Kat. "Topside? Stow?"

"I'm learning all of this from you. You're quite a teacher and you don't even realize it."

"Let's leave three here, you take eight and I'll take eight. I'll put these in the control panel on the bridge and you put those in your room."

They went back to the bridge, Dirk stowed the crystals in a panel he had found in the desk, showing Kat how to get into it if needed.

Kat turned on the monitor and went over to the panel holding the manuals. She took one out and set it in the display panel. They checked out the data on the crystals. The minimum size crystal for power was forty-five krats. There was no definition for a krat in the manual.

What in the hell was a krat? Dirk sat and thought about it. Going to the disc file, he found the one on the English language. He inserted it and went to carat: "a unit of weight for precious stones equal to two hundred milligrams".

"Let's weigh one of these stones."

They went to the tool room and looked for a scale of some sort. Nothing, Dirk found a set of calipers and took the measurements of the stone and they went back to the bridge. Dirk punched the measurements into the computer, three thousand milligrams in this stone. Divided by two hundred equals fifteen. Kat looked at Dirk. "They're fifteen carats each." he said.

"I told you that back on the alien ship. You were singing, 'Diamonds are a girls best friend'. Don't underestimate us girls, we know what we're talking about."

"This explains why our friend back there was coming in this direction. But why were the Arians using substandard crystals?"

"I'll be right back." and Kat went to the reactor room. She was back in a few minutes with the container of the old crystals. She took out five spent stones, piecing them together.

"You measure this while I hold it."

Dirk took the measurements and then put them into the computer. Each cluster was approximately fifteen carats. "Why were these stones being used? I'll tell you, that's all they had left. I'll bet when we get to the mother ship, we'll find that baby running on minimal power also."

"Do you remember, when you resuscitated me how much equipment you had running?"

"Yes, all of the bridge gear and the capsule room power equipment plus some of the tool room equipment."

"That's why the crystal gave out so fast. It couldn't handle the load."

Dirk took the other stones and pieced them together. They had six larger stones.

"These larger stones have a life expectancy of six spans, their time. How long have they been in our galaxy? They could have been here for over a hundred years, our time."

"Well, we know they were collecting specimens from Earth and dissecting some and not others. But why would they be doing this? They were collecting samples of marine life and plants. They could have been testing for edible food sources." Kat thought all this is quite mind-boggling. "But why humans?"

"Let's call it a night. Any more of this and we'll be talking to ourselves."

Dirk took the container of diamonds back to the reactor room while Kat went to her room and put hers away. They then went to get a snack before going to bed.

"This is some of the best ice-cream I've ever had." Kat said.

"What do mean some of the best? It is the best."

"No, my dad makes the best. Makes it in an old hand crank tub." Kat said.

"I'm going to make one more round and see if all's well on the bridge and then I'm going to turn in." Dirk said. "Sleep well."

"Oh, I will." smiled Kat

CHAPTER NINE

Dirk went to the reactor room and checked out the crystal exciter, all's well here. He went into the storage room and then to the airlock, then checked out the shuttlecraft. Dirks last stop was the bridge. Nothing new and exciting here. Everything was running smoothly. Dirk plugged Scaner into the main control computer and went to his room. He took a quick shower and brushed his teeth, shut off the light and got into bed.

***

The door to the galley opened and Kat came in. She stood by the side of the bed with the soft red night light in the galley directly behind her. The light shown through the robe outlining her body perfectly.

"If you get into bed with me tonight, be ready to move in permanently. I don't believe in one night stands."

Kat slid off her slippers and then the robe. She pulled back the covers and got into bed.

"You're even more beautiful than before."

"What do you mean before?"

"Remember, I'm the one who resuscitated you."

He opened his arms and she moved against him. She looked him straight in the eyes and kissed him. A soft kiss at first and then a little harder. Dirk moved his right hand down her back and across the soft rise of her hips. Kat gave a small moan and pulled him tight against her. She kissed him softly and then her tongue darted into his mouth. The sensation Dirk felt was overwhelming. She could feel him against her lower body. She rolled over pulling Dirk with her and guided him. Afterward they lay there holding onto each other for long minutes. Each one not wanting to let go of the moment. Dirk lay on his back with an arm around Kat's shoulder, her head was on his chest. "I can hear your heart beat." and she kissed his chest. Dirk ran his hand over her back gently.

"Are all you girls from Montana this muscular?

"No, just us girl Vets."

She kissed a nipple on Dirk's chest and felt him give a small hug with his left arm. Kat brought her leg over Dirk and felt his member rising.

"Oh, how nice. Is this for me?"

Dirk answered by pulling her all of the way up on him. This time they made love slowly.

***

Dirk awoke at 6:30 am. Having someone in bed with him when he woke up was a pleasant feeling, something he really enjoyed. He leaned over and kissed Kat on the cheek. She uttered a soft sigh and reached over to him. He very gently got out of bed and went into the bathroom.

***

After his morning shower, he went into the galley. Ordering a glass of juice and a cup of coffee. Taking the coffee to the bridge with him, he sat at the main console. Dirk checked out the systems, everything was running perfectly.

***

His instincts told him something was going to happen. Every pilot had them, Murphy's Law. He sat there staring out into space. The stars were still going by. Nothing big coming at them! But? He rechecked the radar, nothing. At long range, it was very hard to pin point anything. What was nagging at him? It was almost like he could feel a pair of eyes staring at him. He switched back to short range radar with a heat-seeking beam imposed on it. There, off the port quarter, range, two hundred fifty miles, another ship. The heading showed it would intersect with theirs in two days. Another Arian ship inbound to the mother ship? <u>I think the proverbial saying, "The shit is about to hit the fan." is about to come true</u> Dirk pressed the intercom and called Kat to come to the bridge ASAP.

Kat came running to the bridge, soaking wet with just a towel rapped around her. Dirk smiled and stared at her.

"Well, you said ASAP, YOU FOOL!"

"Why don't you get dressed and get a cup of coffee and then come back." Dirk was smiling all the time.

Kat stood behind him, took off the towel and draped it over his head. Then took off through the door before Dirk could react. When Kat returned to the bridge she was wearing a light robe and holding two cups coffee. They studied the other ship.

"It seems we're on a converging course. We are slowly over taking it. I've got it, we are still moving at the same pace as the original set up was. But now that we have the bigger crystals we have been moving a lot more smoothly. No power surges. That other ship is running on the older crystals, right? The heat blossom is to small for a full powered reactor. And there's no life form on-board. Scaner and I upgraded this beam. It can pick up the heat blossom from a mouse. I'm going to drift closer and stay a little behind it. If we get closer maybe we can get better info on it." Dirk looked at Kat and smiled. "You've got goose bumps on you big enough to ski off of. Why don't you finish getting dressed, and bring us some chow. We'll eat here. I want to stay and keep an eye on her."

Kat bent down, kissed Dirk and then went back aft. Dirk sat there rechecking the data periodically. His thoughts and feelings went back the previous night. I've been gone from earth for fifteen years, actual years I'm forty-six, bio I'm only thirty-one and a half. Nancy has been dead for fifteen years. No, counting the time was recuperating and then the time after resuscitation, it has been six months. Kat is fifty-six, but is really thirty, bio. I've never looked at another woman in the years Nan and I were together. Kat and I are a strange pair. Normally, we would have never met, but yet here we are.

***

Kat was sitting in the galley with a cup of coffee cradled in her hands like she was warming them, thinking. She was thinking almost the same thoughts. She knew the man in the control room is the one she had waited for. The one she would spend the rest of her life with. She got up, went to her old quarters and moved everything into their quarters. Their quarters, our room. What happens now, will happen to both of us, as a pair, not as two separate people.

CHAPTER TEN

Kat went back into the galley got their breakfast and went to the bridge humming a tune. She set the food on the desk in front of Dirk and sat in the chair on the other side.

"Do you know the name of the tune you were humming?" asked Dirk

"Scotland the Brave. Kind of fitting isn't it?" Kat replied.

Dirk smiled and nodded.

"What do you think we should do about that other ship? I think we should get close enough to really check it out. And if everything looks okay, go aboard it."

"All right let's do it. And if all goes right maybe I'll get a chance to use my roping skill again."

"Your roping skill?"

"Yup, I used to team rope with my youngest brother, Matt. We were quite good at it. He'd head and I'd heel. I bought my first car with winnings from rodeoing."

"I think you will never cease to amaze me. I thought I had done a lot in my life, being in the Navy. I used to get my extra spending money driving stock cars at the local dirt tracks back in Virginia."

***

"You've been picking up Scaners habits to."

Dirk approached the other Arian ship from astern and a little low. They were about twenty-five miles away from it and in perfect firing position, if needed. Dirk locked the radar on the other craft again and sent out the heat-seeking beam. This time he got a faint reading.

"Something's alive on that ship. Whatever it is, it's just barely alive. We are going to go aboard it so let's not expose ourselves to anything until we a find out what it is over there."

"Aye, aye Skipper"

"We will dock in three minutes." Scaner stated

"I'll go get some medical stuff ready just in case." Kat said.

"Put them in the shuttle bay. We can go over through there and get in through the airlock. This way we won't have to wear the bulky space suits. They're lighter suits in the storage area, which are just as good. Each has its own rebreathing and CO2 scrubber units. They're good for about two hours before they need recharging. At least that's what the manual says."

Dirk went to the panel where the lasers were kept and took two out, adjusting the force to stun. Full force would punch a half-inch hole through a steel plate.

They were ready.

"Scaner, stay plugged into the main computer and be ready to fire lasers if need be."

"All right, sir."

"Once we are on board and I send you an SOS, you fire lasers on low power, that'll knock out everyone on board, including us. Then come and get us."

"Aye, aye sir."

"That's more like it." replied Dirk smiling.

Dirk and Kat put on the suits, charged up the oxygen supply. Both had laser in small holsters on their hips. Dirk carried his 9mm in a Navy issue shoulder holster.

"Let's go."

Dirk came along side of the other ship and stopped at the air lock hatch. He rigged out the struts, securing the ships and went to the door.

Kat pushed a button on the panel, which would send out a sleeve and walkway for them. Dirk pressurized the walkway with air from the shuttle bay and opened the door. He repressurized the inner lock of the other ship and shut the door to the shuttle bay. Kat opened the outer door of the airlock and they went in. The outer door was shut. This way the integrity of their ship was kept. Both drew their lasers and Dirk opened the inner door. As both ships were identical they had no trouble getting around.

There sitting at the main console was an Arian, alive, but just barely. Kat gave a gasp and raised her weapon. Dirk put his hand on her arm and gently pushed it down.

"I don't think we will need weapons for this one."

Dirk went over to the main control panel and checked it out. They must share knowledge between ships, thought Dirk. He set up the series of switches and punch the enter light.

"We can talk to him, her or it now, the computer will translate for us."

"Who are you?" asked Dirk

The alien started to bring his hand out from under the blanket covering him. Kat was on that side and saw the laser. Before the Arian could level it, Kat shot. The beam hit the Arian in the middle of his chest. He stiffened, dropped the weapon and went limp.

Dirk came around the desk and kicked the weapon aside. He checked the Arian to see if it was still alive, it was.

Kat picked up the weapon, checking the setting. Full power, damn these Arians.

Dirk suggested they take the Arian to the capsule room and lay him on the table. He motioned Kat to follow, then went into the transporter room.

"Let's lock him down while we check out the rest of the ship." Dirk said.

"Let me do it." Kat said. "I'm not revengeful, but these bastards were going to carve me up like a Thanksgiving Day turkey. I'd like to get at least one lick in."

Dirk stepped aside. Kat moved the locking beam over the Arian and turned the dial on. An aqua colored beam came down and covered the body.

"There's something wrong, the beam should be green." Kat said.

Dirk thought for a second, went over to the storage area and got three straps. He motioned Kat to cut off the beam. He went out to the table and strapped the Arian to it.

"Let's check out the sleeping quarters. He might not be the only one."

They went to the larger one first, no one. They went through the galley and into the next quarters. On one of the beds was another Arian. Dirk went over to it, looked and shook his head. Kat came over checked for life signs. She pulled the sheet over its head.

Dirk said. "I think I know what the trouble is with the power. Whadaya bet they're using the cheap crystals again?"

They went to the reactor room. This ship was down to using the smaller crystals also. Dirk thought, <u>Christ, it's a wonder this ship is even moving.</u> Kat reached into one of her pockets and produced a million-dollar fuel ticket, as she called the crystals.

Dirk started the generator up and Kat replaced the crystal in the exciter. Throwing the switch, the lights brightened. The generator shut off automatically and the battery panel went to immediate supercharge.

"Wow, this ship was down to running on memories." Dirk said. "There's no way they could have made it back to the mother ship. You have got to give them credit for having the guts to try."

"Let's check the one on the table." Kat said.

This one was awake and trying to get free of the straps, when they got there. When he saw them he stopped struggling and looked at them.

Dirk stood over him and said. "I'm going to ask you just one more time and if you don't answer you are going to go to sleep for a long, long time." He pointed to one of the capsules. "Now, who are you?"

The Arian just stared at him.

"Kat, go in the transporter room and switch on the green beam."

Kat started to go to the transporter room. She got about half way there when the Alien spoke.

"You killed my crew mate."

Kat stopped dead in her tracks and slowly turned around. "Your other shipmate, Rega, was going to kill me. She was going to cut me up into small pieces. Anyway, how do you figure we killed your partner?"

"We were sent to your planet to get specimens for research. So we could check to see if we could live there. Our planet is dying. This was our tenth and final trip to your planet. We had just taken two more specimens when we became sick. My crew mate is dead because of your planet."

Dirk looked at Kat. "Asian flu strikes again."

"Well, your Rega was doing a lot of specimen collecting. She was taking humans and dissecting them and then getting rid of the remains. Are you a male, female or what?" Dirk asked.

"I am what you would call a male. My name is Awjer. I am the leader on this ship."

"Well Awjer, we are not going to harm you in any way, but we are going to keep you right where you are for the time being. Do you understand?"

The Arian just stared at him. Dirk nodded to Kat. Kat went into the transporter room and turned on the holding beam. When Kat came back she said.

"He can hear us but he can't see us. All he can do is look straight up. The beam will hold him there."

Dirk motioned her to follow him to the bridge. Once there he went over to the control panel and turned off the translator.

"Now he can't understand us, it is just gibberish to him now. Let's check with Scaner."

Kat switched on the intership channel on the main computer.

"Scaner are you there?"

"Scaner here. All systems are running. No other ships are within range."

"Scaner can you plug into this computer from where you are?" asked Dirk.

"No, there is no ship to ship power cable in place."

"I'll put a cable in place. Then you over-ride this computer and translate everything into English?"

Dirk went to the NanMar and ran a cable between the two ships.

"It will take one half an hour to do the complete system." Scaner said. "Translation commencing now."

Dirk and Kat watched the computer lights start to flash.

"What we've got to do next is find out what killed one and made to other sick." said Kat

"Ok, that's your department, I have no knowledge of medicine but I'll bet its Asian flu. I'll start looking through the capsules. I don't like it but it has to be done."

CHAPTER ELEVEN

Kat went to the air lock and retrieved what Dirk called her bag of medical gadgets.

The first thing she tested was the air for contamination. With the new crystal in the exciter the CO2 scrubbers were working overtime. In the short time they had been on, the air was once again pure. She checked out the filters and found no traces of any poisons or any viruses.

"Dirk, the only thing I can see, with the power so low the scrubbers were not working to full capacity. Just plain dirty air is what they have been breathing. Didn't you say Rega died from Asian flu?"

"Yes"

"I'm pretty sure the combination of the two is what killed the other Arian and made Awjer sick. We can take off these suits now, its all clear and clean."

They went to the airlock and set the suits near the inner door. "Let's keep the gloves on for safety," Dirk said. "We don't know what else is floating around here."

Dirk put his arms around her, hugging her tight, then gave her a light kiss. Kat leaned against him.

"Thanks, I needed that."

***

She went to a monitor and switched it on, punched a few keys and the anatomy of the Arians showed up. Going to Awjer, she drew a fluid sample an analyzed it. Sure enough there was the Asian flu bug. This guy is going to be one sick puppy for a while.

Dirk was going through the capsules one at a time. All that he checked contained small animals and some plants. He was down to the last two, he opened the panels. These two were filled with the mist that covered him and Kat. Dirk cleared the mist away.

"Kat, can you come over here for a minute? We have two humans here."

Dirk called Scaner. All of the systems had been changed to English. Dirk then placed the numbers of the capsules into the computer and the information of two people showed up. John Richard Mayhan, DOB 10 August 1964 brought up 4 August 1994. The other person was Mary Ann Taylor Mayhan, DOB 19 February 1965 brought up 4 August 1994.

"I think we have a husband and wife team here." Kat said.

"There is no doubt in my mind. We're going to have to revive them." replied Dirk "And we're going to have to put Awjer into cryo as soon as he is well. Scaner can do that, he has the knowledge stored in his memory banks." Dirk called the NanMar. "Scaner, disconnect, return to our original course and stop. We will follow." Dirk looked at Kat. "We can stack the ships. Locking them together, we'll have direct access to each ship."

Back at the point where they left their original course, Dirk said. "I don't think any other ship will be coming along this route. So we should be pretty well hidden."

***

Dirk docked the ship they were on to the underside of NanMar. Once the air was checked again for purity before the locks between the ships were opened. They now had access to both ships through the elevator set up. The ships were designed to be able to be stacked one on top of the other. Using the elevator to get to each other, plus a ladder if the elevator was in use. The outer hull panels retracted and the rails extended. The bottom elevator was disengaged and locked in place against the storage bay wall.

Dirk and Kat were in the galley when Dirk said. "We're going to need some time to resuscitate the Mayhans and get them adjusted to this new way of life. It will also give us a chance to get to know them better. If things go well, we'll train them. For what I'm planning, we are going to need all the help we can get."

"I've got this strange feeling you are going to try to capture the mother ship and take it back to Earth." Kat said.

"Not try, do. We know two of the ships have been infected with Asian flu. They must have gone back to the mother ship or have exposed each other in some way. They could have met somewhere out of range of Earth, stacked their ships as we are doing and infected each other. If that's the case, one of the other ships could already be back to the mother ship and infected them too. There are only five of these types of ships out. We know where two of them are. We know they don't have the greatest crystals in the world. So we have an edge there. I'll bet the pirate we captured was coming here to dicker with them for the crystals. That's why we got that guy so easy. He thought we were going to be easy pickings. He must have known these Arians and how they fly, but he didn't know about us."

"You've studied Awjer. He doesn't look to be a physical person. Lots of brains but very little physical strength. They don't react quickly. And I'll bet they don't let a female and a male go out together. Rega was alone and Awjer had a male crewmember. That's three, say there are two on each ship, that's nine. How many more are on the mother ship, five or six? Even if they are not infected, how hard would it be to infect them with the virus? I'd rather have them sick than have to fight them."

Kat nodded. "At least this way no one gets hurt or killed. I'm like you, I don't want to hurt anyone if I don't have to. But I don't want to spend the rest of my life in outer space either. I want to see

Earth again. I can develop an inoculation serum for any human. I don't know about the Arians. I'll have to do some tests on them to find out about their natural immune systems. I'm sure it can be done. Their bodies did over react to the virus. I've got some serums in my black bag. I'll get Awjer up here and doctor him while you resuscitated the Mayhans. We'll have to put the other Arian in freeze."

"We can bring both of them up here. We have two open capsules. That ship doesn't."

"Let's get to work, Cap'n."

"Hold it, I'm the Cap'n and I get to say it. Let's get to work."

***

Dirk loaded the empty capsules in the elevator and took them down to other ship and sent the elevator back for Kat.

Dirk went to look for a body bag of some sort. He found a small mattress cover and used it. Placing the dead Arian in a capsule, he set the dials for freeze and pushed it into the elevator.

Kat, in the meantime, gave Awjer a shot to put him under so he would be easier to handle. They loaded him into the other capsule. Put him into the elevator with his partner, then up to their ship.

Awjer was set on the table in the capsule room and the restraining beam was turned on. The other capsule was set in place and a data printout of him was attached to the body bag. The capsule was set in the panel along side of Rega. Dirk went back down to the other ship and started the resuscitation of the Mayhans.

Dirk and Kat were sitting in the bridge of the NanMar with a cup of "think drink", known as coffee. The other ship had to be decontam-inated and inventoried. This would take up the two days, while waiting for the Mayhans to awake. Kat had put a new purifier in the air recycler, so that was all set. It would take about three hours to recycle all of the air. They went to the bridge of the new ship and checked out all of the systems. Any new information was placed in their computer. Actually NanMars information was more up to date. Leading them to believe this ship had taken off from the mother ship long before theirs.

They inventoried the supplies. Some of the food was contaminated and should be thrown out. Kat made up a lye substance, putting it in with the contaminated food when it was packaged for disposal. The package was jettisoned into space.

Dirk and Kat called it a day and went back to the NanMar. As before Scaner monitored the capsules while Dirk and Kat slept. The next morning was spent replenishing the food on board the new ship.

Dirk stripped down the hand lasers and refitted the selector switches with a stun setting. When he was finished he replaced them in their proper holders. There was not much else left to do so Kat and Dirk spent the rest of the day working in the computer banks on the new ship. Now each ship had the same information plus an intercom channel, just for these two ships.

They went back to the NanMar. After the evening meal they went to the bridge, opened the panel for outer viewing and sat there watching the stars. It was really nice to be able to sit and put everything on "hold" for awhile.

***

Dirk and Kat arose the next morning, had breakfast and got the things they would need before going to the other ship. Kat did a routine check on Awjer.

"He's coming along fine, everything is normal."

"Is it safe to put him in cryo?"

"Yes, he should be able to stand it now."

"Okay sport, you're going into cyro now. You're to volatile to be left loose." They placed him in a capsule and started the process for freeze.

"We'll plug Scaner in to monitor the process just in case there's a malfunction." Dirk said.

They placed the capsule in the remaining panel and Scaner was plugged in. Now all they had to worry about were the Mayhans.

***

That afternoon the alarms on the capsules went off. Kat was already in the capsule room when Dirk got there. The mist was cleared away and Dirk stood over John while Kat stood over Mary. The lids opened and both were covered with a sheet. John opened his eyes first. Pure hatred gleamed in his eyes. He balled his left hand into a fist and was about to swing when Dirk spoke.

"Hi, I'm Dirk and I'm an American, so please, don't hit me."

John was completely taken off guard. He relaxed. Dirk told him to just lay there and move his arms and legs to see if everything worked. John did this. Dirk helped him swing his legs around and sit up.

"Here, drink some of this." Dirk offered.

John sat there.

"It's only water, it'll help you get your voice back."

John drank a little. He could feel his throat loosening up. He sat there for a while and then got up. Dirk motioned him to follow. John looked over to the other capsule and saw Mary lying there. He went over to her.

"Hon, are you all right?"

"She'll be all right in a minute or two. Let's let Kat take care of her. If you'll come with me to the sleeping quarters, you can get some clothes. Then we'll go to the galley and get some juice for you to drink. That'll help get your body functions working again."

John followed him, looking around in amazement. Dirk handed him a suit, explaining why they're so light.

In the galley, Dirk showed him how to operate the ordering system. They were sitting down, drinking a juice when Kat and

Mary came in. John got up and hugged Mary and asked if she were all right.

"Do you want a glass of juice?" John asked. She nodded.

Kat sat down next to Dirk and when John sat back down the four of them just looked at each other. Dirk smiled and said.

"Welcome to outer space. Today is 7 October, 1999." The Mayhans sat there with their mouths open in complete amazement. Not really believing what they had just heard. The real showstopper was when Dirk looked at Mary and said. "You are Mary Ann Taylor Mayhan, Captain, USAF, DOB 19 February 1965. You are stationed at Holoman Air Force Base in Alamogordo, New Mexico." He looked at John. "John Richard Mayhan, DOB 10 August 1964. You are a Professor at the University of New Mexico, and teach Geology at Los Cruces, New Mexico. Your home is in the desert somewhere in between. You were taken onboard 4 August 1994 from the Lincoln National Forest near Jack Peak. That's all we know about you. What in the hell were you two doing up there anyway?"

John spoke. "We were on vacation. We always go to the mountains on the week of my birthday and then to Mardi Gras in New Orleans for her birthday. We were collecting some specimens for my work. On our second evening, while cooking supper, we heard a whirring noise. Looking up, we saw a large, round ship about five hundred feet above us. It came down slowly to about one hundred feet. A greenish colored light came down and engulfed us. We were unable to move. That's all I remember until you brought us around."

After they had talked for about an hour Dirk looked at Kat.

"Let's show them around."

They all got up and went to the capsule room, Kat showed them how to close a capsule and stow it in a panel.

"What's in the other panels ?" Mary asked.

"I don't think you want to know that right now, maybe later." She did tell them the reason for the Arians going to Earth and that they had brought back specimens. They continued into the bridge.

Mary looked around studying the various panels and then sat in the pilot seat at the main console. Dirk showed her how to adjust it. Dirk motioned John over and the seat was adjusted to fit him. They then went to the transporter room and Dirk showed them how the transporter worked and how to work the holding beam. The four finally got to the reactor room. John looked at the reactor and the crystal exciter.

"I know a little about these things, I was stationed on board a nuclear powered sub when I was in the Navy. I went through Sub School in Groton, Connecticut. We never had anything like this when I was in though. Ours were much bigger."

"What rank were you?" Dirk asked.

"Rate, I was a Second Class Sonarman when I got out. I was damn good at what I did."

"And Captain Mayhan, just what do you do for the Air Force?"

"I am an Instructor Pilot for the F16. Call sign "Zinger" Why do you ask?"

"Well, I'm a Lieutenant Commander in the Navy and a Tomcat driver. At least I was. We don't know if there is a United States any more."

After the grand tour they all went to the NanMar for supper. They sat at the table for a while after the meal and talked about the ships. Dirk and Kat asked them about where they were born and brought up and how they met. Kat knew the questions Dirk asked were very important in regards to their up coming quest. He wanted to find out just how angry they were and if they were going to commit themselves to the scheme he had.

They picked up their dishes and went to the panel. Dirk and Kat let the Mayhans go first. After they had put their dishes down the computer vice asked them if they enjoyed their meal. John answered. "Just fine." Then stopped to stare at the panel. Dirk and Kat smiled. John and Mary looked at them with big question marks written all over their faces. Dirk explained the system to them.

"When Kat heard the voice for the first time she almost jumped over me. I just stood there asking 'Who are you?'. At that time it was a man's voice. I had Scaner change it."

Returning to the capsule room, Dirk went over to the three capsules housing Rega, Awjer and the dead Arian. He opened the panels and threw the switch to vent out the mist. Looking at the two new arrivals. "These are Arians." He explained who each one was, and that Awjer was still alive and in protective cryogenic. Rega and the other Arian were dead.

"Their systems couldn't handle the Asian flu. Let's go back down to the other ship."

Kat showed Mary around the storage places and Dirk took John to the bridge, where he went over some of the manuals with him. John was starting to look a little tired so Dirk suggested they go find the girls.

"It's getting a little late so why don't we continue this tomorrow." Dirk said."

CHAPTER TWELVE

Dirk and Kat went back to their ship, got ready for bed. Kat saw the worried look on his face.

"Out with it, something's nagging at you."

"I feel John would be inclined to go along with our idea but I don't know about Mary."

Kat laughed and said. "I quote, 'I don't like what those bastards did to us. I'd like to get some pay-back in.'"

"I really wasn't sure what was going through her mind. But I like her statement. I feel the same way." Dirk said.

"Well, I do too, but I don't think I would have said it like that. You have to remember I grew up in a different era."

Dirk hugged her and she snuggled a little closer. She leaned over and kissed his cheek, then his ear. Dirk rolled over on his side and kissed Kat passionately. They slowly made love to each other.

***

Arising at 7:00 am, Dirk was showering when the door opened.

"Let's see if this shower is big enough for two."

After washing each other Kat looked down. "Well bless my soul, what do you think we ought to do about that?" Dirk opened the shower door and stepped out, picked Kat up and carried her to the bed...

"Time for another shower" Dirk said.

It was almost 9:00 AM when John and Mary came into the galley. They looked as though they had slept well. Mary had a glow to her cheeks.

All's well. thought Kat.

Dirk looked over to Mary.

"I understand you think it's time for some "pay-back" on these bastards." Mary's cheeks turn bright red from blushing.

"Both of us think that. We don't like being yanked away from our lives. I don't know who these Arians think they are. But whatever they're up to, they're going about it the wrong way." Mary said.

Dirk motioned for them to follow him. They put away the dirty dishes. Dirk said. "Great breakfast, Toots."

"Thank you. We are glad you enjoyed it."

John laughed. "Is that what you call her, Toots?"

"Yeah, she loves me."

Kat gave him a poke in the ribs. "Wait till she gets to vote and then see what happens."

***

They went into the capsule room and Dirk opened all of the panels for them to see. All John could say was "Oh my God". Mary just stood there with tears streaming down her face.

Dirk said. "This was what Rega was doing with her time at Earth. The other ship was not like this, some animals and plant specimens and you two." He told them that Awjer had said their home planet was dying. They were checking Earth out to see if it was habitable for them.

"Oh, by the way have you two had Asian flu shots?" Kat asked.

"Yes, we both had them at the base back on Earth." Mary said.

"Okay, enough of this." and Dirk shut the panels. "I'll bet that's how they got the flu. You two gave it to them. They don't have the immune systems we have. Awjer was or is probably a little stronger than the other one."

***

Arriving at the bridge, Dirk checked the systems over. He opened the view screen. John and Mary got their first glimpse of outer space.

"Wow!"

"Awesome."

"Let's relax and talk about what we are going to do." Dirk said.

"The main thing is how are we going to get aboard the mother ship without being shot at, or even killed? We can't beam ourselves on board without getting captured or killed right there." John said.

"Dirk suggested infecting them with the flu virus. We are all immune to it now. The problem is, how can we get the virus onboard?" Kat said.

Dirk switched on the main computer and punched up configuration data on the mother ship. After studying the layout for awhile Dirk said. "I think I know how. They've got a single docking bay. There's room for storing three ships, four in a tight squeeze. If we can get one of the shuttlecraft there with the virus on board we can infect the entire ship. These Arians are not very physical, so two days after exposure should put them all down in sickbay. Three days at the most."

"I vote for three day." stated Mary.

The other three looked at Mary.

"I don't like what they did to us. They took us up here and scared the hell out of us." She looked at Kat. "They were getting ready to carve you up and not think a thing of it. Didn't you recognize some of those specimens? Those are human organs! These Arians are not nice people. We could take Awjer out of freeze and put him in the shuttlecraft and send him there. He alone could infect the whole ship." Mary said.

"Did something else happen to you to make you feel this way about them?" Kat asked.

"My first overseas tour was in the middle east. I saw the unsuspecting "little" people get stepped on a lot. There was not one blessed thing they could do about it, except die. I didn't like it, but there was nothing I could do about it either. I know now how they felt. But now I'm in a position to be able to do something. Does this make me a bad person?"

Dirk spoke. "I've seen some awful things happen to innocent people also. There is a pretty thin line between right and wrong. Let's make sure we don't step over it. Okay, enough said about that. We need to think about where we are and what we are going to do about it."

Everyone looked at each other for a few seconds.

"Why not sent them the dead one that is still contagious. Awjer is on the road to recovery. We would only have to deal with him again." Dirk said.

"Is there someway we can infect the shuttle craft with the live virus?" John asked.

Mary looked at the others. "Put the dead Arian in a space suit, load up the inside with the virus and send him on his way. The first thing they'd do is to take him down to sickbay and strip him down. Bingo, you got most of them right then. There will probably be three or four of them in the docking area. Those will be handling him right away. I think that will take care of at least seven or eight. The rest will get it as a matter of course. We can always decontaminate the shuttle later."

"Mary, I think that is about as good a plan as we can come up with." Dirk said. "Let's T.C.M.O."

John asked. "What's T.C.M.O.?"

"Take Charge and Move Off."

Scaner said. "That is a saying from the fifties."

"I can vouch for that." Kat said

They took the dead Arian out of freeze, put him in a space suit, and then took him to the second ship. Getting ready to put the Arian in the shuttle, Dirk stopped them.

"Wait a minute. Let's make sure there aren't any good crystals in the ship. All we need is one, which will just barely get him there. They'll tractor beam him in anyway. That will put at least four in the docking bay."

Kat went down to the reactor room and came back with a small stone of about three karats. John went to change the crystal.

"There's no crystal in here, they must have been using it in the exciter in the star ship. These two were down to their last legs."

John set in the crystal and started up the systems. Everything should work if they were set on minimal.

CHAPTER THIRTEEN

When John came out of the craft he stated. "There's just enough power in that stone to last for about two days."

Putting the Arian in the pilot seat the controls were set for the original heading of the ship. This way the shuttle would return to the original course of the IV204 to the mother ship.

Just as they were leaving the shuttle Mary, much to everyone's awe, reached over and set the suit's heating system to a little above the normal Arian body temperature.

"There," she said. "That ought to knock their dicks right in the sand when they smell him."

Dirk shook his head and laughed out loud.

"You ought to hear her after a couple of beers." John said. "She puts us sailors to shame."

They had sealed the inner hatch to the shuttle bay. Dirk asked why they hadn't named their ship.

"It's not our ship, it's yours. You're the ones who captured it." Mary said.

"We're all in this together." Dirk and Kat said.

"This ship is yours. All we ask is you help us get back to Earth."

"Have you thought of a name for her yet? Dirk renamed ours the NanMar after his wife and daughter."

Mary blurted out. "I--, we thought you two were married."

"Not yet, I'm waiting for him to ask me. He might be a Lieutenant Commander and a fighter pilot but there are times when he is a bit slow."

Dirk stood there slack jawed.

"Yeah, I know what you mean. I've met a few officers who were that way." John said.

Dirk finally got readjusted and asked what they were going to name the ship.

"We thought up the JonMar, after us." John said. "I just thought of this, all you would have to do is add a 'u' after Mar and we'd both sound like something from a Japanese fleet."

Mary looked at him.

"You know, the "Nan Maru" and the "Jon Maru"."

"Okay, The JonMar it is. Don't take offense at this John but I'd leave the flying to "Zinger". By the way how did you get that call sign?"

"At Holoman, I used to zing my students a lot. It kept them on their toes. Every chance I got, "Zing". My first graduating class, all five of them, got me a helmet with "ZINGER" on it and the name stuck. By the way what's your call sign?"

"With a name like Dirk Conal MacGlashan, what else but "Scotty". I've been Scotty all of my life. All right, enter your name as the Captain of the JonMar and John's as the First Officer in the ships log. Date it two days ago. We'll make up a couple of name placards. One forward and one aft."

***

Kat invited them to come to the NanMar for dinner that night and some homemade ice cream. Dirk and Kat went up to their ship and after checking the systems went to their quarters to shower and get ready for dinner and their guests. As they were dressing Kat looked over at Dirk.

"You've got something on your mind, like you have something to say but don't know how."

"I do, I just don't know how to start."

"Try from the beginning."

Dirk looked at Kat for a few seconds. Kat felt like it was at least two hours before he spoke.

"Nancy and I were never married. I guess in the forties and fifties that's a mortal sin, but in our time it wasn't. Everyone thought she and I were husband and wife and we never corrected them. Even the Navy thinks we were married. A Personnelman in the first squadron I reported to took it for granted we were and did the paper work on his own. I reported it to my Skipper. He told me the necessary paper work evolved to correct this would be enormous. And now that we were expecting a child, leave it as it is."

"Nancy and I were high school sweethearts, after high school, I went on to the Naval Academy and she went to Virginia State Teachers College. I saw her off and on during that time, vacations and such. Everyone thought we would get married, but she and I, by that time were just very close friends."

"I went on to flight school. She came down to Florida one long weekend. One thing led to another. Three months later she called and said she was in the "family" way. She didn't want to get married but she couldn't stay at the school she was teaching at. Too many people with their noses stuck in the air. It was very "Old School", if you know what I mean."

"I told her to pack up and come down to Florida and we'd go from there. She came down at the end of the school year. They had given her a large settlement because of the long-term contract she had with them. After I graduated from flight school, I was sent to San Diego to report to the USS Saratoga. We bought a home there in the foothills and started acting just like the other married couples."

"I really don't think Nancy ever wanted to get married, at least not to me. I loved my daughter and I didn't want to lose her. So we kept up the charade of happily married bliss. When they were killed in the car accident, I felt as though my heart had been torn out. The one thing in my life was gone. That's when I took my ride into tomorrow."

Dirk looked at Kat and saw the tears streaming down her face. He thought. This is the end of her and me Dirk's shoulders slumped as though he had been deflated.

Kat went over to him and held him close.

"You told me if I got into your bed it would be forever. That you didn't believe in one night stands. I moved in the next day. I'm not moving out. You're mine now and the past is just that, the past. We are in the future. By the time we get back to Earth we could be well into the twenty-first century. Even though we've only been gone for a few months, our time, we've really been gone for years."

Dirk pushed her gently back, looked into her eyes and said. "I love you, Kat, I can't imagine my life without you. Would you marry me?"

"Yes. When?"

"Well, we have a Captain on the other ship and Captains can perform ceremonies."

Dirk kissed Kat. Kat leaned backward until they fell onto the bed.

***

When the Mayhans came up to dinner at about 7:00 PM, they found the table already set and a meal fit for a king. The meal was great and the conversation was kept on the light side, just talking about their past lives on Earth.

John looked at Mary. "I think they have something to tell us." John looked back at Dirk and Kat. "Me thinks thou hast come to an agreement?"

"Mary, as Captain of the JonMar, would you perform a wedding ceremony?" Dirk asked.

Mary sat there for a moment staring at them. Realizing she was indeed a Captain of a Ship and she did have the authority to perform a ceremony.

"Yes, it would be an honor for me."

They went to the bridge. Kat opened the view panel at the front of the ship. Mary performed the ceremony there with the stars of outer space in front of them. Not exactly a church wedding but you couldn't get much closer to God.

John told everyone to stay right where they were and left the bridge. He was back in a few minutes with a camera.

"For posterity." John said.

The Best Man made a toast with a libation from a bottle of liqueur found in the stores on the ship.

Mary went over to the main computer, turned it on, and entered the date and time of the wedding and signed it Captain Mary J. Mayhan, Commanding Officer, IV-204 U.S.A., in the ship's log. They had one more drink and the Mayhans bade them goodnight.

Dirk went over to the console and went back to 27 Sept 1999 and entered Bucannan, Kathleen L., First Officer of the NanMar.

"Why did you do that?"

"There are a couple of reasons, one; you deserve it, two; in case anything happens to me, command will automatically go to you, three; you and I make a great team. And besides that, about an hour ago you signed on for life. Dirk went to the door leading out, bowed and waved her through saying. "After you, Mrs. MacGlashan."

"I think I like my new name, Kathleen MacGlashan."

"Like!, what do you mean? I think I like!"

Kat put her arms around his neck, kissed him and whispered. "I know I like my new name."

"If someone throws on the holding beam, we're going to look very foolish." Dirk said.

"What a nice way to spend the rest of our lives." laughed Kat. She turned and led Dirk by the hand. "Come on sailor, this night is still young."

CHAPTER FOURTEEN

As they lay in bed the next morning, the door to the galley opened and in came Scaner carrying a large tray. He came over and set the tray on the bed. "Breakfast is served, Mr. and Mrs. MacGlashan."

"What a nice way to start the day." Kat said.

"I thought you might like it, Madame."

After a leisurely breakfast, Dirk and Kat went down to the JonMar. Meeting John and Mary on the bridge, they discussed plans for that day.

"Item one, will be to send the shuttle off on its trip to the mother ship. Item two, we train. We've got three days to get ready for our trip to the mother ship. Everyone suit up for a space walk." Dirk said.

Kat pressurized the airlock and opened the inner door and everyone stepped in. John closed the inner door, then depressurize the compartment. Dirk attached a lifeline from the ship to himself, then from himself to John and then to Mary and then Kat. Dirk showed each how to leave the airlock.

"Just walk to the door and give a little shove straight out. The life line will only let you go to about fifteen feet."

Kat out went first. This would be her third space walk. When the three were out, Dirk took a fifty-foot lifeline, attaching it to a permanent safety rail that circumvented the spacecraft. He pushed himself out.

Dirk showed Mary and John how to work the small jet blasters. When they could control themselves, he had them all go to the safety railing on the ship. Each hooked up their own safety line.

"Let's go for a ship walk. John and I will go forward and check out the ship and you girls, excuse me, Ladies, go aft and we'll meet on the other side. Check the external gear. No loose wires, that sort of thing. If you find anything you don't think is right sing out and we'll all look. All right, see ya on the dark side."

Kat and Mary walked very slowly around the top of the ship. Checking the different radar gear and antennas, everything looked in order.

While walking on the underside of the ship, it was hard to grasp that they were walking up side down. Kat looked at Mary.

"It's hard to grasp up or down or even sides because of the lack of gravity."

Mary looked at her, nodding. They met Dirk and John on the other side of the ship. Dirk asked if they would like to see a three moon- rise. He motioned for them to follow him. All four walked toward the dome of the spacecraft. Approaching the top, they saw three large asteroids shining off in the distance. Mary said they looked like the moon of earth only in triplicate. They stood there for a while not saying a word. John summed it up.

"Seeing all this really makes one realize just how small you really are. I wouldn't have missed this for all the tea in China."

"Wherever God is, I'm glad he let us see this." Kat said.

Dirk broke the euphoria. "Now we try some space flying. Let's all go out to the end of the lines and use the blasters to get us back around to the airlock."

Everyone tried a small experiment with the blasters on the way around, up, down, sideways and even what they thought was up side down. Once they were at the airlock, Dirk had each one take their shorter safety line and attach it to the inside before they detached the longer one.

"Pure safety" he said.

When everyone was inside the airlock, Dirk had Mary and John work as a team. Securing the outer door, pressurizing the lock, then opening the inner door. Each took care of their equipment. Cleaning the filters in the CO2 scrubbers and replenished the air tanks. The suits were hung next to the air lock and secured in place.

"Let's go up to the bridge and check on the shuttle craft." Dirk said.

***

Mary switched on the monitor and a soft beep was heard. John switched on the Nav plot and there it was, on the original track and about an eighth of the way to the mother ship.

Scaner reported there were no other ships within a five hundred-mile radius of their ships.

The four went to the galley. As Dirk put his tray on the shelf in the food panel a sultry, sexy voice said "Did you enjoy your meal, Darling". The word Darling came out like (Daawling).

It stopped Dirk dead in his tracks. Kat started to laugh and John and Mary joined in.

"That's John's electrical interpretation of Betty Davis." Mary said.

John looked at Dirk, smiled and said. "Gottcha, that's one for me."

Dirk laughed with them.

The rest of the day was spent going through tech manuals and doing some simulated torpedo firing. John excelled at this. Even showed them some short cuts. Learned from his days as a sub sailor. Kat had him go over a couple of the procedures again so she would completely understand them. Torpedo firing was her job on the NanMar.

At five PM they called it a day. Dirk posted Scaner at his usual place, with instructions to call if anything out of the ordinary happened.

***

After dinner Dirk excused himself and went to the tool bay. He worked on a project that took up most of the evening. He finished at about 11:00 PM, went to their quarters, showered and got into bed. Kat was already in bed when he got there.

He held his bride of one day close, told her to close her eyes and hold out her hand. He took her left hand and placed a ring on the third finger. Kat opened her eyes and stared at it. It was a gold ring with a three-carat diamond enclosed in a clasp mounted on the ring. She could read the lettering on the top of the ring, "In God We Trust".

"Oh Dirk, it's beautiful." She looked again at the ring. "You made this! That's what you were doing in the tool room. What did you make this from?"

"I found an old double eagle coin in the store room. I flattened it out by pounding on the edge. The diamond is from the old stones. There's an oddity with this one. Something the other ones don't have."

Kat looked at the stone. "What is it?"

"Hold it up so the light shines light down on it."

She did this. Eight perfect rays of light shone out of the sides. Each showing the colors of the rainbow. It was a perfect prism cut. "That's the way it came out of the exciter." Dirk said.

"It's beautiful. Oh Scotty, I love you."

Kat put her arms around his neck and kissed him. Her eyes looking at the ring on her left hand. He knew she was looking at the ring because he was watching her. They both caught each other looking and started to smile. Kat hugged him, then relaxed in his arms. He took her face between his hands and saw two small tears. He kissed away each tear and held her against him very gently. It was in the wee hours of the morning before they got to sleep.

CHAPTER FIFTEEN

For some reason John rose at four thirty. Getting dressed and with a cup of coffee in his hand, went to the bridge. He opened the outer view panel and switched on the monitor and Nav chart. He punched up the monitoring channel for the shuttlecraft. Something did not look right.

Although it was still on course and moving toward the mother ship, it had slowed down to almost a crawl. He watched it for over an hour, checking its course and speed.

At 6:00 am he went to their quarters, showered and got something to eat. Going back to their quarters, woke Mary. He told her what had been going on and he was going back to the bridge.

The shuttle was on course but still moving very slowly. John figured the crystal had gone bad, which would be the reason for it slowing. Having no way to check the systems in the shuttlecraft, at least none he knew of, without giving their position away. He just sat and watched.

Mary came to the bridge about 7:00 am and studied the chart also. John marked the point where the shuttle had slowed down.

***

Just inside the detection range of the mother ship, the shuttle picked up speed. It was in a direct line to the stern of the mother ship. Right where the docking bay was.

"Bingo," John said. "They've got a tractor beam on it. Right on schedule."

"I'm going to get some breakfast, I'll be back in a little while." Mary said.

As Mary stood they saw a flash of light coming at them. It was so quick neither had a chance to move. It went right on by them. No warning system went off because it was not harmful. To the sensors it was just another light beam, but it was recorded. Mary did an incoming bearing and distance trace. It had originated at the mother ship.

"Those bastards just shot up one of their own. That's what that light beam was." Mary exclaimed.

John looked at her for a moment. Turning to the computer, did an analyzation on the beam. Sure enough, it was a spent laser beam. Not harmful anymore but traveling at the speed of light it should go by Earth in about five weeks. John looked at Mary.

"That ought to really spook the boys at the observatory. Wondering where in hell that came from."

One their best friends, Bob Harwood, who is an Astrologist and also teaches at the University.

"Let's see if Dirk and Kat are up yet?" John said.

John reached over to the intercom and called the NanMar.

"Yo, you guys up yet? Something exciting is happening in the world of Oz."

A very tired female voice said. "Can it wait until after breakfast."

"Sure, nothing happened to us but you ain't gonna' believe what happened to the shuttle. The mother ship has a tractor beam on it. Take your time."

John shut the intercom off and looked at Mary. "I think it's time to strap on the six guns Tex. Cause it looks like the OK coral is dead ahead." John added. "I kid thee not."

"I really don't think this is going to be as easy as we thought. The flying I did in the Gulf War was no picnic." Mary said.

"I know what you're saying, Hon. Things got hairy once in awhile under the ocean when we were playing hide-and-seek with the USSR. Some pretty bad things happened on our last patrol. I've got a funny feeling about this."

Mary looked at John and studied him close. This was a reaction she had never seen in him before. He had never talked about his time in subs. At least not about the missions they had done.

This quiet man who taught school and collected rocks was really a warrior. He had gone, as the Navy says, "In harm's way". She trusted his instincts.

John was one of the very quiet, solid rocks you could lean on, knowing no harm would come to you. She stepped over to him and put her arms around his waist and leaned her head on his chest. John circled her with his arms and hugged her. She looked up to him and said. "I love you." John bent down and kissed her.

"Let's check on our surprise package to the Arians."

The Mother ship was pulling the shuttlecraft in at an alarming rate of speed. Mary did an update on the speed. It had tripled.

"It probably just seems fast because of the speed which we sent it off at." Mary said.

"Probably, but that mother ship has got to have one hell of a big reactor in it. It has to, to be able to push that much bulk and weight around." John said.

The door to the bridge opened and Kat and Dirk walked in.

"What's happening in the world of Oz that is so spectacular." Dirk asked.

John pointed to the Nav chart and reached over to rewind the tape for the monitor. He stopped it and put it on play back. All four watched the view screen.

"There, watch now."

A beam of light came at them and before Dirk could say "Whatinthehellwasthat" it was past them and gone.

"That was the aftermath of a laser shot on our surprise package. It seems 'Mommy' is a little jumpy." John stated.

Kat looked around at everyone. "They just shot up one of their own craft. Those bastards don't give a damn, even about their own people."

Mary went to the Nav chart and showed them the track they had. The course and speed proved they had a tractor beam on. It was moving at three times the send off speed.

"I think," Mary said. "Because they didn't get a life form reading, they shot once to depressurize it just in case. Simple way to solve a problem. I'll bet the inside off the shuttle is a mess. Nasty little viruses all over the place."

"I'll also wager," Kat said. "That in two days there is going to be a litter of sick ,real sick, Arians on that ship. I beefed up the virus strain a little. In fact, I'll guarantee whatever is alive on that ship will be sick."

Dirk said. "Well then, all we can do is sit back and keep checking on the progress of our surprise to Oz. You know, we've been calling it the Mother ship but I think Oz is a better name. All those in favor?"

"Aye"

"Aye"

"Aye"

Dirk put his finger on the location of the ship on the Nav chart "Hello Oz."

CHAPTER SIXTEEN

"John said something before you all came in and I think it's about as true as true can be, 'It's time to strap on the six guns Tex, cause the OK coral is just ahead'."

Dirk looked at these three people, who, in turn, were looking at him. They are looking at me for one reason, Dirk thought guidance. I'm a Lieutenant Commander to John and I should know what to do next. To Mary, I'm the equivalent to a Major and I damn well better know what I'm doing. To Kat, I'm her husband and I had better live up to her expectations.

"What we had better do now is get some flight time in these babies. Mary, John, you two are going to have to learn fly this ship in two days. That's all we've got left now before we make contact with Oz. So let's back away from Oz and conduct some maneuvers. They don't know about us yet so we're relatively safe out here. If we can get some basic maneuvers down pat so we are covering each other, we might be able to get the Arians to think we're a larger force than what we are."

***

"It's 0900 hours now, let's plan on separation for 1200, then do a 180 degree turn and start basic flight training over again." "Captain Mayhan, we'll start with 'S' turns, in formation. When we get those down we'll go to a standard two-minute turns, first to port and then to starboard. Okay, let's make preparations for separation."

At exactly 1145 the JonMar checked in. John reported the ship was ready for maneuvering and they had 110 percent on the reactor.

At 1200 Dirk said. "Break right." In five seconds the JonMar broke right coming into position on their starboard quarter, just a little low. Perfect, he thought, this girl can really drive. At 1215 he commenced an 'S' turn drill, they did these for about 45 minutes. During this time they switched positions and the NarMar became the wingman.

Dirk called the JonMar. "Zinger, standard 2 minute turn to the starboard, commencing at 1301 hours."

"Roger, 2 minute to starboard at 1301."

Zinger put the JonMar at a 45-degree turn to the right and held it there. When she leveled off 2 minutes later she was at the exact position when the turn started. During the turn she asked John to check on NanMar.

"She's right off our starboard quarter. Right where she's supposed to be."

They practiced doing split-'S' turns and Immelman turns to get the feel of the ships and how well they reacted to abrupt movements. These ships were very maneuverable for their size and reacted like cats.

Dirk had NanMar in level flight when Zinger shot past him at full power. First she did a snap roll to the right and then one to the left. At no time was she more than a half of degree off of her axis. She did a loop and was back on station in one perfect maneuver.

Dirk looked over Kat. "That's got to be some of the best flying I've ever seen. I can see why she's an IP." Dirk got on the intership comm. "Zinger, we are about an hour away from our origin. Let's try something out. You shut down, I'm going to go back and shut down. You start up in one hour and fifteen minutes and then come back, hunting. It will be good practice for both of us. You shut down now."

"Roger, JonMar out."

The 208 reached the starting position. Dirk shut her down and they waited. After one hour and fourteen minutes they heard "Zing, gotcha."

Dirk had the cameras pointed at their back trail, looking for the JonMar when this happened. He nearly jumped out of his skin. Kat had to laugh. Dirk started to laugh also.

"I must have looked pretty funny, sitting there with my eyes glued to the screen and then jumping like that?"

"You've got to admit she did sneak up on us. I don't know what you had in mind but she fooled you."

"She is good."

Dirk and Kat checked the Nav chart for the shuttlecraft. The beeper he had put on board showed it in the docking bay.

"I think by tomorrow night there are going to be some very sick Arians in Oz."

Kat turned on the intership comm channel and told John and Mary where the shuttle was now. Mary acknowledged and signed off.

Kat turned to Dirk. "Can you stand some criticism?"

Dirk swallowed hard and said. "Yes".

"You've been treating Mary like she was one of your first day flying students. Assuming she knew nothing about fancy maneuvers. What she did was for one purpose. To show you she really does know how to fly. That the Air Force did not just give her the Captains bars. She earned them. You do know what assume does? It makes an ass of you and me. I'm not a pilot, but I could see what you were doing."

Dirk just sat there for a minute before speaking. "You know your right. I was treating her like a 'Nugget' (fresh out of flight school) and I shouldn't. She's an excellent pilot. I think tomorrow we should practice air-to-air combat maneuvering. So we both can sharpen our skills in these ships."

Dirk went over to the main console and turned on the inter-ship comm.

"Mary, what are your opinions on practicing air to air combat tomorrow?"

Mary told him what she thought they should attempt to be proficient in.

The next day the two ships went off in different directions and then came back towards each other. They did mock dog fighting for about two hours.

"I want us each to fire a dummy torpedo so the other can track it and fire for effect. If Oz fires at us from long range, it will be a torpedo first. So we had better be able to track and fire real quick. John should be okay because of his Sub training, and Kat is doing real well."

Mary reversed course and was soon out of range. She did a split-S coming back at NarMar low. When she had a track on NanMar, she fired.

Kat locked on and had a firing solution in seconds. She fired, full power on the laser. The dummy torpedo was two miles away when it was destroyed. Dirk slipped away and came back at JonMar in a dive on its port quarter. Dirk did a snap roll and fired. He then did a climbing turn to the right. John was on the torpedo and fired. The inbound torpedo disintegrated at little over a mile.

"I would say we are as ready as we are going to get. The virus has had enough time to infect the ship. The Arians should all be down sick by the time we reach Oz. Let's do it Captain."

Dirk called the JonMar. "We're as ready as we'll ever be. Kat says the virus has had enough time and the Arians should all down sick by the time we get there. She says 'Let's do it'. Are you guys ready?"

"Roger, we're on your right wing Captain, so let's start the ball." Mary said.

***

The two ships turned to the inbound heading. Dirk called back to JonMar.

"I want you to get in my radar shadow. This way Oz will think there's only one ship coming at him."

Mary went into position behind NanMar. She was blind forward but she had both sides and aft open for tracking.

Kat looked over to Dirk. "I feel like I'm going elephant hunting with a 22 rifle with nothing but my bra and panties on."

"I feel a little naked too. We've covered every angle I can think of. Just remember, 'He who sleeps soundly and is pure in heart, has the strength of ten.'"

Kat looked at Dirk. "God, that was awful."

The inter-ship com came on. "We concur."

"My head is bloodied but not bowed." Dirk stated.

Finally, "Operation Pay-Back" was on. The small armada was on its way.

CHAPTER SEVENTEEN

When the two ships came in radar range of Oz, Dirk switched on the Arian version of IFF (Identification, Friend or Foe), sending out a message in Arian. It transmitted. "IV-208 returning from earth."

At the end of the second try, a voice came over the air.

"We welcome you back Rega."

Kat got on the transmitter and said in a very raspy, weak voice,

"I look forward to a complete rest. I am sick from a disease I contracted from Earth. Do not come near me when I land."

Scaner was at the transmitter translating all this into Arian and then translating Arian into English. All of this was done in seconds with the computer in hyper-drive.

A message came in. "We are all sick from a virus brought in on the shuttle from Awjer's ship, IV-204. Tepec was dead when the shuttle was tractored in. There are only four of us able to function now. Seven are bedded from this sickness, one is Captain Eugin. Upon your arrival, you will be acting Captain. Request you do not transmit again until you are in range of the tractor beam. We are very low on power. The Beta-Six trader has not arrived yet."

"Wait, what other ship is in now?"

"The IV-205 is in one week now. The IV-202 is still out of commission and attached to the under docking hatch. Ending transmit."

"Good thinking Kat. Now we know there's only one left out here. I'm sure it'll find us sooner or later. We know there are eleven on board, probably the two from each of the ships like ours and seven crew members for Oz. Call the JonMar and see if they received that transmission."

Kat switched to the inter-ship com channel and got Mary. "Did you get the transmissions from Oz? How are things there?"

"We received the transmissions, the translator disc was a little slow working but we got them all. All systems are go here."

"I've got a suggestion to make." Dirk said. "When we get into tractor beam range, let's put out a shuttle craft and let them lock onto it. Just before it reaches the docking bay, we split off, each one goes up a side of the ship. I'll take the starboard and go high. You take the port and go low. Most of the ship's power will be on the tractor beam. It will take them some time to switch power to their armament. By that time we will be along side and have them in a crossfire. You'll be closest to their sick bay. If they light off their laser beam put yours on stun and knock them out. I'll be in sight of the bridge and do the same. We don't want to kill anyone unless it's absolutely necessary."

"Roger, let's go get'em."

"Scaner, go to the shuttle bay, set the course to Oz, open the outer door and wait until I signal you to release the shuttle."

They kept the speed down and approached Oz.

John came on the inter ship comm. "If we send in the shuttle empty they'll know right away something's up. None of us can go anywhere. We've got to think of something."

"Ok, we've got a little time left, so start thinking." Dirk stated.

Kat looked over to Dirk and said. "If we were to put Awjer in the shuttle now we would be showing a life form but without proper resuscitation it would kill him in minutes. We could put Rega in a suit and turn up the heat enough so it would register on a heat-seeking beam. Enough to let us get in close."

"Sounds like a good idea, let's talk it over with JonMar." Dirk got back on the comm channel. "Kat came up with an idea." Dirk told them about it. "Hopefully it will work, just long enough to let us get in close."

"I think it'll work. At this stage of the game, time is against us. If it doesn't work, we've still got speed and maneuverability, which they don't have." Mary said.

Dirk got up. "I'll go get Rega ready and put her in the shuttle. Kat, you stay here and monitor the ship. If they call back for any reason, you're going to have to talk to them. It has to be feminine voice."

Dirk went to the capsule room and got Rega out of freeze. He took her to the shuttle and as he set her in place, he had an idea. He went back to the bridge and told Kat about his idea.

"I can do that." She went over to the main computer and put in a disc. After she had finished she gave the disc to Dirk and he went back to the shuttle. Dirk put the disc in the computer and switched to remote control. When they had reached tractor beam range, Dirk released the shuttle. The shuttle was well away from NanMar when Kat switch on the remote and pushed the play button.

"Master ship, turn on the tractor beam and bring me in. There is not enough power in the crystal to fly correctly. I am to weak to dock the ship."

Everyone waited with their breath held and their fingers crossed. Sure enough, the tractor beam locked onto the shuttle. The two ships slowed down as it they were stopping. The shuttle disappeared into Oz.

***

The Arian who had been running the tractor beam opened the shuttle door and went the pilot seat. He opened the face mast to talk to Rega and was rewarded with an awful stench. With the heat turned up, Rega's body had started to decompose. He ran out of the shuttle and hit the alarm switch. The power was immediately switched to the laser weapons.

Dirk could see Oz shift a little at the loss of power to its drive systems.

"Break now Zinger."

CHAPTER EIGHTEEN

Both ships went to full power and were along side of Oz before any weapons could be brought to bear.

"Lock onto sickbay Zinger. If anyone tries to leave, whack'um."

Dirk switched to the broadcast channel.

"Arian ship, these are the ships NanMar and JonMar of the United States of America. We request you surrender your ship now. We have thermal torpedoes locked on to your bridge and main propulsion room." "Do not do anything which would make us fire upon you. You have one minute to acknowledge. I repeat, we do not wish to fire upon you."

"Someone is moving from sick bay." John said.

"Stun them."

"They're down, no movement."

Dirk waited for a little over one minute. "Arian ship, your time is up." No answer.

He signaled Kat and she fired a laser at the bridge. There were two Arians on the bridge. Now there were only two left standing. One was at the docking bay but where was the other.

Dirk switch the heat seeking beam on auto and started at the stern of the ship. It searched its way up the ship. The beam stopped at the main propulsion room.

Dirk called over to Zinger. "Move forward to the main propulsion room, we have a busy Arian there. Knock him down. I can't do it without punching a hole in the hull."

Mary accomplished this with no difficulty.

***

"Cover me JonMar, I'm going to the docking bay."

Dirk went into the bay very slowly and turned the ship around so it was facing open space. Kat tested the air outside and found it sufficient for humans.

"They haven't closed the outer door to the bay all this time. How can they keep air integrity with it open?" Kat asked.

"I don't know, so let's put on suits before we go out. In fact, let me go first, you stay here with Scaner and run the ship. If this ship gets endangered, you get out of here and nail'em."

"NO!"

"Yes, that's an order. The safety of this ship comes first. With out it you, I, or we can't go anywhere. Do you understand? Nothing is going to happen but I want you to know what to do, just-in-case."

Dirk went to the capsule room, lowered the elevator sleeve and put on his suit. When he emerged from the elevator he looked around for the remaining Arian. There, standing next to the shuttle. He walked toward it. He had the comm channel relayed back to the ship and translated into Arian. Dirk held up the laser for the Arian to see. "I come in peace." Then lay it on the floor. The Arian could not see his right side or the 9mm Berretta in his hand.

Dirk thought. <u>It's up to you now, Sport</u>

The Arian stepped away from the shuttlecraft when Dirk laid down his laser. As he stepped away he raised his right arm, he was holding a laser. Dirk saw a smile come across the Arians face. He stood there, not moving. The Arian started to lower the weapon but brought it up quickly and fired.

Dirk crouched and rolled to the right. Missed, just by inches but still a miss. Lining up the 9mm Dirk fired, the round struck the Arian in the right shoulder knocking him down.

Dirk picked up his laser and walked up to the Arian, kicking his laser aside. The Arian kicked out at Dirk striking him in the knee. Dirk stumbled backward, catching himself before he fell. He raised the laser, stunning the Arian.

"It's all clear now. I tried to get this fellow to give up peaceably but he wouldn't. What is it with these Arians? All they want to do is kill. This guy's knocked out and he's still grinning. Contact JonMar and have them come into the docking bay."

Dirk went over to the Arian and checked the shoulder wound. It was just a flesh wound but the 9mm hits with such force, it knocks you down. There was a little bit of fluid coming from the wound. <u>Christ, these Arians don't even bleed right</u> Dirk found a piece of cord and tied the Arian up. He then went into the shuttle to turn the heat down on Rega's remains. The face cover had been removed. He knew the odor had to be strong. Dirk reset the face cover and turned the temperature down. He brought Rega out of the shuttle and laid her next to it. He looked up to see the JonMar at the bay door but it couldn't get in because NanMar was in the way.

"Kat, move the ship back and to the right so Zinger can get in."

"I've never done any maneuvering like that."

"It's easy, Scaner will help."

The elevator sleeve rose up about three feet and the ship lifted inches from the deck. It gently came back and to the right leaving more than enough room for the JonMar to come in. The NanMar lowered back down and the elevator was dropped down to the deck. Zinger brought the ship in, turned around and then backed up so either ship could get out if need be.

"Kat, retest the air in this compartment, please."

"The air is fine there."

"Zinger, you and John come on down.

The elevator was lowered and both of them got out and walked over to Dirk. They had put on suits before leaving their ship. Kat showed up wearing her suit also.

"What's Scaner doing now?"

"He's translating the computer banks on Oz."

"Who moved the ship?"

"I did."

Dirk smiled at Kat and thought Somehow I knew she'd do it without help

"Has anyone got any million dollar fuel tickets with them?"

John showed Dirk three and Kat had three plus some karat crystals for the shuttlecraft.

"We're going to have to fumigate the shuttle. The one that's tied opened the face covering on Rega. It smells in there."

"It shouldn't." Kat said

"I turned up the heat way up on the space suit."

***

"What's with the one tied up?" John asked.

Dirk told them what had happened. Kat went over to him and looked at the wound. She went back to the ship and got her Vet's bag and put some sulfur powder on it and then bandaged it.

"It's just a flesh wound, He'll be all right in a few days."

"The first thing we've got to do is put all of the Arians in one place that's secure. Let's go round them up." Dirk said.

***

They went forward to the sick bay. There were six in beds and one was on the floor by the door. This had to be the one who was trying to get out. Dirk looked him over. There were five red stripes on his right sleeve, down at the cuff.

"I'll bet this is the Captain."

Dirk put him back in the bed that was rumpled. One of the two females was pregnant.

Kat went over to her and checked her out and then listened for a fetal heart beat. She nodded, then checked out the other Arians. All were knocked out. They were sick but other than that, okay.

Dirk and John went to the main propulsion room and found the Arian lying there dead. His head was at a right angle to his body. Dirk and John looked around to see what had happened. They couldn't figure out what he had been up to. They went to the bridge, got the other two and brought them back down to sickbay. The male Arians couldn't weigh more than a hundred pounds each and the females even less.

When they got to sickbay with the two Arians, Kat and Mary were at work doctoring the Arians. The two who had awakened were tied and strapped to their beds. They were not very happy looking campers, to say the most. Dirk told Kat and Mary what they came across in the main propulsion room. Dirk took out a small inter comm and called back to NanMar.

***

"Scaner, come down to the main propulsion room."

Dirk and John had figured out where the Arian was when he fell but they couldn't figure out what he was doing up there. Scaner came into the compartment. John had him plug into the computer bank for the reactor and the exciter.

There, he had cross-wired the exciter and the leads to the reactor. So when new crystals are placed in the exciter the reactor would over extend and go into melt down. It wouldn't blow but it would kill the ship anyway.

"Not only do these Arians like to kill but their suicidal too. You know, it's getting harder and harder for me to like them. I think the best thing to do is freeze them all." John said

"I don't think the girls would go along. But it's a thought."

"Well, let's fix this and get 'Ole Oz' back on line."

Dirk looked at John and asked. "What do you want me to do?"

"Nothing, really, I can get this fixed in no time."

Dirk plugged Scaner into the main computer panel and started the translation process for the entire ship.

While Scaner was doing that Dirk went looking around. He went into the reactor room and looking at the exciter, went back into the compartment where John was.

"This baby takes four crystals to run at full power." Dirk stated

"That doesn't surprise me. This is one-hell-of-a-big ship and the reactor has got to be two and a half times the size of ours. Dirk, hand me that tester." Dirk handed up the tester and John checked out the leads. "All fixed, we can replace the crystals and get back to full power now."

Dirk and John went into the reactor room. Dirk turned on the emergency generator and John turned off the exciter, he replaced the four smaller three karat crystals with four fifteen karat ones and then turned the exciter on again. The emergency generator shut off automatically and they were back to full power again. A panel opened at the side of the room and a series of lights started to blink.

"Hello, what's this?" John said and stepped over to it. Dirk went with him and they looked it over. "I think we had better leave it alone until we can see the manual on it. It looks to be some kind of energy field."

They left the panel open and returned to the main board. All of the gauges and read out dials showed full power was restored. And the batteries were on super-charge. John tested the reactor out-put, 110 percent. He looked at Dirk.

"She'll go to light speed on a moments notice."

Dirk called sickbay. Kat answered.

"We're back to full power now. The CO2 scrubbers are working fine and are replenishing the oxygen in the tanks. How are things going with you two there?"

"Everyone is awake and very unhappy about being strapped to their beds. The only ones who are being reasonable are Awga, the pregnant one, and the other female, Triga. It seems Awjer is Awga's mate. She's happy to know he is alive and in freeze."

"I've inoculated all of them and done some minor surgery. The one you had to shoot started to act up so I pointed my laser at him and he quieted right down. But I still don't trust him. The Captain is the sickest, probably because of his age. The rest are not resisting like "Ole whatshisface", they're mostly just uncomfortable. What are you two up to now?"

"We're going up to the bridge to see where we're headed. If any one of those Arians gives you two any trouble, wack'em with a laser. The rest will understand that. Don't release anyone, no matter what they promise."

***

Dirk and John went back to the bridge. The interior of this bridge was almost the same as in the small ships. Except it had three seats at the main console, One for the Pilot, in the center, the Navigator was on the right and fire control was on the left. All of the systems had been translated to English. Scaner was plugged into the computer absorbing the main banks.

"Scaner, when you're done with that, switch to the IV-202 schematics and we'll see what's the matter with her." He looked at John. "It could be a small problem, one we could fix. From what these Arians have done as far as space travel is concerned, I don't think they're much on mechanics. There's fifteen sleeping compartments on this vessel and only one head working, I checked. The only one is in the Captains quarters. I had to go the last time we were up here. I almost wet myself before I could find one."

***

"Well, let's find out where this baby is headed." John said. He brought up the navigational star chart on the monitor. "The destination is this star system here. It looks almost identical to Earth's. There's a central star with five planets revolving around it. Look where their home planet is. This doesn't make any sense. From where the home planet is to where Oz is now is a four-month trip. To Earth it's a three-month trip. This other star system is a one-month trip but even further away from the home planet. The star system we are supposed to go to is about a three month trip from Earth. It's a triangle, but in the wrong direction."

Dirk studied the nav chart.

"When we captured the JonMar, we questioned Awjer a little before we put him in cryo. He said their home planet is dying and they were looking for a new planet to live on. I wouldn't be a bit surprised to find out their home planet is dead and they are, right now, in between a rock and a hard place. Just like the Bowivel, 'Just look'n for a home'. Okay, we've got one more ship running around loose. Where is it? Is it headed here? Or is it headed to the other star system and waiting for this ship to arrive?"

Dirk continued. "Let's give it some time, four or five days, to show up here. If it doesn't, I'd say it was going to the other star system, to wait at some point for Oz to show up. If it shows up here, we nail it. The driver has got to be as sick as everyone else. Plus the ship has got to be on its last legs, as far as power goes. You've got to give these Arians credit for one thing. They like living on the edge."

"Let's go down and see what the ladies are doing. We can tell them our latest discoveries."

***

The women had the Arians all secured and sedated by the time they got there and were going through the medical supplies trying to figure out what was what.

John asked. "Do you think we can leave them alone while we get some thing to eat?"

"Sure, they've all been treated for the virus, the only one we had trouble with was "Whatshisface" there. I gave him a shot in the arm and he'll be out for about eight hours. The others are too weak to do anything. The only two really needing attention are Awga and Captain Eugin. The Captain is in pretty bad shape and of course Awga is pregnant. I'm not an MD but I do know a little about the human or as in this case Arian anatomy."

***

"Scaner, we will be in the main galley in case something goes wrong. Change the voice in the automatic kitchens also."

"What voice do you wish to hear?"

"Surprise us, just so long as it's not the voice the Arians use."

They were sitting at one of the tables sipping on an after dinner coffee, discussing what should be done next. Dirk and John explained what had transpired on the bridge and everyone agreed to put that on hold for a couple of days. There was no immediate danger to the ship.

CHAPTER NINETEEN

The first order of business was to look in the cryo capsule compartment. John suggested he and Dirk look first, but was vetoed by the women. They said they were in this crew and they could stand up to the pressures as good as anyone.

They went to capsule room and found sixty panels with capsules, all were filled with mist. Mary took down the numbers from the plates as she went around the room. There were four tables in the center of the room.

Dirk went to the transporter room and went over to the holding beam panel, four beams. Stepping into the storage room, he found it full with clothes and personal items, evidently from the specimens in cryo.

<u>These Arians have been busy</u> thought Dirk. He checked out the tool room. When Dirk got back to the capsule room, Mary had a print out of all the people in the capsules. There were three families, two consisting of four members each and one father and son. The rest were people were taken singularly. The Arians had taken an even amount of men and women. The notable fact is most were somewhere between twenty-five and forty, all in their prime of life. Dirk suggested they go to the bridge and ponder this over. Kat and Mary were for resuscitating everyone.

John said. "This can't be done because the supplies on hand are not sufficient for that amount of people. We can only resuscitate the same amount that's going into freeze. We haven't checked out the other two craft yet. There maybe more people in them.

"Scaner, plug into the computer and check out the other two craft for anything in cryo."

"Aye, Aye, Sir"

Dirk looked at Kat and said. "I wish you hadn't taught him that."

"I didn't, he taught me." Everyone had a good laugh.

"There are no humans in the other two craft, only plants. All of the humans have been transferred here."

Each was deep with-in their own thoughts when John spoke up.

"I know it seems like we're playing God but we can't revive everyone right now. We have to pick about ten people to resuscitate and put some of the Arians in freeze. We are going to have to train people to fly the other two ships and also to man Oz. That's not going to be easy. I suggest we start with the father and son and the two sets of parents. That will give us six empty capsules here."

Kat check the read-out from Scaner. "There are four empties in IV-205 and all capsules in IV-202. Let's resuscitate eight people now and then we can bring Awjer here."

"We can find out a lot more about Awjer from his mate, Awga. He might not be as bad as we think. He didn't harm us and we were the only two humans on JonMar." Mary stated "We've got to do something with Rega's remains. That's one capsule space taken up. "Whatshisface" gets one. I don't think the Captain will be much trouble, if fact I think he might be a lot of help."

"It's agreed then, eight get resuscitated, the two sets of parents and the father and son. Let's go through the list of names and then check on the personal items in the storage. You can get a lot of information about someone from the stuff they carry with them." Dirk said.

"We should start resuscitation on two and then in two hours start two more and so on. That way we won't be busy with eight people trying to figure out what-in-the-hell-happened to them all at once." John said

***

Kat was going through the list of people and she came across a couple who were taken at the same date and time.

"I'm going to check these two out."

Dirk, John and Mary went into the capsule room to start the resuscitation on the father and son, Burt and James Chambers.

Kat came back with a smile on her face and went over to capsules 16 and 17, "May I present, Alicia W. West, RN from Cheyenne, Wyo. and William L. Smith, Electrical Engineer from Cheyenne, Wyo. beamed up Jul 4, 1987. I vote for them to be seven and eight."

Dirk asked. "Why"

"She's a nurse and knows, probably, more about humans than I do and his profession will come in handy around here. Here is his business card. He's an electrical contractor for major building complexes. I figured you guys can use him."

Dirk looked at John, both nodded and said. "That's it."

"Let's start them first then the father and son and then the two sets of parents."

"You know, I just thought of something." Everyone looked at John. "The mothers might want their children resuscitated also. You know, 'What's good for the goose, is good for the gander.', 'Love me, love my children.' type stuff. Some people are funny that way. Especially the people we have here. All were taken from remote places, campers, hikers, and rock collectors. Pilots who crash into flying saucers. Vets who work on cows in the middle of the night. What we have here are family units who do things together. They're adventuresome. We should either take them all or pick some other ones."

They got the first four out of the panels and set the resuscitation for the nurse and the engineer.

"We'll come back in two hours and start the father and son, meanwhile let's check out the sleeping quarters in this ship." Dirk said.

There were six quarters set up with queen size beds and the other nine were two beds each. Each had two swing down beds from the upper walls just in case they were needed.

Most of the sleeping quarters were a mess and needed a through cleaning. The queen sized quarters were located across the hall way from the single bed units. Each had it's own bathroom. And were easily accessed from the main galley. All of this was located on the second level of the ship.

The larger quarters were on the outer side of the ship and had a panel, which opened to a view screen for the outside. It was nice to be able to sit in your own room and watch the stars go by or watch a sunset in private.

Dirk winked at Kat. "I'll bet there were a lot of families started in these rooms."

"Do all Navy pilots think like you?"

"Just about."

John and Mary had to smile at the conversation between Dirk and Kat.

They all agreed there would be no problem in resuscitating the families. There would be no problems in sleeping quarters for the families.

"Now that we have quarters available for all of our new crew members, what about us? Any suggestions?" Dirk asked.

"We decided we would remain onboard JonMar for the time being." Mary said. "She's home to us."

"Dirk and I feel the same way, but we're all needed here on Oz. Why don't we set up temporary quarters here. That way if anything happens, we'll all be able to get to the problem sooner."

"Yes, things have a habit of happening real fast out here." Dirk stated. "Kat, why don't you and Mary check on our patients while John and I explore the rest of the ship. There are two decks below this one. If anything happens, call us, if not we'll see you in one hour in the capsule room and we'll start the father and son on the road to recovery.

***

The women went to sickbay. John and Dirk went down to the lower level. There was a machine shop set up in one of the compartments with tools for fixing almost anything on the ship. Another compartment had spare parts stored in it. They went through a hatchway into the next room and found the filtration plant. There was a foul smell lingering in the air but the plant was working.

"I'll bet, that running on such low power clogged up the sewer systems." John said. "Now it's trying to catch up. We could shut this down and clean the filters and then package the solid waste and jettison it. It shouldn't take long for all of the heads to be working again."

"Ok." Dirk replied.

They went to the next compartment and found what looked like a large cool room and a freezer. They opened one door and were rewarded with awful stench. Dirk slammed the door shut. "I think we had better put on a breathing unit before we go back in there."

They didn't go near the door to the freezer.

"It's time to go to the capsule room." Dirk said.

By the time they got to the capsule room Kat and Mary were already there. They had the father and son's capsules out and were switching the systems on for resuscitation. Kat looked over to Dirk.

"The Captain requested to talk to the Commanding Officer of our crew. He doesn't look so good, so maybe you ought to go to him as soon as possible."

"Sure, I'll be over as soon as we're done here." Dirk said.

"You know there is still something funny about these Arians we have here." The other three looked at John. Dirk motioned to John to continue. "There are to many things going wrong with this ship. A normal crew could fix this as matter of course. Low power doesn't mean all of the bathrooms should back up. The rooms are a mess. Bad food stuffs, like the cool room and the freezer. Dirk, you were attached to a Flight Squadron and used to the freedom of either a shore station or a very large carrier."

"I spent five years on a Submarine, fast attack type. We were in tight quarters just like it is here. Everyone knew the others job and knew the ship inside out. Even though I was a Sonarman, I could run Engineering and even the Torpedo room. These people can't do a damn thing except fly the IVs and they don't do that very well. Something is screwy here."

"Well, maybe after I talk with Captain Eugin, we'll know more about what's happening here. Let's go down to sick bay."

When they got to sickbay, everybody was awake and looking very uncomfortable, except for Awga, the pregnant one and "Whatshisface". He was still out from the shot. The Captain lay there, not moving. Dirk went over to him and pulled a chair over to the side of the bed.

"I'm Lieutenant Commander MacGlashan, United States Navy. I was taken onboard the ship IV-208 before the Pilot Rega died. I was resuscitated by the robot Scaner, your people beamed up from Earth. What can I do for you?"

"You know who I am, so I will not go through all of the formalities. I don't have much time left. All is not what it seems to be here. Do not trust any of the Arians here except the two women. They just happened to be in the wrong place at the wrong time. That's why they are here. I believe your people, humans, call them prostitutes. Awjer is my Second in command and is a loyal Arian. The one called Awga is carrying his seed. She should produce in three weeks if all goes well."

"There are discs in the safe in my quarters. I made them up as we came out here from our home planet. I was told that we, Awjer and I, were getting a new crew and were to go back out, as soon as we took on fresh supplies. We did get a chance to off load all of our specimens. At the time all we had were plants and small trees, which grow on your planet. We needed to re-seed our planet. After a long draught, all of the eatable food products on our planet were about gone."

The Captain grimaced as though he was in pain. Dirk said for him to take it easy, and they would talk again soon.

"No, I don't have much time, I am dying and I know it. The virus we contracted from your people plus what I had before will kill me."

"What did you have before that could kill you? Maybe Kat can help you."

"Old age, you can not cure that. The new crew I was supposed get were killed by these Arians. They took their place. There were three female pilots in the new crew, which explains Rega and the other two females."

"As we got further away from Arian, I was under guard all of the time. I was forced to bring the ship here and stay, while they went to Earth to get specimens. I did not know what they had in mind to do at the time. I took the extra crystals we use in the exciter and hid them. The note will tell you how to retrieve them. What these escaped prisoners want to do is all on those discs."

Dirk could tell the Captain was failing fast.

"You rest easy now, we'll figure something out. We are going to need you here on Oz."

"Oz, what is Oz?"

"That's the name we gave this ship as we were heading for it."

"Ahhh, the little girl from Kansas. We have an extensive library of films from your planet. We put them on discs to study your ways. Some thought that is the way your people lived. That was, until we saw your space films. We knew, it was just entertainment. Some of them are quite good, not the space films. Your people need to learn a lot more before you are capable of space travel. Now the way to get into my safe is." He whispered the directions to Dirk so none of the Arians could hear and neither could John, Mary or Kat. "All you will need to know is on those discs. This ship, Oz?, is in your hands now. It is a good ship, treat her right." The Captain gave a sigh and closed his eyes.

Kat leaned over him and tried to rouse him. "I think he's lapsed into a coma."

Dirk motioned everyone outside.

"I think in lieu of what the Captain said we had better consider putting all of the Arians in cryo. I'll go get the discs from the Captains safe and we can check them out. Who wants to go with me to the Captains quarters?"

Mary looked at John and shook her head no.

"You two go" John said. "We'll meet you in the small galley here on this deck."

When Dirk and Kat got to the Captains quarters, they found a very spacious room with a large bed, a desk with a computer and monitor, a lounging area with a couch, an easy chair, end tables and an extensive library. A very large bathroom with a sunken tub and shower. A walk-in closet, with the Captains clothes hanging there.

Kat said. "I'd say Captain Eugin lived in these quarters for a long time. By the looks of things, this is the only home he has."

Dirk pushed the button on the underside of the bed. The desk turned sideways. A slide panel in the deck exposed the safe. Dirk retrieved the discs. Also the note, directing the way to the crystals.

"Whew, you're not going to believe where he hid the crystals."

They were on their way back to back to the galley when Kat's pocket beeper come on. Sickbay flashed on and off. Kat took off on a run with Dirk right behind her.

They were at sickbay in less than a minute. Kat went over to the Captain. His neck was broken. One of the bunks was empty. Not "Whatshisface", he was still out cold. Another Arian was on the loose. Dirk pulled out his laser, raised the power on it, handed it to Kat and told her to stay in sickbay.

"You shoot anyone coming through that door that doesn't look like me, Mary or John. You shoot to kill, because that's what whoever it is, is going to do."

Dirk went toward the galley, walking as quietly as possible. He peeked though to the window in the door and saw John and Mary sitting at a table with their hands flat on the tabletop. Both were looking at a corner of the room he couldn't see. He took out the 9mm and waved it in front of the window. Mary saw it.

She went back to staring at the Arian. Out of the corner of her mouth she told John when she reached up to plug her ears he should do the same. John bobbed his head once.

Dirk crept down the hall to the entrance to the food storage area in the back of the galley. He went to the first panel and opened it a little so he could see into the galley. There against the wall sat an Arian. He had a laser in his hand and was waiting.

What's he waiting for? I know, the discs. He wants the discs and then he is going to shoot all of us.

Dirk raised the 9mm so just the muzzle was sticking on of the panel. He tapped on the panel door with the ring on his finger. Both Mary and John lifted their hands up slowly and then stuck their fingers in their ears.

The Arian stood up, pointing the laser at them, not knowing what they were up to.

Dirk fired. The bullet struck the Arian in the center of his forehead. The force of a 9mm parabellum, hollow-point at close range is similar to being struck by a speeding freight train. The projectile exited out the back of the head creating a hole big enough to put your hand in. The vacuum created by the expanding projectile on the way through, literally pulls what's inside, out.

The Arian never knew what struck him. He dropped the laser. His hands were half way to his head when his body realized there was no more brain to guide it. He was dead before he hit the wall and slid to the floor. Dirk went through the door to the galley from the food storage area. There was a faint odor of burnt powder in the air. Dirk look at John and Mary.

"You two Ok?" They both nodded. "It does get noisy when one of these goes off, huh?" Dirk looked over at the dead Arian. "He wanted the discs and then he was going to kill us, right?"

John said. "That's what he had in mind. He said they couldn't go back their home planet because of a death warrant against all of them. They must be real desperate to think they could get away with something like this."

Dirk went into the storage area and came back with a cloth bag.

He went over to the Arian and put it over what was left of his head and tied it in place. "Did you know he killed Captain Eugin? Broke his neck."

***

Dirk picked up the body and carried it back to sickbay. Before he got there he called out to Kat.

"I heard a shot."

"Yeah, what I'm going to show these Arians is not a pretty sight so if you want to turn your back."

"No, I can't."

Dirt understood. He told her to stand in front of Awga so she couldn't see. Mary stood in front of the other female. Dirk dropped the body of the Arian on the floor and took off the hood. He looked at each Arian. They knew exactly what he was thinking.

"We will not tolerate anyone trying this sort of thing again. We do not wish to hurt anyone but this is what happens when you Arians leave us no choice. This male killed the Captain and planned to kill us."

Dirk covered the Arians head again. He went to "Whatshisface" and asked Kat if she could wake him up. She nodded.

"Wake him up, please?" She looked at him.

"Nothing is going to happen to him. I'm going to get him to help me."

She went over to a tray and got a syringe and gave him a shot. In about a minute his eyes were open.

"John, I'm going to untie one of the others, you keep him covered. Then I'll untie "Whatshisface". Dirk looked at the one he untied and told him to tell "Whatshisface" what had happened.

The Arian spoke to him in his native language, not realizing these humans had translators.

"When he unties you, I will jump on this man and you jump on him. We will take their weapons away from them and kill them."

Mary very calmly drew her laser and stunned him. She turned toward "Whatshisface". He cowed backward.

She looked at him for a second and said. "Your nothing but lousy bully and coward to boot." It was all she could do just to keep from spitting on him. The Arian understood exactly what she meant, just by the tone of her voice.

She looked a John. "God, I despise people like that." Looking at Kat and Dirk, "I apologize for that outburst."

"You don't have to, you were just a little faster than we were. We thank you for doing what had to be done." Dirk said

John retied the one Mary whacked, and untied a different one.

Dirk motioned "Whatshisface" to pick up the body and led them through the door. Mary was right behind with her laser pointed at him. Dirk led them all to the air lock. He pressurized the lock and opened the inner door. He motioned "Whatshisface" inside and told him to undress the body and to take the hood off. He did exactly as he was told. When he saw the condition of the Arians head he sat down and stared at him. Dirk had to reach in and physically remove him from the lock. He stood there at the door of the lock looking at the remains with the clothes in his arms.

Just as Dirk pushed the button to close the door to the air lock he dropped the clothes and jumped into the lock. The door shut. Before anyone could move, 'Whatshisface' opened the outer door, whoosh, out they went.

Kat turned to Dirk and put her head on his chest. "Oh my God" she moaned. Dirk held her tight.

"Alright let's take this one back to sick bay."

When they got back the Arian went over to his bed, laid down and put his hands up to be tied again. He was completely convinced humans were not to be trifled with. After they leave I will tell the rest what had happened.

Dirk told everyone to stay there while he went to the galley and cleaned up the mess he had created. John said he'd help but Dirk said "No, I made it, I'll clean in up." He went to the storage area behind the galley, got a bucket, rags, and disinfectant and went to work cleaning up the mess. He took the bucket back to the utility closet and cleaned it and the rags.

Calling the others to come down, they sat there listening to the discs Captain Eugin had made. It seems "Whatshisface", Rega, Tepec and the one out in the last IV were the ring leaders. Tepec was a space pilot who had gone berserk and killed two of his crewmembers. He was allowed to work in the main prison office because of his knowledge of spacecraft. Where they were incarcerated, the inmates were used to construct spacecraft parts. He had found out about the in coming ship, returning from earth with restocking trees and food plants. It carried many tons of seeds, which would help replenish their world. There was going to be a crew transfer also. Everyone but the Captain and the First Officer.

The three of them planned an escape and enlisted others in their plot. The ones they enlisted were ones that were literate about space- craft. These Arians were there for what would considered minor offenses back on earth. But on Arian, stealing food was damn near a hanging offense. There was not much food left on their planet. The one Mary whacked was there for murder.

Dirk suggested he be first to go into freeze. The others were really not much of a problem. Most were to scared to do anything. Plus were in an environment they knew nothing about. No wonder this ship is a mess.

"We could keep some of the Arians out of freeze for a while, if for no reason other than to clean up the ship." Dirk said, looking at Kat.

"Most of the Arians should be strong enough by tomorrow to be able to do some light tasks. What are we going to do about these bodies?" Kat said.

"I'll get them ready and put them in the air lock." Dirk said. "We'll hold services for the Captain tomorrow."

John looked at Mary and then at Dirk and Kat.

"This ship is now without a Captain, Captain. Are you going to rename it or leave it ISS 04."

Dirk looked at John. "What do you mean?"

"Are you going to switch your Flag from NanMar to this Ship. We can't go zooming around in space without a Captain. You are the ranking Officer here. You were the Executive Officer of your Squadron and used to command. The NanMar will always be the NanMar. There has got to be someone in cryo who can fly her."

Kat looked at Dirk. "He's right. You should be Captain of this ship. If you were back on Earth would you always be an Executive Officer or would you go up in rank?"

"You're the one who put all of this together. For us and for those who are in freeze. You are a Commander and I'm still going to be a Veterinarian, John is still a Professor and Mary is still a Pilot and the Captain of the JonMar. She should be Executive Officer of the Ship."

"You people drive a hard bargain. I'll change my 'Flag' over to Oz and take Command of her. What are we going to call ourselves?"

"I think IS-101, Interstellar Squadron #101. 101 for the first of its kind. Like Basic Grab-Ass 101 in college." John stated.

"Ok, people we are now Task Force IS-101 and we are onboard the ISS Oz of the U.S.A.S.F." Dirk said.

"What does that stand for?" Kat asked

"United States of America Space Force. Kat do you feel like moving in to the Captain's quarters?"

"I'll go to NanMar and move our things. But first we should pack up Captain Eugin personal belongings and clean it up." Kat thought for a minute "Let's do it tomorrow, after the funeral services."

Dirk took the note out of his pocket that showed where he had hidden the crystals. He handed it to John and they began to laugh.

The ladies wanted to know what was so funny so John showed them the note.

"What's so funny about that I'll bet no one would look for them there." Mary said.

"If the Arians had checked why the toilets didn't work they would have found them right away. that's probably one of the reasons why the system is clogged up. Now we have to go digging around for this package. Would you girls like a job?" John asked

"I've got to check on some stuff on JonMar."

"I've got to look in on my patients."

Both women were gone in a flash. Dirk and John sat there laughing.

"Well, it's a dirty job but someone's got to do it." Dirk said, standing up.

John went with him to get air rebreathers. They got some space bags and scoops and went to the lower level into the filtration room. Closing the face covers, they went to work.

In about fifteen minutes they had recovered the package, washed it off and then cleaned out the rest of the pit. All of the solid waste was put into bags and secured. The pit washed and with clean filters, began to run normal.

Dirk called Kat on the intercom and asked her to flush all of the toilets. John turned on the plant and put in a package of bacteria to help break down waste. Dirk and John stood there watching the plant work. All fifteen toilets were working perfectly.

They filled the pit with water from the Grey water tank to the mark and closed it up. That's one dirty job done. Dirk looked at John.

"In all the years I spent in the Navy I never saw a Ship's Captain do this. The next project is getting Rega and Tepec ready for burial, right." John said.

"Let's go do it."

Getting Rega ready for burial was no problem and fumigating the shuttle was easy. They went over to the other shuttle and open the hatch. When the laser struck the craft it holed it, on the way through it took the right arm of Tepec's body off. They put the remains in a body bag (a mattress cover). They took the bodies to the air lock and placed them inside and then closed the door. Dirk looked through the window and said. "May God have mercy on your souls." He pushed the button opening the outer door. 'Whoosh', both bodies shot out into space. They secured the airlock and went back to the damaged shuttle- craft. They cleaned up the small mess inside and then checked the ship for damage. Dirk said he didn't think it could be repaired but at least they could use it for spare parts. Pushing it over to the elevator, they took it to the lower level storage area and secured it to the deck.

"I think it's time for dinner."

John said. "I wonder what the girls are up to?" He went to the inter-comm.

"You guys go get cleaned up and then we'll meet for supper in the galley on NanMar." Kat said.

Each went to their respective ships and got cleaned up. In about forty-five minutes John call over to NanMar and got Dirk. "I'm on my way. Where are the girls?"

"I don't know." said Dirk. "I'm up on the bridge. I meet you at the elevator."

John came up and they went to the galley, both of the girls were there. John came to a complete stop.

"Wow, will you look at this meal. This was not done by "Otto" (the name they called the automatic meal vendor)."

"Nope, this was cooked by two home town girls from the good ole U.S. of A., Sport. Sit down and enjoy. There is tossed salad, soup, baked potatoes, steak, done to your personal liking, and dessert. Tapioca pudding, Dirks favorite."

"There is some great wine in those decanters, I don't know where it comes from but I, excuse me, we guarantee the quality." Mary poured two glasses and handed one to John while Kat handed the other to Dirk.

She raised her glass to Dirk. "Salung-ne-vaugh, Captain." They clinked glasses and took a sip.

John asked. "What does that mean?"

Dirk said. "To your good health. It's Gaelic, err, Scottish."

John raised his glass. "Erin-go-brauh, that's Irish."

After the meal was over and the dishes were put away on the panel shelf, there was no voice asking how they liked their meal. John looked at Dirk.

"Boy, is she pissed." They all started to laugh. Filling the decanters with wine, they went to the lounge on Oz. Opened the outer panel and sat there staring out into space.

"I have another surprise for you all." Kat said.

She reached over and pushed a button on a console. The screen turned white and a movie came on. They sat and enjoyed "A night at the Opera" staring the Marx Brothers. It was a very much earned and enjoyed night off.

They walked back to their ships, arms around each other, swaying a little. They were singing "Till I Walk You Home Again Kathleen". They said good night to each other between the two ships and called it a night.

CHAPTER TWENTY

The next morning Dirk and Kat were in the galley for breakfast when the inter-com came on.

"How is everyone feeling this morning?" Dirk and Kat looked at John.

"How could anyone, who drank as much as you did be so chipper in the morning?" Dirk asked.

"Because I'm Irish. We always could out drink you Scots. We've already had breakfast so we're coming over for coffee. By the way is "Toots" talking to you this morning?'

"We don't know yet."

Mary and John came over and they discussed the jobs that had to be done that day. Going to the sick bay, they found everyone awake and very hungry. Dirk had gotten some extra clothing the day before and had it piled up on an extra bed. He went over to the male who went with them to the air lock the day before.

"Can you hear me?" He nodded. "If you can understand me? Lift your hands." He lifted his hands. Dirk untied his hands and then the straps.

"Get a suit that fits, go to the shower and clean up. I'll be right here waiting. Don't take all day."

The Arian bolted toward the shower. He was back in a few minutes. By then Dirk had another standing there waiting. He told the first one to sit down, the other went into the shower. He took a little longer.

Dirk took them to the galley and sat with them while they ate. After they had finished, he took them over to the meal panel and ordered four meals. When they came out he told them to take two each. They would carry them back to the ones who could not get out of bed. The second Arian said. "If they want to eat, they can come down and get their own." The first Arian said something to him that Dirk could not really hear. He just looked at the Arian. The second Arian looked at Dirk with an idiotic sneer on his face and picked up the trays. When they got back to sickbay they distributed the trays. He told the second Arian to lay back down but the male just stood there not moving. Dirk very calmly drew his laser and "Wham" down he went. Dirk picked him up and put on the bed, tied his hands and strapped him in.

Looking at John. "There's number three for freeze. Who are the next two for breakfast."

John pointed to two Arians. They almost fell over each other getting up. They ate a very fast breakfast and were standing next to the panel waiting for more trays to come out. <u>Quick learners these two</u> thought Dirk.

After everyone was fed and cleaned up.

Dick said. "We're going to hold a burial service for the Captain at the air-lock now and everyone goes. Those who are to weak to walk will be helped by the others."

On the way over to the air lock John came up to Dirk and said he had three more for freeze. When they got to the airlock Dirk took out a copy of the New Testament and read from it. He looked at the Arians and asked if anyone would like to say a few words about the Captain. The first Arian Dirk untied stepped forward.

"I did not know the Captain long but he was a very fair man with this crew and tried to teach us about running a space ship." He bent his head and whispered something. Four others bent their heads also. When he was finished he stepped back into line. Dirk said a finial prayer and said.

"Into your hands I commend the body of our brother, Lord."

He nodded to an Arian who went over to the panel and opened the outer door. All could hear the "whoosh" of air as the airlock cleared.

Kat looked over to the women and saw there were tears streaming down their faces. She went to them and put an arm around each of them and led them to the galley. Dirk motioned for the males to follow. Dirk told them to get something to drink if they wanted to. He got a cup of coffee and sat at a table and waited for everyone to finish.

After they were done he had five males stay while Kat and Mary took the women and three males back to sick-bay.

"You five are going to be restricted to quarters until something can be done with you. You will be brought out for food and then placed back in your quarters. I suggest you keep them clean because no one will be in there but you. There is no way to get out of the spaces so don't even try. We are not going to harm you in any way nor are we going to return you to your home planet right now. We don't know what we are going to do with you but you have shown you can't be trusted. That is all I have to say. Now follow John, he will show you the way. I'll be right behind you." Dirk looked at John and nodded.

John led them up the passageway to the last two quarters. He stopped in front of the last door and opened it.

"Three in here."

He shut and locked the door. He backed up to the next door and opened it. The other two went in. Dirk said to wait before locking it. He would get the other one in sickbay. The two males turned around quickly and one of them spoke.

"If you put him in with us, we will hurt him bad."

Dirk looked at them for a moment, he believed them.

"Why?"

"He likes other men, that is why he is like that. No one will have anything to do with him."

"All right, he stays in sick-bay." Dirk said.

John shut the door and locked it. They went back toward sickbay.

Dirk exclaimed. "Christ, that's all we need, a fairy. Well, it's nice to know the human race isn't the only one to have them."

***

When they got back to sickbay, Dirk went over to the one in question. He untied him and motioned for him to follow. He went to airlock, pressurized it and opened the inner door. He turned and looked the Arian straight in the eye. He could see the Arian was getting a little nervous. He let him off the hook.

"I just found out you like other Arian males." The male swallowed hard. "I don't care what your sexual preference is. I'm trying to keep everyone alive. I'm not going to put you in freeze yet. You were a nurse back on your home planet?" The male nodded. "We need your skill here with the other Arians. If I even think you are getting friendly with another male, I'll slap you in freeze so fast your head will spin. Do you understand?"

"Yes"

"I am either Captain or Sir, a plain yes will not do." Dirk just looked at him for a minute.

The Arian got the message. "Yes Sir."

"Now I'm giving you a choice right now, here or there. Here you live, but you will follow the rules. I don't need to tell you about there. The choice is yours. Make up your mind right now."

The Arian walked over to the airlock, looked at Dirk and shut the door.

"Okay, let's have a cup of coffee with Mrs. MacGlashan. You can tell her what she will need to know about the up coming birth." Dirk reached over to the intercom and asked Kat to join them in the galley for a cup of coffee.

"Walk with me to the galley." Dirk pointed to a spot right along side of him.

"Yes Sir." There was pure admiration in the eyes of the Arian. The man would have laid down his life for his new Captain if asked. When they got to galley Kat was all ready there with three cups of coffee. They sat down. Dirk looked at the Arian.

"I don't know your name?"

"When I was found out on my home planet my name was taken from me and stricken from the rolls. As far as they are concerned I am dead."

Kat said. "That's terrible. What an evil thing to do."

"We'll call him Bruce" Dirk said.

Kat looked at Dirk. "No, that won't do."

"Oh yes, Mrs. Mac, that will be a good name for me, I like it. I am Bruce, Yes."

"Ok, that's done. Now what are the others doing?" Dirk asked.

"They're cleaning up the quarters and generally getting ready for our new arrivals."

"What new arrivals, Mrs. Mac?"

"We are resuscitating some of the humans, Bruce."

"Can I be of some assistance to you?"

"Yes, I need to know about the up coming birth of Awga's child."

Dirk stood. "I'll leave you now and go do some work on the bridge." He looked over to Bruce, who had jumped up when Dirk stood.

"You okay now?"

"Yes Sir, Captain Mac."

Dirk left, he went to the storage room and found some storage bins and took them to the Captains quarters. He started with the bathroom and cleaned out Captain Eugin's personal things. Leaving the towels and face cloths.

Going to the closet, he started to put the clothing in the storage bins. Finding a box on the top shelf, he took in down and opened it. It held the Captain's service hat. Dirk looked at the emblem on the front. It was round with a Star Ship embossed on it, there were five stars on top of the ship. Underneath were the initials I.S.S. (Interstellar Star Ship). Dirk put the hat on and looked at himself in a mirror. The hat fit perfect. I'm going to keep this out and put it somewhere, where I can look at it once in a while thought Dirk. He looked at the emblem again. He didn't know what the white metal was, but the ship, stars and the lettering were gold.

He finished packing the Captains clothing and went into the main room and started to pack things away there. Captain Eugin had collected a lot of memorabilia. Dirk found a book, which looked like a diary. It was written in Arian. Taking it to the bridge, he put it in the computer reading panel, and went through the pages. It told of his life, when he had married, the birth of his daughter and the death of his wife during the birth of their son. The son had died at age five. There was an address for his daughter. Dirk wrote it down and then took everything back and put it into the storage bins. When he finished he took the bins to the storage area, and secured them in a locker. He called Kat and said he was going to the capsule room to check on the resuscitation. He would meet her for some lunch in the small galley. Kat came in and kissed Dirk on the cheek and went over to the order panel.

"I like the voice Scaner put into "Otto" it sounds like Charles Boyer, the French Actor." She brought her meal over to where Dirk was and sat down. "Well, how did your morning go?"

Dirk told her what he had been doing and what he had found out about Captain Eugin.

Kat told him about her morning with Bruce and Awga. She had been studying most of the morning learning about Arian anatomy. "Not much different than ours. I found out why our departed ones were collecting humans."

"Tell me."

"They had decided to colonize a new planet and decided to use us as breeding stock."

"You've got to be kidding."

"No, I'm serious. I'm doing some cross checking on our systems."

"Did they really think we would go alone with some thing like that?"

"They were planning some frontal lobotomies. Also Bruce told me the other ship is on its way to the other planet, where there is another Oz. That one has only two star ships. He is going to stay there until we get there. They were planning to capture it and force the other crew to go along with them. I imagine that meant they were going to kill anyone standing in their way."

"That's a few weeks away yet, but it's nice to know what we're going to be going up against. Right now it's the resuscitation of the rest of our crew. As of right now we only have nine members."

"You are accepting the Arians into our crew?" Kat asked.

"Why not, they know we are not going to harm them. They weren't part of the bizarre plot, Rega, Tepec and "Whatshisface" and the other one had hatched up. Does anyone know what the other one's name is or the number of his spacecraft? I can find out what the number of the ship is from the log. But see if you can find out what his name is."

"It's time I got back to the books." Kat said.

"I'll walk back with you." When they reached sick bay Dirk stepped inside to see how things were going. Bruce stood at attention, for a minute Dirk thought he was going to salute him.

Awga came up to him. "I wish to thank you for all you have done for us, Captain Mac."

"You are quite welcome Awga." Dirk looked around, noticing all of the beds had fresh linen and the deck had been scrubbed.

"Good work, Bruce, keep it up."

"Aye, Aye Sir."

Dirk looked at Kat. She smiled. Dirk thought, Great work Kat.

Going to the quarters for the crew, he found Mary working along side of the three men and Triga. She looked up, saw him and stood.

"Good afternoon, Captain Mac."

"How's it coming Mary."

"We're doing fine, Skipper."

Dirk looked at her. "Would you mind if I borrowed Triga for a while?"

"No, we can finish up with no problem."

"Have you people eaten yet?"

"Yes, we ate about an hour ago."

"Where's John?"

"When he found out about the other Oz, he said he was going down to the shop on the lower level. He said he had been thinking of something and wanted to work on it. I found out a long time ago when he gets an idea the best thing to do is leave him alone. Whatever it is, I'll bet it works."

"Triga, would you come with me."

"Aye, Aye Sir." Dirk looked at Mary and she too, smiled.

Dirk took Triga to the storage area. Found some cleaning equipment and went to the Captains quarters.

"Let's clean this up." Dirk started to roll up his sleeves. Triga stopped him.

"It is not right for the Captain to do this kind of work. I will do this. You must run this ship."

"Ok, I want to move our things from the NanMar so we can stay here tonight."

"It will be ready for you and Mrs. Mac tonight." She opened the door for him. He took the hint and left.

<u>What in-the-hell am I supposed to do now. No one will let me do a damn thing. I don't know if I like being a Captain.</u>

Dirk went to the lower level and into the shop where John was working. He looked up and was about to say something when Dirk cut him off.

"Don't even think about running me off."

"Huh?"

"Everywhere I go and try to help, I'm reminded I am the Captain, and I'm not supposed to get my finger nails dirty. You're my last hope for keeping my sanity."

John laughed. "Ok, I won't run you off."

"Now what is it that you are working on?"

"It's an active pinger."

"Explain?"

"You know what sonar is?" Dirk nodded. "Well, underwater it's a way to measure the distance from yourself to another object. Whether its another Sub, the bottom or an under water range."

"Well, there's a lot of drag from the water so you have to figure the density of the water and allow for that to get the proper distance. Out here in space there's no drag."

"I'm building a pinger, it can be mounted outside on the pressure hull. I can direct the beam to fire at any direction. With the power we can generate, the strength of that beam will be awesome. You would never know it was coming at you until it hit. Can you imagine what it would be like sitting in a tin can like this and have it hit you. The sound would just about blow out your eardrums. I'll bet it would knock you down. You wouldn't have to sneak up on anyone. Just get close in, say fifty miles and 'wham'. They are history. It would be lot easier then trying to infect them the Asian flu bug."

"Do you really think it will work?"

"Yes, I played around with it a little back on earth. One time in the mountains, I knocked a Deer out with it. He was down for about five minutes. I'll bet he's still running."

"You get something together, we'll mount it on the roof and check it out. How are you going to get a cable to it?"

"I all ready checked that out. There is a main junction box just forward of the elevator shaft opening with all of the cables I'll need."

"How long before you'll have something ready?"

"I figure three days."

"Do you need any help?"

"Not really, I can work on this faster by myself. I've got most of it in my head."

"Ok, I'm going back to my lonely vigil on the bridge."

Dirk went through the other compartments checking. Everything was in its place and secure. I'm starting to act like a Captain now. He went up to the next level and into the reactor room. Everything looks fine, the crystals look normal. He turned to leave and noticed the panel John thought was an energy field of some sort. He stepped to the intercom and called John.

"Do you remember the extra panel in the reactor room?"

"Yes"

"Would it help in developing your pinger?"

"Yes, that's where I'm getting the boosting power for it. I traced the wiring to the junction box on the roof. All the wiring I need is there and it can be controlled from the bridge. I have no idea what that panel was going to be used for but I'm glad they put it in."

"Ok, if I can be of help, call."

Continuing, Dirk checked on the progress of the resuscitation. All looks well and coming along smoothly.

Going to the galley, he got a cup of coffee and headed for the bridge. He took out the manual for armament and looked for that control panel. It was located in the back as an add on. It was an energy field designed to over ride the propulsion unit of a craft and render it useless. It was tested once and brought back to the lab for alterations. They probably blew something up by mistake. Dirk called John again, and told him what he had found out.

"I was right. The Navy was fooling around with it for awhile. All they managed to do was knock a bunch of fish out. I've got a glitch here, could you do me a favor?"

All right, now I get to do something besides sit. "Sure, what do you need."

"Call Mary and ask her to bring me supper here. I'm going to be working late. Thanks." He switched off.

Dirk put the manual back, called Kat and asked her to tell Mary to bring John's supper to him and why. He then went over their quarters, Triga was all finished cleaning up and had some clothes on the bed and was going through them.

"What are you doing?"

Startled, Triga jumped up. "I was getting some new clothes ready for you, I have put Captain stripes on the sleeve and your gold leaf on the shoulders. I went to the storage compartment and got them. Was I wrong?"

"No, this is fine, thank you. What did you do before, back on Arian?"

"Before I became, what you call, a prostitute, I was at the Arian National Space Academy. I was training to become a Star Ship Officer. In my third and finial year, I became pregnant when two Senior Pilots covered me. I was expelled from the Academy and sent to a house for bad women. When the child was born it was taken away and I was sent to a house for prostitution. I had been there for five spans when these people took Awga and me away."

"Why didn't you say you were in the Academy before?"

"I was afraid of them. I did not want to do what they were doing. It is not right. I told Captain Eugin and he promised he would not say anything to them. He was teaching me how to run this Star Ship. Every time one of the others would come near us he would put his arm around me and act like I was his favorite woman. No one knew he was teaching me."

"Are you proficient in flying one of the IVs? Do you know how to maneuver one in combat?"

"Yes Sir. I was first in my class in aerial gunnery and in torpedo firing."

"Ok, Ensign Triga, you are now our newest Fight Officer. Come with me, Ensign Triga."

Dirk took her to the bridge and went directly to the main computer. He brought up the crewmember list, found Triga's information packet. Everywhere it showed her profession as a prostitute he erased it and Student Officer was typed in. Promoted to Ensign, 11 Nov 1999, onboard the Star Ship Oz, ISS-04 U.S.A.S.F. (Renamed from ISS-04 on 10 Nov 1999).

"I think you had better be sworn in." Dirk got on the intercom and called Mary.

"Captain Mayhan, would you please lay up to the bridge at 1600. ------ No one else. ------- Just you, Thank you Captain."

"What I would like for you to do, is go to the storage area and get an officer's uniform for yourself and put it on and then come back here. You can use our quarters to change. Be back here at 1555 hours. That's 3:55 PM." Triga was gone in a flash.

Dirk finished his coffee, went down to the storage area and rummaged through some of the bins. He found what he was looking for. Arriving back on the bridge with two minutes to spare. Triga came in at exactly 1555 and Mary walked through the door at 1600. She stopped, came to attention and reported.

CHAPTER TWENTY-ONE

"Mayhan, Mary A., Captain, United States Air Force reporting as ordered, Sir."

"Stand at ease, Captain. I want you to witness this. Ensign Triga step forward, place your left hand on this Bible and raise your right hand. Repeat after me. I, (your name), do solemnly swear to defend the Constitution of the United States of America; --- against all enemies, foreign or domestic; --- and will faithfully execute the duties of the office upon which I am about to enter. --- I will obey the orders of the officers appointed above me by competent authority. --- I am taking this oath without any mental reservations whatsoever. So help me God."

Dirk took one step back and saluted the new Ensign. He then stepped forward, put his hand out and shook hers.

"Congratulations, Ensign Triga."

Both Dirk and Mary attested to the fact Triga had been sworn in as an Ensign in the U.S.A.S.F. on this date 11 Nov 1999. All of this is being entered in the disc holding Triga's information packet.

"Ensign Triga, your rank is noted by a single one-half inch gold stripe on both cuffs. Although these uniforms only use one sleeve. When you get a chance put one on."

Triga pulled out a gold stripe from her pocket.

"This is what a new officer wears in our service. All the others are silver until you get to Captain, they are red."

"Let's call the rest of the crew to mess and introduce our latest officer to them."

"John wanted me to bring his supper to him down on the third deck."

"I'll take care of that right now." Dirk switch on the inter comm. "Attention all hands, this the Captain speaking. All hands, I repeat, all hands will take the evening meal at the second deck galley at exactly 1630, there will be no exceptions." Dirk looked at Mary.

"That settles that."

Mary went over to Triga, stood at attention and saluted, Triga returned the salute. Mary smiled. "Congratulations"

"Mary, I want you to take Ensign Triga out tomorrow for a check ride."

She looked a Triga. "Have you any time in a Star Ship?"

"Yes Captain, The first half of our third span is spent in space. Captain Eugin was our fleet Commander then."

Mary looked at Triga in awe. "You went to a space academy!"

"Yes, Captain. Sir, can I ask a question?"

"Certainly." Dirk said.

"How come you are a Captain and she is a Captain also?"

Dirk looked at Triga. "In our country, on Earth, we have five branches of service, The Navy and the Coast Guard, call their Officers one way. The Air Force, the Army and the Marines, call their Officers another. It's not all the hard to understand. I'll write it down for you."

***

Dirk looked at his watch it was time to go to chow. They arrived fashionably five minutes late. Dirk and Mary came in together stood on each side of the door.

Dirk called out. "Attention on deck." Everyone stood. "I wish to introduce the newest addition to the Officer Corp of the U.S.A.S.F., Ensign Triga."

Triga came through the door. Kat and John clapped. The others followed, when they figured out what they were supposed to do. Everyone sat back down and there was quite a buzzing sound as the whispers flew back and forth. Dirk, Mary and Triga got their meals and sat at the table. Dirk sat at the head of the table as befitting a Captain. He clinked his glass and stood up.

"Ladies and Gentleman, I would like to clear something up before we eat. It concerns Ensign Triga." He then told the crew exactly what had happened to Triga, leaving out no details. He continued.

"I know we have a very courageous young lady here in our wardroom. The humiliation she has suffered is no more. I have read the information handed to me by Captain Eugin, it speaks very well of this lady. She will be taking over as Commanding Officer of the NanMar. Her duties here, onboard Oz will be Supply Officer, Berthing Officer and Master-at-Arms. People raise your glasses. To Ensign Triga."

Dirk sat back down, reached over and refilled Triga's glass. <u>Now the other Arians know I will have their heads if they disobey her in any way, shape or form.</u>

After the meal was over and everyone was relaxing, Triga came over to Dirk and asked.

"Captain would it be correct if I moved into the quarters across from sick bay?"

"No, I would like for you to move into the quarters next to sick bay."

"But those were for the married people." Triga said.

"The first four quarters are what we call in the Navy 'Officers Country'. The nine, four bed, quarters are going to be for single people, if we ever have any. You will have the first double bed quarters and John and Mary have the next."

***

Dirk looked over to Kat. "Madame, would you like to help me move our meager belongings to the Captain's quarters?"

"OH! kind sir, it would be my pleasure." They started to laugh and everyone joined in.

As they left everyone followed right along with them. With nine people in a ship designed for three, it got a wee bit crowded. Soon everyone had their arms full and off they went to the Captain's new quarters.

Dirk thanked everyone for their help and said. "Tomorrow is going to be a big day, we've got a lot of people coming out of cryo. It should start about 11:00 am. You people that don't have uniforms, get some." Dirk looked at his officers and asked them to stay.

"Mary, you worked with the Arians today, which one or ones would you recommend for petty officers. These people need to know they are wanted and a reward is in line."

"We have another no name. He was actually in charge today during clean up. The man is a perfect housekeeper. He knew what to use for clean up and how to start cleaning a room up. Made a perfect bed and set each room in order as we left. I believe he should be working for Triga as a Chief Petty Officer. The other two could be made Airman First, excuse me, Third Class Petty Officers. They are not really what you would call housekeepers."

"Triga what do you know of the one which has no name?" Dirk asked.

"He was a Manager of a Restover and was convicted of selling on the open market. He took the throw aways, cleaned them up and then sold them at his vendor stand at a market place. He did not have enough for a pay back so he was sent to detention and his name was taken from him. The other two are Gorex and Tribec. They were convicted for stealing food for their families. I do not know what they did before the famine. I can go to the storage area and get the rank markings for these men tomorrow, if that is what you want to make them."

Dirk looked at Kat, John, and Mary each nodded their heads.

"Okay, do it."

"I think Bruce should be made a Chief Petty Officer also. He is an excellent nurse. If I were to open a practice here, I'd hire him in a New York minute." Kat said

"Good, then it's all settled. Have a nice night."

After they had all gone Dirk took Kat in his arms and asked. "What do you think?"

"About what?"

"How things are going here on Oz."

"So far so good, tomorrow is going to be the test, remember, we have twelve people coming out of freeze."

"Twelve?"

"Have you forgotten about the children already?"

"Yes, I did."

"What are you going to do with five Arians in lock up?"

"They are going into cryo tomorrow."

"How are you going to get them to cooperate."

"Gas'em."

"WHAT!"

"I told Bruce what I wanted. There's a gas we can put into the air conditioning, which will put them to sleep. He's to do it at 1100 tomorrow. It will put them out for about six hours. I know they don't like each other, but Bruce knows what will happen if he screws up. It's really harmless, I checked it out in the computer. The Arians use it quite a lot on their own people."

"Dirk, I just don't like seeing anyone hurt if it's at all possible. To many have been killed just in the short while I been awake." She laid her head against his chest and held him tight. Dirk kissed the top of her head and hugged her.

"Shower and the sack? That sound good to you?"

"Yes"

After the shower, and lying in bed, Kat snuggled up to Dirk and ran her fingers across his chest and then bent down and kissed the nipple closest to her. Dirk and Kat made love slowly, falling asleep holding each other tight.

***

Dirk and Kat awoke at 6:30 am. Dirk went toward the shower and called out. "I'll let you scrub my back if you promise not to fool around."

"The offer is tempting but I'm going to take a nice long bath. A nice, long, hot, bubble bath." She held up a bottle of some kind of oil. "Triga got it from stores yesterday for me. She said Rega loved to take bubble baths and used this tub when ever she was at the ship."

Dirk said he was going to get a cup of coffee and go to the bridge.

"Wait a minute." Kat went over to the intercom. Dirk stopped her by asking "What are you going to do?"

"I was going to order your coffee and juice sent to the bridge. You are a Captain now you know."

"Yes, I am a Captain, but I don't have my own steward. I'll get my own at the galley. If we were all at the bridge and wanted coffee or a snack, I would send for some. That would be the only time."

Kat looked very hurt by his comment. "I was only trying to make things a little easier for you."

"I know and I appreciate it, but I'm in the Navy and that's not how it's done. At least not the Navy I was in. You know what I would really like for breakfast, a couple of donuts, two, nice, round, fat, plain donuts. The kind that you break in half and dunk in your coffee and slurp over." Grinning, he looked over at Kat. "You're drooling, wipe off your chin."

"I am not." She still brought the back of her hand up to her mouth.

Dirk laughed. "See, I told you so." Kat had to laugh too.

He went over to Kat and kissed her on the cheek. "Thanks for thinking of me."

***

When he came into the galley, everyone stood up.

"I might be the Captain, but you people have things to do and standing at attention every time you see me is a waste of time. If I want you to come to attention I'll call for it, understood?"

There was a chorus of "Yes Sir".

"Be seated and carry on."

He went over to the coffee panel and got a cup and started to go to the bridge. He stopped, turned to Ensign Triga.

"When you finish your breakfast come to the bridge."

Dirk was sitting at the control desk went she came in.

"Ensign Triga reporting as ordered, Sir."

"Sit at the Nav station. Bring up the star chart for our destination." Dirk was watching as she did this. They studied the plot to where the other Oz was.

"At our present rate of speed, we should reach it in eighteen days. If we go to light speed we will be there in sixteen hours, I figure."

"At light speed we will be there in twenty and a half hours, Sir." She held her breath for fear of his reaction.

"How did you come up with that figure?"

"Sir, didn't you want to go back to the Beta Six ship and salvage it?"

"Yes, I do, there's some equipment on her we can use."

"From here we can be there in one and a half hours. If we spend two days there getting what the ship needs, we can go to light speed and be at the other Oz in nineteen hours, Sir." Triga went over the figures again and showed them to Dirk. Studying them, he checked them on the star chart. <u>She's right. She knows her stuff.</u>

"If we do we will be coming in at a different angle to "Ozzie Too", which they won't be expecting and neither will the other IV craft. Maybe we can surprise them both. Do you have any duties which would prevent you from staying on the bridge and setting up course changes?"

"Sir, all of the men have been put work cleaning up the remaining quarters. Then they are to go to the second deck and clean. I have told them not to go into the reactor room for any reason. I am to take a check ride on the NanMar this morning with Captain Mayhan."

"Right, set this up and then get Captain Mayhan."

"Yes Sir."

"I'm going down to the galley and have breakfast, and then go to the capsule room."

Dirk went over to the inter-com and called Kat. "Are you ready to have some chow?"

"We're waiting on you."

"Who's we?"

"John, Mary and me."

Dirk left the bridge and went to the galley. There they were sitting and chatting. He got his breakfast and sat down. He asked John how the pinger was coming along.

"It should be working by day after tomorrow."

Dirk told Mary what Triga was doing up on the bridge and that she really knows her stuff when it comes to star navigation. Dirk explained he had set up a problem for her and gave her the wrong numbers. She had done the figures and had come up with the right answers and very tactfully gave them. Captain Eugin spent a lot of time with her.

"Mary, you're going to give her a check ride today in NanMar right?" Dirk asked.

"Yes, I was, but if you want her on the bridge."

"No, what I would like you to do is go to the bridge and check on the course changes she'll be putting into the main computer, don't offer any options unless it is absolutely necessary, call me when that has been done. The check ride is still on for this morning." He looked over to Kat. "Hon, what have you got going this morning?"

"Bruce and I have to get some clothing ready for our new guests. By then they should be about ready to hatch."

"That's a new way to call resuscitation but it's appropriate."

Mary said. "I'm off to the bridge."

***

Dirk went into sickbay with Kat and sat down, reached for a book and thumbed through it. In about five minutes Triga called and said the course changes were entered and were ready for execution.

"I want you to go to light speed in two minutes, calculate for arrival at the asteroid in one hour and thirty minutes. That should bring us to a range of fifty miles from the asteroid. Inform the crew of the jump to light speed." Kat, Awga and Bruce just stared at him.

"You had better sit down and hold on. If you don't, your going to look awful funny pinned against that wall for three or four seconds."

Ensign Triga's voice came over the inter comm. "Attention all hands prepare for jump to light speed in one minute thirty seconds."

"The others have gone through this so they should be all right."

At exactly one minute and thirty seconds later Dirk felt the ship excellerate with such force he was pinned to the back of the chair for about five seconds. Kat looked at him.

"You had this planned from the beginning didn't you?"

Dirk stood up. "Yup, I wanted to see how fast my navigators could react to a sudden change. And they're right on the money. They did a great job. Now we will be at the junk pile in an hour and a half, and two hours before hatch. We'll be able to get started on getting the rest of the material from the junk pile. Mary will be able to check ride Triga and everyone can be used to shuttle the equipment. I'll be on the bridge if anyone needs me."

When Dirk got to the bridge, he found Mary sitting in the pilot seat just staring at the view screen. The stars that used to lazily go by now were a white blur streaking by. He reached over and closed the panel.

"You're going to fall over if you continue to watch that, Captain Mayhan."

Mary shook her head and turned to look a Dirk, her eyes were way out of focus. She was about to fall. Dirk grabbed her, told her to shut her eyes and then pushed her head down between her knees. He held her there until she waved a hand and gave him a thumb's up, signaling she was all right.

"Wow, now that's a rush, that's awesome. You should have seen it. One second you're lounging along and then "Wham", your slammed back in your seat. The stars seemed to stop for a split second and then it's a streak. You can't help but just stare at it."

"You had better get used to it, because the star craft will go to light speed also. If you don't set your course right you could slam into a big rock and then it's all over."

"Excellent work Ensign Triga, well done."

Triga spoke. "Captain, the star craft are unable to go to light speed at this time. The new exciter boards were never put in. They were with the crew which was killed on Arian."

"I was under the impression they were able to jump to light speed. Now that does present a problem. We'll work it out." Dirk reach over to the inter comm. "Is everyone alright, Report in." Everyone reported in.

"Captain, why don't you and Ensign Triga go and check how the space craft fared after the jump to light speed? Report back, if all is well, go and have a coffee or something. Be back here by 0900."

"Aye, Aye Sir."

Dirk called John on the intercom. "How are things going down there?"

"The next time, please give a little more warning, all my tools went aft at a high rate of speed and I damn near went with them. That's some kind of a rush, huh? It's coming along fine, Tribec is down here helping. He worked on these big babies before the famine. It's a shame, a guy goes to jail because he wants to feed his wife and child. He knows these ships inside out. Tribec told me that Gorex is what we would call a rigger back on Earth. These two guys worked together back in the good old days. How's our expectant mother coming along?"

"Doing just great, I was in sick bay when we jumped to light speed. If you can leave for little while come up to the bridge, I've got something to show you."

John and Tribec came up to the bridge and Dirk opened the panel and turned on the view screen.

"Now that's something to see. Tribec have you ever seen this before?"

"No Sir, we were never allowed to go into space. All we did was build them."

Dirk asked. "How many are there?"

"Only four, Sir. This is the last one. It has many improvements over the first three. All four can go to light speed." Gorex said.

"Well, with the new plants and seeds your people have the famine should be over. And that means back to work. I'll bet their building more ships as we speak. I'm sure they found the dead crewmembers by now. It wouldn't surprise me if they came looking for Oz with both barrels out. Before this is all over, we'll probably meet one."

"Bad news, Ensign Triga tells me the star craft are unable to go to light speed. They need a new motherboard. That's a problem. What part of the ship did you work on Tribec?"

"I was a structural Supervisor. Sir, I can fix the shuttlecraft "Whatshisface" shot with the laser."

"Alright, when we get to the junk pile, see if you can salvage what you need off of it."

John asked. "What junk pile?"

Dirk told them what had happened with their first encounter and why they hid it.

At ten minutes to nine Mary and Triga came to the bridge. Dirk looked at John and Tribec.

"We'll be dropping back from light speed at ten past nine. That should put us at fifty miles from the junk pile. We'll stay there for three days. Get what we need and then it's off to see Ozzie Too. If you want to see the drop back from light speed, stay." Both stayed.

Dirk and Triga set the speed changes into the computer and waited for ten minutes after nine. Dirk started the count down, three, two, one, mark! Everyone watched the view screen.

Stars that were streaking by literally stopped. Triga checked their position. They were right on target.

"We will be over the asteroid in fifteen minutes, Sir."

"Very well, Ensign."

***

"Incoming torpedo, impact in three minutes." Triga said.

Dirk reached over and switched the laser on high power and set the tracking systems on.

"Fire."

A red streak shot out from about ten degrees to port.

"Impact -------- Now." Mary said.

A tremendous explosion occurred. Dirk turned to look at Mary and Triga.

"You two, man your craft. John, you and Tribec go too." Dirk turned the inter-com on. "Kat to the bridge, ASAP."

The four left the bridge on a dead run. Kat came in, "What's happening?"

"We are being fired at, someone shot a torpedo at us. I've got a back track going on now. Can you man the fire control panel?"

Kat nodded and sat down. She turned on the panel and set two torpedoes on warm up and switched to heat seeking mode.

"All set, here."

The inter-com came on,

"JonMar on and ready."

"NanMar on and ready."

"Roger, I am going to switch on the radar with a heat seeking beam and locate our not so welcome guest. Stand by, ----------- I have a lock on. Target range three hundred seventy-five miles, launch, I say again, launch." Dirk felt the ship move slightly as the weight of the two star crafts lifted.

"JonMar, NanMar you're inbound heading is 340 degrees."

"Roger, 340 degrees."

"Heads up, we have an inbound torpedo, we will fire. Kat, firing point procedure."

"I have lock on."

"Fire."

The laser beam streaked out-------- another explosion.

***

Mary switched to the inter-ship comm channel and told Triga to stay on her right side and a little low. "At my command break right and down. Then make a turn toward the target. I'll break left and up, and turn toward the target. When you get on target, fire. Laser on full power."

"NanMar, roger." She clicked the mike twice. Triga heard Mary click twice. Three, Four, Five minutes went by.

"Break now, NanMar."

Mary peeled high left. Triga literally shot down and to the right, did a roll back to the left. She turned on the cameras. As she leveled she spotted the target. Pulling the nose up a little, she fired.

Another red streak was headed toward the target, a little behind hers.

Triga's beam caught the other ship on the underside to port and exited on the starboard side top. The ship was slowing down. Mary's shot struck just over the starboard bow. There was an explosion. The target ship was not there anymore. At least, not in one piece. There were pieces flying in all directions. Triga banked away from the wreckage and went to a safe distance. Her view screen showed Mary had done the same.

"NanMar this is JonMar. That was good shooting. The kill goes to you, I have it on film."

"Click, click."

"Form up on me and we'll go home."

"Click, click."

They went back to Oz at about fifty percent power.

"Triga, come up along side, when we get close to Oz you snap roll to the right. I'll snap roll to the left. You peel off and go down the right side and I'll go down the left. It's what we call buzzing the tower. We're entitled to it, we worked hard for it. Rogooo!"

"RogoooO!" Repeated Triga.

When they came in range of the view screen, Mary called in.

"Oz this is JonMar switch on cameras."

"Roger"

"Break now"

Both did a perfect maneuver and streaked down the sides of Oz. They met aft at about five miles and turned back to the fantail, approaching the docking bay. Triga approached first. She turned on the auto lighting system and backed into her docking slot.

Mary had seen the maneuver and asked what it was.

"It is an auto lighting system. When you turn around it will guide you backward to your docking spot." She told her how to engage it.

Mary tried it. She was a little shaky but got it on the first try. After both ships were shut down and secured to the deck, the four met in between and walked toward the evaluator. Mary turned toward Triga.

"That was some of the best flying I have ever seen. Where did you learn to fly like that?"

"When we went out on our training cruise in our third year, Captain Eugin had us flying everyday. We would practice maneuvering in close order flight and then attack some small asteroid. We took films of the attacks to study afterward. Whoever struck it first got extra rations. I did not get fat but I ate well. Since you people have taken over the ship I have gained weight. I do not expect an extra ration."

Mary and John laughed.

"You don't have to be the best to get extra rations here. But you are expected to do your best at all times. You can eat at anytime you want and eat all you want. Just eat all you take." John said.

The four arrived on the bridge, Triga gave Dirk a film disc and they watched the attack. The alien ship fired as the two star crafts split. It happened so fast the other ship could not bring its laser to bear on either one. Dirk froze the film and they all looked at the craft. It was identical to the one that Dirk and Kat had hidden.

"Looks as though these Beta-six traders stick together."

Dirk switched the film back to play. When they had seen the film Dirk looked over to Triga and with a smile on his face said. "That is the best flying I've seen in a long time. Mary had the advantage for a shot but you beat her. How?"

"There are small jet blasters located on the bow, top and bottom, and on the stern, top and bottom. When you are in an attack mode you switch them on. You can activate them from the main control panel. What they do is either push the bow up or down. You can bring yourself out of tight turn faster with them also. That is why I got the first shot. If I had known Captain Mayhan was unaware of them, I would have told her. When she takes me for a check ride, I will show her how they work."

"I think Triga should take me on a check ride instead." Mary said

"Let's look the area over and see if anything can be salvaged from this mess. Scaner, are there any more craft in our general area?" Dirk said.

"There are no other craft within a five hundred mile radius, Sir.

"Very well."

Just then a red light started blink. "I think we have some people coming out of freeze. Let's give them a proper welcome." Kat said.

"John, Tribec, do you two want to come down to the capsule room with us?" Dirk asked

"I think we had better get back to my project in the machine room. Besides, if they see to many people they're libel to faint. We'll get to see them later."

"Ensign Triga, you have the bridge watch, report if anything out of the ordinary happens. Bring us over the junked Beta-six craft and hold there." Dirk said. "John, hold on a minute. Do you need Tribec?"

John thought for a minute. "No, not right now, but I could use him later."

"Tribec, what I would like for you to do is go with Ensign Triga and see if you can salvage some of the parts floating around where you two shot up that other Beta Six craft. Anything that might be of use to this ship. Ensign, check out the area real good after you have brought us over our junk pile. Before you leave, plug in Scaner. He can hold us over the target."

"Aye, Aye Sir."

Dirk left the bridge and went down to the capsule room. Kat and Mary were all ready there and had sheets ready to put over the young couple when the lids of the capsules lifted. Mary handed Dirk one and he went over to the one William Smith was in. The fan started to clear away the mist and Dirk could see the face of William Smith, Nice looking young man. The mist was extracted and the lid lifted open. William opened his eyes and just stared at Dirk.

"Don't try to move just yet." Dirk said "Try moving your hands and arms and then your feet and legs."

William did this, all the time keeping his eyes on Dirk. He tried to sit up but fell back. He lay there, staring at Dirk. Dirk reached over to a tray and got a glass of water and held Williams head up so he could drink. William took a sip of water and tried to speak. All that came out was a croak. Sounded something like a frog. Dirk grinned and spoke.

"I am Lieutenant Commander Dirk MacGlashan, United States Navy, you are onboard the Star Ship Oz. of the U.S.A.S.F. Just relax for a minute and you'll be OK. I'm the Captain of this space craft and now for the surprise of your life, today is 12 Nov 1999."

"Is this some kind of a sick joke?"

"No, it is not and if you promise not to go berserk, you can get up now and we'll tell you all about it."

William swung his legs over the side on the capsule and sat up. Dirk handed him a robe to put on. Dirk helped him to stand up. William looked over and saw the two women helping Alicia to stand.

"What in the hell is going on here? You're telling me we are on some kind of space ship and it's November 12th, 1999. I don't believe it. Alicia, are you OK?"

Dirk looked at William wondering.

"Young man, you are in a space ship and this is 12 Nov 1999 and you have been in a cryogenic capsule for about five years. You are about twenty-five days travel from Earth, if we travel at light speed and now you are going to go with me. I will not tolerate any more of your attitude. Do you understand me?"

William stared at Dirk, as though this was the first time in his life anyone had ever talked to him that way .

"Do you understand me?"

"Yes."

"Yes, what?'

William looked at Dirk and then understood. "Yes Sir."

"Very good, William, you're learning."

Dirk started toward the door to the passageway to the sleeping quarters. Took William into one of the rooms for four people, pointed at some uniforms.

"Take a shower and get dressed, I'll wait."

William went into the shower and when he came out he had a uniform on, much to Dirk surprise. Dirk thought he was going to have some more trouble from him.

"I apologize from my outburst back there. I was a little shaken up to say the least. Alicia and I were on a fishing trip in the hills northwest of Cheyenne. When this round shaped flying machine hovered over us, and the next thing I know you are standing over me saying 'HI' my name is."

"Nothings damaged, come on let's go to the galley and get you something to drink and eat."

When they got to the galley, Dirk took him over to the ordering panel and showed him how it worked.

"It is about 11:45 AM so you might want to order lunch, I am."

They got their meals and had just sat when the women appeared. Alicia was looking around the galley with a big question mark on her face. Mary motioned her to the panel and she was shown how to order food.

Kat had come over to where William was and introduced herself.

"I'm Kathleen MacGlashan, wife to this grump, most people call me Kat."

William stood up and shook Kat's out stretched hand. "It's a pleasure to meet you, Ma'am."

"Please, sit down and enjoy your first meal in outer space." Kat went over to the panel and got a cup of coffee. When Mary and Alicia came over and introductions where made. Dirk started to explain how all of this came about but changed his mind.

"I know there are a million questions you two want to ask, but we have a small situation here. We have ten more people coming out of cryo today and five going in. We are going to be very busy, something similar to a "one armed paperhanger". When we get everyone on their feet, we'll explain all this to everyone at once, then answer any questions."

Ensign Triga's voice came over the inter comm. "Captain, we are in position over the junk pile, at an altitude of three miles. Petty Officer Tribec and myself will be going to check out for salvageable parts from the other Beta-six now." Dirk went over to the inter comm.

"Roger, carry on, report in on what you find." Dirk came back and sat down.

"How many crew members do you have on this craft?" asked Alicia.

"We have ten, twelve counting you two. There are six humans and six Arians."

William and Alicia's eyes opened wide. "Arians, what are Arians?" asked William.

"They are the prior owners of these space ships. Some of them have joined us and some are going into cryogenic capsules, these are the ones that can't be trusted. I'll explain it later. If you meet an Arian, be nice. The ones here with us have been through just as bad a time as you have. The ones that captured you are dead, mostly by their own hand. I repeat, these are the good guys. Ensign Triga and Petty Officer Tribec are Arians and they are a valuable asset to this ship. Ensign Triga is a product of their Space Academy and a terrific pilot. Treat them with respect."

Kat looked at the young couple for Dirk had said this in his 'I will be obeyed voice.' <u>Good, no problem there.</u>

A red light started to blink on the inter comm panel. Kat said "We have two more hatching out."

"Mary, would mind taking Bill and Alicia to their quarters and help them get adjusted.

"Aye, Aye Sir."

Dirk and Kat got up to go to the capsule room. Dirk went over to the panel and put their trays on the shelf.

"Great meal, Toots".

"Thank you Captain, We're glad you enjoyed it."

"Was that an Arian?" asked Alicia

Mary answered. "No, it's an automated voice from the main computer. Come on, I'll show you how it works."

William set his tray on the shelf and said. "Great meal, Toots." No answer. He looked at Mary.

"The Captain is the only one who calls her Toots. She won't answer to anyone else who calls her that. Pick your tray back up and set it back down but don't say anything."

He did and a voice asked. "Did you enjoy your meal?"

"Yes, I did, thank you."

"Your welcome, we are glad you enjoyed it."

Alicia put her and Mary's trays down and the same thing happened. "That's pretty neat, I like that."

Mary took them down the passageway to the quarters.

"This will be your quarters William. Alicia yours will be over there."

"We have been co-habituating." William said. "Do you have a room with a double bed we can have?"

"You will have to take that up with the Captain. We are going to be having children coming out of freeze and I'm not sure the Captain will go for it. In the mean time, I'd leave things as they are, if I were you."

"Well, I plan on talking to him as soon as possible about this."

Mary looked at him. Boy, are you ever thick. Oh well, it's your ass not mine. Mary smiled.

"OK, let's go down to the storage area and get some new clothes. You can also pick up your personal belongings too. What you had on you when you brought on board. There are a lot of buttons and gadgets on this craft so don't play. You push the wrong button and you may be in space all by yourself. Oh, and also very dead. In about one tenth of a second you'll explode. I'm telling you this for your own safety."

Dirk and Kat were on their way to the capsule room and Kat stuck her head into sickbay and asked if all was all right. Gorex, Awga, Bruce and the unnamed Arian were sitting there drinking coffee. Dirk looked at Gorex.

"What I would like for you to do is go to the IV-205 and get three cryogenic capsules. Take them to the quarters with the three detainees and put them in the capsules. Take, Ah --------, Jasper with you."

They all looked at the Arian that had lost his name while in prison back on Arian. He stood up.

"Thank you Captain for giving me a name again. Jasper, Jasper." he repeated it over a couple of times. "I like this name."

"I'll meet you there with two more capsules, for the others. We'll start them as soon as possible. Is doing this going to be a problem for you? Putting your fellow Arians in freeze?" Dirk asked.

"No Sir, they were not very nice Arians, they caused a lot of trouble here and on Arian." Jasper said.

"OK, let's get to work." Dirk looked at Awga. "You look lovely today. How do you feel?"

"Very well, thank you, Captain."

Kat and Dirk left to go to the capsule room.

"That was a nice thing to say to Awga. She feels kind of useless, not being able to do any work."

"To me, there is not a more beautiful sight than a pregnant woman. They radiate a very special inner beauty, it's kind of hard to explain but that's the way I feel."

Kat put her arm through his. "You never cease to amaze me." and kissed him on the cheek.

***

When they reached the capsule room, they checked the units holding the father and son. Everything was coming along fine.

Dirk said he was going to take the two empty capsules to the passageway in the quarters area and be right back.

By the time he got back Kat had sheets and robes ready. The mist was clearing in the capsules.

Dirk looked over to Kat and said. "Ready or not, here they come."

The lids opened and Dirk and Kat placed sheets over the two men.

The capsule Kat was at held the son. He looked up and said. "Wow, an Angel."

Kat smiled at him and said. "Not yet, but thanks for the complement. Just lay still for a moment and we'll see if you are alright. Can you move your hands and feet? Now try your arms and legs."

She reached over, got a glass of water and gave him a sip. "Now swing your legs over and I'll help you sit up." She help him put on the robe and then to stand up.

Dirk was standing over the father when he opened his eyes. Dirk asked him if he felt okay.

The man answered "Yes" but it came out as "Ayah"

"You can tell he comes from Maine." and he smiled. He helped the man stand up.

"Well, Mr. Chambers welcome to the Space Ship Oz of the U.S.A.S.F. I am Lieutenant Commander Dirk MacGlashan of the U.S. Navy. You two are doing fine. I know you have a lot of questions to ask. But first, some clothes, then something to drink and eat. Then I'll be glad to answer any questions you have. The lady is Kathleen MacGlashan, my wife, she is First Officer onboard. Most folks call her Kat."

After they had a drink of water and felt a little better, Dirk took them to their new quarters.

"Mr. Chambers, if you would like to have private quarters, we have some available.

"No, this will be fine."

"Yes, he does. He snores something awful." James said.

Dirk laughed. "Okay, private quarters it is. We have three quarters available to senior Petty Officers. They are single bed quarters, located at the end of the passageway. James, you'll find a shower stall and bathroom through that door. There are clean uniforms on the bed. So why don't you clean up and I'll take your father to his new quarters. Are you ready Sir."

"Major, excuse me, Commander, I'm a retired Master Gunnery Sergeant, USMC. It is I that will be calling you Sir, Sir."

"Gunny, I am glad you are here. We can really use you. Come on, I'll show you where your quarters are and we can talk." Dirk took him down the passageway toward his living quarters.

***

Kat was seeing to the loading of the Arians being put into the capsules when they went by. Dirk could see Burt was interested in what was going on.

"Is this some kind of a funeral, Sir."

"No, these Arians are very unfriendly to humans. We are placing them in cryogenic capsules. We can't have them running around loose. I'll explain it all to you a little later on." Dirk stopped at the last door to the outer quarters. "This will be your quarters."

Dirk showed him how to open the door, by pushing lightly against the amber light. These quarters were not as big as the married quarters but still had all the benefits. Dirk went over to the console and opened the panel for the view screen.

"Gunny, welcome to outer space."

"Well I'll be damned. Will you look at that!"

"I'll leave you now. The galley is straight back down this passageway. You'll see the double doors. I'll stop by and get James. We'll meet you there."

"Aye, Aye Sir."

***

Dirk went back to where Kat was working with Jasper and Gorex.

"How is it going?"

"All right, they were still out. I checked them over and each is in good physical shape. The flu bug is about whipped."

"If they're ready to go, I'll help you move them into the capsule room."

"They're ready. God, I feel like I'm killing them."

"Oh no, Mrs. Mac, please don't feel like that. These are very bad Arians. All have been convicted of very serious crimes. They would not think twice about killing us, if they had the chance." Jasper stated.

"Let's get them into panels so we can clean up these quarters and get back to running this ship." Dirk looked at Kat. "Our Mr. Chambers is a boon for us. He's a retired Master Gunnery Sergeant from the Marine Corps."

"I don't know what that is?"

"I'll explain it to you later, but trust me, it's good."

***

They took the capsules and stowed them in the panels. Dirk had asked Jasper to get a print out on each Arian and put it in the slot on each of the capsules for later identification. Dirk and Kat went toward the galley. Dirk stopped to get James and they went on toward the galley. Kat stopped at sickbay after stating she'd had enough coffee.

"I'll see you when the first family is ready to hatch." Kat whispered in his ear. "This would be a lot easier if it were just you and me back on the NanMar, zooming toward Earth."

Dirk put an arm around her and gave her a little squeeze. "I know what you mean, but we've come across this responsibility and we can't turn our backs. You're doing a great job. Just in case I forget to tell you before we go to bed tonight, I love you."

Kat put her arms around Dirk's waist and laid her head on his chest just for a second and whispered "I love you too."

Dirk and James continued on their way to the galley. When they arrived, Dirk showed James how food was ordered and how to get something to drink. He showed him where to put his tray after he was done eating. They were sitting down when Burt Chambers came in. Dirk took him over to the ordering panel and explained the system to him. They had just sat down when Mary and Alicia and William came in. Introductions were made. Alice and William went to get a cup of coffee and came back and sat down.

CHAPTER TWENTY-TWO

The inter-com came on "Captain, this is NanMar, we have checked the area where the Beta-six was and pick up some crates of weapons, a box of crystals, some machinery and some large pieces of metal plating. We are returning to Oz at this time.

Dirk went over to the inter comm. "Roger NanMar, report to the bridge upon arrival, Oz out. Let's all go to the bridge. I've got some things to do and it will be a learning experience for all of you."

Dirk led the way to the bridge. He checked on Scaner and as usual, he was doing his assigned job perfectly. Dirk opened the panel to the view screen and trained the cameras on the wreck of the Beta-six ship. He told the new comers how he got the ship, emphasizing the fact that not everyone in outer space was friendly. It was shoot first and ask questions later with them.

"If we come under attack everyone will have a job to do and it has to be right the first time because everyone's life is at stake." Dirk looked at each person to see if it had sunk-in.

"What we have to do is strip the wreck and get everything onto Oz. We only have three days to get the job done."

The ship gave a small shake. "That'll be NanMar coming in. Scaner, did you ever find out what was the matter with IV-202?"

"The wiring to the exciter was burned out. It can be fixed with spare parts in storage."

"Captain Eugin never told them it could easily fixed. That crafty old fox." Dirk said. "Chalk another one up for him. We'll explain everything to you all soon. I'm waiting until all the people are out of cryo so we won't have to go over it three or four times, Okay?"

***

The door opened and Ensign Triga and Tribec came in. "People, this is Ensign Triga and Chief Petty Officer Tribec."

Burt Chambers went over to them and extended his hand.

"It is a pleasure to meet you, Ma'am ---- Sir."

James went right behind his father and extended his hand also, Alicia went next and Bill was last.

Dirk had the feeling Bill was not pleased. I'll straighten his ass out real quick. These people are saving his life and he's to damn stupid to know it.

Burt Chambers was watching Dirk and could read his mind just by the look on his face.

James was also watching Dirk and his father. Oops, looks like Bill is going to be the recipient of a brand new anal orifice. I've seen that Master Gunnery look before. This is not going to a pretty sight but he still had to smile.

Dirk looked over to James and asked what he was studying in school. James said he was in his third year of college and was studying electronics and computer programming. He already had an Associate Degree and was working on his Bachelors on a part time basis.

Dirk switched on the inter comm. "John can you come to the bridge. I believe I have something for you."

It took John a couple of minutes to get to the bridge. When he was introduced to everyone, he looked at Dirk. "What is it you have for me, Dirk?"

"It seems James is an electronic whiz and also a computer programmer. I thought you two might get along."

John looked at James and asked him what he knew about sonar. James told him didn't know too much about it except in theory. But he did know a lot about the old APS 56 and APS 57 radar and started to describe how he and a friend had boosted one up to reach over seven hundred miles. John took him by the arm, inviting him to come down to the machine shop, where he was working on a little project that might interest him. And off they went.

Dirk turned to Mary and asked her if she wouldn't mind taking Alicia down to sick bay and leaving her with Kat. He looked at Alicia.

"I know we can use a nurse down there. Bruce is an Arian nurse but we sure could use some one who knows about humans."

"I thought Mrs. MacGlashan was a Doctor." Alicia said.

"She is, in veterinary medicine."

William looked at Dirk. "You mean to tell us a Veterinarian has been checking us over." Everyone could hear the disgust in his voice.

Much to everyone's surprise Dirk kept his temper.

Burt Chambers thought. <u>This man is an Officer through and through.</u> <u>Anyone else would have punched this clown into next week.</u>

"Ensign Triga, Petty Officer Tribec, you both have done an excellent job in retrieving the parts of the Beta-six craft. How long do you think it will take to get it all stowed?"

"It should take about one hour, Sir." Ensign Triga said.

"Good, get Gorex and Jasper and I'll sent someone else down to help you. William, why don't you go to your quarters and take a break."

"Captain, I'd like to discuss the sleeping arrangements of Alicia and myself. We have co-habituating for sometime. Mary said I would have to talk to you about getting a room for us."

"William, the lady you speak of is a Captain in the United States Air Force, in the future you will address her as Captain Mayhan. As far as the sleeping quarters go, togetherness is for married people only. We will be having children coming out of freeze and they will not be subjected to a type of free-style living. Subject is closed. Now Mr. Smith, why don't you go to your quarters and relax a while."

William was about to say something else when he caught Burt Chambers motioning with his head to leave. Without saying a word he left.

Burt looked at Dirk. "When I was an active Gunny, every once in awhile I had to discuss the right way to a few that had strayed. It would be a pleasure to relieve the burden of William from your shoulders, Sir."

"It seems he does need to learn that this is a team effort."

"That he does, Sir."

"After you're done instructing him, have him report to Ensign Triga. He can help moving the spare parts into storage. And then come back here, Mr. Chambers."

"Aye, aye, Sir."

Dirk was studying which would be the best way to get the shot up Beta-six up to Oz when Burt came onto the bridge.

"William is down at the docking bay working his heart out, Sir."

"What am I going to call you by, Mr. Chambers, Burt or Gunny?"

"Gunny will be just fine, Sir."

"So, Gunny, what did you do while you were in the Corp?"

"Sir, I was a flying Sergeant, they reopened that slot during the Korean War."

"Are you still flying?

"Yes Sir, James and I bought an old Cessna 150, rebuilt it. Now we fly it all over."

"How would you and James like to be pilots in the extra IVs that we have?"

"That sounds great Sir, but what is an IV?"

"An Interstellar Vehicle, we've been renaming them and calling them Star Ships. With the proper crystals in them they are capable of light speed. Right now the motherboards have to be overhauled, to be able to produce light speed. They have to be to be able to keep up with this be baby. Do you still want to try it?"

"Yes Sir."

"While we are alone, why don't we skip the formalities, I'm Dirk and your Burt."

"Yes S--, Ahhh, Dirk.

"Tomorrow we'll line up some training flights with Triga and Mary. I want you to know Triga is one hell-of-a-driver. Do you think James will be a good student for her to train?"

"Dirk, I think it will be a good combination."

"Let's go to the docking bay, check things out and talk with Triga. I'm sure Mary will jump at the chance to teach again. She was an IP at Holoman A. F. Base. We can talk to James. John will probably squawk about loosing him for awhile. He's building a space pinger that's supposed to be kick-ass. He can explain it better than I can."

***

They found Triga in the NanMar directing the unloading of a welding machine. When they had it on the deck, Dirk asked Triga to join them on the bridge. He told her about Burt and James both knowing how to fly and would she mind taking James under her wing and teach him how to operate an SS.

"It would be a pleasure to teach someone to fly a Star Ship, Sir"

"Thank you, Ensign, when would you like to start."

"We have to start getting the Beta-six wreck dismantled, so I can start tomorrow morning, Sir."

"Would it be possible to do a ground school tonight for the Chambers. They could learn a lot just sitting here in the docking bay."

"Mr. Chambers,-------." Triga started.

Burt interrupted her by putting up his hand. "Call me Gunny, please."

Triga looked at Dirk, who nodded his head.

"Gunny, would 7:00PM tonight be alright for you and James?"

"Yes, that would be fine."

"I will have the manuals ready for you. These are not very hard to operate once you know where everything is. A little practice and you will have no problem."

Dirk and Burt walked off to see James. Burt said. "She makes it sound like you were just going to take a bath. Would you mind if I asked you a question?"

"No, Burt, go right ahead.

"Were you ever a cowboy?"

Dirk smiled. "No I can't say I was ever a cowboy. Why?"

"One of the Officers in my old flight squadron was. He said people are a lot like cattle. If you nudge them in the right direction slowly, they'll think that's the way they wanted to go in the first place. If you don't mind me saying, Sir, that's exactly what you do. James is developing that same trait."

Dirk looked at Burt for a second. "You're a wise man, Gunny."

***

When they got to the machine room, both John and James were standing looking at a weird looking contraption.

"Do you think that it'll live?" Dirk asked

The two looked up. "Dirk, if you get hit by this baby inside of one hundred miles I guarantee it'll knock your dick in the sand and you right behind it. James did a tremendous job on the programming. He really souped this up."

"Well I guess you won't be needing James for a while." Dirk looked at James. "How would you like to learn to fly a Star Ship?"

"Yes Sir, I'd like that fine."

"OK, it's all settled. Ensign Triga is going to start a ground school tonight at 7:00 PM for you two. And then tomorrow you start flying. James, you'll be with Ensign Triga and Gunny will be with Mary. Now the next item. We've got to get SS-202 on the line. John, you take these two gentlemen and Scaner, go and see if you can fix her. Scaner says it's the wiring to the exciter. Also Ensign Triga picked up a box containing twenty-five more million dollar fuel tickets, we now have thirty-five in stores. Plus numerous three karat ones for the shuttle-craft. Oh, I forgot about the package Captain Eugin hid. John, what did you do with them?"

"I put it in the storage locker in the reactor room."

"Alright, you men take care of 202 and I'll go and see our latest hatch. Oh, by the way, our bad guys have been put in freeze, panels one through five. I threw the safety locks on."

Dirk went up to the galley.

"I'm sorry to have run off on you all like that but a couple of things had to be taken care of. Welcome to outer space. Did Kat or Mary explain to you the whats, whys and wherefores of all this?" They all nodded. "Good, I won't have to go into opening speech #1. I know you have a lot of questions and if you'll be a little patient a little longer, we'll answer all of your questions. I'll try to explain what's happening and what's going to happen." Dirk looked over to youngest Ross. "Susan, right? Where did you get that red hair and all of those freckles?"

Susan blushed bright red and started to giggle. Dirk smile and in his best Scottish accent said.

"Aye, you're a bonney wee lass."

Susan looked up at Dirk as though he could walk on water. Kat looked at Dirk and thought <u>You might have started something you know nothing about.</u> Then she remembered Dirks daughter, Marnie. <u>This girl must remind him of her. All will be okay, I'll explain this to the Ross's.</u>

Dirk looked at Samatha. "Tell me a little about you, are you still in school? What are you studying? Things like that."

"I was to start College this fall I am hoping to get my degree in English History and Literature."

Dirk noted she looked a little devastated realizing where she was right now.

"Don't you worry, you'll get your education. And in the mean time look at the education you're getting right here. You'll be the only one in your class to ever been in space and you'll be able to prove it."

"But I'll be twenty-nine on my next birthday, that's a little late to be starting college."

"No, your still eighteen, you've be in a cryogenic capsule for the past ten years. You haven't aged one day since you were beamed up. None of us has, it's like getting a second chance when we get back to Earth."

The red light started to blink. Kat said. "It's time to get the third family out of the hatchery." Everyone started to laugh. Mary Jane asked if there was something she could do to help, that she was not used to just sitting around. Kat look at Mary and Ally, as she was now called, they all nodded. "Sure, come on along, you know what's going to happen cause you just went through it."

Dirk looked over to Allen and the girls.

"I've got to go to the bridge, why don't you go with me."

***

Each group went their different ways. When Dirk and the Ross's got to the bridge Susan went over to Scaner and looked at him. Scaner rotated his dome like head. "Hi, I'm Scaner, what can I do for you?"

"What are you?"

"I am a Self-contained, Analytic, Electrical, Robot. I am called Scaner. What are you?"

"I am a sixteen year old human female."

"Oh, is that why you are so short?"

"I am not short. I am very tall for my age."

"Scaner, show the Beta-six ship on the view screen."

The panel opened and the view screen came on. Dirk looked at the Ross's and the expressions on their faces. Allen and Susan were in awe but Samatha had a look of extreme interest. Like she wanted to be closer so she could really look it over. I think this young lady has found a new nitch in life

"Sam, can I call you Sam?" she said yes, that was what everyone called her.

"Sam, come over here and I'll show you how to enhance that picture. We're looking at something that is three miles away." Dirk showed her the way to get the main computer to enhance the image. Enhanced the ship looked as though it was only fifty feet from them.

"What we have to do is get all of the equipment and as many spare parts off of it as soon as possible. We have to be on our way in three days. It's going to mean that all hands work. Everything has got to be inventoried, labeled and stowed away. The information has to be put into the main computer. All of this information will be sent to each Star Ship, so each will know what is available."

Sam was soaking this information up like a blotter.

"Go ahead and look around, but don't touch anything unless you know what's going to happen. You push the wrong button and we could be shooting at something. Or worse, we could be floating around in space, wondering how we got there. Feel free to ask any question you want. I'm a firm believer of, 'There's no such thing as a dumb question. I don't like correcting dumb mistakes.'"

The intercom went on. "Dirk, the Jones's are up and in good shape. What do you want do?"

"Let's get everyone down to the main galley on the next deck. We'll have dinner there. Then we can let everyone know what's going on. Jasper should have it all set up by now. Check with him and we'll all be there by 1730."

Dirk looked over to Allen. "Are you alright? You look a little shaky."

"I'm alright. Probably a little hungry."

Dirk reached over to the inter comm. "This is the Captain, the evening meal will served in the main galley for all hands at 1730."

CHAPTER TWENTY-THREE

Dirk, Allen and his two daughters went down to the main galley. Everyone was there, including John. As Dirk went toward the head of the table he past John and asked. "How's the pinger going?"

"Excellent, it'll be ready for testing day after tomorrow."

Everyone had their meals and was sitting, relaxing over a cup of coffee and whatever the younger ones were having. Dirk stood up, clinked his glass a couple of times to get everyone's attention.

"I think the only people I haven't met are the Jones's, Richard, Clare, Richard Jr. and Rebecca. It is a pleasure to see you all up and looking well. I'll introduce myself. I'm Lieutenant Commander Dirk C. MacGlashan of the United States Navy, I'm Captain of this Star Ship, the Oz. We call ourselves Task Force #101, we called it 101 because that's what we are. Just like college, the first year, freshman classes were 101. All of us are in our freshman year so to speak."

"It's pretty obvious all of us are here because we were abducted. That is everyone but me. I'll tell you about that later." Dirk went on to tell them why he was resuscitated and who resuscitated him. "Scaner is quite an invention. For one thing while everyone was working at one thing or another for the last two days, he has been piloting this ship. And here we are safe and sound. He eats nothing, gets paid nothing but he does get a grease job and an oil change once a week. That's my job, or one of them. There are six people here who do not look like we Earthlings. These people are Arians.

Their names are." Dirk looked over to the Arians. "Please stand when I call out your names; Ensign Triga----, Chief Petty Officer Bruce----, Chief Petty Officer Jasper----, Petty Officer Gorex----, Petty Officer Tribec----, and Awga----. Not one is here by their own free will. They were abducted just as we. These people are trusted, valuable members of this crew. They've been on this ship longer than we have. Ensign Triga was a student at the Arian Space Academy. This lady can really fly a Star craft. She's good, damn good."

"When I was resuscitated I was on the IV-208, which stands for Interstellar Vehicle 208. The pilot Rega had died from an acute case of Asian flu. I am a Navy pilot. I had to learn about the 208. With the help of Scaner, I resuscitated Kat. It takes two days to resuscitate a person, and three hours to freeze one in a cryogenic capsule. On the same day she came out of freeze, we had to shoot down an alien spacecraft. He fired upon us first. He missed not once but twice."

"We got the last shot in." Dirk switched on the view screen, "That's it right there. We tucked it away because we knew we would be headed back this way. There are a lot of things on that ship we can use here."

"We went on toward the Mother Ship. Along the way we encountered another Arian ship, the IV-204. Kat and I boarded it, found the pilot very sick with the Asian flu and the co-pilot dead. Kat developed an anti-serum and nursed the Arian back to health. Because of his nature we put him in a cryogenic capsule. The Mayhans were onboard that ship. John is or was a teacher at the University of New Mexico, now he works on a space ship. His lovely wife Mary is a Captain in the United States Air Force and is an IP or Instructor Pilot on the F16, her call sign is "Zinger". They renamed their ship the JonMar. I had renamed mine the NanMar."

"When we came upon the Mother Ship, we had already started to call it Oz, after the young girl in Kansas. We had to figure a way to get on board the Oz with out killing anyone. We did, we sent the dead co-pilot in a shuttlecraft loaded up with the live virus, after three days waiting we came aboard with very little resistance. There was only one fatality, an Arian was trying to sabotage the ship, literally kill it. He was knocked out by a laser and fell to the next deck, breaking his neck. He was one of the bad guys."

"After Kat and Mary worked on the remaining crew, nursing them back to health. One of the bad guys got loose, killed Captain Eugin and took John and Mary as hostages. Hoping Kat and I would rush in and he could kill all four of us and retake the ship. He didn't make it. That day we held funeral services for the dead. One of the bad guys rather than risk going back to Arian, opened the outer door to the air lock. He went along with the dead into outer space."

"We held a military funeral for Captain Eugin the next day. The Arians, which could not be trusted were put into security quarters. As you people were resuscitated we refilled the capsules with them. And that brings us to today. Literally right now. Let's take a break, I need a cup of coffee."

As Dirk and Kat stood talking, he noticed John looking the new people over. He kept coming back to William. Dirk could see his eyebrows knot up every time he looked at him. <u>John is thinking the same thing Gunny and I feel about him. He's going to be trouble. I'm wondering if we really need him as much as we first thought?</u>

"Okay folks, if I could have your attention again. I'll try to go a little into the future." Dirk went to the view screen and brought up a star chart. "This is Earth and this is Arian. These lines here, here, here, and here are the routes the star crafts used to go to Earth and back. There are five star crafts assigned to this ship. The fifth is some where between here," He pointed to Earth. "and here." He pointed to a 'X' marked on the chart. "I don't know what's happening with him or to him. He had to have been exposed to the virus while he was at Earth. But the 'X' is what we're interested in. That's the ISS-01, Ozzie Too as we call it. We know they have two Star Ships. One of the things we do not know is, are they good, loyal Arians or are they bad guys too. If they are the bad guys, you can bet there are humans onboard. If so, we plan to get them. If not we leave them alone and go about our merry way back to Earth."

"All these people are doing is trying to find a new planet to colonize. Their home planet is not doing so good right now. The Arians that mutinied back on Arian were mostly harden felons and killed the replacement crew for this ship. They needed a few more to make the count right and these six are those. What they had in mind was to colonize the new planet and use humans as breeding stock for a new race of people. Okay, now you can see what we are up against."

"We can leave right now and head back to Earth and say to-hell-with-it. Along with that, we're going to get up every morning and look ourselves in the eye. I don't think I can do that. The responsibility was thrust upon us, meaning John, Mary, Kat and myself. We brought you into it."

"If you look around at each other, I think you'll notice most are all between the ages of twenty and forty-five. We are all physically sound. Ask your neighbor where they were when they were beamed up. Right, in the country. Everyone here and the ones still in freeze were picked up somewhere in the country, except for me. Rega was in the process of beaming up a newborn dolphin when I struck her ship with my F14 Tomcat. She switched the beam over to me and brought me onboard instead. I was pretty well busted up. With the help of Scaner, she was able to put me together again."

"The theories we came up with check each other out. I would like for each and every one of you to think on this and we'll talk about it in the morning. Tomorrow is going to be a busy day. If anyone wants to stay, there is going to be a movie and I think, some ice-cream." Dirk look over to Jasper, who nodded. "Yes, there will be ice-cream. Oh, by the way the movie is a Disney classic. The Arians became addicted to our movies. They've even got some silent ones. So get to know each other. We'd probably be surprised at just how much we have in common."

Ensign Triga came over to Dirk and said. "Awga and I would like to thank you for not telling everyone what we were forced to do back on our home planet."

"That is your own business and no one else's. As far as we are concerned it never happened. Now are you ready for you students?"

"Yes Sir, I will take them down to the NanMar for a couple of hours and we will go through some of the manuals." Triga walked over to where Gunny and James were standing, talking to the Ross family.

"Excuse me, Gunny, James, it is time for your first lesson on the Star Ship."

As they went to leave Sam asked. "May I go to?"

"Please wait here." Triga said and went back over to Dirk. "Captain, the young girl Sam wishes to come too."

Dirk looked over to Sam. "Yes, I think you'll have willing student there. She soaked up the bridge today like she was a blotter."

***

The four went down to the NanMar. Triga started on the airframes manual. Owning an airplane and having rebuild it, Gunny and James had very little difficulty with the SS. Sam was absorbing it like it was gospel. The two-hour lesson turned into four hours. They broke off and called it a night.

Gunny turned to Ensign Triga. "Ma'am, we thank you for your time tonight. It was very informative."

"It was my pleasure. I enjoy being here in outer space. It is so quite and peaceful. You are always seeing new things. Let us see if there is any ice-cream left. I have never had any."

When they sat down to enjoy the ice cream. Triga said.

"I have something to show you." She went over to the view screen. A picture of the Beta-six wreck was there. She turned the cameras around, pointing toward the port side. "I will bet you have never seen two moons before as big as these."

The three sat there with their mouths open.

"Ayah, we have'm althuh tyme down Maine." Gunny said, looking toward Triga. It was her turn to stand there with her mouth open. She didn't know what to say.

"Just kidding, it is quite the sight. And we only have one moon on earth."

Triga smiled and then started to laugh. After they had finished the ice cream. Triga said. "I'm going to make a turn around the ship to check the systems. I will see you all here at 0700."

"Wait I'll go with you." Gunny said. Triga looked at him. "Old Marine habit, I used to be a Master Gunnery Sergeant, the last thing I did was to check my duty station over before going to bed. James will you see Sam to her quarters?"

"Yes Sir."

James walked Sam back to the quarters she shared with her sister and Rebecca Jones. Standing at the door, Sam said.

"I asked Ensign Triga if it would be alright if I went out with you and her tomorrow. She and the Captain approved it. How do you feel about it?"

"I think it's great. You know there are going to be two star ships open for pilots, the 202 and the 205."

"I know."

"Goodnight Sam."

"Goodnight James."

"Just JT, that's what everyone back home used to call me."

"OK JT, what's the T stand for?"

"Tyrone, it's a family name, on my mother's side."

"Your mother must miss you two something awful. Just 'poof' and you're gone. I'm glad that we are all together."

"My mother was killed when I was twelve. Dad was stationed in Turkey. There was some rioting. My mother was struck by a stray bullet... I miss her." JT said

"I feel a little foolish talking about my family like I did. I'm sorry about your Mom."

Sam had put her hand on JT's chest when she said that. James reached up and took her hand in his.

"There's no way you could have known. No harm done. Well, I'll see you in the morning, good night again." JT turned and walked to his quarters.

Sam stood there and when he had reached his door he turned, and looked at her one more time.

Unbeknown to them, there was a witness to their parting. Dirk had been making a walk around of the ship and had just come to the far end of the passageway. Standing in the dark, JT and Sam could not see him.

At first he almost called out but thought against it. They have only known each other for part of one day. Let them have a private talk. They are a good looking couple. If a small romance starts up, it will be good for the morale of the ship.

Dirk continued on his way toward the galley. When he got to the galley he went over to the ordering panel.

"I'll have a cup of coffee, black, Toots. The coffee appeared and Dirk heard. "Aye, there you go you handsome devil." It came out in a Scottish brogue "Eye, t'ere ewe goo ewe 'anhsoom deavil." Taken by complete surprise, Dirk almost dropped the cup.

There was laughter behind him and he turned to find Ensign Triga and Gunny standing by the door.

"Don't blame us, we just got here." Gunny said.

"We were making a check of the ship and decided to have a cup of drink before going to bed, Sir." Triga said

"Well, I'm sure it wasn't you Triga." He cocked an eyebrow at Gunny.

"Honest. It wasn't me."

"I was just making a turn around the ship myself, it seems all is well." Dirk said

"Captain, tomorrow, if you get the chance, talk to James about an idea he had about the IVs. We were going though the manual on the propulsion unit of the star ship. They are not capable of light speed in they're present condition. He has an idea which might just put them up to light speed."

"I just saw JT saying goodnight to Sam, They didn't see me, so I left them alone. I'll talk to him in the morning. What time are you meeting them, Ensign?"

"At 7:00 AM Sir, here for breakfast."

"How did you know his nickname is JT?" Gunny asked

"I heard him tell it to Sam. Why?"

"Well, that was his mother's pet name for him. Very few call him JT. If you're not in his close circle of friends, he'll tell you his name is James and not JT. He's kind of possessive about that."

"I guess Samatha's status has risen somewhat, wouldn't you say, Gunny."

"Yes Sir, she's a lovely girl. Smart as a whip to."

"I've covered the forward part of the ship and all's well. I would think the after end is secure or you two would have reported something. I believe I'll go to bed. Scaner is on the bridge. Good night to you both." Dirk said

"Good night, Captain."

Gunny looked down at Triga. "I think I will forego the cup of coffee. I'll see you in the morning Ma'am." Gunny turned to leave.

Triga decided to leave also. "It's going to be a long day tomorrow."

CHAPTER TWENTY-FOUR

The next morning when Ensign Triga came into the galley she found Sam and James having breakfast with their fathers.

"Good morning." Allen said. "Won't you join us?"

Triga went over to the ordering panel, got a breakfast and came back.

Mary and John came in, ordered and sat down with them.

Everyone was talking about the up coming day when Dirk and Kat came in.

Gunny saw them first and said. "Attention on deck." Everyone started to get up when Dirk said.

"As you were. Please, you don't have to do rise every time I come in. In fact, while we are on our daily routine, don't. That's an order. I know it will be hard for you Gunny. Really, to me it's a waste of time. When we get busy, we won't have the time to spare."

All he could hear were "Yes Sir's."

Dirk and Kat got their meals and sat down.

Sam got up, went to the ordering panel and came back with a glass of milk. She was going to take a sip when JT put his hand over hers and shook his head.

"If we have to get into a pressure suit today we will be breathing compressed air. Compressed air will make the milk curdle and probably make you throw-up. Just drink coffee."

Sam put the milk down and pushed it away from her. She looked a JT as if he were Moses and he had just read to her from stone tablets.

Allen looked at Sam and then at James. If anyone else said that, she'd have told them in no uncertain terms just what to do and how to go about it.

Dirk caught Allen's look and though I was right, this girl's got it bad, love blooms. Just what this ship needs, Yes.

Dirk looked over to James. "If you're done, would you come with me to the docking bay?"

James stood. "I'm all done, Sir."

Going to the docking bay silence, Dirk could almost hear James's mind working. When they were standing by the NanMar Dirk said. "I understand you have an idea which can make the star craft capable of light speed?"

"Yes Sir, it's in the exciter. We were checking the manual last night when I saw it. The exciter is the same as the Oz but the control panel isn't. There are smaller chips here. If the mother board was upgraded with hyper chips they would able to go to light speed."

JT continued. "I talked with Ensign Triga about this last night, Sir. She said the original design was to keep pilots from straying and going off on their own. There is one big problem. The system won't handle two fifteen-karat crystals. She'll go into melt down. The most she'll handle is a single twenty-two and a half-karat crystal. Which we don't have."

"Yes, we do. The package Captain Eugin hid had forty, twenty-two and a half karat crystals in it along with twenty more fifteen karat crystals. Can you work this up so it's feasible?"

"Yes Sir. I can."

"Make it happen."

"Yes Sir."

"Today, you will be going with Ensign Triga and Sam will be going with you. Your father will be going out with Captain Mayhan. Don't think about the souping up of the star ship. You just pay attention to flying and get back here safely. One thing at a time, Mr. Chambers. One thing only."

"Yes Sir."

"Scaner reported the wiring in 202 was burnt out. You work on it. Rebuild it to your specs and we'll test it out."

"Yes Sir." Translated, that means she's mine

"Okay, here come the crews and the work parties for the salvage. Go on board and get ready Mr. Chambers."

James literally flew up the ramp to NanMar. Dirk smiled and thought of himself at that age. God, this being Captain is getting old real quick. I wish that were me going out.

Dirk turned to Mary and Triga. "I'll be monitoring the progress from the bridge. Only one ship down there at a time. I don't want any mid-airs understood? Let this be a safe day."

Dirk noticed William was not in any of the work parties.

Going through the galley, he got a cup of coffee and headed toward the bridge. Stopping by sickbay, on the way.

Ally and Bruce were going through the supplies and entering what they had in the computer. Kat was studying about deliveries. He went down to the quarters William was in and knocked. No answer. He opened the door and found William laying across his bed fully clothed and an empty bottle on the floor next to him. Dirk picked up the bottle and smelled it. It was some of the wine they drank when they first came onboard. Dirk reach over William, pulled the bottom sheet back over him, dumping him on the floor. William groaned and opened his eyes.

"Whajadodatfo"

"Mr. Smith, get your sorry self on your feet. Clean yourself up and report to me on the bridge in twenty minutes. Do you understand me?"

William lay there. "Yezsur"

***

Dirk went to the bridge and sat down at the control panel, turned the view screen on and waited.

He felt the ship lift a little and then settle back down. <u>There go the star ships</u> He turned the cameras on wide angle and watched the craft go toward the junk pile.

First the JonMars shuttle went down along side and parked and then the NanMars. <u>Everything's good so far</u>.

The door opened and William came in. He was not in good shape. Dirk looked at him. <u>This man is a danger to himself and to this ship. I can not and will not tolerate it. If this were the service, he'd be spending time in the brig</u>

"Mr. Smith you have been nothing but pure trouble since you came out of cryo. You do not wish to be a working part of this crew. I believe you would rather just be left alone to do what ever you wish to do. I am the Captain of this ship and its well being is in my hands. I will not allow one person to drink himself into a stupor, and then let it go as though nothing has happened. You will be restricted to quarters until further notice. You will take your meals back to your quarters and eat there. If you stray from your quarters at any other time, your ass had better be on fire. That is all, you are dismissed. Stop!" Dirk reached over to the inter-com and called sick bay. "Mr. Smith is going to stop by for a couple of aspirins and then retire to his quarters."

William finally spoke. "You know, I really don't want to be a part of this ship or anything you people have in mind. I would rather be brought back to earth. I believe I have the right, as a citizen of the United States, to demand that. I personally don't give a damn who you are. I will talk to the others about this outrageous action." He turned and walked out of the door. Dirk checked the disc to make sure all of this was taken down.

***

Dirk turned his attention to the star craft and watched them go through some maneuvers. <u>If James and his father are driving, they</u>

are very good. It shouldn't be to long before they could be going out on their own. The next two days should tell the tale.

While Dirk was watching the NanMar go back to the junk pile and land along side to begin receiving spare parts. He noticed two people get out of the NanMar to help transfer material. One was James. The other had to be Sam. I hope they know how to use the space suits, Christ, that's all we need chasing them as they float off into space.

***

Dirk was so involved in watching the loading, he failed to hear the inter-com until Kat yelled at him.

"Bridge here."

"Dirk, I think you had better come down to the galley right now. William is creating a scene. He said some awful things to Awga when she went into get us all something to drink. I don't know what he said, and she won't tell. Ally is in there talking to him now."

"I'll be right down. Dirk reached over and took the laser out of the holster and stuck it in his waistband at the small of his back. I've had all of this stupid son-of-a-bitch I'm going to take. He's going back to bed, in a capsule.

Dirk went down the passageway and looked into sickbay, saw Kat sitting next Awga who was sobbing and trying to say something. Going toward the galley, he heard a stifled scream. Dirk went through the doors to galley like an avenging angel. Took one look, drew the laser from his waistband and fired. The impulse struck William in the chest. He fell to the floor.

Dirk put the laser away and went to Ally, who was lying on the floor. Dirk helped her up and told her to take her hand away from her eye. The eye was starting to swell. The lid was already half shut.

"He popped you a good one, Huh." She nodded her head. "Well, it looks like your going to have a nice shiner."

Ally pointed. "What are you going to do wi----?"

Dirk interrupted. "With shit-for-brains? He's going back to sleep." Dirk went over to the inter-com and called Kat. "Go to the capsule room and get a bed ready. And have Awga bring in an ice pack. Ally's gonna have a shiner. Let's try and keep the swelling down."

Not waiting for an answer, he switched it off. Dirk went to William and took him by the front of his shirt and lifted. Letting him fall over his shoulder, he carried him in a fireman's carry. Dirk didn't look right or left, going straight to the capsule room.

Kat had a capsule out and ready. Dirk walked over and dumped William in, like he was a sack of grain. Kat could tell by the look on Dirk's face this was not a good time to talk. She stripped William down to his shorts. After taking his vitals, she closed the lid. Let in some mist and set the dials for freeze.

Dirk went back to the galley and found Awga holding an ice pack to Ally's eye. He went over to the ordering panel and got two cups of coffee and soft drink. He went back to the two women and sat down. He pushed the drinks toward the women and said.

"Awga, Ally, I'm very sorry this happened. It's my fault. If I had done what was necessary in the first place, none of this would have happened, I apologize to you both."

"Oh Captain, do not be feeling that way, he would done something at a later time that could have much worse. What he said to me has been said before. It is Miss Ally that is hurt."

"Well, it's over and done with. We'll get on with our lives and say no more about this incident." Dirk said.

"Captain, if I could talk to you at a later time when you are not busy. I would appreciate it." Ally said

"Anytime Ally, just come up to the bridge." Dirk reached over, gave her a hand a little squeeze and did the same to Awga.

"Well, I've got to go down to the docking bay and see what they brought back."

***

Dirk was standing next to the docking bay opening in a glass enclosed platform. When the NanMar came in, turned around and backed into place. Not as smooth as she usually does it. But it's probably better than I could

The NanMar was shutting down when loading hatch opened. Two women stood there. Dirk came down off his perch and went to the NanMar.

"James did a nice job docking. How is he at flying?"

Taken by compete surprise both Triga and Sam jumped.

Triga turned and looked at Dirk. "James is already a fine pilot. He will make an even better Star Ship pilot. The landing on the asteroid was done by Sam. She too will make a fine pilot Sir."

Dirk looked at Sam. "Well done."

"Thank you, Sir."

Dirk could see her straighten up a little. Well at least I did this right. Dirk was still a little down because of the William incident.

"All we need to do is unload and we can go back for another load." Triga said.

"Let's leave everything up here. While you're getting another load, I'll separate it by items. That way we can stow things group by group."

While they were talking James had a load by the hatch. Dirk looked up.

"That was a nice piece of driving James. I don't think I could have done better. Well done."

Dirk could see James puff up a little too. Dirk went over to the compartment that held the forklift. It looked a lot like the ones he had seem back on Earth only a little more stream-lined. He went over to the loading door, lifted the forks. James guided him under the load. He saw Sam standing next to him. Watching his every move. She is either in love or is in a heavy duty learning mode. I'd wager a lot of the former and a normal on the latter.

Dirk backed away from the ship and lowered the forks to deck level. Turning the machine he saw a flash of light. Looking up, saw Kat with a camera.

"For our grandchildren, so they'll know you did manual labor once in your life."

She promptly stuck her tongue out and made a funny face. Dirk had to laugh. When he dropped the load and went back for another he saw the crew of NanMar laughing also.

It took about fifteen minutes to unload the ship. Dirk backed the forklift over against the bulkhead and wait for NanMar to take off. He saw the elevator lift back up and the hatch close over it. Dirk could hear the reactor starting to whine. She lifted about three feet further from the deck. The four struts were rigged in. She moved slowly toward the door to space. I'm glad she is driving slowly so the kids could get the feel of the ship moving about in a tight place. Kids! they're not kids, they're adults now. They're learning to survive in space. This is making veterans out of them. Damn, I must be getting old. Dirk suddenly realized it was James piloting the craft out and probably it would be Sam piloting on the next trip.

He was bought out of his reverie by a soft feminine voice. Dirk looked down. "Hi there Susie Q, what can I do for you?"

"Will you teach me how to operate the fork lift? I don't have a thing to do."

Dirk look at her for a minute. "Sure, climb aboard." Dirk slid over and Susan sat behind the wheel. Dirk showed her how the levers worked.

"OK, I've got it. I've driven tractors back home during haying season and also trucks."

Dirk told her to go over to a load, pick it up and then move it a round. She was slow at first but as she gained confidence, she became faster.

I think I have just lost a forklift to a sixteen year old. Dirk looked out bay door to watch the JonMar come in she turned around, backed into position, lowered her struts and landed. The ship shut down and the elevator lowered, Mary came out and walked over to the forklift.

"If James is anything like his father you could turn them both loose now. I taught him everything I know about her and now we are teaching each other from the manuals." Mary looked at Susan behind the wheel of the forklift and then at Dirk. "Aren't there child labor laws in space? Sir."

"She's good at it, watch."

The unloading hatch opened. Gunny pushed the first load into place. Dirk spoke to Susan.

"Keep the forks down until you reach the ship, and then lift them. Watch Gunny's hands and arms for directions on how to place the forks. Don't pay any attention to anyone else, just him."

Susan drove over to the ship and raised the forks and Gunny directed her under the load.

"Tilt the rails back so the load will clear the deck of the ship." Dirk instructed. "Now back away slowly, when you're clear of the ship, stop, then lower the forks to the deck."

She did this perfectly. Dirk got down and checked it. He told her where to put it and stood back. As she drove away he told Mary "I wish I had a camera. Mary, you kind of watch her, I'll be right back." Dirk was back in five minutes with the camera that Kat had. He showed it to Mary and winked. He took some shots when Susan could not see him.

When the ship was unloaded Susan backed away from the ship and stopped. She stood up, hooked one arm around the roll bar, leaned out and looked up at Gunny. He was watching her all of the while smiling. As she leaned out, she threw him a salute. He came to attention and returned it.

They waved at each other. Susan gained an "Uncle Gunny". Dirk got a long distance shot of the salute. Going over to Susan, they watched the ship get underway.

"Tomorrow, do you want to go with Mary and Gunny?"

"Oh, Yes, can I?"

"I'll talk to Mary. But you've got to promise me you won't get in the way, because Gunny is learning to fly."

"I promise, cross my heart." and she did.

"Park the forklift in that compartment, secure it and let's go to the bridge." Susan drove over to the compartment. She saw two slots, lowering the forks, put them into the slots and shut the lift off. Dirk showed her the tie down for the back and they were off.

***

When they got to the bridge Dirk switched on the view screen and Susan watched the two ships go through some maneuvers. Her eyes were glued to the screen. Dirk suspected a bomb could have gone off and she wouldn't have noticed it.

A red light started to blink, Dirk told Susan to sit down at the fire control panel and turn it on. She sat down at the panel. Studying it, found the power switch. She turned it on. Looking at the bearing director and distance read out of the target. Laser lock on, auto and manual. Torpedo warm up switches for tubes 1 though 5, automatic reload for each tube. Without being told she pushed the warm up switches for all five tubes. She waited.

Dirk was busy searching for an inbound ship. A tiny blip appeared on the view screen. Dirk set condition red through out the ship. All the main passageway doors were shut. He got on the inter comm.

"Kat, are you on?"

"Yes"

"Who do you have with you?"

"Mary Jane"

"OK, take her with you and go to the 205. Get her underway, we have an incoming ship. Form up with the other two ships. Report when you are ready for launch. I have Susan here with me, over".

"Yes Sir, don't worry about us. I used to be a BAM, out."

MJ said.

Susan looked at Dirk. "What's a BAM?"

Dirk contemplated for a second. She's a country girl and she's probably heard worse.

"A 'Broad Ass Marine', she was in the Marine Corps, like Gunny. But don't you call her that. She's libel to pin your ears back. They're kind of touchy about that. Okay, Susie Q."

"Yes Sir." Susan almost said "OK, Dirkie Do." but common sense and fear of a spanking from her father prevailed.

Dirk looked at Susan "Don't even think that"

Susan's eye widened. Christ, he reads minds too

"You're damn right I can and don't use the Lords name in vain."

They looked at each other and grinned.

***

"Clare, are you on this channel?"

"Yes Sir."

"Get the two R's and go to sick bay. If Ally and Bruce need help they'll tell you."

Dirk got on the inter-ship channel and got both ships.

"Condition Red, we have an inbound ship you're bearing 270 degrees. The 205 will be launching and forming up on you. Captain Mayhan you are wing leader."

"Bridge, 205 warmed up and ready for launch, over."

"205, Launch, I say again, Launch. Form up on JonMar. You've got some time so show MJ how to use the fire control panel. Susan's already got it figured out. Oz out."

Dirk turned to the view screen, split the cameras, one on the NanMar and one on the JonMar.

The NanMar was still at the loading site. "What in the hell is the hold up" Dirk said aloud. Then he could see it, a piece of equipment half in. Someone pushed it back into the junk pile and secured the hatch. He could hear a female voice yell "Go" over the inter comm. The NanMar rose up, shot ahead and did a turning climb. She did a snap roll and was in position off of JonMars right, a little high. Right on the money.

When push got to shove, Triga could really fly. Dirk thought.

He turned the inter-ship channel up a notch so they could hear what was going on between the ships. Dirk motioned Susan to turn around and watch him.

"This is a heat seeking beam. It literally rides on the directional radar. I beefed it up some. It'll pick up the body heat of a mouse at fifty miles. OK, now watch the screen." There were no heat blossoms. Dirk got on the inter ship channel.

"Oz to JonMar, I have no, I repeat, no signs of life on this inbound ship. Approach with caution."

"Click, click"

***

When they got to within a hundred miles of the incoming ship the JonMar called back to Oz.

"JonMar to Oz, what is the reading on Bogey one?"

"Still no signs of life. I smell a rat JonMar. Be careful. Out."

"Click, Click."

"NanMar, split right, go high right and look behind him. This stinks."

"Click, Click."

"JT, keep your eyes peeled and your ass down."

"10-4, Gunny."

Two minutes went by. Both Dirk's and Susan's eyes were glued to the screen.

All of a sudden Susan blurted out. "Shit, somebody say something."

"It'll hit the fan soon enough." Dirk said.

***

"NanMar to JonMar, We have a bogey in the shadow, correction not one but two bogeys. I say again, two bogeys. They've seen us and are splitting. Break left JonMar."

The JonMar and the 205 broke left, the 205 going wide.

***

The reason the NanMar was late taking off back at the junk pile was the machine they were loading had shifted, knocking Triga down. Striking her head, she was knocked out.

Sam pushed the machine back into the junk pile and shut the hatch, yelling "GO" to JT over the inter comm. JT had taken off like a shot, maneuvering like he was driving an F4 Phantom. Sam lifted Triga, carried her to the bridge, set her in the navigators seat and strapped her in. JT gave her his belt and told her to strap her upper torso to the back of the chair so she wouldn't fall over.

JT looked over to Sam. "We're going to have to do this on our own. We can't go back to Oz, cause there's no one there to fly her except the Captain and he's busy with Oz. If we tell the others what happened, they'll get paranoid. My Dad's on JonMar and your Mom is on the 205 with Mrs. Mac. So we're on our own."

"There's an ex-fighter pilot at home who's got an AD5E Sky Raider. It's a two seater. He's been taking me up as a bonus for flying him around in our Cessna 150. It's a teaching bonus; we've been doing combat maneuvers. If we have to get into with another ship and I tell you "tap it". I want you to keep hitting the laser as fast as you can, okay."

JT reached over and turned on the cameras, as Triga had taught. <u>Always turn on the cameras, so you can study your flight later on. And you can prove what you did.</u>

***

An alien craft broke left, came at the NanMar and fired a torpedo.

"Lock on and fire laser."

Sam did and felt the ship rise, literally straight up.

There was a tremendous explosion. Their laser struck the torpedo. JT inverted and brought the nose down.

"Sam, Fire one torpedo ----------- NOW!"

The ship gave a slight shudder as the torpedo left. JT inverted and once again, rose straight up. He nosed down. The alien ship moved to the right, to dodge the incoming shot. Alright, I've got you now you son-of-a-whore. JT slammed the throttle to 110 percent and went into a dive toward the alien. Before firing another torpedo he shifted to the left to lead him. Doing a snap roll to the right, JT said. "Tap it".

Sam had her finger on the trigger waiting for the command. As fast as she could, she fired. A ring-of-fire went out. No matter which way the alien ship went there was a laser beam waiting on it. The ship, struck twice, pitched to the left. The torpedo holed it dead center. It exploded.

JT yelled. "Yeah, KICK ASS. Great shooting, Babe." JT did a victory roll and went after the other alien. "Reload the torpedo tubes."

"I already did."

"I know, that was for the record."

He spun around and looked at Triga. There was large swelling on the side of her forehead. He looked over to Sam.

"Check her out. She doesn't look so good."

"NanMar to JonMar. Splash one bogey. Am going to engage with you." He had no more than said that, when there was another explosion. It had to be the other alien ship.

"JonMar to Oz, both bogeys splashed, anymore visitors?"

"Negative, Check out the decoy ship and report."

"Click, click."

***

Sam got the first aid kit. Took the stethoscope and listened to her heartbeat. Then took her pulse. Every vital statistics checked out all right.

"I don't like the way this is swelling" Sam said. "She checks out, but the swelling is getting bigger."

JT maneuvered over to JonMar and fell into place low and right. He looked over to Triga and then to Sam.

"Break, Break. NanMar to Oz. We have an emergency, over."

"This is Oz, go."

"Ensign Triga has what appears to be a concussion, her vitals check out. There is a swelling on the right side front of her head by the temple, advise?"

Kat jumped in. "James, I want you to take a scalpel, make an incision at the bottom of the swelling. Then put a pressure bandage over it and get her back to Oz ASAP."

"I was afraid you were going to say that. Roger, will do, out."

"NanMar this is Oz, Bruce concurs with 205. Hit the burners."

"Click, Click."

"Okay, Babe, you want me to do it?"

"No, I can do this. You get us back."

"Hang on."

JT hit the throttle. The ship shot out ahead of the other two. Sam reached over with a scalpel, made the incision and put a cloth up to catch the fluid. She smeared some ointment over the incision, put a compress on and rapped Trigas head. Adjusting the chair, laid it back with Trigas head slightly lowered. Knowing nothing else could be done went back to her seat.

JT hit 110 percent. They were at the ship in five minutes. JT slowed the ship down and went toward the docking bay.

"As soon as we're inside and turned around, go aft. When you feel the ship settle on the struts, lower the elevator, okay."

"Aye, Aye Captain."

"Come on Sam, this isn't anytime to be joking."

"I'm not. You did a great job out there and I'm proud of you." Sam went over to JT and kissed him on the cheek.

JT went into the docking bay, switched on the lighting system and backed into closest docking spot to the elevator. Sam lowered the struts and as the ship settled JT could feel the elevator lower.

He was in the process of shutting down when the Captain and Bruce came up to the bridge. They put Triga on a gurney. Bruce pushed her toward the elevator. Ally was waiting for him on the main deck. Dirk looked over to JT and said.

"When you get your ship secured come up to the bridge."

"Aye, aye, Sir."

Sam came back to the bridge to help shut down the ship. She set the first aid kit back in place, making mental note to replenish it. Changing her mind decided to take to sick bay herself. She reset the Nav chair and sat down while JT recapped the ship's log explaining the cause of Ensign Trigas injury. He took the camera disc and he and Sam went to the bridge. On the way Sam dropped the first aid kit off at sickbay.

JT looked over to Sam. "Every once in awhile when Dad gets upset about some stupid thing I did, he'd say 'Your ass is grass and I'm a power lawn mower.' I think this is going to be one of those times."

James stood outside of the door to the bridge, took a deep breath, squared his shoulders and knocked.

"Come."

James opened the door and stepped into the bridge. Going to the front of the Main console, he stood at attention.

"Sir, reporting as ordered, Sir.

Sam really not knowing what to do stood along side of her JT, as she now thought of him, at the best attention she could muster. Only she was looking directly into the Captain's eyes. JT was looking about six inches over his head, trying to stare a hole in the wall.

Just before they had come to the bridge Dirk told Susan to go to the galley and eat some ice cream. She had been trying to find a reason to flee but couldn't. This is her sister and she'd be dog-goned if she'd run. The Captain made her mind up for her.

"Explain, Mr. Chambers." that's all Dirk said.

Sam wasn't used to military jargon. Dirk could see the question marks in her eyes.

JT explained what had happened down at the junk pile. How he knew the chain of events to take place. He then told how they put Ensign Triga into the chair and strapped her in. Explaining the reasons why he had not reported in immediately. He then told of the events of the battle, handing over the camera disc.

"What is this?" Dirk asked

"It is a film disc of the incident, Sir. Ensign Triga has taught us to always take a film of any engagement, Sir."

"Continue, please."

JT told the rest of the facts. What transpired when they were aware of Ensign Trigas condition.

When JT stopped Dirk asked. "Is that all?"

"Yes Sir. Sir, the responsibility for this action is completely mine, Sir. Miss Ross followed my orders and did her duty. Sir."

This young man did exactly the right thing. He carried out the orders given to the ship. He took over command after the Captain was injured and carried out the battle plan. He did this to the best of his ability. He has presented the facts precisely as they happened. And now he has taken any blame off of his second in command. Gunny, you've every right to be proud of your son. Dirk looked over to Sam.

"Do you have any thing to report Miss Ross?"

"Yes Sir." She told the events that lead up to Ensign Triga's injury.

"Is that all you have to add Miss Ross?"

"Yes Sir."

"Very well. I was watching what went on down at the junk pile and I saw the load shift. It was you who pushed the load back into the Beta-six craft?" Sam nodded. "I heard you yell 'Go'. The NanMar took off even before the hatch was completely shut. You brought the ship up out there like you driving an F4 Phantom. The maneuver that put you in position on Captain Mayhans right wing was a classic. When you approached the dead ship and went high and right, it was right on the money. The reporting of the alien ships was correct. When the alien shot the torpedo at your ship, your firing and evasive action was perfect."

"The way you suckered the alien ship into turning left by firing a torpedo was text book. What gave you away was the way you dove at the alien and did a snap roll and fired a tapping burst all of the way around. This was very inventive of you, Mr. Chambers. We learned to do that in the Korean War against MIGs. Who taught you?" Dirk waited for an answer.

"Sir, there's a gentleman in my home town who was a Navy pilot in the Korean War and he owns an AD5E. He used to take me up every once in awhile and teach me some aerial combat maneuvers. I used to fly him around in our Cessna 150. This was his way of giving me a bonus Sir."

"Is his name Lieutenant Commander Richie by any chance?"

"Yes Sir."

"Well, Mr. Chambers you have learned from one of the best."

"Yes Sir, I believe that to be true."

"There is only one thing I'm going to add, 'Well Done, Mr. Chambers, Miss Ross.' Now back to the business at hand. We still have some men down at the junk pile. Miss Ross, do you believe this man can fly safely?"

"Yes."

"Then I believe you two should start moving parts. Off with you now and be careful. Remember, one thing at a time, just one thing. I don't want any more of my pilots getting injured."

James took a step backward, did an about face, just like "The Gunny" taught him. Sam tried to do the same and almost made it.

***

They left the bridge. When they got to the passageway Sam grabbed JT's arm and spun him around. She threw her arms around his neck and kissed him. It only took JT a second to get his arms around her and hold her tight. They broke off the kiss and JT looked at Sam.

"Let's go flying."

On the way down to docking bay they stopped by sickbay to see how Triga was doing. She was awake but she would not be doing any flying for a while. JT and Sam stood by her bed looking down at her smiling.

"Thank you both for saving my life. Bruce told me if you had not cut the wound open the pressure of all that fluid would have killed me."

She reached over and took a finger of each of them in her hand and said thank you again. There was a tear in each eye. Sam had to wipe her eyes. JT found it hard to swallow. "We've got to go now but we'll be back tonight and talk." JT said. They left.

When the got to the docking bay they found Susan sitting on the forklift eating a bowl of ice-cream.

"Better stand back cause we're going out and down to the junk pile." JT said.

"Well, hurry up cause I'm running this damn fork lift and I don't like sitting around on my ass."

"Does she always swear like that?"

"Most of the time, you ought to hear her when she really gets mad."

Sam and JT went to the NanMar started her up. Sam opened the side-loading hatch, whistled to Susan and motioned her to drive over. Sam pushed a load over to the door and Susan picked it up and backed away from the ship. She lowered the forks and backed out of the way. She jumped down and looked at the load and then drove it over to where it was supposed to go. After she dropped it she put the forklift in its proper place and secured it. She didn't even look at the NanMar on its way out of the docking bay. She had somewhere to go and that was the bridge.

***

When the NanMar cleared the bay, Sam strapped herself in at the Nav chair. JT increased the power, did a snap roll and yelled "YeeHaw". Sam turned on the view screen and saw the other ships just coming into view.

"They're back, JT. That must be the IV 207, it doesn't look to good." She switched the view screen cameras to the junk pile and told the men they were on they're way down.

"Do you have any food onboard, we're hungry."

"Yes, we do. We'll land and you can come in through the airlock."

JT set the ship down and adjusted to the struts so the sleeve and the walkway would reach the junk pile.

The men came over to the NanMar, got out of the suits and went to the galley. Mr. Ross looked at his daughter.

"What in the hell went on? All we could hear were bits and pieces."

Sam proceeded to tell them all about the fight and what JT had done. What had happened on the bridge with the Captain. By then everyone had eaten and were ready to go back to work. When they put their dishes down, Dirk's female voice asked if they enjoyed their meal. Allen Ross turned to Dick Jones.

"God, that's got to be the sexiest voice I've ever heard."

"I heard that and I'm telling Mom when she gets back. "Back! What do you mean back?"

"Ummm,... she went with Mrs. Mac on the 205. Everything is okay, they're bringing in the 207. She's been shot up. We'll load up, go to Oz and then come back to reload."

"Then everyone climbs on board for a wonderful, fun filled trip back to Oz." JT said.

It took them about 45 minutes to load up. JT looked over to Sam.

"That was the slickest changing of subjects I have ever heard."

"Well, I know my father. He gets carried away sometimes when one of his 'girls' does something outrageous."

"He didn't even bat an eye when you told him of the gun fight at the OK corral up there in never, never land."

"You're right. I'm going to have to talk to him about that. Anyway Mom's pretty tough, she used to be a BAM. That's how they met."

"You don't say that to her face do you? My dad said that only once in front of my mother and she reamed him out good."

"Anybody who's got a lick of sense wouldn't say that in front of Mom."

"My, my how time does fly when you're having fun. Here we are back at Oz." JT brought the ship around to the docking bay and stopped. Looking at the two ships hovering at the bay opening while the crippled ship was tractor beamed in. JT turned to Sam.

"You know what Gunny would call this?"

"Probably the same thing my father would, 'A cluster fuck.' right?"

"Right."

JT looked at what was going on and then got on the inter ship channel.

"NanMar to JonMar."

"Go NanMar."

"Ma'am, if you break off, and go to the junk pile, get a load and bring up the men. We can do this. We're loaded."

"Roger that, Oz this JonMar, did you copy."

"Roger, do it."

The JonMar backed off, rolled to the right and dropped down to the junk pile.

"That's my Dad driving."

"How do you know?"

"That's his style of flying. He's one of the 'Flying Sergeants' the Marine Corps had. He's been flying most of his life."

***

JT placed the 207 against the port side bulkhead, out of the way of the elevators.

"Mrs. Mac, if you use the center slot and go back to the rear of the bay, 205 will be out of the way. I can park on the port side and turn a little. This way Susan can unload us and we will have enough room left for JonMar to come in and park."

"Click, click."

***

When all of the ships were docked. JT and Sam started to push the load to the hatch for Susan to unload. Kat and MJ stood at the sidelines and watched. MJ looked over to Kat.

"They work together as a team, don't they?"

"Yes they do, Susan is doing a great job on the fork lift. Like she has been doing it all of her life." Kat said.

"I'm not talking about the three, I'm talking about the two, up there." MJ said.

Kat looked at JT and Sam and then back at MJ, then back at JT and Sam. She watched them work together. Saw the looks each of them stole while they thought the other wasn't watching.

"Oh, I see what you are talking about now. It looks as though Sam is forming a plan of attack." Kat said.

MJ looked at Kat smiling. "I don't think she'll do any better. James is a fine young man. She'll get him if I know my daughter. You had better watch out for Dirk, Susan has a bad case of 'puppy love'."

"I saw it coming the first time he said something to her and I told him so. He really enjoys her company. I'm going to tell you something but you've got to keep it under your hat."

MJ looked at Kat and saw that she was completely serious.

"I will."

Kat told her about Dirk and Nancy and his only daughter Marnie. "I think Susan reminds him an awful lot of Marnie. I know her heart is going to be bruised when she finds out he's not madly in love with her. But is really a very tolerant, lovable uncle. The kind of guy she can tell her secrets to and know he won't laugh. And here's a clincher for you."

"You're pregnant."

Kats mouth dropped open and she stared at MJ. "How, did you know?"

Mary Jane took both of Kats hands in hers. "I've been pregnant five times, I know the look. How far along are you?"

"I should have started my second period yesterday. I'm going to give it five more days. Then it's a positive. This will be my first."

"You'll love it."

"Do you want to know what Dirk thinks? He said a pregnant woman is the most beautiful person in the world, and they have a glow about them no other woman has. I thought that was rather nice."

Dirk and Mary were talking on the bridge about how the operation went. Kind of a post mortum. The proper word is debriefing. Mary was telling how it went and Dirk was picking it apart. Typical Captain's way of making sure it was done right and no unnecessary chances were taken.

"This was a good win for our side Mary. Now what do you think of our new pilots?"

"Triga and I decided to let the new guys get all the flying time. We would stand back and advise. I can't really say about JT or Sam but Gunny is a great pilot. He doesn't need any more training from me. In fact, as I told you before, he and I were teaching each other from the manuals. He's ready for a ship of his own."

"JT did some fancy flying out there to day. Back on earth, in my service, he would have had his ass chewed out by some desk warming REMF. But the fact remains he got the job done and done right. I've watched that maneuver done on film but my people won't let us teach or use it. Too aggressive for them. Sometimes I think they fought in the Revolutionary War. You know, first rank on one knee, the second rank getting ready to shoot. The training we've had has given us the upper hand so far. These aliens don't know how fly all they can do is shoot and hope for the best. I guess I ran off at the mouth a little, I apologize, Sir."

"Nothing bent, Captain. Did you know the man who taught JT that maneuver is the one who perfected it? He lives in the same town as the Chambers. I hate to burst an Air Forces balloon but a Lieutenant Commander Ritchie U.S.N. retired is the one. He has been giving JT sometime in his own AD5E. The man must have won the lotto. Those are very expensive to go joy riding in. Evidently, he thought JT has what it takes to be a warrior of the sky."

"Sir, he also saved Ensign Trigas life today, he and Samatha. Shouldn't they be commended for that?"

"Captain Mayhan, you are right. The night before we sail off into murky waters we'll have a small ceremony for all hands."

"Murky waters? Aye, aye, Captain Hornblower, Sir." Mary snapped to attention and gave him a palm out, English type, salute.

They laughed.

***

Dirk continued. "JT says he can fix the 202 and get her up to light speed. One of the Arians in the replacement crew had the new boards, which would enable the star craft to go to light speed. Captain Eugin had crystals of the correct karat weight JT said they would need to get them up to light speed. I told him to go ahead and do it. Now that everyone's aboard I'll bet that's where you'll find him and Sam."

Just then there was a light tapping at the door and soft 'Ahem'. Dirk turned and saw Susan standing there.

"Just how long have you been eves-dropping young lady." He motioned her in.

Mary could see what was coming. "By your leave, Sir." She left, shutting the bridge door on the way out. Dirk turned on his best scowl.

"There's a rule in the service everyone, and I mean everyone, abides by. You just broke it. 'Thou shalt not eves-drop.' You have broken the faith. What you have heard here in this room will go no further, do you understand?"

Susan just stood there frozen in place.

"Do you understand?"

Susan nodded, tears started to stream down her face. She was completely crushed.

"I still can't hear you."

"YYYYes Sir."

"Good."

"Now, what is it you want?"

"NNNothing." She turned and bolted though the door.

I feel like I just pulled the wings off of a butterfly. But it had to be done. I hope she doesn't stay mad, I like her company.

Susan ran to her and Sam's quarters and threw herself on the bed and cried her eyes out. How could he talk to me like that. I didn't hear all that much. After she had cried herself out, she went into the bathroom and cleaned herself up. Took a good look, squared her shoulders and went back to the bridge. When she got to the door she knocked loudly.

"Come."

Susan walked up to Dirk. "I apologize, Sir, I won't do anything like that again."

Dirk looked down at her. "Apology accepted. There will be no more said about it."

Dirk returned to the star chart and was busy plotting a new course to the Alfa system. Everything had to be exact. They might have to come back this way. All of the course changes were fed into the main computer for storage.

Dirk noticed Susan walking around aimlessly. He stopped and looked at her.

She stopped, looked at him. "I'm hungry."

It was time for dinner. "Me too, go get your Mom and Dad and Kat, I'll meet you all in the galley."

Dirk went into their quarters and cleaned up before going to the galley. Everyone was there waiting for him. "I stopped to clean up, sorry I'm late."

They all ordered and were eating when James and Sam came in both looked as though they had been wrestling in a mud pile.

Dirk excused himself and went over to them. "Working hard?"

"Yes sir, we've been up to the 202, we thought we'd get a bite to eat and go back up."

"That's fine, go get cleaned up, then come back. This is a galley not a pig sty." Dirk started to smile. "Do it again and I'll ship you both out."

"Yes Sir." They left.

Dirk went back to his dinner. Kat leaned over and asked.

"Did you send them off on another job?"

"Sort of."

MJ looked over to Kat and raised her eyebrows and then looked at where Susan was sitting. Susan was at the end of the line sitting next to her father. Kat and MJ smiled at each other. Dirk had straightened things out.

***

Allen was telling Dirk about his job as a Deputy Sheriff back in the wilds of Colorado. Dirk was completely taken in by what Allen was telling him.

When Samatha and James came back, both were freshly showered and had on clean clothes. Gunny, Mary and John came in, got their dinners and came over to the table.

The subject immediately went to the problem at hand. The extra parts they were getting from the junk pile. They all had to be stowed and inventoried. The data put into the main computer. Soon the galley began to fill up with ships crew. Except for Triga, Ally, Bruce and Awga. Bruce came in and got two trays and started for the door when Kat stopped him.

"What's going on?"

"Awga is in child labor. She is a little early but who knows."

"Do you need me?"

"No, not now, Mrs. Mac."

"Well, it looks as though our family is about to be increased by one." Dirk said

Kat looked at Dirk. This has really got to be a strain on him. Not only does he have a ship to run but he has a huge family with him also. It's got to be hard for him to keep the two separate. And if I'm pregnant, he's going to be like an ant on hot sand.

Dirk looked around at the people here. What an awesome responsibility I have here. They are all looking at me for direction. But any one of them could do the same if they were in my shoes.

"Well, we've go some work to do before bed time." Dirk started to assign work parties and everyone, including the twins, R & R, as everyone was starting to call them now, had jobs to do. Susan stood up and said.

"Well, it's back to that, ---- Ahhh, fork lift for me." This surprised everyone. It seems as though Susan is starting to grow up.

Dirk told James and Sam to go back to work on the 202 and asked Tribec if he would check out the 207 and report on it.

The inventory and stowing went smoothly. They were done in about two hours.

Dirk went to the 207. He found Tribec crawling around in the lower level superstructure. It was quite a job for him to get there. He looked at Tribec.

"I don't think you Arians had humans in mind when you built these ships."

"No, we didn't even know about you then."

"What do you think?"

"It can be fixed. There are four holes in her bottom. None of the main spars or ribs have been damaged. The reactor is sound but the exciter is beyond repair. We have extra exciters in stores. That's not a problem. She should be ready in about a week." Tribec stopped, looked at Dirk. "Sir, it is not me alone but have you seen Mr. Allen, he does not look well. I noticed him while we were at the junk pile today. He is a very sick man. I think he should go to sick bay and have Mrs. Mac look at him."

"I did notice him tonight, he isn't looking to good. I thought he was over working himself. I'll talk to Mrs. Mac and see if she can get him to come to sickbay. Are you about done here?"

"Yes, all done. I have written everything down, the parts needed and the time it should take to replace them. The biggest time loss is the welding of the new skin. All of the skin can be taken from the Beta Six craft." Tribec handed Dirk the list.

Dirk stared at it for a second and then started to grin. Tribec realized what he was grinning at and had to smile also. It was written in Arian.

"Make a copy of it and bring it up to the bridge. I'll put it into the translator, no problem."

"That is good because I could not translate it to English."

"Alright I'll see you in the morning."

CHAPTER TWENTY-FIVE

Dirk went on a walk around. When he got to the machine shop he found James and Sam hard at work, making a new motherboard for the 202s exciter. He asked how it was coming along. James answered.

"It's done. I'm testing it out now. If it checks out I'll put it in and light her off. First with a small three karat, then with a fifteen karat. If she works then, we'll try the twenty-two and a half. I can make up more boards for the four other ships. Before I started I checked with Tribec about these ships going into light speed. He said the 200 series were designed for light speed. But the motherboards were not made in time for the last trip into space. The relief crew had them with them."

"When you get ready to test, call me."

"Yes Sir, and Sir could you spread the word it would be alright if everyone called me JT."

"Alright I'll do that, JT. Sam, walk with me. I've got something personal to ask you."

When they were in the next compartment Dirk looked at Sam. "There's only one way to say this. How long has your father been sick? And what's making him sick?"

Sam leaned back against a desk. "He has leukemia, its proper name is acute myelonic leukemaia. We all know about it. Dad has sworn us all to secrecy. He doesn't want anyone feeling sorry for him. We were on a gold panning expedition when we were taken. I know he's failing fast. Maybe being here in outer space has sped up the process, I don't know. I think he has only days left."

"Is there any medicine here he can take to help?" Dirk asked.

"No, we looked. I talked to Ally. She hasn't any medicine here that could help him."

"If you need to talk at anytime you know where I'm at. Kat lost her mother to cancer so she knows what you are going through. Please, Sam, don't hold it back, talked to someone. If you don't, it will eat you up. I lost my family in a car accident the morning I was taken aboard NanMar. Kat knows all about it. Nancy was the lady I lived with. We were never married, but in our own way, we loved each other. We were very comfortable together. We had a daughter Marnie, she was twelve. Nancy was taking Marnie to school when the accident occurred. I took a plane and flew straight out, as hard and as fast as I could go. Before I could react, I struck the 208, and here I am. I look at Susan and I can see Marnie in her. "

"Kat and I were married by Captain Mayhan onboard the NanMar. What I'm saying is life goes on. It has for me and it did for Kat. You might not think so now, but it will for you. You have JT to lean on and Susan and your mother will have you to lean on. You're a lucky girl to have JT. As far as I'm concerned, he's one in a million. I know Gunny is proud of him. Let's go about our way now, but you remember, anytime."

Sam stood up and went over to Dirk. Standing on her tiptoes she kissed him on the cheek.

"Thank you."

***

Dirk went on with his inspection. When he reached the galley Kat was there with Ally.

"Well, how's our almost mother doing?"

Ally looked up, smiled and said. "It'll be a while yet. Probably around what should be dawn. You know, not seeing daylight does get a little depressing. I always enjoyed seeing a sunrise."

"When we get back to earth, you'll probably be up every morning watching one." Dirk said.

"Captain, I want to apologize to you for the actions of William. It was my fault he drank that night and into the day. He wanted me to go to you and ask about he and I living together. I wouldn't do it. I did not want to for one thing and I knew, because of the children, it wouldn't be right. At the time we were taken, I was packing my things to go back to town. I had told him I didn't want to see him anymore. Maybe, if I had been a little stronger and told him to leave before we went on the fishing trip. None of this would have happened."

"Do you realize if you had taken that route we would never have had the pleasure of meeting you. You are a valued member of this crew. As far as William is concerned, if he had done that back in Cheyenne he would be in jail and probably lost his job. This way he is sleeping quite peacefully for however long it takes to get back to earth. Hopefully he'll wake up with a hangover. Don't worry about apologizing to us about anything."

"Kat, I don't know about you but I'm ready for bed. It's been a long one for me."

Kat looked at Ally. "If anything comes up, call me."

Dirk and Kat went off to the Captains quarters.

***

Sam had gone back to the machine shop and was watching JT put the final touches on the motherboard. He looked up and smiled at Sam.

"This is going to be 'Kick-Ass', I kid-thee-not."

Gunny walked in and heard the last explicative. "What's going to be kick-ass."

The remark caught Sam unaware and she jumped up. "Whew, you scared me. You're the last person I expected see."

Gunny smiled at her and said. "Old habits are hard to break. When I was in the service I used to make a walk through, to see if all was well, before I turned in for the night. Okay, what's going to be 'I kid-thee-not'?"

"This is the new mother board for the 202. I was talking to Captain Mac about upgrading the ship's capabilities. This will enable the star craft to go to light speed. I thought the Arians didn't know how to do it. I found out from Tribec the 200 series of IVs were designed for light speed. They didn't install the right boards when they went out the first time. The new boards were with the replacement crew at the time they were killed."

"Captain Mac said to go ahead and repair the 202 and up grade the board. I just finished this board. Now we put her together. The Captain wanted me to call him when it was ready for testing. Okay, Babe, let's go up to the 202 and install."

<u>Okay, Babe?. I think my son has found a kindred soul here. Now that I think about it, she is just as adventuresome as he. She certainly is a very intelligent young woman. I like it.</u>

Gunny followed JT and Sam up to the 202. He stood to the side and watched the two put the heart back into the ship. As JT hooked up the wires Sam was checking them out with a meter. JT would look at her and she would nod as they were checked.

<u>These two work as a team. Each knows what the other wants without asking. A combination like that is hard to beat. Reminds me of Marlene and myself.</u>

***

Everything was in order. A three-karat crystal was put in place. She was ready to light off. JT stopped and stood back. He did a mental read back of the steps involved.

"Sam, start the auxiliary generator up. She'll be ready to light off in five minutes." JT saw the look on his father's face. "It takes a few minutes for the wiring, equipment boards and the main propulsion systems warm up. If you light everything off at once, after she has sat dormant for so long, something might blow or melt down." JT looked at Sam. "You want to call the Captain and let him know she ready for testing?"

Sam nodded and reached over to the inter-com and buzzed the Captains quarters.

"Captain here, Go"

"Captain, this is the 202 calling, we are ready for light off and testing."

"Very well. Test at three karats, then at fifteen and at twenty-two and a half. Call me if anything goes wrong. And I mean anything."

Gunny was listening to the voice, more than what it said. <u>I think the kids just interrupted what could be considered 'Dirk's night'.</u>

"Yes Sir." Sam looked at JT. "We've got a go." Sam's eyes were flashing with excitement.

JT looked the systems over and went to the reactor and took the leads of the meter, testing one more time. He nodded to Sam. She reached over and turned the dials to start. When all of the lights turned Amber the auxiliary generator shut down. They could feel the ship come to life.

JT turned the dials to run and she really came to life, as though someone has given her a shot in the arm. JT and Sam high fived each other and then looked over to "The Gunny". He smiled and held up both of his hands, palm outward. Everyone high fived. Gunny had become one of the boys.

***

Going to the bridge, they checked out all of the panels. Every panel was working perfectly. Sam opened the view panel and turn on the screen. All three stood there looking out into space. Sam hooked her arms though the arms of JT and Gunny and rested her head against JT. Gunny cleared his throat.

"Don't you think it's time for the other crystal."

"Okay. Dad, Sam, let's go do it."

Back at the reactor room, the exciter was shut down and the generator was turn on. The crystal was changed, and the exciter was restarted. The generator shut down automatically. The process was repeated. Everything worked perfectly.

They went back down to the reactor room. This time JT shut the exciter down and started the generator up. He went over to the main panel, turned the dials to off and switched the crystals. JT went over to the main panel and turned the dials to start, They watched the crystal start to glow. The generator shut off. JT waited a minute or so and then turned the dials to run. The 202 came back to life with a sudden surge. The twenty-two and a half crystal did the trick. This was what this ship was meant to do. JT put a hand on the dome, which covered the crystal exciter and smiled.

"Sam, Dad come and do this."

Sam went first and said "Wow". Gunny put his hand on the dome. "Well I'll be." Gunny could feel a slight tremor in his hand it went up his arm, into his body.

"It's like this ship is giving me life. Sam put your hand here, James put your hand here where mine was."

Gunny then put his hands over theirs. The three of them could feel the slight tremor go up into their bodies. Like the ship was conducting a ritual of it's own. Making them a part of her.

They took their hands away.

***

There was a loud pop. A circuit breaker let go and started smoking. JT turn to the dials back to start. Reaching in his back pocket for a pair of pullers. He took out the breaker, looked it over and smiled.

"It's old and a little under specs. No problem."

He went over to the spares locker and took out a higher rated one. Replaced it and turned the dials to run again.

Everyone was looking at the panel waiting for another to pop out. Nothing, JT went over to the panel, put his hands on it, moving up and down feeling for overheating. They started back through the ship checking on different panels in each of the compartments. Everything was working perfect.

When they came to the bridge all of the panels were lit-up. JT said. "Watch this." He went to the door and turned a switch. The white lights went off and red lights came on. "Pretty neat, Huh?" It took a few seconds for their eyes to get accustomed to the change.

"I heard the Captain talking about rigging for red at night on the ships. So I decided it could done here also. I had nothing to do for awhile this afternoon so I came up here and did this." JT said

"What did you use for power?" Gunny asked.

"Scaner showed me how to switch onto shore power."

"I wonder if the Captain will let us use Scaner to translate everything into English." Gunny said, thinking of the 205. "The 205 is only partially done."

"We don't need Scaner, as long as we are on shore power" Sam said. "Watch." She went over to the main computer and brought up the main keyboard. She typed in a command and a job window came on. She put the cursor on an icon and pressed enter. First one panel of lights flickered and then another, until all of the panels were done. "That job is all done. Is there any other little job you would like done, Sirs?"

JT and Gunny had to laugh at that remark.

***

"Well, I can't see anything else to do here but call the Captain and report she's ready to go." JT said.

Sam looked at Gunny and then at JT. "I don't think the Captain wants to be interrupted again, so why don't we wait until morning."

"Why do you say that?" JT asked.

"If it were me, doing what I think they are doing, I wouldn't. As my sister would say 'I'd be pissed'."

Gunny almost choked trying to keep from laughing.

It finally dawned on JT what she had meant and his face started to turn red.

"I think we'd better call it a night." Gunny said.

JT and Sam went over to the panels and shut them off. Then went to the other compartments and rechecked on the way down to the reactor room. JT turned the power down on the reactor just to keep it warmed up. They left the 202. As they past through the lower hatch, JT and Sam patted the doorsill as if to say goodnight to her. As far as they were concerned she was their ship now.

CHAPTER TWENTY-SIX

They went down to the galley on Oz and had a soft drink. Sam excused herself, saying she would be right back. Gunny finished his drink and said he was going to bed.

"Good night Dad, I'll have another mother board ready in the morning."

Gunny knew it would be for him. He just nodded. "Good night Son."

Sam came back with two large placards. She stood on the other side of the table and lifted one up so JT could see it. It was a drawing of a large boot kicking a donkey on the backside. Under it was U.S.A.S.F. and above was the lettering JT's.

JT motioned her to come over to him. She did.

She had her arms up and around his neck before he had her gathered in his arms. The kiss started out at what one could call a medium force but soon reached about 9.5 on the Richter scale. JT could feel her lips move against his. He pulled his head back.

"What did you say?"

"I love you. I know it's only been a couple of days but I knew the first time I saw you. Do you think I'm nuts?"

"No, I don't think you nuts or anything else like that. The first time I saw you I thought. "My God, she's beautiful. I saw my father looking at me and I could feel my face turn red. I thought, Oh shit, I'm in for it now. He's reading my mind again. But he didn't say a word. And yes, I love you too."

Sam pulled his head down to hers and kissed him again. He could feel her tongue touch his lips. He opened his mouth and their tongues met, ever so slightly, but enough to rekindle the fire. JT could feel the blood pulsing through his body. He felt Sam's body shiver. She moaned softly.

"Walk me home." she said.

JT released her and picked up the signs.

She took his other hand and led them down the passageway, past her room to his. They went in. Putting the signs down on the empty bed, he turned to her.

She had unbuttoned the top to her uniform. As she stepped toward him, her breasts moved slightly back and forth. The curvature and swell along with pink tips and pert nipples was breath taking. He unbuttoned his uniform top. He could feel her breasts against his chest as she put her arms around his neck. They kissed long and passionately. He kissed her cheek, then her ear. He heard another small moan. JT kissed the side of her neck gently. Sam lifted herself up by the strength of her arms. JT reached down, picked her up in his arms, carrying her to his bed.

Sam slipped off the top to her uniform. This was much further than she had ever gone before. Not knowing what to do next, she would have to rely on JT and Mother Nature.

JT took the top of his uniform off and lay down beside her. Gathering her in his arms once again, feeling the soft, warm breasts against his chest sent JT's blood coursing through his veins. He ran his hand down her back until he could feel the top of her uniform pants. Hooking his thumb, he gently pushed down.

Sam shifted her hips, helping him. The feelings she felt now pushed her on. She reached down, trying to undo the belt at JT's waist. She wanted to feel his naked body pressed against her.

JT reached down and undid his belt, he pushed his trousers down and off. They lay there, feeling the warmth of each other.

JT ran his hand down her body, over the swell of her hips. Sam copied his move, learning from him. Breaking the kiss, JT kissed her neck and then a breast.

Sam felt warm sensations coursing throughout her body. Her leg found its way over JT's as if it had a mind of it's own, pulling him toward her.

JT traced Sam's body with his hand. He ran his hand over her hips and down her leg. Mimicking, Sam did the same. JT bought his hand up the inner side of her thigh. As he touched her, she pulled again at him with her leg and with her arms, pulling him over on top of her. She felt him enter. Pushing he felt a restriction. JT's mind clicked in. She's a virgin.

Sam's body by this time didn't give a damn, virgin or not, it demanded more. She felt him hesitate. Placing her legs around the backs of his thighs, pulled.

Sam thought. There was no pain like the girls back home had said there would be. In fact it felt nice. The warm sensations flooding her body made her feel as though she was floating on air.

JT made love to her slowly. He felt her body respond. She could feel a warm tingling sensation rising through her body. She didn't know what it was, but "Oh God" did it feel good. Sam could feel her body start to shake as the sensations grew. It was like lights were flashing in her brain as she started to climax.

JT could feel the climax build up inside of her as it was with him. He felt Sam's legs tighten against him and her body quiver as the climax flooded over her. He gave two hard thrusts and his climax exploded from him.

They lay there for a while not wanting the beauty of the moment to slip away and become part of the memories that last a lifetime.

JT rolled to his side, holding her tight against him. He marveled at the thought that she had given him her most prized possession, her virginity. He kissed the top of her head and gave her a hug that would put a bear to shame. She hugged him back. They laid in each other's arms for a while just enjoying the comfort of it.

This is the first time I've thought of this but she fits perfect against me. It's like we were molded for each other and no one else.

I feel as though we were made for each other. We fit together perfectly. Sam thought and leaned over kissing his chest.

JT looked into her eyes and saw a little gleam come on. She threw a leg over him, pushed herself up and over so she was kneeling over his stomach. She leaned forward and put a hand down on each side of his head, lowering hers. Her hair fell down around him like an auburn umbrella. He reached up with his hands and placed them on each side of her face. He then brought her head down to his and kissed her. Sam looked down into his eyes and felt as though she could see right into his soul. She liked what she saw. She lowered her head and softly kissed him. She thought her heart would burst from joy. This was her man and nothing was going to take him from her. She stretched her legs out straight and lay on top of him. She could feel something between her legs rising. Her eyes widened and she grinned. She lifted her head and looked at him. "Ready?"

"Ready."

They both nodded. This time was not slow and easy. The demand's of their body's was tremendous.

She collapsed against him spent. She rolled off of him and laid her head against his chest. They lay there for a while. JT heard her breathing change. She gave a soft gentle snore. As much as he wanted her to stay here forever, he knew, right now was impossible. He woke her up by gently shaking her. Sam shot straight up.

"What! what?" She shook her head and looked down at JT. She smiled. "Again?"

JT laughed. "No, you've got to go. It wouldn't be right for us to get caught here in the morning. Come on I'll help you get dressed."

She was trying to get one leg into her uniform pants and he was trying to get the other one in. She finally stopped him.

"I think you spell help, H I N D E R. I can do this faster alone."

JT put on his robe.

"What are you going to do, walk me to my room?"

"Yes, and then I'm going to go on to the galley. If we stay in step to your door you can slip in and I'll just continue on to the galley. If anyone is awake they'll think it's just one person."

It was a good idea, and it fooled no one, at least not the two that were awake.

Ally had just come back from sickbay and had almost shut her door when she heard another door open. She peeked out and saw JT and Sam come out of his room.

That's one!

They walked to her door. He went on toward the galley. She shut her door as quietly as she could. Sam slipped into the room she shared with her sister and Rebecca, quietly got undressed and slipped into bed.

"Well, how was it?" Susan asked.

Sam yanked the covers over her head. "Shit, Ssshhhh."

That's two!

JT came into the galley and found Bruce getting a cup of juice. He went to the ordering panel getting one for him self.

"How's the almost mother coming along?"

Bruce looked over to JT. "She is doing good. It should not be long now." He noticed what looked like teeth marks on JT's lower neck. Smiling to him self. I'm glad. They are a beautiful couple. He leaned over to JT and said. "I would wear a high topped shirt for the next couple days if I were you."

That's three!

JT's face got beet red. Bruce smiled at him in a friendly way.

"I'll do that, my friend."

They sat down and enjoyed their drink. JT asked him if he like being out here in space.

"I do but I miss my friend an awful lot."

"It's too bad she can't be here with you."

"It is not a her, it is a him."

JT thought for a moment. One of my best friends back home is gay. There were a few people who knew this. All of us were close friends. It didn't matter one way or the other to us then, why should it matter to me now. Ed was still Ed and Bruce is still Bruce.

"God, that's got to be hard leaving a good friend behind."

"Thank you for your understanding. You are good person. You and Miss Sam are a lovely couple. I am happy for you. Our lives here are to short, do not waste it."

"Bruce, you are a wise man."

JT looked at his watch 3:00 AM. "Well, time flies when you are having fun. I've got to be up and at'm in four hours. And my backside can't be dragging. Good night, Bruce."

"Good night, James."

"Bruce, my friends all call me JT."

"Good night JT."

JT went back to his quarters and went directly to bed. He was asleep before his head hit the pillow. The night passed without any interruptions or at least what was left of it.

***

Dirk woke at 6:30 AM and went to the shower. The door opened and he heard a sweet voice.

"Is there room for two in there, sailor?"

"Oh yes, fair maiden."

After a nice leisurely shower Dirk and Kat dressed and went to the bridge. Kat looked at the stars through the view screen.

"It is so calm and peaceful out there."

Dirk looked up, watching his wife for a second. "Yes it is. All done here. Nothing went on."

They left for the galley. As they passed by sick-bay, Kat looked in. Awga was still in labor. Soon I hope, the poor thing has been in labor to long

"I'm going to get some breakfast, then I'll be back." she told Bruce.

Dirk and Kat went into the galley and went over to the ordering panel. Allen, MJ and Susan were seated and having breakfast. As they sat down Dirk said.

"JT and Sam must have worked real late last night."

"Oh yes, real late." Susan said smiling.

Gunny came in and got a cup of coffee and sat down with them. He noticed Sam and JT weren't there but didn't say anything. Most of the crew trickled in. The Jones's came in, got something to eat and sat at the table across from them. Dick Jones asked Dirk what the orders were for the day.

"Back to stripping the junk pile. Tribec looked the 207 over last evening. She can be repaired with little time lost on her. Nothing damaged but skin and a few spars and ribs. JT is going to make up some new motherboards for the star craft, enabling them to go to light speed. Did Sam and JT get up early and go to work?"

Susan giggled. "Sam is still in bed."

Dirk looked at her. She put her head down and resumed eating. Susan looked up at the inter comm. There were two lights on. "They should been here in about fifteen minutes"

Now everyone looked at her, like she was some kind of fortuneteller. Sure enough, in about fifteen minutes Sam walked in, looking fresh as a daisy. She came over to her Mom and Dad and kissed them on the cheek and said. "Good morning, everyone." Sam went over to the ordering panel, got breakfast and sat down next to Gunny. She had no more than sat down when JT came in.

"Hi, sorry I'm late. Over slept." Getting something to eat, he sat next Sam. He leaned over and said something to Sam making her smile. She looked at him still smiling.

From the time Sam had walked over to get breakfast Kat watched her. The look Sam gave JT proved what she was thinking. Kat went back to her coffee and smiled to herself.

Now there were four!

MJ was watching her daughter also, and was thinking the same as Kat.

Now there were five!

Clare looked at MJ and then at Kat and then back at MJ.

Now there were six!

The men sat there and ate breakfast, discussing what had to be done.

John and Mary walked and got coffee. Dirk looked at them and motioned at his plate. John said.

"We ate on the JonMar."

Dirk told them about what Tribec has said about the 207 and they all went to talking about the up coming day.

"Captain, I've got the 202 ready to go. We worked on her last night. Everything is working perfectly. Only one breaker let go. It was underrated. I've left her in the start position, to keep the systems up, and warm, Sir."

Dirk looked at JT. "Very well, is she ready for a test flight?"

Both Sam and JT said. "Yes Sir."

"Alright, after we get the men down to the junk pile, we'll take her out. Gunny, you take the 205. Mary, you and Gunny fly chase?"

"Yes Sir."

John spoke up. "At 12 noon there will be a demonstration of the 'Mayhan Space Pinger System, Model #1', for all those interested parties."

"You've got it ready to go."

"Yes, all tested and the only thing I've got to do is to mount it on the bracket on the roof." He pointed up. "If I could keep Allen with me today it would help. I need someone on the inside to push buttons and stuff."

"OK, Allen you want to work with John today." Dirk said

"Sure."

Dirk looked at JT. "Would 9:00 AM be a good time for test #1, JT."

"Yes Sir, we'll have her ready to go." JT elbowed Sam and they both wolfed down their breakfast.

"Excuse us." JT said and they both got up went to the tray panel. "Great breakfast."

"Thank you, we are glad you liked it."

"I wonder who the other one is?" Sam mused.

JT looked at Sam and said. "Let's go talk to Triga. There are some things that we have to know about light speed." They went to sickbay.

***

"OK, people let's get to work. I'm sure we are going to have a new member of the crew today, right ladies."

"We'll let all hands know just as soon as it happens." Clare said.

"Susan, you man the fork lift again."

"Aye, aye, Sir"

***

Sam and JT went into sickbay and found Triga sitting up eating when they got there. She looked up, smiled. "And what can I do for you two this morning."

"We need to know all there is to know about light speed, so we are here to pick your brain." JT said.

Triga's eyes widened.

Sam said. "No, no, we're just going to ask you questions. You start by telling us what the manuals don't say. That's what we mean by 'pick your brain'.".

"There is only one thing, the navigation. You must always be sure of the path you are going to travel in. Nothing can be in your way. If you strike an asteroid you are going to be just a lot of plasma floating around in a dusty cloud. Always check the star chart to plot your course. Not the regular nav charts. It must be the star chart. Oz here has the best."

"We have them too. I zoom loaded them last night to the 202." Sam said.

"But Star craft do not have light speed capabilities."

"202 does, I beefed up a new mother board when I repaired her. The master wire loom and the motherboard were burnt out. Some goof over loaded her."

"You are going to need a twenty-two and a half karat crystal to make her jump to light speed."

"We've got them too. Captain Eugin had them all along. He had them hid somewhere."

"Alright, check out the heading of 090 degrees. I looked it over when we got here. It is a good way to go, no obstructions. How long will you be gone?"

"Two hours, max."

"That will be a good time length, I will see you in three days when you return."

JT looked at Triga. "Time warp. Right?"

"Yes." She smiled and looked at Sam. "If you did enough time at light speed, by the time you got back your sister would be older than you. It's funny but that's the way it works. An hour at light speed is about a day and a half of your time at a normal sub light speed. On a planet it would be weeks. By the time I get back to Arian the people there I knew will be thirty or forty spans older than me. You have to stop and think about whether or not you want to spend your lives here in space. You are young and it is an adventure but the price you pay is a terrible amount."

Sam looked at Triga. "Wow, that's a heavy load. But we are here and I like it. Looking back at north central Colorado, the prospects were very dim to say the most. Yes, I glad I'm out here."

JT looked at his watch. "Its 8:30 AM, we had better go to the 202 and get her ready."

"What are you going to navigate by?"

"Star chart." they said in unison.

"Have a good flight and be safe."

"We'll have to tell your Mom what's happening as far the time warp is concerned. She can tell Dad when he gets back onboard."

"Aye, Aye, Skipper."

***

They found MJ at the docking bay with a clipboard in her hand talking to Mrs. Jones. JT and Sam went over to them, told them about time warp and that they would back in three days.

MJ shrieked. "Three days but you're only going out for two hours."

"Ma'am, if you talk to Ensign Triga, she will explain it all to you, in detail. Right now we don't have the time." JT said.

Sam went over to her Mom and kissed her on the cheek. "JT will take care of me, Bye."

"Tell Dad I love him." she called out over her shoulder as they headed to the elevator.

When they got onboard they went to the reactor room. Checking everything out before turning the dials to run. JT set the dials to run and the 202 came to life. "Good Girl." They patted the exciter.

Sam looked at JT. "When we get back, this baby is going to get a complete cleaning, everything gets washed."

When they got to the bridge they found Scaner there. JT looked at him and said. "Hi big guy, what are you doing here?"

"I am taking the Captains place. He cannot leave Oz for the three days we will be gone. Too much work has to be done. In one day the ship will be leaving for the Alpha system. We are to meet her along the way."

"Okay, let's bring up the star chart. Scaner, monitor and check our figures."

"Aye, Aye, Skipper.

JT looked over at Sam. "Did you teach him to say that?"

"No, he taught me."

"Set your computer for 0915 departure. I will be back." Scaner scooted out the door.

***

JT and Sam went to work, plotting a course at 090 for one hour at light speed. They worked out the course and speed Oz would be taking and plotted a return course to her. It would take them an hour and a half to get back. They would be getting back on the evening of the third day. At 0900 Scaner came back to the bridge and plugged in to the main computer banks.

"The course, speed and time difference is correct. We have 110 percent on the reactor. We will be ready to cast off in seven minutes."

JT went back to the elevator. Rigged it in and secured it. He shut the outer hatch, making sure it was airtight and went back to the bridge.

At exactly 0915 JT increased the power.

"0915, 202 light on the skids. We are clear. Landing struts up and locked."

He moved to the starboard, clearing the ship. Increasing power, he brought them to the position for light speed.

"Strap yourself in Babe, lock yourself down Scaner. Cause, we are gone."

JT engaged the drive for the jump to light speed. The 202 hesitated for a second, then disappeared in a streak of light.

Sam was looking at the view screen. "Wow, JT look!" The stars were going by them in a steady white line. Scaner closed the view panel.

"Why did you do that?" Sam said as she turned. If she had not been strapped in she would have fallen to the deck.

"That is why I shut the view panel. The passage of the stars at this speed effects the optic nerve and in turn makes you dizzy." Scaner replied.

"Are you OK, Babe?"

"I'm fine now. But that was something to see."

"I'm going to check the exciter, you've got the con, Babe."

JT went down to the reactor room. He felt the panels for over heating, okay. Going back to the bridge, he went over to the fire control panel. Checked out the laser and the torpedo loads. Something was wrong with the tube lights. They showed empty,

"I don't understand this" he said aloud.

"What?"

He told Sam. "I'm going down to the loading area and physically check them, Scaner you check the system out here."

JT opened the hatch to the torpedo room. Smelling smoke, hit the emergency shut down switch. JT turned on the exhaust fan. He went over to the inter comm.

"Babe, shut down the torpedo panel, we had a little fire here. I'll keep checking."

JT was back on the bridge in fifteen minutes. "Old wiring. If you don't use this stuff on a regular basis, sitting idle like she did, the wire coating dries out and flakes off. Two wires rubbed together and short out the system. We're back in business now."

He went to the panel and turned it on. Every light showed green. Turning the switch to stand-by, went back over to the con.

He stood behind Sam and put his hands on her shoulders. She reached up and held one of his hands. He bent down and kissed the top of her head.

"It's time to down shift. I'll sit at the fire control panel."

"No, you drive. I'll look out for 'Cops'." Sam stood up, went to the fire control panel and strapped herself in. JT took the con.

***

At 1015 the 202 came to a stop. JT opened the view screen. They were staring at another ship. JT could see the red lights warming up on her nose.

"Oh shit, hang on." JT exclaimed.

He set the throttle at 80 percent, pushing the nose down, shot under the other ship. JT threw the switch, closing all the airtight integrity doors. The 202 almost cleared the firing radius when she was hit.

The laser had struck the 202 on the stern. "Weapons on, ready two tubes. Fire on my command."

JT turned on the cameras, getting a view of the other ship. It was like the ones they'd had a run in with before. JT pushed the throttle to 90 percent, shot straight up, inverted and came back at the ship.

"Medium power setting on the torpedoes."

Sam set in the changes and said. "It's time to Kick-Ass." JT fired the laser, and moved one degree to the right.

"Fire one"

They could feel a slight shudder as the torpedo left. He moved two degrees to the left "Fire two, ready three and four, reload one and two"

"Done."

JT eased the throttle back. "Scaner, anyone else around?"

"Negative, Sir."

They watched the alien ship turn to the right to evade the laser. When it saw the torpedo coming on to it, it turned hard to the left, directly into the path of number two.

The torpedo struck the ship on the port side just forward of the center. There was an explosion, internally, but the ship did not disintegrate. The other torpedo exploded against a small asteroid.

The alien ship came to a halt. Debris was coming out of the hole the torpedo made, as the ship equalized pressure. JT stopped the 202 behind and a little low of the alien ship.

"Scaner can you detect any life form onboard that junk pile?" JT asked

"Scanning now. There is no life form on that ship, Sir."

"Scaner, rewind the disc and restarted." JT said.

It was in slow motion and enhanced. There, JT could see a form shoot out of the hole. It had no more than cleared the opening when it disintegrated. Sam look like she was going to be sick but she held on. JT didn't feel all that good either.

"Babe, that son-of-a-bitch was trying to kill us, just like his two butthole buddies the other day. The Captain's right. Everyone out here shoots first and asks questions later. It ain't right, but that's the way it is."

"Scaner, log this incident. Babe we've got to check-----, Belay that. Scaner, you check out the damage to the ship. I'll log the incident."

***

"We have a rupture of the outer hull at the shuttle bay. Air tight integrity is still in effect in the remainder of the ship."

"OK, we're doing alright. Next question. Do we go over and see what we can salvage, or go on to Oz?"

"Can we get a message off to Oz?" Sam asked

"Yes, we can, but what frequency are they monitoring? I know, UHF one twenty-one point five." JT leaned over the comm panel setting in the proper numbers.

"What is UHF 121 point 5?"

"Ultra High Frequency 121.5 on your radio dial, national distress frequency. Every station monitors it." He set the computer to record and reported the action as it happened. The damage they sustained and asked for further orders. Setting the transmitter to hyper speed, sent the message.

"Babe, could you get us some of the Captains think drink."

"Sure I'll be right back. Wait a minute, I don't think we have anything except water."

Scaner turned. "I loaded the food pallet JT ordered in the galley before we left. It is set in the automated kitchen."

"Scaner, you're a darling." Sam said.

"Ohhhh." and Scaner lit up like a Christmas tree.

Sam was back in a couple of minutes with two cups of coffee.

"Scaner, you get high detergent next P.M." JT said.

***

The light on the comm panel lit up. "Our answer awaits."

JT put the disc into the speaker system and pushed play.

"Oz to 202 Attn Capt. Chambers, If possible, board alien craft. Check for salvage. We are on base course and speed. Authorized delay two days. CYA. KMA. Captain Mac."

"OK, let's look her over real slow. Babe, keep your six guns out. Here we go."

"What does CYA and KMA mean?" Sam asked.

Scaner said. "Cover Your Ass and Keep Me Advised."

"Well, that's rather direct and to the point." Sam said.

They went around the alien craft and found an airlock hatch. JT decided they could pull up along side, put out a sleeve and walk ramp out.

"Scaner, bring us along side. We'll secure it to us." "Aye, aye, Sir."

They went to the second deck and over to the air lock. Scaner brought them alongside and stopped the ship. JT rigged out the side struts and secured the ship to them.

Sam rigged the sleeve out. She turned on the magnetic field on the mouth of the sleeve. Then sent the walkway out.

They went through the capsule room to the shuttle space. They took the oxygen rebreathers over to the charging station, refilling them with fresh oxygen. Putting on the space suits and rebreathers, they were ready. Both had hand lasers. Sam was carrying a dart thrower.

"Looks like an old M1 carbine doesn't it?"

JT nodded his head. "Yeah, they're not much on range but up close it packs a hell-of-a-wallop." They went to the air lock. JT opened the outer door to the alien ship. They stepped in and went through the inner hatch. Looking around they saw they were in the main storage area. JT motioned Sam to follow him. He went up to the bridge through an open hatch, empty.

"No wonder the guy went out in such a hurry, he never shut the air tight hatch. You know, for people who go around shooting at other people, they're dumber than a post. They fly around in these over sized tubs that can't maneuver worth a damn. The only thing they can try to do is 'dry-gulch' you. And they can't even do that right."

They went back through the storage area and into the reactor room or what was left of it. This was where the torpedo blew. There was nothing left. Down on the second deck there was more storage area. It was full of crates, all lashed down. JT looked for a pry bar. He found one and opened a crate, electronic equipment. Okay, we can use that. He checked the labels on the other crates, all the same.

"Sam do you see a loading hatch anywhere?"

She walked along the wall until she found a window. "Here's a shuttle craft bay with an outer door. Maybe we can lower 202 to this level and go straight through."

"We should be able to. If we close the doors to the lower level and depressurize, we should be able to load everything in there for the ride back to Oz. We can use the rollers here and be loaded by tomorrow night.

They went back up to the first storage area and looked through the crates there. These looked like panels for a temporary hut of some type.

"Looks like an outer space version for a modular home." Sam said.

"Everything goes home to Oz. Scanner can you hear me?"

"Roger"

"Shut all doors to the lower storage room. Then depressurized it and open the inner door to the airlock. We're going to start moving crates onboard."

"Aye, aye, Sir."

Even from where they were they could feel the depressurization. They set the rollers into place and moved crates across to the 202. It took about three hours to move everything across and get them stowed and secured.

***

They decided to call it a day. They brought the rollers over to 202 and shut the outer door. Sam rigged in the walkway and the sleeve, she looked at JT.

"Just in case we've got move in a hurry all we would have to do is turn the junk pile loose and we're outtahere."

JT pressurized the storage room and shut the inner door. They got out of their suits there and hung them up next to the airlock, securing them. JT took the rebreathers to the air tank outlet and recharged them. These too went over by the airlock.

They went up to the bridge and check the area for anything that looked hostile. Nope, all's well.

"Scaner we're going to get cleaned up and then get some thing to eat. KMA.

"Roger, Captain."

***

JT and Sam went to the larger quarters. It didn't look too bad. The bathroom was clean and had fresh towels and wash cloths. There were supplies on the shelves and clean sheets for the bed.

"Let's make up the bed and then take a shower."

"Your wish is my command, fair maiden." and JT made a fancy bow.

"Oh, thank you, Sir James." and she curtsied.

Before they made the bed JT went over to the inter-com and turned on some music.

"This was in the main computer on Oz."

They made the bed. JT looked at Sam. "I'll flip you the shower."

"If we play this right we can both fit in there." Sam said as she started to undress. JT was not far behind. They looked at each other unashamed. Even though this was the first time they had seen each other naked.

"God, you're beautiful." JT said.

"So are you."

They stepped to each other and embraced. The kiss started out every lightly but ended when they fell to the bed.

Each could not get enough of the other. They made love to each other. Not one doing all and the other receiving. After a days work, and the not so much sleep the night before, they almost fell asleep.

JT slapped her on the rump and said. "Let's take that shower, we smell like a dead whale."

"What an awful thing to say." She lifted one arm and sniffed, sat up and sniffed again. "You know, you're right."

They went to the shower and washed each other, taking their time, making doubly sure the other was really clean. JT washed Sam breasts at least three times. Just to make sure, he even gave them the squeaky clean test with his right index finger. Sam reached down with a washcloth and started to clean. JT stopped her.

"Easy, the 'Wee fellow' is a little sore around the edges."

"Well, he ain't the only one. You get frisky tonight and I'll wallop you so hard, your back side will think it was born all alone."

They dried each other off and got dressed. Remade the bed and went to the galley. With a hot drink in their hand went back to the bridge to check in with Oz.

"Sam, do you want to make the message up and sent it? I'm going to check on the torpedo room."

"OK."

Sam thought for a while at what she was going to say. She recorded the message, hit the play back and listened to what she had said, making sure the facts were correct. She reached over to the transmitter and threw the hyper speed switch and zoom it was off.

***

It seemed everyone including Awga and the newest addition to the crew were in the galley when the message came though.

Trigas voice came over the inter comm. "Captain this is the bridge, I have received a message from the 202, Sir."

Dirt went to the inter comm. "Put it on play and let's hear it. If you please, Ensign."

"Aye, aye, Sir."

"Oh, Wonderful Wizard of Oz, this is 202 in Never Never Land sending a KMA. We have onboard eighteen crates of space type modular homes. Will be loading thirty crates of electronic equipment tomorrow. Plus Nav equipment and all spares from junk pile. Interesting data on ships comings and goings. Will call in AM. All is well. We are CYAing and we did KA. 202 out."

"What is KA?" Kat asked.

"Kick Ass." said Susan. She jumped up and went to their room and then went to JT's room. She came back with the placards that Sam had made. She stood up on the end of an empty table and said "Ta-Dah", holding up a placard. It showed a large boot kicking a donkey on the butt, on top it said JT's and on the bottom it said U.S.A.S.F.

"Bring it over here, Please, Susan."

Dirk reach inside his uniform flap and came out with a marker. He crossed out the s after JT and added & SAM's. It now read JT & SAM's. "I think that's more like it. Don't you?"

A chorus of "Aye, Ayes" rang out.

Dirk looked over to the Rosses and then to Gunny "How are you folks doing. It's your children out there?"

Gunny looked at Dirk. "I am real proud of those two out there. They are doing something none of their peers at home would never think of doing. They have had to do a lot of adlibbing and they're doing it right. They're using their heads. Oh, and I don't think we can call them children anymore. That's a man and a woman out there. They've proven that."

Allen spoke up. "Gunnys right. They're not children any more. I always knew our daughter," Susan's head snapped up. "Excuse me, daughters, would leave the nest sooner or later. But to have one fly off into space is a little mind boggling to say the least. I can't think of a better young man to have my oldest with. I'm very proud of them myself."

"Well, we'll be seeing them again in a couple of days."

Dirk said.

***

JT came back to the bridge and asked Sam if she had sent off the message. She said Yes, and the disc was still in the transmitter. JT switched it back and played it aloud. His eyes widened.

"You sent this?" He started to smile.

"I thought the people back there could use a little humor. You should hear the reply. It's short but it's sweet." Sam hit the incoming switch.

"Oz to 202. Well done. Family out."

"Well, how's that grab ya, Buster?"

"Com'ere." Sam came over, sat on his lap and rested her head on his chest. She played with the buttons on his uniform shirt and opened it up. JT had a silver necklace on. There was ring on it.

"Whose ring is that?"

"It's my mother's engagement and wedding band, all rolled into one. There are two, half karat, diamonds on it"

"It's beautiful."

"My father gave it to me when I turned twenty-one. I put it on this chain. It reminds me off her. She was a beautiful lady."

Sam held up her right hand, she had a ring with a ruby set on it. "My folks gave this to me the night I graduated from high school. I feel the same as you. It will always remind me of them."

Scaner came over, held his arm out. "May I see that ring." Sam held her hand out. Scaner lifted her hand up so it was directly in front of what would be called his face. A thin white beam projected from an aperture.

"This a very rare stone. It comes from India and only from a small area in the northern mountains. If you hold it so the light shines through the bottom you will see a star shinning in the center of it."

***

"I'm going to get a hot cup of chocolate, do you want one?" Sam asked.

"No thanks. I'm drinked out. I'm going to check out the reactor room and the lower storage room and then I'll be right back. Let's look at some stars."

Scaner opened the view screen. JT left and went to the storage area and Sam went for her drink. When she got back there was soft music playing. She had changed into a robe. Sam curled up in the pilot chair and was soon fast asleep. JT came back to the bridge and found her there all bunched up. He put the cup in a holder and picked her up, carried her to their quarters and put her to bed.

During the night he dreamt someone was touching him. He opened an eye. Sam had one leg draped over his. <u>I guess it's because I'm not used to having someone sleep with me. But I like it</u> He kissed Sam on the forehead, and was sound asleep again before his head hit the pillow.

***

JT woke up at 7:00 AM and kissed Sam awake. She reached up and grabbed him and wrestled him back on to the bed. She pinned his arms back over his head and began to take small nibbling bites down his body. When he moved she would bite a little harder. He lay there and took his medicine. She moved down lower. She stopped and looked at him. Unknowingly she had backed up to an erection, She dropped her head and looked down between her legs. She looked up at JT and said. "Oh My."

JT started to get up on his elbows but Sam pushed him down. She sat straight up, making love to him.

Sam let out a soft moan and lay on top of JT. There were tears of pure joy coming from her eyes as she held him close. She stayed that way, happy to be where she was.

Suddenly she sat back up. Put the palm of her left hand on his chest. Holding him down, raised her right fist.

She's going to punch me!

"When we get back to Oz, you'd better make me an honest woman."

"Will you marry me?"

"Did you hear what I just said?"

"For the second time. Will you marry me? I won't ask you again."

"Huh!" Sam looked a JT. "Oh Yes,yesyesyes." She dropped back down hugging him. "I love you."

"Hummm. I love you too."

***

They sat there cross legged looking each other. JT reached up and took the necklace off, holding the ring, which had been his mothers.

"Hello, what's this?"

Between the two diamonds was another larger one of about one karat. JT reached over and lifted Sam's right hand. "Well, bless my soul."

There were two small diamonds, one on each side of the ruby. Each clasp was identical to the original. Sam looked up at JT, both had tears running down their faces. JT finally found his voice.

"That little bugger."

JT took Sam's left hand and as he slid his mother's ring onto the third finger said.

"You're mine forever just as I am yours forever."

Sam took his left hand and held it to her lips.

"You're mine forever just as I am yours forever."

They leaned forward and kissed. This wasn't a kiss of passion or just a quick buss on the lips. This was a promise, a life long commitment. This whole wide universe was theirs at this moment. They broke off and looked deep into each other's eyes.

"I think I'm going to like being married to you, Mr. James Tyrone Chambers."

"And I know I'm going like being married to you, Mrs. Samatha Jean Chambers."

Just then the door to the galley opened and Scaner came in carrying a large tray with two breakfasts on it.

"Good morning, may I be the first to say congratulations." as he set the tray down on the side of the bed.

Sam reached over and put her hand on Scaners "head".

"You didn't have to but thank you."

"This is the second wedding breakfast I have served. It is a pleasure. May I say that is a beautiful ring you have."

"Oh Scaner, your a Darling."

JT looked at Scaner, he had figured it out. How Scaner had gotten the ring sizes, and had gotten the rings to work on them. But who's driving the ship?

"I know you're a crafty little devil, but when and how did you get the rings?"

"I came and got the rings as soon as you where asleep. Went to the machine shop and remade them. I sized the ring you had to fit her hand." Turning to Sam. "When I looked at your ring last night I took the measurements. The only problem was when I put them back, you almost woke up Sir. I reached over and put her leg over yours. Then I shut down."

"And now for the big question. Who's running the ship?" JT asked.

"Auto is Sir."

"Who's Otto?" asked Sam

Two antennae arose from the top of his head. They laughed.

"Who was the first breakfast for?" Sam asked

"The Captain and Mrs. Mac. They were married a week before you were resuscitated."

"Scaner, you're a wealth of information." Sam said.

"Thank you, Ma'am"

The red light came on at the inter comm station. "Read it Scaner."

Scaner looked over to the inter comm. It started," 202 this is Oz, Plans remain as is. No new course change. Continue salvage operations. Also new member yesterday. Trimac, strapping young lad. Call, if needed. No reply required. Oz out."

"Reality strikes, Babe, its back to the grindstone. Scaner, go to the bridge and plug your self in. We'll be up in a minute or two."

***

They took a quick shower and got another cup of coffee and went to the bridge.

"We have got to move to the other ships lower level to get the other crates out. Let's do it now."

JT released the holding struts and told Scaner to bring the ship down to the shuttle bay door. The ship lowered and they locked on again. JT and Sam went to the air lock and put on their suits. Sam rigged the sleeve out and engaged the magnetic seals on the end. The walkway was run out. The green board on the bridge showed all hatches closed and airtight. They put on their helmets and rebreathers. JT depressurized the compartment and opened the inner door. He stopped. "Do you have your laser?" Sam shook her head no.

"Get one, Hon, you never know."

Sam was back in a minute. "Let's go"

They opened the outer door and went over to the alien craft.

These crates were smaller and the transfer went faster. Going back to the 202 they secured the crates.

"Let's take another walk around and see if we missed anything down here."

JT and Sam looked in every nook and cranny but could find nothing. Leaving the alien ship they crossed to the 202. Went into the air lock and shut the outer door. The walkway was rigged in and then the sleeve.

Going inside the 202, Sam shut the inner door. The compartment was pressurized. After recharging the rebreathers, they placed them in the lockers by the air lock. Sam was taking off her suit while JT released the alien ship.

"I'm going to try something." JT said and reattached the struts and brought the ship in closer to them. He released the alien ship, pushed the struts out fast. Stopping, as the two ships grew further apart. Doing this, he felt their ship move in the opposite direction.

"Something's wrong. The 202 should not have moved." JT said as he looked at Sam. He could see the alarm in her eyes. JT rigged the struts in and they went to the bridge.

CHAPTER TWENTY-SEVEN

Arriving at the bridge JT saw a stranger standing by the com-panel. He turned and pointed something at JT and fired. It struck JT on the chest, knocking him backward against the wall. Everything went black. The last thing he heard was Sam's scream.

The Alien came toward Sam.

"I have a human female at last. After I take you I will give you to Korac to play with. This ship will be mine to go back Balarac."

Sam was frozen in place. The alien came up to her and grabbed the front of her uniform top and ripped it way exposing her upper body. That got her moving. She lashed out with her foot aiming for his crotch or where a crotch should be. He moved to the side and caught the blow on his upper leg. Sam backed around the main console. The alien advanced toward her. *If I can get you out in the center you'll be wearing your balls up around your neck. I didn't play soccer for nothing, Buster.* Sam backed to the center of the room and crouched, rocking from side to side, waiting. The alien came at her. He came slowly, on guard, not knowing what was going to happen next. Sam was watching his eyes when she saw a bulge rising at his crotch. *This idiot is thinking of a something he'll never get. Not, if I can help it.*

She motioned with her hands, come on. He did. As she started to kick he dropped down. The kick went over his head by inches. He grabbed her leg and yanked her down. He was at her in a flash.

***

JT shook his head trying to get the cobwebs loose. His eyes started to focus, he could see Sam backing away from the alien toward the center of the room. He was starting to get movement back into his arms and legs. JT saw the kick and the maneuver the alien did.

The alien had Sam and dragging her to her feet, pushed her against the view panel. He held her there with one hand and reached down with other to undo his pants.

JT knew exactly what he was trying to do. He reached down and got his laser out. The selector was in the full power position. He turned it down, not wanting to hurt Sam. Even if she was free and out of the way. Full power could possibly punch a hole in the hull at this range.

The alien moved to the side a little. Sam saw JT moving. She suddenly relaxed. The alien reached down and opened the front of his pants, freeing himself. Thinking he'd won, he let go of Sam and attempted to pull her pants down.

Sam reached down, got a hold on him and twisted with all her might. The alien screamed and struck out. Sam was all ready moving, down and away. The alien was holding on to himself with both hands when he heard.

"Yo, asshole."

Turning to look at JT, he saw the red beam streak out, striking him in the chest. The alien could feel the molten heat created by the laser burning inside. He knew he was dead even as he dropped to his knees.

JT got up and very calmly walked over to the alien and stood in front of him. He held the laser on its side and turned it to not quite stun.

The alien looked at JT with pure hatred in his eyes. JT raised the laser and point it at his head. Still the alien glared at him.

Sam came over, put her hand on JT's arm and pushed it down. She reached over and took the weapon from him. The alien sneered at the pair of humans. Sam very swiftly put the weapon against his head.

"You tell Korac, when you see him in hell, that this is from Sam and JT." She pulled the trigger. Sam stood there for a second, dropped the weapon and turn to JT, holding onto him. She cried and JT held her. In between sobs she said. "I've killed a living person." JT held her until she got it out of her system.

"Hon, all you did was to put a rabid creature out of its misery. It was already dying. Come on Babe, let's get into some clean clothes.

Sam stripped down where she was and threw the clothes at the alien.

"I'll never wear those again, they're filthy. I'll be right back, I want to be alone for a while." Kissing JT, she turned and walked toward the door.

JT took off his space suit and examined it. There was a scorch mark dead center, but did not go through the material. He too threw the suit over by the alien. <u>It isn't dirty like Sam's but I won't be wearing it anymore.</u>

***

JT went over to Scaner and checked him. When he bent over he felt a pain in his chest. <u>I've got to sit down</u> He was still sitting there with his eyes closed when Sam came back into the room.

She saw him and rushed over. <u>He's dead! Oh No, Please God, No!</u> When she reached him she saw he was breathing. She came back to life again. She had died inside at thought of JT dying. She kissed him again and again.

JT opened his eyes, surprised, at what she was doing. He put his arm up and around her. She stopped.

"I thought you had died."

"It's my chest, Christ, it hurts."

She very gently opened his uniform shirt. Dead center was a bruise and swelling such as she had never seen before.

"You ought to see my space suit. It's got a burn mark on it like you won't believe."

JT reached up and touched the wound and pressed around a little. "Nothing broken, man, I took a hell-of-a-wallop. I should be all right in a couple of days. Could you get me a cold compress to put on it Hon."

Sam turned. "Scaner get a cold compress." No answer. She look over to Scaner, There was a scorch mark on his side. "It looks like Scaners done for too."

Sam was up and out the door in a flash. She was back with towels and a plastic bag fill of ice. She flattened out the ice bag and rapped a towel around it and put it on his chest. She buttoned up his shirt and then put a band of tape around the bottom of the bulge.

"There, that should hold it for a while."

"OK, let's look at Scaner."

JT got up slowly and moved over to Scaner. He took off the side panel and looked at the wiring.

"Hand me a flash light, Hon." It was there in a heartbeat. JT flashed around inside looking for any kind of damage, he could see none. He replaced the panel and went around to the rear. He opened the panel up and there it was. He looked up at Sam. She had a horrified look on her face.

"You've heard of people getting mad and blowing a fuse?" She nodded. "He blew three." JT pushed the circuit breakers back in and touch the restart button.

Scaner came to life. JT buttoned up the panel. Scaner started making funny noises as his systems came back on. In two minutes he was back to normal.

"I hope he hasn't lost any memory. Scaner how many fingers do you see?"

"Three"

"Good"

"Your memory banks? Are you OK."

"Yes, the circuit breakers stop the electrical currant from doing any damage. How many breakers went out?"

"Three."

"When all six go, it will be a problem. That means some of my wiring has to be replaced."

JT thought for a minute. "Can you put your wiring diagrams and schematics into the main computer banks?"

"Yes I can."

"Do it right now."

"Yes Sir." Scaner plugged himself into the main banks and hyper sent it. "It is in HIMEM now."

JT looked at Sam. "You know I'll bet this computer has never been defragged."

"What's defrag?"

"It's a process that lets the computer rearrange itself. When you put information into a computer it tries to fill in all the holes. Say you sent a message to it requiring three doors. It would look around for three doors side by side to put them in. If it came upon one door it would drop off enough to fill it and then go to the next. If it couldn't find two doors next it would drop off at the next open door and so forth. It takes time to jump from door to door find the information you want."

"Okay, knife, fork and spoon, wouldn't be easier for you if you had them side by side instead of one here and one over there and the other over there." Sam nodded "Well, that's what happens to a computer. Defrag let's it police itself, putting all those nuts and bolts in the right place, side by side. This baby has 5000 megs of RAM, megabytes of Random Access Memory, right now she's getting a little confused. So we'll defrag her. Should take about an hour. And for that hour we'll be blind."

"Is it worth the risk?" Sam asked

"Let's think about it."

"Where did 'whatshisface' come from? He mentioned a place called Balarac." Sam answered her own question.

"Well, that's a Balaracian ship. The information is on the disc from its main computer."

"First let's get this off of the bridge. It doesn't look good, especially if we have company."

Good, she's back to her old self again. "Right you are love, I'll get a capsule and we'll freeze him for future reference."

JT got a capsule and the Balaracian was safely tucked away. He took the suit and the uniform and put them in a disposable bag. For later discarding.

***

"Let's get some more ice for me."

They came back to the bridge. Sam was walking around, mulling something over in her mind. "Scaner, from the time we started filming this latest escapade, run it through one frame at a time, enhanced. There were two spaces on that ship for shuttles but only one shuttle. I bet 'gizmo' left his buddy in the lurch and screwed."

The film came on, there on the fifth, sixth and seventh frames.

"Stop, go back one frame. There, that is the same type of shuttle left in the junk pile. And it's around us somewhere."

"That's good thinking, Babe. When we find it, we can load it and take both back with us. We'll know a little more about them. Now with this body and the computer discs we'll know a lot about them. Our shuttle is trashed. Let's stow it in board and put theirs in the bay."

"OK, Scaner turn on the cameras and search for that shuttle."

"There over by that little asteroid in the shadow." Sam said.

JT looked, yup, Sam had found it. "What do you have 20/15 vision."

"As a matter of fact. Yes, I do."

"Let's go, I've got an idea on how to get that one onboard without going on a space walk."

"Shoot, I was looking forward to one." Sam said.

"Babe, I couldn't get a suit on right now."

They went back to the bridge. JT maneuvered the ship to the alien shuttle and got right in front of it. The nose, nearly touching the 202. They went back down to the shuttle bay.

"I think this will work. If not, it's out we go."

JT rigged the struts out past the shuttle. Then put the sleeve out over the struts. He engaged the magnetic field on the ends of the sleeve and they closed. He gently drew the shuttle into the bay. When it was almost inside, he rigged the struts in.

"When I say to, you shut the outer door."

The shuttle was over lapping the outer edge. JT brought the sleeve in the rest of the way. It pushed the shuttle in.

"Now."

Sam shut the door behind it as it thumped the inner door. The shuttle settled to the deck on its skids. Sam pushed the lever for the hold-downs and the shuttle was secured to the deck.

JT looked at Sam and smiled. "Good job. Now it's back to the bridge and compile a 'Message to Garcia'. We'll word in a way the Captain will see there is more to the message than we are telling and it's of a personal nature. OK, Mrs. Chambers."

Sam leaned over to him and whispered in his ear. "I like being Mrs. Chambers." and kissed him on the cheek. When they got back to the bridge Scaner was plugged into the main control panel, running the ship.

"Good job on holding us steady, Scaner." JT said. Scaner was a little down in the dumps about the Balaracian sneaking up on him.

"I have been going through the known hatches on this ship and I can't find out how the Balaracian got onboard."

"Well, we've got to get a message off to Oz and then we'll study it some more."

"Scaner, would get me a nice hot cup of chocolate, please?"

"Yes Ma'am" She looked at JT and he nodded

"Make that two."

"Yes Ma'am" and off he went.

JT showed Sam the message. She read the message and nodded.

"I'm going to put it in code. Don't want other folks reading our mail."

JT put a disc into the com-panel and typed the message to the disc. Played it back, then sent it out at hyper speed.

CHAPTER TWENTY-EIGHT

Ensign Triga was standing the bridge watch when the message came in. Part of it was in a code of some type. The message started out:

202 TO OZ

EYES ONLY, CAPT MAC

FCA VYQ X HKPKUJ UCNXCIG X 202 KPVGTKVA DTQEJGF X

WRQP GPVGTKPI DTKFIG LV UJQV, YQWPF UWRGTHIEICN X

UCO CVVCEMGD X LV CPF UCO FKURCVEJGF DCNCTCEKCP,

KP HTGGBG X PCOG MQTCE OGCPKPI X FOYP QPG JQWT FGHTCI X

LWOR VQ NU CV 0700 QP UGXGPVGGPVH VJ GUV 3 RQKPV 5 AQWT FAC X CNNU YGNN

LVE, ECRV, 202 QWV.

Triga switched to the inter comm. "Bridge to Captain, Bridge to Captain."

Dirk and most of the crew were in the galley having lunch when the call came over the inter comm. Dirt looked over to Gunny.

"Must be important, by the sounds of it." He got up and went to the inter-com and picked up the handset.

"Captain here."

"Captain, a message just came in from 202 and it is in some type of code. It starts out, '202 to Oz, Eyes only, Capt. Mac, and the rest is in code."

"Thank you, Ensign. I'll be right up."

Dirk turned and saw Gunny and Allen looking at him. Everyone else was still eating or talking. He motioned with his head. They got up and left. Everyone else was still eating or talking. Going through the passageway that brought them by the storage room office. Dirk stuck his head in and MJ looked up. He again motioned with his head and she got up and went with them.

They arrived at the bridge. Triga handed Dirk the clip board with the message on it. He looked it over and said this was going to take some time to decipher.

Gunny reached over. "May I, Sir." He looked it over. "If I can have a pad and a pencil I can decipher it right now."

Dirk looked at Gunny and motioned with his hand, come on tell me.

"This is a code JT and I use every once in a while when we felt like screwing with someone's mind. For him to use it, something heavy duty has hit the fan."

Gunny sat down and started to decipher it. Everyone was trying to lean over his shoulder at once to see. He stopped, turned around and looked at them. He was giving them each his best Master Gunnery Sergeant "Don't mess-with-me right now I'm working" look. They all backed away, knowing, even Officers can be silently told off. It took him about five minutes to finish the job. He handed it to the Dirk. Dirk looked it over and then read it to the rest of them.

"202 TO OZ EYES ONLY CAPT MAC

DAY TWO FINISHED SALVAGE 202 INTEGRITY BROACHED UPON ENTERING BRIDGE JT SHOT WOUND SUPERFICIAL SAM ATTACKED JT AND SAM DISPATCHED BALARACIAN IN FREEZE NAME KORAC MEANING DOWN ONE HOUR DEFRAG JUMP TO LS AT 0700 ON SEVENTEENTH

EST 3 POINT 5 YOUR DAY ALLS WELL JTC CAPT 202 OUT

MJ looked around at the other members of the crew. "As a mother, I'm worried about the attack on Sam. It could be worse than what we are reading. I think there is more to this than a plain attack. And what is a defrag?"

Gunny spoke up. "Defrag is an operation on the computer." and he told her how it works and why it should be done. "By the time we compile an answer to him it ought to be done defragging." Dirk looked over to Ensign Triga. "Does the name Korac mean anything to you?"

"Korac is, I believe, the other member of the original crew which came out here on the first run with Captain Eugin. I thought all of those members were killed."

"OK, we'll check with original crew manifest. What does he mean by integrity broached? And how bad is his wound? Let's get Tribec up here and see if he can shed some light the integrity part." Dirk switched on the inter comm. "Chief Tribec report to the bridge."

Gunny said "I don't think the wound is serious or JT would have stated so. If it were real serious Sam would have written the message. He's telling us he was temporally out of it and that was why Sam was attacked. Evidently the Balaracian tried to get Sam. She fought him off long enough for JT to get back on his feet and nail the bastard."

Chief Tribec came to the bridge.

"Yes, Captain."

"Chief, look at this message and see if you can shed some light on the integrity part."

Tribec looked at the message and thought for a while. "What he is asking is, how did the intruder get on to the ship without being noticed? It had to be through a hatch of some sort which doesn't show a light on the main panel." Tribec went over to the main computer and brought up the structural plans for the IV-202. He sat at the nav station and went over the layout. "Here Sir." and enhanced the area where the cursor was. It showed the elevator sleeve, which extends to another ship.

"That's how he did it. All you have to do is drop the sleeve six feet and the hatch can be opened. There is not a light for it because you need a correct set of numbers to open it from the outside."

"We are going to have to modify all the ships green boards. Chief, put that down on your high priority list. How long do we have before their computer is up?"

"Sir, It has been an hour and a half since we received their message." Triga said.

Dirk sat down and wrote a message to the 202. He showed it to the people standing there.

"Anyone got anything they what to add?" Everyone shook their heads. Dirk set the disc in the computer, about to send it off, he stopped. Took it back out and handed it to Gunny.

"Code this and then we will send it off. We don't want any one reading our mail yet. We'll send it out over UHF 121.5. I'll bet no one monitors that channel out here but us."

Gunny sat down and wrote the message in code, and handed it back to Dirk. Dirk set it in the translator and it was put on a disc. The disc was then set in the transmitter and sent out at hyper speed.

"All we can do now is wait." Dirk said and brought up the star chart. "Here is where we will be at 0700 tomorrow. And here is where they are. In three and half days we will be here. From this point back to them is a 2.66 hour trip for them. We can expect to see them around 0907 on the 17th. Anyone want to start an anchor pool?"

Gunny looked up. "I believe I still know how. And by the way the 17th is JT's birthday. I'll let Jasper know and maybe he can whip up a cake."

CHAPTER TWENTY-NINE

The red light came on at the transmitter on the 202. The message was received:

OZ TO 202

KPVGTKVA NQYGT JCVEJ VQ GNCXCVQT UNGGXG.

MQTCE DCF CTKCP MGGR GAG RGGNGF. INCF AQW

CPF UCO QM. UCHG VTKR VQ QB RCTGPVU QM

WFUV 0700 NU ECRV OCE

JT handed the message to Sam. "You decipher it. And I'll send back a receive message."

JT switched the transmitter to the main computer and sent out.

"202 to Oz, msg rec 202 out."

Sam had a little difficulty in the translation.

OZ TO 202

INTEGRITY LOWER HATCH TO ELEVATOR SLEEVE KORAC BAD ARIAN KEEP EYE PEELED GLAD YOU AND SAM OK SAFE TRIP TO OZ PARENTS OK USTD 0700 LS CAPT MAC

"What does USTD stand for?"

JT read the message "Understand 0700 light speed."

He brought up the blue prints for the 202 on the view screen and went to the elevator sleeve. He and Sam looked it over.

"Scaner, there's the villain. One hatch on this whole ship that doesn't have a warning light. It doesn't need one because it's always rigged in for flight. We'll rig a light on it and then I'm going to booby trap it. If any one tries to get in that way again they're in for a big surprise."

"What are you going to do?"

"I figure a sand bag swinging down ought to put someone about twenty miles away by the time they start to slow down. As we say in Maine 'Adios Mother'. Scaner, plug yourself in to the main computer and we'll go down to the elevator door. Inform me if this light flickers on and off." He pointed to a light on the green board. "I'm going to wire the two doors together until we get back to Oz and then I'll rig a permanent light up for it."

As they were leaving the bridge Sam went to the weapons panel. She took a belt out and put it on. Then stuck a laser in the holster.

"I've learned a hard lesson today. It won't happen again. If one of these alien bastards looks at me like that again, he's going to be one hurting unit."

They didn't have any sand but a sack full of lead would do the trick. JT rigged up a light. Scaner told them the light flickered.

"OK, I'm going to test it." He opened the door.

Scaner reported the red light was on. JT shut the door.

"We have a green board, Sir."

"Very well."

JT looked at his watch, "Let's eat and then go back to the bridge and plot our course for tomorrows jump to light- speed."

"OK, I'll cook."

"You can cook?"

"Of course I can cook. What do you think us country girls do. Just sit around polishing our fingernails. Now, what do you what to eat?"

"Surprise me."

"You stay on the bridge and I'll call you when dinner is ready."

Sam went to the kitchen and looked through the food locker. She found what she wanted. Sam started to make her first meal for her man. In about thirty minutes she called JT and told him that dinner was ready.

JT came to the galley. There sitting on the table was a tossed salad, toast, steak, baked potatoes, peas, and thanks to Scaner, some strawberry ice cream. They sat down and enjoyed their first meal together.

"Babe, this is one of the best meals I've had in a long time. Every once in a while one of Gunny's lady-friends would cook. Most of them couldn't boil water without burning the pan. None of them could hold a candle to this meal. My mom was a great cook but it's been ten years since I've tasted her cooking. I really can't remember but I know it was good. This is better."

"Well, thank you kind sir. I'm glad you liked it. Really, I was worried you wouldn't. Now I'm happy." She got up, went to his side of the table and sat on his lap. She leaned her head on his chest and stayed like that for a minute or so before looking up to his face.

He leaned down and kissed her.

"Come on let's get the dishes put up and then go to the bridge and set up the course to Oz for tomorrow."

They cleaned up the mess and went over to the tray shelf and put them down, no voice.

"I'll bet she pissed at me for cooking for you, whadathink?" Sam stated

"Automated voices don't get pissed." JT said

"The Captains does, and I'll bet this one's got her back up."

The trays disappeared into the scullery.

"Maybe your right, but I ain't gonna loose sleep over it. Speaking of sleep. Do you know what night this is?" JT said.

"Yup, and you had better carry me across the threshold to, I expect the whole nine yards tonight, Buster."

They walked to the bridge hand in hand. JT brought up the star chart and plotted a course to the point where they would meet Oz.

"I'll bet this left turn we have to make is going to screw up the anchor pool."

"What's an anchor pool?"

"It's a bet on what time we show up. Probably down to seconds. See, here I'll show you." JT plotted a straight course to Oz. "Calculated time, 2 hours decimal 6666 minutes."

"Now the real course is going to take us to here, to avoid this asteroid, and then left to Oz. And that is going to take and extra fifteen minutes. So our flight time will 2 hours and 23 minutes. I'm plotting to come up in front of Oz. About five miles in front. And I'll even tell you who is going to win the pool."

"Triga." replied Sam. "She's the only one that will take the asteroid into consideration. Woman's intuition."

"You got it, Babe. 0700 is going to come around real soon. Let's get some sleep, reveille's at 6:00 AM. Scaner you've got the ship. Call us at 6:00 AM. or if anything comes up, 10-4?"

"10-4, Skipper."

CHAPTER THIRTY

Sam and JT went to their quarters and true to her word, made JT carry her across the threshold. Standing her on the side of the bed, he slowly took her clothes off and started to kiss her. Sam stepped down and did the same to him. Only she started to kiss his body as she took off his clothes. When she lowered his pants she could see that he was ready. As they embraced, she lifted herself up and rapped her legs around his waist. She slowly slid down. JT sat down on the edge of the bed and rolled over. They fell asleep holding each other in their arms.

JT was up at 5:45 AM and was in the shower when Sam opened the door and joined him. They scrubbed each other and Sam started to fool around.

"You know we are going to start suffering from TOMBANES Syndrome." JT said

"What's Tombanes Syndrome?" Sam asked

"To Much Bed And Not Enough Sleep." JT said

"God, I love it. I hope there's no known cure."

Sam looked down and took JT by the hand and led him back to the bed.

"This ones for the road."

***

After breakfast they took a cup of coffee up to the bridge and prepared for the jump to light speed. Sam did the count down.

When she said zero, JT hit the switch for light speed. They lifted their cups and sang together.

"We're off to see the Wizard, the wonderful Wizard of Oz."

***

Gunny had posted the anchor pool list up on the wall in the galley and everyone would wanted to join in picked a time which they thought the 202 would appear. Triga came up and looked at the numbers. She did not see the number she wanted. She looked at Gunny and asked.

"Can I post my own number or do I have to pick one of these?"

"You can choose your own number."

She took a folded piece of paper out of her pocket and taped it to the list.

"Don't worry about anyone looking at that, everyone's number will be a secret until after 202 shows up."

***

Time kind of dragged by for the crew of the Oz waiting for the 202 to show up. Susan, a bundle of nerves, was hopping around the ship, making everyone else a nervous wreck too. Finally her mother told her to sit down and be quite because she was driving everyone nuts. That lasted for about two minutes and she was off and going again. She went to the bridge at 9:00 AM and sat at the fire control panel chair. Turning to the view screen she waited, not saying a word. The minutes ticked by. Starting at 0906, you could hear people say. "Well, I didn't win." Triga didn't say a word.

At 0923 the 202 appeared directly in front of Oz. Susan nearly jumped out of her skin. "THEY'RE HERE!"

Triga looked at Gunny and said. "YES, right on time."

Gunny took the piece of paper down from the list and opened it up, the time was 0923.

"Ensign Triga wins the pool. How did you know this was the time?"

"As your Sherlock Holmes would say, "It's elementary my Dear Watson".

***

The 202 came at Oz slowly and down her left side to the stern. She lined up to the docking bay, came in, turned around and switched on the light landing system.

"JT look."

Over the docking bay door was a large banner. WELCOME HOME 'KICK-ASS' and just below it was HAPPY BIRTHDAY 'JT'

JT looked at Sam and said, "That's right, I'm twenty-three now."

Sam backed 202 into the docking space, lowered the landing struts and set her down. JT reached over and patted Scaner on his dome like head.

"We couldn't have done this with out you, buddy." and Scaner, again, lit up like a Christmas tree.

"Happy Birthday, Captain."

"Thank you, Scaner."

The three of them left the bridge and went to the elevator and went down to the main deck. As they stepped out, the whole crew came toward the 202.

Sam looked over to JT. "I wonder who's driving the bus."

Two antenna came up out of Scaners dome. "Otto." They both laughed.

***

"Holy Shit! Look at that rock!" Everyone looked at Susan. She was pointing at Sam. "Look!"

JT and Sam put an arm around each other and Sam held up her left hand. There were cheers and hand clapping. Dirk came over and put out his hand. "Welcome home."

Sam's parents and Gunny were standing in front of them. Everyone was crowded around them. Gunny looked at his son and said. "Well done, Son, Well done." Gunny put out his hand. The next thing he knew JT had his arms around him and was giving him a big hug. Gunny put his arms around JT and hugged him back.

"I love you, Dad."

"I love you to, Son."

Allen, MJ and Susan were hugging Sam and after that everyone had to get a hug in.

Triga came up to JT and Sam and held out her arms and the three of them embraced. She stood back and JT asked.

"How much did you win from the pool?"

"How do you know I won?"

"He knew you would be the only one to see the asteroid and the left hand turn."

"Ahhh, the star chart. I taught you well. I am proud of you two."

JT looked over Triga to see Bruce standing there. "Excuse me." and stepped around her. He put his right hand out and grasped Bruce's and then put his left arm around him and gave him a hug. "It is good to see you, my friend."

"Oh, I am so happy you have returned safely. Welcome home."

JT looked around, saw Susan standing there. "HEY RUNT. Don't I get a hug."

"Who in the hell are you calling runt." and she jump into his arms, squeezing him tightly around his neck. She let go of him and he asked "Where's R & R?" There was a slight tug on his right uniform sleeve and he looked around. He bent down and gave the twins a hug. "How you guys been?"

"We missed you very much JT. You're not going to go away again are you?" Rebecca asked.

"Not for awhile, if I can help it.

The women were crowded around Sam looking at her ring, talking all at once. MJ looked in her daughter's eyes and saw a woman looking back at her. <u>She's made her choice and it is a perfect one. If any two people were made for each other, they are.</u> MJ put her arms around her daughter and whispered in her ear. "You have my blessings." Sam held her mother close.

"Thank you, now all I have to do is convince Dad.

"He knew from the very beginning JT would be the one for you."

"Huh, you're kidding."

"No, the second night we were here, he said you would pick JT. I guess your father knows you better than you think."

"Dad, can I talk to you in private for a minute?" JT and Gunny walked off, away from the throng of people.

"I want to asked Mr. and Mrs. Ross for permission to marry Sam."

"Son, if you're looking for my blessing too, you've got it. I think she'd make a fine wife for you. You two are going to make a mark out here together. Just don't make me a grandfather just yet."

"Yes Sir, Gunny, Sir. Would you walk back with me? He wouldn't dare say no with the U.S. Marines standing behind me."

"You're forgetting Mrs. Ross was a U.S. Marine also."

"You're right. I did."

JT and Gunny walked back to the small group of people standing there and found Allen and MJ talking with Sam. Susan was standing on one foot and then the other waiting to get a word in. When JT and Gunny walked up she saw to look on JT's face and stood still. Whatever was going to happen next she knew it was going to be a beauty. JT stood over by Sam. She took his hand in hers and gave it a little squeeze.

"I--- ahhh," He took a deep breath. "Mr. and Mrs. Ross, I'd appreciate it very much if you'd say yes to Sam and I getting married."

Allen Ross smiled. "That's a rather unique way of asking for our daughter's hand in marriage. Yes, you do have our appreciation in the upcoming nuptials

"Yes Sir, thank you Sir, Ma'am."

Allen said smiling at his wife. "He's more nervous than I was when I asked your parents for your hand." That broke the ice and everyone relaxed.

"Hot damn, I get my own room, Yes." And Susan crooked her arm, made a fist. Then pumped it back and forth and kicked out.

"When would you two like to get married?" asked MJ

Sam looked at her mother. "How about this afternoon."

"So soon."

Sam leaned over and whispered in her mother's ear. "Mom, we've been together for a few days in space. When you are out there, even for a few days, it seems like a life time."

Gunny reached out to Sam. "May I see the ring?" Sam held out her left hand.

"That's a beautiful diamond. I hope this ring brings you two as much happiness as it did for Marlene and I." and he leaned over and kissed Sam's cheek. "Well, we were going to have a birthday cake and ice-cream for JT. We may as well use it for a wedding cake too."

Allen looked at Gunny and said. "1:00 PM out here." Gunny nodded. "Everyone's invited, let's spread the news.

"Sam and I would like Captain to perform the ceremony. So before everyone gets to carried away we had better ask him."

JT and Sam went in search of the Captain. They found him on the bridge making a plot on the Star chart.

Sir, can we talk to you for a minute?" Dirk noticed JT had brought a packet of computer discs with him.

"Sure, relax your among friends."

They told him about wanting to get married and asked him if he would perform the ceremony. And told him the time Mr. Ross and Gunny had set.

"Yes, it would an honor to perform the wedding ceremony." They thanked him. JT handed him over the discs and told him what they were.

"Well, Miss Ross, I'm sure you have some pre-wedding things to do. I'll keep JT here while you get them taken care of."

"Yes Sir and thank you sir." and she left.

"Now, Mr. Chambers, would you explain the first coded message to me."

JT told the Captain what had happened when they had gotten to the bridge and what happened after the Balaracian had shot at him.

"We searched for a weapon but couldn't find one. I looked the body over and all I could find was a bracket on his wrist. If I hadn't been wearing my space suit I would be dead now. Whatever he shot me with knocked me backward, burned the suit and raised a bruise on my chest." JT opened his uniform shirt and showed the Captain the bruise. When he was coming to he told the Captain what the alien was trying to do and how Sam had gotten away from him. He told him he had finally got a shot at the alien. How Sam had finished him off and what she had said to him.

"That's quite a gutsy girl you've got Mr. Chambers. There are not to many women who would take on anyone that way. Gunny and I thought something like that had happened. You two make a good team. And now you want to make it permanent."

"Yes Sir, She is quite a woman. We made it permanent yesterday morning. This is for the benefit of the world and her little sister."

"Gunny said you'd do the right thing."

"Actually Sir, she held me down with one hand, cocked her fist and told me that I had better make her an honest woman when we got back to Oz. I believe that's how she said it."

"She did? I'll bet you didn't fight to hard."

"No Sir, I didn't fight at all."

Dirk laughed. "I don't blame you one bit. She's one in a million. Now I think you had better go and get dressed for the up coming event that is going to change you life forever."

At twelve noon Dirk went down to their quarters and cleaned up for the wedding. He found a complete ISS Captains uniform laid out on the bed. I wonder where this came from. This is some fancy uniform. A set of gold wings were embroidered over the left breast. There was a knock on the door "Come" and Jasper came into the room. He was holding something in his right hand.

"Yes Jasper, what can I do for you."

"Sir, I thought these might come in handy at the awards ceremony you have planned." He handed Dirk four patches, which had names and ranks embossed on them, with a set of Gold Wings on the top. Dirk looked at them and then looked up at Jasper.

"Sir, this is my ship and I am the Chief Steward. It is my job to make sure all is run right. When I got the information you and Gunny had this planned, I made these up."

"Very good Chief, thank you." Dirk read the top one. Chambers, James T. Lt. U.S.A.S.F. Commanding Officer SS-202. The second was for, Chambers, Samatha J. Ens. U.S.A.S.F. First Officer SS-202. The third was, Chambers, Burt T. Mstr.Gun.Sgt. U.S.M.C. Commanding Officer SS-205. And the fourth was for, Triga, LTjg, U.S.A.S.F., Commanding officer NanMar SS-208.

Dirk looked at his watch. "It's time to go to the docking bay. I wonder where Mrs. Mac is?"

"Right here behind you."

Dirk turned and Kat was standing behind him wearing a striking light blue cocktail dress.

"Where did you get that, Saks, Fifth Ave.?"

"No, there are many dresses and other feminine stuff in the main store room. MJ came across them while doing her inventory. Wait till you see the bride. MJ and I have been planning this for a couple of days."

"You have! I didn't find out about it until this morning."

"Men, you just don't read between the lines, like we women do."

When they got to the docking bay there was a small alter set up with it's back to the open bay, there was a long red walker type rug stretched out leading to the alter. Dirk could even hear bagpipe music, faintly in the background.

"Where did you get the bagpipes?"

"It was in the file of discs the Arians had. Evidently they recorded every type of music we have on earth. Wasn't that nice of them? And besides she's a Ross."

"I'm surprised you didn't find a Kilt for me to wear."

"We looked, but alas, no Kilt. You look just fine in your Sailor suit."

"Sweet Jesus Kat, I worked hard for this uniform and these gold oak leaves."

Dirk went and took his place in front of the alter. JT and his father came in and stood by the side. JT heard the pipes break into Mari's Wedding and he turned to look up the isle. Sam came down the isle escorted by her father. She was wearing a beautiful white gown, a small tiara and a veil over her face. There was even a short train of white satin trailing behind her.

JT stood there mesmerized. He blinked his eyes and whispered to himself. "God, She's beautiful."

"Your right, she is." said his father.

Sam and Allen reached the front and JT took his place beside Sam. Dirk said the time honored words and then said "You may kiss your Bride." Which JT promptly did and Dirk said. "Ladies and Gentleman, it is my honor to be the first to present to you, Mr. and Mrs. James Tyrone Chambers." Everyone clapped and whistled. Sam and JT walked back up the isle arm in arm.

***

After all the hugging and kissing was done and everyone had their fill of cake and punch and the toasts were made. Sam changed back into her uniform.

Dirk came to the head off the table, tapped a glass and got everyone's attention. He called JT, Sam and Gunny to "Front and Center."

"Attention to orders: You will raise your right hand and repeat after me." He recited the Officers oath. "Lieutenant Chambers, you are hereby directed to take command of the SS-202 as Captain." JT stepped forward and received the patch Jasper had made up. JT saluted Dirk and stepped back. Dirk stepped over to Sam.

"Ensign Chambers you are hereby directed to take over the duties of First Officer on the SS-202." Sam stepped forward and received the patch and did her very best to give a proper salute. Dirk returned her salute. She stepped back. Dirk stepped over to Gunny. "Master Gunnery Sergeant Chambers, you are hereby directed to take Command of the SS-205 as Captain." They saluted and Gunny stepped back.

"Ensign Triga, step forward for receipt of orders." She came forth and stood in front of Dirk.

"Ensign Triga, you are hereby promoted to the rank of Lieutenant junior grade." They saluted and Triga stepped back to stand along side of Gunny.

"Officers, you are dismissed." Dirk saluted them.

CHAPTER THIRTY-ONE

After the party was over and everyone had gone back to their duties. Dirk and Mary were going over the star chart plotting a new course to 'Ozzie too' when Dirk said.

"We aren't even sure where this ship is. We could over run it by miles or it might not be on this track anymore. Why don't we call the pilots up here and go over this?" Dirk went to the com-panel and called the machine shop.

"Are JT, Gunny and Triga there?

"Yes Sir, they are."

"Have them come up to the bridge, please."

When they arrived at the bridge. Dirk looked up. Sam had come with them.

"Well folks we have a small dilemma here. Where is the Ozzie too? I think it is safe to assume she has moved. Now that the Balaracians have not shown up, I'm sure whoever is running the ship is smart enough to hide somewhere. I'm sure he or they have no knowledge about we humans being up and about." Dirk looked at JT and Sam. "Did you find any crystals on that ship?"

"No Sir, we check the ship out from stem to stern and found nothing."

"Where there any hidden panels?"

JT and Sam looked at each other and thought. JT said. "No Sir, we had the diagrams of the ship and Scaner could not find any."

"Well then, we'll have to go with the idea they have gone looking for the Balaracian ship. What did you do with the shuttle from the 202?" Dirk asked.

"We stowed it inboard. Then retreived the Balaracan shuttle" JT said.

Sam spoke. "Sir, we didn't check out the alien shuttle. All we did was load it and then came back here. If there are any crystals, they might be on it, hidden."

"Check on that the first chance you get."

"Yes Sir."

"The discs we brought back might have some knowledge of where they were to meet."

"Yes they might. Where are they?" and he held out his hand.

JT went over to the com-panel disc storage and took them out. "You put them here Sir, just before we went down to the docking bay earlier."

Dirk put in a disc and found nothing, which would indicate where the ship might be. All the disc had on it was information where it had been.

There was one small planet in a system just at the edge of their star chart that this craft had visited four times.

<u>I wonder what's on this little fellow that warrants four trips? It's way off the beaten path</u> Dirk reached over and circled it and put a question mark next to it. He took that disc out and placed in another. All this disc held was the transactions it had done and how much profit was turned. Dirk put in the last disc. There was a course plotted in and he transferred it to the star chart. It showed a course to the outer edge of the Alpha system.

"I'll bet this is going to be the rendezvous point. Triga plot a course to this point and how many days travel to it. Sub-light and at light speed."

"Sir, the Star Ships lack the capabilities of going to light speed."

"Captain, I can have four new mother boards made up by noon tomorrow and in place and checked out by 5:00 PM."

"All right JT, do it."

They left the bridge. JT looked at Gunny and Sam, "Before we left I had one almost completed. It won't take long to finish it. If I start now, I can have it completed in about an hour. You two can start on the other ones."

"Sounds good to me, son. If we run into any problems you can help us along. It really shouldn't take all that long to get them started."

"You two guys go down to the machine shop and I'll stop by the galley and get some cups and a thermos of hot chocolate."

"Good idea, Sam. Now that I have a new daughter, what am I supposed to call you?"

"How about Sam. Now what am I supposed to call you?"

"How about Gunny or Dad."

"Okay, see you guys in a couple minutes."

By the time Sam got down to the machine shop JT almost had the motherboard complete. He set out the parts for the other three and Gunny and Sam went to work. JT finished the board he was working on and started the last one. Sam and Gunny were having a little problem with one step and JT showed them how solder the micro-chips in place. Making sure there were no cold solders.

"If it's a cold solder, it won't work and will take time to find. It's not hard to fix, just to find."

They stopped for a drink break and Sam looked over to Gunny and asked. "How's the flying coming?"

"Well, I've got the 205 up and running at full capacity now. I changed over a lot of breakers and had to rebuild some of the wiring in the torpedo room. She's got a full stock of food and after we install this new board she'll be ready to hit the streets."

"We've got to fix a hole in the after end of 202. That's where the Balaracians hit us when we first popped into view." Sam smiled. "I'll bet that kind of spooked them, when all of a sudden we popped into view. JT slammed to throttle forward and we scooted under them but they still got a shot off. He turned on the cameras and when we finished the job, we looked the disc over. You could see the alien being pushed into space. We ran the disc over, one frame at a time, and saw the one we killed on the 202 leave. He hid out until the second day and then came aboard through the door in the elevator sleeve. You know, when you stop and think of it, he ran off and left his crewmember to fight us. That's probably what killed him. He then sneaked back and entered the 202, tried to kill JT and then rape me. To me, that's pretty cowardly."

"Well, the 202 is getting her hull patched now. She'll be ready to go tomorrow afternoon. Dad, have you been talking to Triga about jumping to light speed?" JT asked

"Yes, she has been holding classes and teaching Dick and Clare Jones how to fly a star ship. He's coming along fine but I don't think that she'll make it. She's a very good navigator and an excellent shot on the simms we've been holding on laser weapons. It seems she was on a woman's pistol and rifle team back in Idaho."

"Have you been studying the star charts?"

"Oh yes, that is something Triga has been pounding into our heads. When you go to light speed you always use the star charts."

"When we were plotting our course back to Oz, we looked at the regular nav chart. It didn't show the asteroid we had to avoid. If we hadn't used the star chart we would be in a dust cloud somewhere."

"OK, the mother boards are all ready to go. We can test them in the morning and then we'll all be able to jump to light speed."

"Let's button up here and then you kids hit the sack. I'm going to take a walk around then hit the sack myself."

JT and Sam took the empty cups and thermos back to the galley. They went to their old rooms to get their clothes and things and found they had been moved. There was a sign on one of the quarters on the outer side of the ship. It read "Bridal Suite and New home of Mr. and Mrs. J.T. Chambers". JT opened the door and was getting ready to walk in when Sam stopped him.

"Aren't you forgetting something?"

JT looked at her for a moment, reached down, picked her up and carried her across the threshold. Sam kissed him on the neck and whispered "I love you"

"I love you too."

He set her down. Looking around, saw a bottle of wine in a cooler and the view screen was open. There was a note by the cooler, "Congratulations, complements of the House." JT opened the bottle and poured two glasses and handed one to his bride.

"To us"

"To us" she repeated.

They sat down on the couch and relaxed. Sam looked at JT.

"I miss the 202, I feel like I'm staying in a motel." "Well, we can always go back to the 202 and stay onboard her. I think the Captain will okay it. After all, John and Mary are staying on the JonMar. If we have to get underway fast we'll be right there."

"Let's stay the night here and then we'll move everything on to the 202 in the morning. It's not like we have a whole lot."

***

They got up early the next morning, moved their clothes and few personal belongings into the 202. Went back to the galley for breakfast. Gunny came in, got breakfast and sat down with them. While they were talking about the installation of the motherboard on Gunny's 205 Susan came in.

"They just took Dad to sick bay."

Sam jumped up and went with Susan back to sick bay. Their mother stopped them at the door.

"I don't think your father is going to last the day. Ally is giving him a couple of tests now and asks us to be patient for an hour or so. Let's go back to the galley and sit for awhile."

"Let's go to your quarters and sit. I'll tell JT where we will be. Susan you go with Mom, I'll be right along." Sam went back to the galley and saw Mary and John, Dirk and Kat sitting with Gunny and JT. She went to JT and sat down.

"I'm going to go and sit with Mom and Susan. We'll be in Mom's room."

"Is there anything I can do?"

"Walk me back."

JT stood up and held his hand out to Sam. They walked back up the passageway to her folk's room. JT put his arms around Sam and held her tight. Sam leaned against him as if to draw strength from him.

"Hon, I'm going to be on the 205 first and then to the NanMar, the JonMar and then over to the 207. You call me if anything happens." He gave her a hug and said. "I love you." JT went back to the galley.

"Dad, I'm going to get the new board and install it on the 205."

Gunny looked up and nodded. He knew JT wanted to be alone. To get all this straightened out in his mind. After JT had left the rest of the crew there looked at Gunny.

"He'll be alright. He just needs to be alone for a little while. I know him, he'll work like crazy for a few minutes, think about the passing on of his new father-in-law. And when he gets it all settled in his own mind, he'll be a rock that Sam, MJ and Susan can lean on."

"Gunny, you have a fine son there. He's had to shoulder some terrific responsibilities in the past couple of weeks. I wish I had ten more like him in my squadron back on the 'Sara'. John, you've got the pinger up and running so why don't you, Mary, Triga, Dick and Clare come up to the bridge and we'll form a plan of attack. Gunny, you're going to be with JT. When he gets your ship checked out, call me and I'll send down the Captain of the next ship."

"Aye, aye Sir."

***

Gunny took his time going to the 205. Wanting to give JT some more time to himself. He had just walked onto the docking bay area, when he saw a small figure standing by the open bay door. He walked toward it. It was Susan, standing there with tears streaming down her face. Gunny didn't say a word. He just reached over and put his arm around her, pulling her to him. Susan leaned over. She put her arm around his waist and held on. "Gunny, what's Mom going to do now. She'll be all alone."

"No she won't, she'll have you and her friends here on Oz. And when we get back to Earth she'll have all of her friends there also."

"I expected to have a new brother but I didn't expect to loose my father."

"Hon, Your Dad's been a sick man for a long time. You knew that, and you knew he was going to pass on. Now it's up to you to carry on. He would want you to put your head up, square your shoulders and walk proud."

"I think it's time for me to go back to Mom and Sam." Susan stood on her tiptoes and kissed him on the cheek. "Thanks, Gunny." Gunny gave her a little hug and let go.

Susan walked off toward the elevator. Gunny saw her lift her head and bring her shoulders back. He saw her then as a very self-assured young woman. I wish Marlene and I had had a daughter. Gunny turned and went into the 205. JT was putting the finishing touches on the motherboard installation.

"Son, why don't you go to your wife and her family. I'm sure she could use you to lean on. I'll finish up here and check it out. If I need help, I'll call you."

"Thanks, Dad."

JT went over to the inter-com and contacted the bridge. "Captain, if Triga could come down to the 205. Gunny is finishing up here, then they could go over to the NanMar. They should be able to finish her tonight. I'll get the other three tomorrow. If you don't need me, I'd like to be Sam."

"You go to Sam. We're not getting to far here. In fact we're about ready to call it a night."

"Thank you, Sir."

JT looked over to his Dad. Gunny nodded. "I'll see you in the later."

"Good night, Dad."

JT left the 202 and went to sickbay. Ally met him at the door to the small room where Allen was. Ally told him it wouldn't be to long now. His vital systems were shutting down.

"How he hung on this long is a miracle. I've been around cancer patients for a few years and this is one for the books."

JT went into the room and went over to the side of the bed. Allen lay there not moving but his eyes were open. He recognized JT and lifted his hand. JT took his hand and held it.

"James, the girls are going to need you now more than ever. Susan is the one that is going to take this the hardest. Watch over her, she's my baby." JT just nodded his head. Allen started to gasp for air and JT called Ally back in. Ally looked up at the monitoring machines.

"You had better get MJ, Sam and Susan."

JT went down to the Ross's quarters. He knocked and went in. Sam looked up, saw the look on JT's face and came over to him.

"I think you all should come back to sick bay now."

The four went to sickbay and into Allen's room. MJ sat on the side of the bed while Sam and Susan were standing by his head holding his hands. Allen let go of Sam and motioned MJ closer, she bent down and he whispered something in her ear. MJ smiled and nodded her head. Allen reached up and took Sam's hand again. He let out a long soft sigh and the monitors went to straight lines. Allen had passed on. Sam reached over and placed her father's arm across his chest, Susan did the same. They both looked at JT. He held out his arms and they came over to him. JT held his wife and sister-in-law close. MJ stood, bent over and kissed Allen good-bye. She turned and said. "Let's leave, so Ally and Bruce can do what is necessary now."

MJ went out to the passageway and turned right toward the galley. She went over to the panel and got a hot drink and sat down.

When JT, Sam and Susan sat down with their drinks she looked up.

"Do we have a funeral here in space or wait until we get back to earth?"

"I think out here in space is right." Susan said. "He said it was so peaceful out here. Dad really wished he could have come out here sooner."

MJ looked at the three of them. "I think out here will be just fine. I'd like to think he will be near all of the time. Wherever heaven is, it can't be any closer than where we are right now."

"Ma'am, I'll talk to the Captain and asked him to perform the services, if you'd like."

"Yes JT, that would be fine. Susan, would you stay with me tonight?" Susan nodded.

MJ and Susan got up and reached for their cups. JT stopped them. "We'll clean up."

After they had left JT looked at Sam. "Let's go find the Captain." Sam nodded. JT picked up the cups and went over to the panel.

"Did you enjoy your drink?"

"Not really, thanks for asking."

JT and Sam went to the bridge, found Dirk and Kat looking out at space through the view panel. They turned as JT and Sam walked in.

"Our sincerest condolences, Sam, JT."

"Thank you Ma'am, Captain, would you hold services for Mr. Ross tomorrow?"

"Yes, it would a privilege. Would 0900 be acceptable."

"Yes, that would fine Captain." Sam said.

Kat came over, hugged the two of them and stood back.

"Thank you again Sir and good-night to you and Mrs. Mac." JT took Sam by the arm and they left to go to their quarters. They got ready for bed and as they lay there JT held Sam close while she cried away the passing of her father.

***

Dirk called down to the NanMar. "Gunny, can you do me a favor?"

"Certainly, Captain."

"Go to the torpedo room and prepare a shell for Allen. Paint it blue and gold. We'll use it for a casket. There'll be a small planet abeam of us tomorrow at 0900. We'll aim the casket at it. Place a homing device at the foot of the coffin. I'll fire a beacon to the planet. The casket will home in on the beacon. That'll keep it from floating around in space."

"Aye, Aye, Captain."

***

At 0900 the services for Allen Ross took place at the docking bay door. Kat had found the disc that she had been looking for and placed it in the inter-com panel. She took the remote with her and just before the closing she turned it on. The beautiful notes of "Amazing Grace" could be heard. Played by a single Piper. Dirk finished the service with an excerpt from a poem, "Home is the hunter, home from the hill, and the sailor home from the sea." Gunny pushed a button and the remains of Allen Ross shot out and into space, heading directly toward the small planet.

***

The Captain said. "I'd like the Captains and First Officers on the bridge at 1300. We have some work to do." The group broke off. At 1300 the Captains and First Officers arrived at the bridge.

"What we've got to do is figure out where 'Ozzie Too' is or approximately where she is. I'm sure she can't get to light speed. In fact, I believe she can't get full power. At least not enough to run everything at once. We have a lot of 'Ifs' here." Dirk put the star chart up on the view screen. Everyone studied it for a while.

Triga said. “If I were running ‘Ozzie Too’, I’d head to this position here.” and she pointed to a position between the fourth and fifth planets in the Alpha system. “First of all you would have a hiding place for a very large ship. Second, you would be in a position to guard both space routes.”

Sam pointed to the fourth planet. “You would also be able to get down to the Alpha planet for food and water. This is the planet they were looking to repopulate?”

“Yes, it is. That’s according to their information. It could be they have over looked something and wouldn’t be able to colonize it.” Dirk said.

“Sir, I don’t think that should be taken into consideration. The Arians have been at this a lot longer than we have. They had to do some serious investigations and tests before they would just land and say let’s live here. Sir.” Sam said.

“Well, they did come to earth and contracted the Asian flu. That knocked them down and killed some of them.” Dirk said.

“There could be a bug or virus down there we don’t know about, one that could knock us down. It could be in the food taken from the planet or the water or even the air.” Kat said.

Triga spoke. “It wouldn’t be from any of those. Because the food, water and air that we have here on Oz has all come from Alpha. The Oz went out here several times on its first run. In fact, it spent a few months here planting seeds and seedling trees from your planet. If my figures are correct, it has been over one hundred and fifty of your earth years, since Oz came here the first time. Ozzie Too has been here for quite a while and has probably visited it quite often.”

“Which way would you conduct an attack on an element of force you knew was right here?” Dirk asked, looking at Mary.

“Sir, I’m not a strategist, but I think we should form a V formation and come up at light speed and then spread out. We can form a semi-circle and have the Ozzie Too in a cross fire position.”

JT looked over to his father, who nodded.

"Sir, If two SS's were to flank the Oz and the other three went in, one on each side and one behind 'Ozzie Too'. We could capture it without too much of a fight. If Oz and two SS's jumped to light speed a little after us, we could all be in position at once." JT picked up a grease pencil and went to the star chart. "This is Ozzie Too. We are coming from here. He knows this and will be expecting it. If Oz were to maneuver to a position over here, it would give us a straight shot to the other ship. The likely hood of them watching this route is almost nil. He'd have all his weapons pointed in this direction. The three SS's fly right by him. Positioning themselves at points here, here and here. We would have the back door and you covered. If anyone tries to sneak up on us, we'll be covering each other. There is only one thing he can do. And that's put his hands up."

"He could choose to blow up the ship and kill everyone near him too." Triga said.

John spoke. "We could give him a minute to surrender and then I could hit him with a single ping. I guarantee at this range no one will be standing up. They'll all be laying on the floor holding onto their ears wondering what-in-the-hell hit them." John looked over to JT and Sam and said. "While you two were off on your scavenger hunt, I tested the pinger out on an asteroid. It shook 'All' of the dust off of it and returned a reading as to distance. This hummer packs a hell of a wallop."

Dirk went over to the star chart and ran off a copy of it. It showed an identical set up of the plan JT had suggested.

"It took two of us a day and a half to come with the exact same plan JT took ten minutes to come up with. Only I didn't have the center SS down low covering the underside. Did you and Commander Richie ever go over battle strategy?"

"Yes Sir, We went through all of the missions he flew, trying to figure out if there was a better way. Most of them were done right."

"Most of them?"

"The only things we could improve on were the angles of attack."

"OK, I can see that now. That's good thinking. I like that in my pilots. Well done." Dirk looked around. "Does anyone have anything to add. OK, we've got six and a half days now to get to point 'A'. We've got three ships to convert to light speed. If we jump to light speed in two days, no, let's make it three days. That will put us in position in 2 hours and 30 minutes. Let's get back to work and worry about the small things as they come up. Would the pilots please stay behind for a minute. Thank you people for coming up."

JT wondered what the Captain had in mind. <u>A scouting mission maybe. That would be the thing I'd do. Just to take a peek at where the other guy was.</u>

***

After they had all left Dirk turned to JT. "Could I see you out side for just a moment." Looking at the others. "Would you excuse us?"

JT looked at his father. He followed the Captain. JT closed the door and looked at the Captain.

"Before you came up here for this meeting, did you discuss your plan with anyone?"

"No Sir."

"Did you know what this meeting was going to be about?"

"Sir, I thought it would a briefing about the upcoming event. I had no prior knowledge it was to set up a plan of attack."

"Good."

Dirk and JT went back onto the bridge.

"What I'm going to say now is by no means to be construed as a lack of faith in anyone's abilities. Lieutenant Chambers is appointed Commander of the SS fighter group. Each pilot is to follow his orders as if they came from me."

"Yes Sir."

"Aye, aye, Sir."

"Yes Sir."

"That will be all, dismissed."

JT stayed behind. "Captain, could I have a word with you, Sir?"

"Yes Lieutenant."

"Sir, there are people who have more experience than me at command, Lieutenant Triga, Captain Mayhan and my father."

"I want Captain Mayhan to guard the flank of Oz because of her experience. The other ship will be piloted by Lieutenant Triga. Triga is a fine pilot but she has had no combat experience and doesn't react quick enough. If she did, she wouldn't have been injured back at the junk pile. I was watching the operation from up here. She had time to get out of the way of that piece of machinery. She's just lucky to be alive. How are you coming along on the other three ships?"

<u>I think that was the beginning, the middle and the end of this conversation.</u> thought JT. "They will all be ready to go at 5:00 PM, Sir.

"Very well." and Dirk turned back to the star chart.

JT left the bridge and walked to the elevator. Gunny stepped in along side of him.

"Had to ask, huh?"

"Yes Dad, I did. I don't think he should have put me over Captain Mayhan, Lieutenant Triga or you. All of you have more experience at this than I. He did tell me why though. And I have learned a lesson here too. The next time it's 'Aye, Aye Sir' and go do it. He's got his reasons. And besides, he's the Captain."

"Son, let's go down to the docking bay. I've got something I want to tell you, about you." When they reached the bay they walked over to the outside view stand.

"First thing, the Captain did pick the right man for the job, you. He didn't say a word to me or ask me what I thought. I'm a Master Gunnery Sergeant and that's it. I knew he'd pick you because of your abilities. You react fast and correctly. You have the ability to think even when you're at a dead run. If you couldn't, you wouldn't have been the Captain and Quarterback for three years at High School and for two years at college. Triga is not that type of person. If it's not spelled out in the manual she's lost. She's learning by her mistakes. She's getting a lot of bumps and bruises but she is learning."

"Captain Mayhan is a great teacher but she's to slow on the up take about a fast fire-fight. She's a great wingman, but she's got a lot to learn about instant command decisions. She doesn't even realize you saved her bacon the other day back at the junk pile. After you took out the first one and came over to help us. The one we were after had us dead to rights. Your quick maneuver made him hesitate just long enough for her to get a shot in. She shot at him with a damn torpedo when she should have been at 110 percent and using a laser. I asked her about that and was told the manual called for that type of a run. Fuckin' near got us killed."

"Son, I've been though Korea and Vietnam. I know a good Officer when I see one. I'm talking about one that doesn't mind throwing the manual away and doing what's right. You let this little talk go to your head and we'll have another. One about your health and welfare. When you are out there, you've two things to worry about, your ship and your men. Now you've one more, your wife, she's your First Officer. If I didn't think you could handle this. I'd be the first to talk to the Captain. Now let's get back to work."

"Gunny, that's the longest pep talk or ass-chew'n I ever got, even from you, Thanks."

After they climbed down from the platform, they both had a new spring to their step. "Did you get the BurMar checked out, after I left last night?"

"Yes, she's working fine ----- BurMar?"

"Yeah, the BurMar, I figured you would never rename her, so we did. You know, Burt and Marlene. BurMar, just like that."

JT pointed to the bow of the 205. And there in big block letters was the name BURMAR and under it, SS-205 U.S.A.S.F.

"Sam and I were thinking of a name for ours but JamSam or SamJam, just didn't get it. So we decided to just keep the painting on each side of the 'Kick-Ass' and let it go at that. And besides Sam was the one who named her. Up front and astern are just the letters SS-202 with U.S.A.S.F. under that."

"Triga and I have almost got the NanMar done, so let's check her out. And then go on to the JonMar and then the 207."

***

They went up to the reactor room in the NanMar and found Triga trying to get the last of the wiring together. JT pointed to a couple of wires, which were attached, wrong and fixed them.

"What would have happened if I tried to start the ship with those on backwards?"

"Nothing, she just wouldn't start. No problem now."

They tested the NanMar out and everything worked fine. JT made sure she had extra crystals and all of the circuit breakers were at specks.

"She's ready, let's go over to the JonMar."

When they got there Mary had the old panel out and all of the circuit breakers were open. Good, at least she doesn't screw around with anything that she's not sure of thought Gunny. JT slid the new motherboard into place and secured it. Attaching the wiring harness, he looked over to Mary.

"Start the generator up."

He pushed the circuit breakers in and the SS-204 came to life. Gunny set the twenty-two and a half, carat crystal in place and nodded to JT. He set the dials to start and the crystal started to glow. As it warmed up you could see the changes in the hue. They gave her a couple of minutes to warm up and then JT stood aside while Mary switched the dials to run.

She checked the circuit breakers and felt the sides of the panel for over heating. They went around the ship checking the panels and firing control systems. Everything was perfect so they went back to the reactor room.

Gunny put his hand on the dome covering the crystal. He looked over to JT and Mary.

"Mary, put your hand here." and pointed to the other side of the dome. She did, if she could feel anything she didn't say a word. For some reason Gunny thought I'm glad that I'm not flying with her. I believe a pilot has to have certain awe about the craft that's his or hers. She doesn't have it. To her this is nothing more than a machine. He took his hand away and looked over to JT. "One more to go." and they left.

JT thought, She didn't even say thanks or even good-by. Ooops, here comes trouble again.

They left the 204 and went towards the 207. JT looked at his father.

"Is there any truth in the saying, 'That hell has no fury like a woman scorned' or as in this case one who thinks she has?"

"Damned right. Right now she bears watching. It's those railroad tracks your wearing that really pisses her off. Along with not being made Commander of the SS's. You just do your job Lieutenant Chambers. Your First Officer and the Gunny will train the troops."

***

They got to the reactor room to find the whole Jones family there. The twins were standing there doing their best to look like attentive crewmembers. JT smiled at them. Rebecca took that as an okay and ran over to him and hugged him. JT hugged her back.

"OK, guys let's get her ready for light speed."

JT explained the process step by step and point out some of the hot spots to look, in case something went wrong in flight. All four soaked it up like they were blotters. It took a little while longer than normal to get her up and running but it was worth the effort.

They all asked questions, even the twins. Clare and Rebecca left the reactor room but were back in a few minutes with hot chocolate and homemade cookies.

Gunny stepped over to the dome covering the crystals. He looked at the Jones. "If you put your hands right here you can feel the life you've given her."

The twins came over and set their hands were Gunny showed them. They started to grin. Dick and Clare came over and Gunny took his hand away and pointed to the places to put theirs.

"She is alive." Clare said. "It's like she's making us a part of her."

"I know what you mean, Hon. You know Gunny, I was in the Navy and it's the crew that makes a ship come alive. Just like we've done here with the 207." Dick looked at his family. "We gave this ship life and now she's sharing it with us. Thank you, Gunny and you too, JT. Come, put your hands with ours."

When all of their hands were placed on the dome they could feel a slight acceleration from the dome as the crystal picked up the heat from their hands. It was indeed as if the 207 was welcoming them.

JT knew the reason for the increase in power was from the lesser heat of their hands. The sensors inside the dome were telling the exciter, 'more heat, please', but he didn't say anything.

"It's time I called the Captain and reported all of the ships are up to par and should have no problem going to and maintaining light speed."

When they were getting ready to leave JT leaned over to Clare.

"If you get a chance, sneak that cookie recipe to Sam, I'd appreciate it. They are delicious."

Gunny and JT were walking back to the elevator when JT stuck his hand in his pocket and came out with a couple of cookies.

"Want one?"

"Yeah, what did you do, 'cop' a hand full?"

"Ayah", they both laughed.

Sam came out of the Elevator and heard them laughing.

"OK, what are you two thieves up to now?"

JT held out a cookie. "Want one?"

"Wow, these are good. Where did you get them?"

"From Clare. If you talk to her real nice, I'll bet she'll give you the recipe."

"I was coming out to ask you if you had eaten yet."

"That's what Dad and I were getting ready to do. Ask you and MJ and Susan if you had already eaten."

"Mom and Susan have, I was waiting for you."

"Dad, eat with us on the 202."

Gunny knew the invitation was not for dinner only. JT had something on his mind and he wanted to talk about it. Something, which would include his wife.

"Well, I've never tasted any of this young ladies cooking yet. Is it safe?"

Sam reached over and punched Gunny on his arm. "Watch it Buster or you'll get warmed up cat food."

Gunny had to laugh and held onto his arm faking sever pain. They turned around and headed over to the 202. Gunny put his arm around Sam. "Thanks for renaming the 205." And gave her a little squeeze.

Sam kissed him on the cheek. "You're welcome."

***

Gunny and JT went up to the bridge and brought up a nav chart.

"What I want to do is take the ships out tomorrow for a little training exercise. I want to set up some kind of scenario and take it to the Captain, then let him shoot holes in it. But before I do, I wanted you and Sam to look it over."

"Just what did you have in mind?"

"I thought by sending two craft out as ducks and letting the others go out to hunt them down, then get into a dog fight. It would be good practice for all of us. But now with the trouble Mary is going start. I've got to give it a great deal of thought. She's going to try to live up to her call sign and zing everyone. If for no other reason than to show off."

"Well, you set up the scenario you want and we'll go over it after dinner. I'm going to go down to the galley and pester Sam. You work up a battle plan."

"OK, I'm going to get Scaner up here and plug him in. He's pretty good at punching holes in ideas."

JT walked over to the inter-com panel and brought up Scaner. He was in the machine shop getting his batteries charged by Tribec.

"Tribec, when you get Scaner charged up, would you send him to the 202, please."

"Roger, Sir."

***

Mary had been sitting in the pilot chair on the JonMar, fuming all this while. She was thinking of the ways she used to trick her student pilots into making a mistake. Just so she could zing them over the airways. She didn't even go to the main galley for dinner. Mary chose to eat onboard "her" ship. She was still sitting there went John came aboard.

He came up to the bridge, saw her sitting there and thought she was working on a piloting problem. If he knew now what he was going to learn tomorrow, he would have booted her on the backside. Telling her to straighten up and start acting like an Air Force Officer. Not like some ten-year-old that didn't get her own way.

***

Sam had made BLT's and a potato salad. She called up to the bridge and told JT that "Soups on". JT stopped by their quarters and washed up and then went into the galley. Gunny and Sam had just sat down when he got there.

"These are the best BLT's I have ever eaten." Gunny said.

JT took a bite. "What's in them?"

"It's and old family recipe. And don't beat around the bush. Out with it." Sam said.

"What I plan on doing is this." and JT told them what he wanted to do tomorrow.

"I wanted you two to look at it and shoot holes in it."

"Well, I'll look at it but I don't know if I'll be able to shoot holes in it. First of all I really don't know much about battle plans and I'm not a good pilot." Sam said.

"Three sets of eyes are better than one and you might just surprise yourself."

"OK, I'll do my best."

***

Going to the bridge. They looked over the scenario JT had made. The planning of it was perfect as far as the navigation was concerned. Gunny asked if letting the 207 lead a head on like that would be a good idea.

"If he got left out there alone and against two ships, one of them would get him."

"Not if his wingman does her job. There is going to be three ships out there, me, you and Triga. I'll be off over here and then come in slow. With you flying on Triga's wing. Dick should come in and break to her open side and then come around and shoot. If his wingman does her job and swings under and covers his left side, he'll get his shot. Then they can come after you. The rolls will be reversed and he will then become wingman. It's a slick maneuver and it works. I know, we used to do it back home in our light planes."

"About the time Dick goes in for his shot, I'm going to come out of here", he pointed at a spot "and attack his open side. You should be doing a turning climb to the right and come back toward me. Then they will have to take us on, one on one. I don't think Dick is going to be hard to combat, but Mary will. One thing we've all got to remember if the Captain buys this he's going to be watching us like a hawk."

"Hon, like I said I'm no expert but aren't you dumping a little to hard on Dick." Sam said.

Gunny interrupted "No, I don't think it's to hard. I think JT's trying to teach Dick two things here. One, rely on your wingman and two, this could have been for real. All of us here know what combat is like. You've been in two scrapes and I've been in one. All we know is he used to be in the Navy. Mary has been in one scrape out here but she was in the Gulf War we had back on earth. Triga is a product of the National Space Academy on Arian. Dick is the one we have to train. I personally think he will do all right." Gunny looked around at JT and Sam. "Any one else got any ideas? Well, I think what you should do now is show this to the Captain. We'll be waiting for you in the lounge."

Gunny looked at Sam. "New daughter of mine, let's go see what the other half is doing. If you act right and promise not to get silly. I'll let you buy me a beer."

"Huh! First of all, there ain't no beer. And second, I could drink you under the table. How do you like them apples? New Pop of mine."

Gunny stood up and extended his arm and she took it. The pair strolled out of the bridge and down onto the deck of the docking bay.

***

JT rolled up his nav chart and told Scaner to unplug and the two of them left the 202. When JT got to the bridge he knocked and stepped in. The Captain was also looking at a nav chart. Susan was there, watching and asking questions.

"Could I speak with you for a minute, Captain?"

"Certainly, what's on your mind?" Spotting the nav chart.

"I'll leave." Susan said.

"No, it's all right if you stay." JT said. "If it's alright with the Captain?"

"Stay, sometimes three heads are better than two. What have you got there?" Dirk said.

JT rolled out the nav chart and explained what he want to do. Showing the Captain the scenario he had come up with and why he had placed the ships in such a manner. Dirk looked at the nav chart for a long time. He even stood back and looked at it.

"This is a good plan. Safe to, no big rocks floating around for people to run into. What time did you want to start this."

"Sir, I thought 0800 would be a good time. Everyone will be done with breakfast. After a short briefing, we could be airborne at 0830 and then the two hunters could come out after us at 0845."

"OK, that's sounds good to me. We'll be watching from the bridge."

"Yes Sir." JT turned and left the bridge, with the chart tucked under his arm.

***

JT went forward to the lounge and sat down next to Sam. "Hello, what's this?" Pointing at the glasses in front of them.

"Home brew, my son, home brew. It seems our Mrs. Jones is a lass of many talents. It was made right here in space and properly aged, four days. And has been deemed suitable, by me, for human consumption."

"He tricked me. He knew about the home brew all of the time. He was just trying to get me to buy. But I told him I would wait awhile before I drank him under the table."

"Well, seeing that no one is going to jump up and say 'Stay here, I'll buy', I'll just go and get my own." After JT came back, he raised his glass and said "Tomorrow".

Sam looked at him. "It's on?"

"It's on."

MJ walked in and saw the three of then sitting over in the corner with very suspicious looking glasses in front of them. She walked over and sat down next to Gunny. Reaching over she picked up Sam's glass and took a sip.

"Aren't you a little young to be drinking this stuff?"

"Mother! I'm a married woman now."

JT looked at his Dad. They both shrugged their shoulders as if to say "That's that".

Gunny looked at MJ. "We're going out on a little test run tomorrow and I need a First Officer. Tribec is going out with Triga and Gorex will be with Mary. Would you be interested in going along as my First?"

MJ didn't say a word, just got up and went over to get a glass of home brew. JT looked at his father and then leaned over to Sam and whispered in her ear.

"How many brews as he had?"

She extended three fingers.

<u>Oh boy, this is going to be a duzzie</u>

Gunny leaned out, looking around Sam and said, "Hey BAM, I asked you a question."

MJ stopped in her tracks and turned around. "Who are you calling a BAM, you piss-pot jarhead."

"You really got her attention now, Dad."

Gunny sat there smiling and looking at MJ. Sam and JT were watching MJ, getting ready to duck. All of a sudden she started to smile, then turned around to get her drink. She came back and sat down next to Gunny.

"I ought to pour this in your lap."

"Now that would a waste of good beer. I was serious about First Officer."

MJ looked at Gunny, "Yes, I'll be your First Officer. And you had better be a damn good pilot. No screwing around out there cause you're not going to get me air sick."

"You got it." and they clinked glasses.

The three had another home brew. Gunny had three.

"Is your Dad going to be all right in the morning?"

"Sure, the only time you have to worry is when he gets to numbers 23 and 24. Then he jumps up, sings bawdy songs and dances with all of the pretty girls. Then he'll have a hang over. Other than that, he's fine."

***

JT and Sam got ready for bed set the clock for a 6:00 AM call and got in between the sheets. JT rolled over onto his stomach and asked.

"Would you rub my back and shoulders? I bet you could play a tune on my shoulder muscles. I'm beginning to understand why the Captain is a little short with people once in a while. I don't think this command stuff is all it's cracked up to be."

Sam sat over JT's lower back with her knees under her and started to give JT a massage. After finishing there she slid down over his buttocks and sat on his lower legs. She started to massage his lower back and thighs. JT started to squirm a little and she looked up at his face. He was smiling back at her over his shoulder. She rolled him over and then laid down full length on top of him. After they had made love. They lay there in each other's arms. "You've got another problem about tomorrow don't you?"

"Yes, I do. I'm sure it will work out. It has to work out, if this mission is going to be a success."

"Does this have to do with a certain female pilot?"

"Yup, but I'd rather not talked about it right now."

"Pardon the expression. If she 'fucks-up', she's going to have the Skipper to contend with, and that ain't gonna be a fun trip."

"I know, and there's got to be away to prevent it from happening."

"Have you talked to Gunny about it?"

"We talked, he saw it coming long before I did. You know twenty-five years in the Marine Corp, you get to read people real well. We'll just have to wait until tomorrow morning."

They fell asleep in each other's arms.

***

As far as JT was concerned 6:00 AM rolled around to fast. They got up, showered and put on clean uniforms. As they were getting ready to leave to go to the galley Sam stopped JT. She turned him around and gave him a big hug. They went down to the galley. All the pilots and First Officers were there. Except for Mary. Dirk and Kat came in, got breakfast and sat down at the table with crews.

"Lieutenant Chambers, I informed the crews there will be a briefing on the docking deck at 0800."

"Thank you Sir, I was about to call Captain Mayhan and inform her."

At 0745 people started to file out toward the Docking area. JT went over to the corkboard and pinned up the nav chart. At exactly 0759 Captain Mayhan came in sat down, speaking to no one.

JT thought. <u>She's really got her back up straight. And will you look at all those "I was there ribbons"</u> He looked at each person before speaking.

"What we're going to do today, is a couple of mock battle scenarios. After each one there will be a debriefing, done by the Captain. He will be going over the exercise after each one's told him what he or she did and why. Each of us will be able to improve our flying techniques."

JT outlined what he wanted done. He pointed to Dick. "Captain Mayhan will be flying as your wingman on the first problem. Each team has a channel to talk over. Everyone will monitor 121.5. The defenders will wait here until 0845 before entering their ships. That will give the aggressors a little edge. I don't know how they say this in the Armed Forces but at home it's; 'Fly safe and be safe'. OK, it's 0820, let's go and get warmed up. Take off is at 0830."

I don't know why but those ribbons aggravate me. This is a training mission not a bloody parade JT went toward Mary he saw she was not going to stand as due his station, as Flight Commander. It was a simple courtesy all pilots give their Commanders. Gunny had taught him that. He stopped, looked down for a few seconds before speaking. The others were watching.

"Captain Mayhan, I sincerely hope those ribbons will not hinder your ability to fly. Also, Captain, isn't it a common courtesy to stand when the Flight Commander leaves." JT left her there as she attempted to stand.

Dirk looked over to Gunny. They were reading each other's mind. JT was right in saying that to her, she deserved it

Dirk turned and went back to the bridge with Susan tagging along right behind. I know one Air Force Captain that had better shine today she thought.

JT and his team set out for their designated spots. They arrived on station at 0930.

"We'll hold here until 0955 and then go slowly toward the Oz. Just before we get into their range we'll go to 80 percent and after we are in range we will go to 100 percent. Don't use 110 percent unless you have to, like avoiding a collision. I'm going to my station now. Fly safe and be safe. 202 out"

"Click, click."

"Click, click."

JT knew the Captain would be watching both flights and did a short prayer for his team, all five of them.

"0955, commence run."

"Click, click."

"Click, click."

They surged forward. JT powered a little more and went wider. The two hunters came into view on their screens. JT saw the two ships in his team go to 80 percent. Then when they were in range, go the 100 percent. Everything went as he planned it. Dick pulled high and to the right and started to make his turn toward Triga. Dick was doing it right, without any coaching. JT turned in and went after Dick.

Mary picked JT up on her screen and immediately broke off and came at him. The fight was on. JT told Sam to hang on. She was coming at him at 110 percent. In a manner one would call, very aggressive. JT watched her go a little wide and then do a quick roll back to the left, trying to get her guns to bear.

JT faked a left turn and slammed on the brakes causing Mary to fly right by his nose. He didn't fire. Instead he poured on the power. The 202 leaped ahead like a mad cat. He maneuvered in behind her and once again did not fire.

All Mary heard, both times, was 'click, click'. She knew she was dead meat both times. Mary had let anger and frustration kill her.

Unknown to JT, Sam had the cameras split. Half were on what they were doing. The other half on their group. JT called over the inter ship channel.

"Break off. Let's go to the barn. Form up on the 207, 50 percent throttle. That was good flying Dick."

***

After they had formed up, Sam replayed the fight between Dick, Triga and Gunny. JT saw Dick do a snap roll as soon as he found out Mary had deserted him. He brought his ship back out and underneath the NanMar. He got a clear shot but he had lost track of Gunny and couldn't recover in time to find him. Gunny had done an Immelman turn (which is a half loop up and then a half roll at the top). He had flown straight out and then did a

Split-S (A half roll and then a half loop down. Back over your own head, decreasing the throttle to minimize altitude loss.). When he came out of this, he was right on Dick's tail. If Dick had done a Split-s then, he could have broken off and went for a better try at Gunny.

When the formation approached Oz, JT told them how he wanted to stow the ships. Mary was to go in and take the extreme starboard spot, Triga to take the extreme port, Dick to take the center and go all the way back and then Gunny in last. He would dock outside on the roof.

"Be careful going in. Break now." JT said.

The ships broke formation and they started to land one at a time. JT went up and over the roof to the last docking sight. The one which would put them over the elevator to the docking bay.

Sam went down to the elevator compartment. As soon as the struts had locked onto Oz, she started the rails down. When they were locked into place she lowered the sleeve, and pressurized it. JT shut down the 202 but left the power switches in the start position. He met Sam at the elevator. She saw he had the film disc with him. They went to the docking bay and over to the debriefing table. The other pilots were just leaving their ships. JT handed her the disc.

"Sam, would you mind waiting here with the other pilots and the Captain." and he turned on his heel and walked toward Captain Mayhan. Sam didn't even get a chance to say okay.

Everyone could feel the sparks jumping. JT slowly walked up to Captain Mayhan.

"Would you please join me over here, Captain." and he walked over to the far side of the bay, out of sight of the crew, turned and looked at her.

"Is it not proper in the Air Force to stand at attention while your Commanding Officer is talking to you." Mary snapped to attention.

"Captain, you are to be congratulated. Your display of flying killed ten people." JT waited for that to sink in. "You killed yourself and your First Officer, Dick, Clare and R & R, Lt. Triga and her

First Officer. You broke a major rule of combat flight, 'Don't ever leave your wingman'. Captain, you broke the faith. You hung your wingman out to dry because you have an attitude problem. You came after me like an avenging demon. Throwing caution to the winds got yourself and your First Officer killed."

"Like I said, all those pretty ribbons got in the way of you're flying. You want to see ribbons? Ask Gunny to show you his sometime. He's got the Navy Cross, Silver Star with a cluster, Purple Heart with four clusters. He even did a 'Walk-about' with the Army and received the CIB (Combat Infantry Badge) for that."

"Those, 'I was there ribbons' don't impress me and like I said, they got in the way of your flying."

"For your general information. I started flying when you were a sophomore in high school. I had my private, my commercial, and was being instructed in air-to-air combat maneuvers along with a ground school when you were in your third year at the Wild Blue School (Air Force Academy). Get a pencil and paper out sometime and figure it out."

"'YOU' stand at attention, Captain Mayhan. I'm not done talking to you yet. If I had the authorization, I'd ground you right now. As far as I'm concerned you have neither the right to fly nor the right to command a Star Ship. I do not want you in my fighter group if you cannot take orders and carry them out. Do I make myself clear, Captain?"

"Yes Sir. I offer no excuse for my actions. Sir."

"Captain, what happens now is up the Skipper. He has my report on the matter in front of him. Along with the last part of what I said you. That is all I have to say. You are dismissed.

Mary took a step backward and then saluted, waiting for JT's return salute, which he did. She then did an about face and walked away. She stopped and turned around.

JT thought. Oh shit, what now!

"Sir, you said ten people."

"I let you go twice. Didn't you hear the double click?" She nodded. "That was Sam, she's the one who did the 'Kick-Ass' on you, twice. We're a hell-of-a-team, aren't we, Captain."

Little did JT know, but the way the docking bay was built, everyone on the other side of the bay could hear the ass chewing he was giving her, including Captain Mac and her husband. Everyone pretended they didn't, but it was very clear to all. And everyone could swear they heard an "anal orifice" hit the deck. Most were thinking. I'm glad that's not me.

Gunny thought. That was even better than Marine Gunny could do. And he never raised his voice.

Susan thought. Wow, I hope I never piss him off.

I hate to do this but I'm going to have to chew her out again. Dirk said to himself.

John thought. She really screwed the pooch this time.

The twins just stood there with their mouths open.

MJ thought. That was even better than I could have done.

JT walked up to the pilot area. Chief Tribec stood and called out "Attention on Deck" even though the Captain was standing there.

All JT could think of was Dirks usual reply. "As you were."

As far as this crew was concerned, JT had all their respect. He had proven himself in battle twice and now he acted as a Commanding Officer should have. He gave a subordinate a dressing down in private. And the beauty of it was he never raised his voice. The art of tactfulness is defined as, "The ability to tell someone to go to hell in such a manner, they look forward to the trip." JT has tack.

JT went up to the Nav chart and turned around "I apologize for the delay, Captain."

"Carry on."

"I have a film disc I would like to show. Everyone look at the maneuvers these ships did."

The lights were shut down and the film came on. It showed the 207 and the JonMar coming in to attack. How Dick had maneuvered to make the turn shot keeping the 205 on the other side of the NanMar. It was a perfect side shot set up. It showed the JonMar leaving its post as wingman and going off on its own, leaving the 207 to fend for its self. They saw the maneuver Dick did to save his ship and then come up underneath the NanMar. Also the maneuver the Gunny did to get the shot at the 207.

JT turned the lights back on and turned the briefing over to Dirk by saying one word, "Captain" and stood back.

Dirk came to the front of the nav chart and faced the crews of the Fighter Group. "What I saw today was some very impressive flying and I'll show you why. Jasper, would you turn on the projector." A grid map of the combat area showed up on the screen. "You will notice how the 207 came right and then went into the attack, good maneuver. The 204 at this time should have gone under and protected the left. Blocking the 205 from making a counter attack. The 204 did not and broke off on its own. The 207 realizing this, broke, dove down. Then moved in behind the 208 getting a shot off. The 205 did an Immelman and then a Spilt-S enabling it to come up behind the 207 and getting a shot."

"After the 208 was killed, the 207 should have done a tight turn to the right and thus bringing it around to set up for another shot at the 205 and also protecting it's wingman. Dick, I noticed there was only one film disc from the 207."

"Sir, the aft cameras were not functioning." Dirk turned and looked at JT

"I'll check into it, Captain."

"If your cameras were functioning you would have been able to see the 205 coming up behind you. Seeing they weren't, that is reason enough to shoot and then break off, hit 110 percent and then relocate. We are going to have another flight this afternoon at 1500, so prepare your-selves. All in all, this was some good flying. The main thing is fly right and stay safe."

Dirk started to leave and Gunny said. "Attention on deck".

Dirk went up to Captain Mayhan and said. "Report to me on the bridge at 1300." and kept on walking toward the elevator.

***

"Dick, let's go over to the 207 and check out the aft cameras. They need to be working if you're going into combat." JT said.

"Aye, aye Sir.

As they were walking toward the 207 Rebecca came up between the two of them, slipping a hand into theirs. JT looked down and winked at her and gave her hand a little squeeze.

"There's something I would like to ask you, Dick. Do you and Clare plan on taking R&R out all of the time?"

"JT, we talked about it. Weighed the pros and cons and came up with, we're a family. Being out here is no picnic. What if we left the kids here and Oz was attacked. Or we were attacked. Clare and I would be devastated if anything should happen to them and they feel the same way."

"They're fourteen now and old enough to make up their own minds. We're a family and we fly as a family. We're good and we're getting better. Each person has his or her own jobs to perform. What I'm saying is, 'We stick together'. Is this going to be a problem with the fighter Group?"

"No one has said anything to me nor to the Captain that I know of. It is certainly not a problem with me. In fact Sam wanted me to ask if we could take one of the twins out with us sometime. One, one time and the other the next."

"That would be OK with me. I'll talk to Clare about it. The next thing to do would be to ask them."

"Oh Daddy, could I go out with JT and Sam, Please?"

"Ask your Mom."

Rebecca took of running toward the 207 in search of her Mom.

***

Dick and JT reached the 207 and went to the bridge. Dick turned on the aft cameras and both check the breakers, okay. They checked the wiring harness, okay. Dick Jr. turned on the main computer and brought up the schematics on the camera systems.

"The schematics on the main computer show no breaks or shorts, Dad. It has to be the cameras."

JT looked at Dick "He certainly got to the heart of the matter."

"Well, lets go check the cameras out."

"Dad, I've got an idea."

"OK, lets have it." JT and Dick both listened "That's good, son, do it."

Dick Jr. went over to the inter-com and contacted the bridge. "Bridge here."

"Captain, this is the 207. Sir, is Susan up there and may I speak to her."

"What's up DJ?"

"Can you get the fork lift and a people box, then come over to the 207? We need to check out the aft cameras."

"Sure, I'll be there in five minutes, SeeYa."

"What's with the DJ?" Dick asked.

"Susan started it. She said that Richard Junior was just to damn long and stuck DJ on me. We all decided that Rebecca was to long. Now it's Reb, DJ and SR." DJ reached over and threw the switch, rigging out the aft cameras. The three of them went out and around to the after end of the ship.

Susan came up with the forklift and the people box. "Who goes up?"

"We do." DJ said. All three got into the box and set up the safety chains. Susan lifted them toward the first camera. They knew what the problem was before they got all the way up. The camera lenses were broken. DJ stuck his fist out and Susan stopped them. DJ pointed to the next camera.

"Hang on." and she moved them over, same thing. DJ pointed to the next, same thing.

All of the camera lenses were broken. On the last one JT signaled her to bring them up all of the way.

"I want to check inside to see if any thing in the casing could be the cause of the breakage." JT looked inside to compartment. There were traces of soot and burn marks inside.

"I think I know what caused this." He stuck out his hand and pointed down. Susan lowered them to the deck. JT went to the nearest inter-com and called down to the storage area. Tribec answered.

"Chief, this is JT. Check if we have any camera units in stock?"

"Aye, Aye, Sir."------"Sir, we have twelve on hand."

"Bring five up to the 207 and some tools to change them. All five of the aft cameras have damaged lenses."

"Yes Sir, I'll be up in ten minutes. Would you ask SR to meet me at the elevator with the fork lift."

"Consider it done and thank you." JT walked over to Susan. "Meet Tribec at the elevator in about ten minutes. He'll have five cameras. To replace the ones here on 207." JT turned to Dick. "I'm sure the reason the lenses are broken is when she got hit. The heat created from the laser was too intense for them. You could see the soot and burn marks in the compartments. If anyone can change them in record time, it'll be Tribec."

Tribec came over to the 207 while Susan carried the skid of cameras. He set the toolbox in the people box and climbed in, motioning for her to raise him up. She took him to where he wanted by hand signals. Tribec looked the compartment over and then the camera.

"Sir I'm going to change the lenses on this camera, then check it out. Usually when things get a little to hot in these compartments it's the lenses that go. The cameras are encased in a pretty secure housing. They have to be because of the forces working against them."

Tribec changed the lenses, then opened a panel on the side and attached a monitor to it. He pushed a lever back and forth. Everyone could see the camera moving.

"Working perfect, Sir. I'll just change the others and I believe you'll be in good shape." It took Tribec all of twenty minutes to complete the job. DJ had gone back into the ship and had checked the cameras out one by one. By moving them to point around the bay and also into outer space. He had it all down on film. Susan secured the people box and then took the skid of cameras back to the elevator. And then secured the forklift. She walked over to the monitor that was set up for the crews of the SS's.

"God, what's that ugly thing."

"That's you at close range." DJ said "I needed a subject for a close up. You were handy. You know, you're right, you are ugly close up." With that statement DJ took off at a dead run with Susan close on his heels. Swearing she was going to kill him if she caught him. One thing about DJ, he was fast on his feet.

***

The crews of the ships were at the pilot area talking about the flight that morning. JT walked over and sat down.

"I don't think we'll conduct any more war games this afternoon, just concentrate on maneuvers. Dad, if you'll go with Dick, I'll go with Triga. We'll start with standard S turns and then go to two-minute turns. Then we'll go into Immelmans and then to Split 'S's. These are all easy to learn and are very effective in loosing someone on your tail or for going in the other direction real quick."

"Dick, Triga, we're going to throw the book away while we're out there. I want you two to snap those SS's around like you were going to break them. If they break now, that's good, we'll fix it. If one breaks in combat, you might just be kissing your backside good-by. We're going to shake, rattle and roll out there this afternoon. I'll meet you all at the docking bay at 1400. We'll take off at 1430, OK.

"Aye, Aye, Sir" was all that he heard.

"By the way, Triga what was that meat we had for lunch? It tasted like venison."

"That's exactly what it is. On the first ten trips to the Alpha planet the ships brought only animals, which could be used for food. There are deer, elk, cows, sheep, and swine. Also, many, many types of birds. The birds were all mating pairs. The transporting of these animals started at your year 1875. It took eight weeks at sub light speed to transport them from one planet to the other. Some of your big cats are there also. The herds have to be kept in check some how."

"I have never been on the planet but I was there to replenish supplies. There are vast plains with plenty of feed. The average rainfall is approximately thirty-five inches. Some mountain ranges there have your snow on them year round. It is a beautiful planet. We have kept it a secret for over a hundred and fifty years of your time. One SS tried to get a pair of your Elpants but the beam was not strong enough to lift them."

Dick looked a little strangely at her and she stopped. "OH, you mean Elephants, okay. Please, go on, I didn't mean to interrupt you."

"We took pairs of animals which were on your endangered species list and brought them out also. We tried to get pairs of whatever you had on earth out here. There are no poisonous creatures there that I know of. All I know is what I have read and heard."

JT looked at Triga. "You're a wealth of information. How did you get the larger animals here? There are no capsules larger enough. You didn't let them run loose in the ships, did you?"

"The larger animals were brought on board. Eggs were taken from the females and placed in containers. Seaman extracted from the males then eggs were fertilized. The host animals were released.

Once at Alpha these containers were place in an incubator. The animals were then turned loose."

"You should talk with Chief Gorex. He has been there three times. The last time he was there for over one of your years."

"You keep saying, one of your years, or two of your years. How do the Arians record time?"

"Because of our physical differences, we actually live longer than you earthlings. Two of your years is a span to us. In your way, six months is one year to us. So if you lived to be eighty, I would live to one hundred and sixty. We both would age approximately at the same rate. Captain Eugin was one hundred and forty two of your years but in our time it was only seventy one spans."

***

At exactly 1300 hours Captain Mayhan knocked at the door to the bridge and reported.

"Sir, Mayhan, Mary A, Captain, United States Air Force, reporting as ordered, Sir." and stood at attention in front of the main console. Her eyes were riveted six inches over Dirks head. She was trying to bore a hole through the wall.

Dirk did not put her at ease but sat there looking at her for a minute or so. What I see in front of me is well formed female, no fat, muscular build. Keeps in shape. According to what I know of her, she's an Instructor Pilot on the F16 (bug). She had the good life at Holoman, AFB. Got there because she's good and also because she a female. She was beamed up about the time all of the 'Bull shit' was happening in the Navy. She's an average pilot. A real good one when she doesn't let her emotions get the best of her. Normally, I'd put her mess cooking for the major screw up she did today. But we need every pilot we can get our hands on.

"Captain, what you did today was not in any way, shape or form, conduct becoming to an Officer of the United States Armed Forces. You have, I believe an attitude problem. Whether or not it's ego or feminist, I don't give a damn. You, above all, should know what's going on here and what we, as a crew, are trying to accomplish. You threw all of that away with your fancy flying. The one thing that really pisses me off, Captain, is Susan at age sixteen could have shot your ass down. That was the worst display of flying I have ever seen. All JT did was fake a left, slam on the brakes and you flew right by his nose. He killed you, then he jumped on your tail and killed you again. Lady, excuse me, Captain, if that is how the Air Force teaches it's pilot's now, the U.S.A. is in for a lot trouble."

"Captain, you broke the faith today. If I were Dick Jones I'd come looking for you and kick your ass. You got him killed along with his crew. Which is, in this case, his family. If you had John flying with you, would you have pulled that stunt? Don't answer that. I don't want to hear your voice. If I---, we didn't need pilots for the up coming engagement, I'd ground you right here and now. You'd be counting mess kits and dirty dishes. You had better throw the manual away you teach from. Out here in the real world, it's brains and a big set of balls that's going to save your ass. Not books and tests. Your wingman just might save your ass sometime. This is not your private Air Force, Captain."

"One other thing, LT. Chambers stayed behind last night to say there are other people, which are senior to him, that should have had the job. I appointed him because he's an excellent pilot, he can think on his feet and he gets things done even if he has to do it himself. Maybe you ought to start thinking like that. Captain Mayhan, if I were you I'd go to my quarters and reflect. You are dismissed."

***

Mary took one step backward and saluted. Did a right face and marched out of the bridge. She went straight to their quarters, opened the view panel and sat there staring out into space. She was mentally exhausted. This had been the worst day of her life. She searched her mind. I'm the one to blame. It was me and me alone. JT gave me two options and I hung myself out to dry. It was my damned ego and pride that got in my way. I'm damn good at what I do. I really am not fit to Command, at least not yet. "At least not yet". There goes my ego again. The rules and regulations of the Air Force have been pounded into me for so many years, I can no longer think and act on my own. Is that it, I can no longer think and act as an individual. I surely wasn't thinking straight out there today or for that matter, the past two weeks either.

Mary sat there and reflected on her life up to date. Finding her self wanting in some cases. She felt the ship shudder a once and then again. There they go She started to cry. She fell over on the couch and cried herself to sleep. She didn't feel the ships land when they came back in.

***

At 5:00 PM John came in with two trays. He set them down on the coffee table in front of the couch, knelt down and gently shook Mary. She woke up, saw John and smiled.

God, she's got a beautiful smile "Hi babe, you hungry?" She nodded and stood up. John held his arms out and she literally fell into them, put her head on his chest and started to cry again. John held her and letting her get the hurt out of her system. She was talking and sobbing and crying all at the time. John couldn't understand a word of it. But he could understand the hurt she was feeling. When she stopped, he took her into the bathroom and ran some water. He cleaned up her face and took her back out to the couch and pointed to the meal.

"Eat."

Mary ate. She felt better after. "I really screwed the pooch, didn't I?"

"Yeah Babe, you did."

"What can I do to make this up?"

"Try being yourself and not some premadonna. I feel this is my fault. I didn't see it coming because I was to busy wrapped up in my own ideas. I didn't take the time to see what was happening with you."

"When I felt the ships taking off, I knew all I wanted to do is fly. And now I can't because of my stupid pride. I don't know how or what to do, right now. I feel so lost."

"Things always have a habit of working out for the best, Babe, Just hang in there.

"Do you know where JT is?"

"He was in the galley with Sam eating when I got the trays"

"I've got to talk to him."

Mary started to call around the ship trying to find JT.

The last place she tried was the 205. Sam answered the call.

"205. Ensign Chambers."

"Sam, this is Mary. Is JT there?"

"Yes, he is. He, Gunny, Triga and Dick are up in the bridge. He said not to disturb them, unless it was the Captain or someone was bleeding and near death."

"Would you tell him I called and would like to see him, Please."

"I'll tell him, Mary."

Sam got the coffee and then went back up to the bridge. They were just as she had left them. All hunched over a star chart. She set the tray down.

"Mary called and would like to see you."

JT looked up and nodded. He didn't look too happy about that. Sam stepped over to JT and in a soft voice said.

"Do it, Hon. Right now she needs a little reassurance."

JT smiled at her. "I'll do it, thanks." JT leaned back over the chart. "Ladies and Gents, I think we will go with plan 'B'. The Skipper didn't ground her.

Gunny looked around, "Well, I'll bet he took a sizeable chunk off her back side. She didn't leave her quarters all afternoon."

"How do you know that, you were flying all afternoon?" JT said.

"Lieutenant Chambers, You have forgotten, I'm the Gunny. I know what's going on all the time."

"Let's run through this one more time and see if we can punch some more holes in it. I don't want to take a piece of garbage up to the Skipper."

They went through Plan 'A', which is with four ships, Plan 'B' is with five ships. Everything looked good. JT stepped over to the inter-com "205 to bridge."

"Bridge"

"Captain, this JT could I have a minute of your time, Sir. I have a plan worked up."

"Report at 1930."

"Aye, Aye, Sir." JT switched the inter-com off and turned "I'm hungry."

"You just ate two hours ago."

"Well, I'm hungry again. If this works out, no booze, it's got to be clear heads tomorrow."

They all went to the galley to get a snack. JT made a big milk shake and looked as though he was thoroughly enjoying it.

***

At 1925 JT got up and went to the bridge. He knocked and went in.

"Captain."

"Come in Lieutenant Chambers. What have you got there?"

"Sir, this is a tentative battle plan for the up coming event."
"Spread it out and let's take a look."

JT went to the Nav table and set out the star chart and the three plans that he had made up. The Captain looked at them.

"I see you have three plans here. One for four ships and one for five. What is this one, plan C? Oh, I see just in case they're not where we think they are."

"Yes, Sir. I didn't know if Captain Mayhan had been grounded or not. Sir."

"I feel that decision should be made by you. Although, I did agree with what you said to Captain Mayhan this morning. I'm dumping it back into your lap, Lieutenant. You're her boss."

"Ahhhh----, Sir, how do you know what I said to her this morning?"

"It's the design of the docking bay. You can hear people talking anywhere around the edge. I don't think anyone knew until this morning."

"I feel a little embarrassed for both, Captain Mayhan and the crew."

"Don't be, it couldn't have been helped. One thing, the crew now knows you will accept nothing but the best from each of them. Also there will be no independent action when there are two or more ships in a formation. Let's go over these plans."

The Skipper asked a few questions as JT told of the plans.

"Isn't this 0515 takeoff about twelve hours ahead of schedule."

"Yes Sir, Lieutenant Triga states that on all Arian ships reveille is at 0700. They should be at breakfast."

"Where do you plan to have your ships stationed at the time of departure."

"The 202, 205 and 207 will be ready to jump to light speed at 5:13 AM. The Oz, 204 and 208, will jump to light speed at 5:15 AM. That will put the SS's at these points here, here, here, here and here, Sir. The Oz will be here. The 207 will be in the center low and the 205 will be on your right and the 202 will be on your left. The 204 will be on your right flank and the 208 will be on your left."

"I noticed the 208 is always on the left, why?"

"Sir, Triga is left handed. She is more comfortable on the left. She's doing much better now that I've showed her how I wanted the ships to be flown. She has an aggressive nature, but it was suppressed at the Academy. I understand they want meek and mild, try not to break our machines, type people. The truth is she can out fly Captain Mayhan."

"This a good plan, we'll go with it. In fact, all three plans are good. I'll call an all hands meeting at 2030 in the docking bay. You'll give the plan out then. It's 2000 now, that should give you enough time to do what you think is right."

"Aye, Aye Sir." JT gathered up the star chart and the plans and left the bridge.

***

He went directly to the Chiefs quarters and found Gorex. "Chief, how do you feel about flying with Captain Mayhan? Truth?"

"She scares me. The last two times we went out, it was like she was trying to show the universe she is the very best. Sir, are you ordering me to fly with her?"

"No Chief, that decision is yours and yours alone to make. It is strictly voluntary."

Gorex thought for a minute. "Yes Sir, I'll fly with her."

JT looked hard at Gorex while he was making up his mind. "Very well, Chief. Thank you for being honest. Would you mind if I said that to her, about her scaring people?"

"No Sir, I told her myself today coming back in."

"Chief Tribec, I'm asking you the same question about Triga. Truth?"

"Yes Sir, I'll fly with her."

"Very well, thank you gentlemen.

***

JT went to the Mayhan quarters and knocked at their door. John came to the door.

"Is Captain Mayhan available?"

This is not a social visit. The Skipper is all business now. And I don't blame him thought John. "Come in, JT."

Mary was sitting on the couch but stood up when JT came in.

"Thank you, John, Good evening Captain." JT went over to the coffee table, set the Star chart and the plans down. He looked at Mary.

"Captain, can you be ready for a 0515 jump to light speed tomorrow?"

"Yes Sir."

"There is going to be a crew briefing at 2030 at the docking bay. I'll be going over the plans. I wanted you to see the set up first." And he opened the star chart. As she looked down and read the chart and the plan, JT could see her facial expression change.

"This is plan 'B'." and handed it to her. The meaning was quite clear to her.

Just then the Captains voice came over the inter comm. "Attention all hands, there will be an all hands meeting in the docking bay at 2030. This is for all hands."

JT looked at his watch "It's almost time."

"I've got to go to the head, you two go on ahead and I'll see you there. Save me a seat, Hon." John said.

"OK Hon." Mary said.

That was very astute of him. He knows I would like to talk to her some more, but in private. Also she'll be seen walking in with the Commander

JT held the door for her and they stepped out into the passageway.

Before I came here, I stopped at the Chief's quarters and spoke to Gorex." He looked at Mary "He said, you scare him. But he volunteered to fly with you."

"Yes Sir, he told me that to on the way back today."

"Are you going to have a problem with that?"

"No Sir."

"Call me JT."

"No Sir, not yet."

Walking into the briefing area, JT went over to where Sam was sitting. Mary found two seats, for her and John. Dirk walked in JT called "Attention on Deck" and everyone stood.

"As you were." replied Dirk.

John came in and sat next to Mary. Dirk stood by the display board and briefed everyone about the upcoming trip. He then turned the briefing over to JT.

"At 0513 the 202, 205 and the 207 will jump to light speed. The courses will be preset in the main computers on each ship. The first course will be 055 degrees to this point. Then a course change to 354 degrees. This will be the final destination, here."

"At 0515 the Oz with the 204 and 208 will jump to light speed. The courses will be the same. As soon as we stop and I do mean stop. We should have Ozzie Too and the other two SS's boxed in. We will give them one minute to surrender. If not, John will fire a single ping."

"During the one minute time limit the 204 and 208 will extend to these points, here and here. Guarding the starboard and port quarters of Oz. The 202 will be here on your left, 208. And straight ahead from you, 204. The 207 will be low center behind the Ozzie Too. 205 will be here on your right, 204. Directly in front of you, 208."

"With six heavily armed star ships looking down his throat, the smart thing for him to do is put his hands up and hope for the best. If for any reason we have to fire at the other ships, we will use lasers at 50 percent. All that does is knock them out. We don't want to hull those ships. Once the big ship has surrendered the SS's should follow suit. Shoot to kill only if you are fired upon. Don't play games with them. You shoot, then we'll ask some questions. If there are any other type ships there, knock out the 'Ozzie Too' and the two SS's, then go after the others. Don't hang around to watch."

"The 204 and 208 will team up and attack if needed. Depending which side the intruders come from, that side will be the lead ship.

204 if they come at you, the 208 will be your wingman. vice-a-versa. Are there any questions so far?"

"All right, it might be hard for Triga, Gorex and Tribec to shoot one of their fellow countrymen but remember what happened to Captain Eugin. They will be shooting at you. I've grown fond of you all. I don't want to see you hurt or killed. Once we have them subdued, the Command of the SSs will fall back to Captain MacGlashan. Any questions--------No. OK, the flight crews will muster here at 0430. That is all I have, Captain."

"The only other thing I have to say is, 'let's get ready tomorrow is going to be a long day'." Dirk started to leave.

"Attention on deck."

Everyone hung around awhile and talked. Sam looked over to JT and motioned with her head, they said good night to all and headed toward their quarters. The others followed suit. 0400 was going to come around to fast.

***

Back in their quarters Mary took John to the bed and started to take his clothes off. They made love the first time like it was going to be their last. The second time was very slow and they enjoyed each other. Mary had loosened up and was back to her old self again.

***

Kat and Dirk lay in each other's arms. She ran her fingers though the hair on Dirks chest. "Do you like the name Conalea for a little girl."

"I suppose. Yeah, it has a nice ring to it. Why do you ask?" "What about Conalea Lyn MacGlashan?"

Dirk sat straight up and looked down at Kat. "Are you telling me what I think you're telling me?"

Kat looked up and smiling nodded her head. She reached up and pulled him back down.

"When did you find out? How far along are you? When is she due?"

"Whoa, easy big feller, Today, about a month and a half, sometime around the third week of June, 2000 AD."

"I've got to wait that long for a daughter. Wait, how do you know it's going to be a girl?"

"All of the women in my family have had a girl first. I'm talking every woman, bar none. First we get a Conalea, then we'll work on a Conal, I promise."

"Kat, you don't know how happy this makes me." They fell asleep holding each other.

***

Dirk was up and out of bed at 0345, showered and shaved and was down at the galley at 0400. The flight crews came in and had a big breakfast.

At 0430 the five flight crews were in the briefing area, each had a cup of coffee. Susan was there with her mother and Gunny. <u>No need to ask where she's going</u> thought Dirk.

JT stood at the view panel. "Does everyone have a copy of Plan 'B'?"

Everyone nodded and said. "Yes".

"OK let's set our watches with Oz." and he looked up at the clock. "0440 on my mark." Everyone set their watch to 0440 and zeroed the second hand.

"Three, Two, One, Mark. Set the clocks on your ships to this time. Everyone will monitor UHF 121.5, we'll use it for a master channel. 204 and 208 will use channel 'Alpha' and we three will use channel 'Baker'. You will notice there is a Plan 'C' attached. This is an alternate route and meet up in case something goes screwy at Point Intersect.

We are to be logged as U.S.A.S.F., TF-101 (United States of America Space Force, Task Force number 101). Remember, Fly safe and be safe."

"Let's go warm up and be on station five minutes before jump time. As Sam and I say 'It's time to Kick-Ass', let's mount up."

They started toward their ships. Jasper was standing at the end of the isle, handing each one a shoulder patch. Mary was the first to get one, "Well, I'll be go-to-hell, Yeah." It was a four inch in diameter round patch, showing a boot kicking a donkey. On the top half of the circle it said, 'KICK-ASS SQUADRON' and on the bottom 'U.S.A.S.F.----T.F-101'.

Susan, RJ and Reb yelled, "All right", and at the same time made a fist and kicked out a foot and then high fived.

The display brought morale to an all time high. Both Dirk and Gunny thought. <u>Now we have a squadron.</u>

JT was the last to go by. "Jasper, you're a Prince among men."

"Sir, this is my ship and you all are my family now. This small patch will help bring us all together." And Jasper took a step back and saluted. JT gave him the sharpest Marine salute he could, in return.

When all the ships were on station and ready JT came over 121.5. "All ships, recheck to see if everything is rigged in." He had his aft cameras on, checking each ship himself. Everyone was OK. He rigged the cameras in, making sure they were secured. He switched the selector to talk on the transceiver and watched the clock.

"You all set Sam?"

"As ready as I'll ever be, but I'm as nervous as a cat on a hot tin roof."

"Me too."

"205, 207 on my mark. Three, Two, One, Mark."

Three streaks of white light shot straight away from Oz.

"204, 208 on my mark, Three, Two, One, Mark."

Three more ships left streaks of white light fading out behind them.

***

"Scaner you've got the ship." JT said. "KMA"

"Yes, Sir."

Sam stood up. "Give me your flight jacket."

JT handed her the jacket. She went to their quarters and sewed the patches on the left sleeve up by the shoulder. Coming back to the bridge, she saw JT at the fire control station checking the firing selector switch panel. He looked up.

"Two of these have got to be replaced. They're starting to get sloppy. Here I'll show you what I mean." He took her hand placed it on one and moved it. "See".

"Yes." She tried the other ones. "This one and that one are bad."

"Right, I'll go get two from stores."

"Here, how does this look?"

"Great, you're amazing, you can cook, sew, shoot, fly a space ship and your great in bed. I believe I'll keep you."

Sam cocked back a fist. "Don't get flip Buster, I'll nail ya."

Holding up his hands. "I quit, I quit." and smiled.

JT left, went to the storeroom, got two switches and went back to the fire control panel.

"While I'm doing this, call the others for a check in."

"205 from 202 check in, over."

"202 from 205, 5 by 5, and we're CYAing, over.

"Susan is that you? over."

Susan's voice came back over the air. "No unnecessary talking over the channel. Out."

Sam looked at JT "Did you hear that? Fresh brat."

"I guess she told you off, huh. I'll bet Gunny told her what to say."

"I wouldn't be to sure of that."

"207 from 202, check in. Over."

"202 from 207, all's well, 5 by 5, CMA please, out."

"What in the hell is CMA?" Sam asked.

"Cover My Ass, remember he's out in front and in the middle."

***

Time has a habit of flying by when you're not watching the clock.

"Twenty minutes to touch down. It's time to do a radar check."

At 0715, JT switched the radar from sniff to emit. Searching the area ahead, nothing. "202 to 205 and 207, emit radar and check. I get no joy."

"Click, Click"

"Click. click"

JT swung the radar sweep from 60 degrees left to fifteen degrees right, still nothing. Where in the hell are they?

"205 to 202, no joy."

"Roger

"207 to 202, no joy."

"Roger"

JT flipped up plan 'C', calculated, six minutes to point x-ray.

"202 to 205 and 207 In five point five minutes execute plan 'C', I repeat plan 'C'. Mark.

JT switched to the guard freq. "Oz this is 202"

"202 this is Oz, go"

"We have no joy, I repeat no joy, Am executing plan 'C' in four minutes on my mark.----- Mark."

"Roger on plan 'C', will comply. Oz out.

JT switched back to Baker channel. The minutes slowly ticked by.

"202 to 205 and 207, on my command execute, now, now, now." The two outer ships turned two degrees outward. One minute they turned back to the original course. One minute and all three ships stopped. Radar on, cameras rigged out and the view screen was opened. Two minutes went by and the other ships stopped as planned.

CHAPTER THIRTY-TWO

"All ships report." This came over the guard channel. Captain 'Mac' had taken over Command of Task Force 101. All the ships reported their sectors were clear.

"202 and 205 return ASAP, out."

JT and Gunny hammered down and returned to Oz, landed and went directly to the bridge.

"Alright, we know they are around here somewhere. Dirk point to the nav chart. JT, take the 204 with you and search this area. Gunny, take 207 with you and search this area. If you make contact don't engage, I repeat do not engage. Wait until help arrives, understood? JT inform the 208 I want her to maintain a guard on our six. We're helpless back there."

"Aye, aye, Sir.

"Good hunting."

JT and Gunny went to their ships and got underway. When the 202 cleared the bay door, JT did a roll to the left, dove down and under the Oz, heading straight at the 204.

"202 to 204, fall in on my right wing, sending mail on Alpha, hyper."

"Click, Click."

JT was coming up on Mary at a high rate of speed. Mary slammed the throttle forward and fell into position on JT's right, a little low. They looked like two runners in a relay race.

JT said. "Let's throttle back to 40 percent and maintain an altitude of ten miles. You search high and I'll search low."

Sam sang. "And I'll be in Scotland before you."

JT and Sam could hear Mary and Gorex laughing. The ice was broken. Mary was back on the team again.

"202 to Oz, no joy, out."

"Click, Click."

***

The minutes ticked by. Even at this altitude and the gravitational pull of the planet, they where doing Mach two. Still nothing.

"207 to Oz, Bingo, three bogeys on the ground floor." He gave the coordinates.

"Roger, 207 the Calvary is on the way. Scout pack one did you copy."

"Click, Click."

"Roger, come in angels thirty and spread."

"Click, Click."

"You got it, 204"

"10-4"

"You got a CB too."

"Not with me."

"Let's go to 80 percent"

"Click, Click."

They were there in six minutes. JT and Mary slowed down to 30 percent and came in at thirty thousand feet. The cameras were moving about like multi-eyed bug. Nothing was moving.

"Susan, strap on your six guns."

Susan's voice came back over the air. "We'll be okay."

Sam screamed. "You wear a laser. That's an order. I out rank you. I mean it."

"Alright, you don't have to shout."

Sam looked at JT, "I'm going to kick her butt so hard, she'll start to hum like a nail hit with a greasy hammer. Her sixteen-year old mouth is starting to piss me off. All I can think of is that

'Bastard' that tried to rape me. And I wasn't wearing a laser, like you told me to." Sam didn't know it but the 205 heard what she had just said along with the 207 and the 204.

Susan looked over to Gunny and her Mom. "Wow, no wonder she got upset."

"I hope you learned a lesson, young lady." Gunny said. "Safety rules are written in blood. Don't you ever forget that."

"Yes Sir."

"Gunny, I knew something awful had happened when that coded message came in." MJ said.

"Nothing happened back there. The key word was tried. That's a blessing and I'll bet she sleeps with a laser under her pillow."

Gunny landed and tested the out side air. The gas read out was almost the same as earth. Just a little more oxygen than Earth, but acceptable. Better a little more than not enough. Gunny lowered the elevator rails and rolled the elevator in place.

They went to the locker where the dart throwers were and each took one and an extra clip. When they reached the ground, the 207 had landed and so had Oz. Dirk had a head set on and told everyone to be very careful. The 202 and 204 landed and they also came out heavily armed. John elected to stay on board and monitor the systems. He watched the view screen and saw the different crews come up on the Ozzie Too. Dirk and Gunny went on board but were back out in two minutes. Both were gagging.

"They're all dead. There are twelve dead Arians in there. They have been executed, hands tied behind their back and shot in the back of the head. Sweet Jesus, how can anyone kill their own people like that." Dirk almost vomited just thinking about what he had seen.

Sam and JT had gone in the IV-206 and came out. JT shouted "It's empty" and then went over to the IV 201 and went inside. In about one minute Sam came running out and down the ramp. She grabbed the rail with one hand, spun around, bent over and vomited. JT slowly walked down the ramp saw Sam and got sick himself.

Gunny and MJ came running toward them. JT waved them off and straightened up. He went over to Sam and held her. JT looked at his father and shook his head. He motioned to his father to follow him. When they were out hearing.

"There are two Arians in there. Their hands were tied behind their backs and their heads were blown off. It looked like someone took a double barreled 12 gauge to them." JT said.

"That's what happened to the people on 'Ozzie Two' also. It's a shame what fanatics do. These Arians were probably just like Triga and Gorex and Tribec and the others. The only thing we can do now is to give them a proper burial." Gunny said.

***

They walked back over to the women just in time to hear.

"I'm going to punch her in the mouth."

"Hey Babe." JT asked. "Who are you going to punch in the mouth. Hummm.... Susan, right?"

Sam nodded.

Gunny looked at Sam and then MJ. "I'll take care of this."

He walked to MJ and leaned over and whispered in her ear. Sam and JT saw her face get red. Gunny went right on walking.

Susan saw Gunny walking toward her. She smiled at him. He motioned for her to come to him. She met him more than half way and stopped. She didn't like the gleam in his eye. <u>Shit, I've done nothing, so why is he looking at me for like that?</u>

"Do you what's worse than a gossip?" She shook her head.

"A blabber mouth. If I hear one word out of you about what we overheard. I take my belt off and you will be eating your meals standing up for a least a week."

Tears welled up in Susan's eyes. "I would never say anything about that to anyone. That's my sister. I would never do anything to hurt her."

"Baby, I'm sorry I talked to you that way but I had to know. It's your mother who's the blabbermouth." Gunny held out his arms and Susan flew into them sobbing. He hugged her close and said he was sorry again.

"Wipe you eyes, pretty girl and give me a smile. That's my girl. I'll be right back ."

Gunny strolled back over to MJ and the two kids.

"Why don't you and Sam go back over to the group and we'll be right along."

They left and Gunny turned

"Do you know what's worse than a gossip?" MJ shook her head. "A BAM with a blabbermouth. I went over to Susan about half cocked and it's your ass I should eat out. You might be her mother but she didn't need the shit you handed out. Now she's mad at Susan. I ought to take my belt off and let you stand up and try to eat."

"Don't you dare talk to me like that."

"I'll talk to you like that any damn time I feel like it. And besides I already did."

"Did what?"

"Dare."

"You son-of----" Gunny stopped her by wagging his finger at her.

"I don't think you want to finish that statement, do you?"

MJ just stood there with her mouth hanging open and her face getting red. She finally got herself collected and said "Damn you Gunny."

"That's better.

"Better?"

"Better than what you were going to call me. If there's a next time, try to act like a friend instead of a dolting old, back fence hanging gossip. Remember, you used to be a Marine. Let's go back to the group."

JT, Sam and Susan were standing there watching. They couldn't hear but they knew what was going on.

JT smiled. "I'll bet she hasn't had a good Marine chewing out in years, huh?" They all looked at each other and started to laugh. Gunny and MJ came over to the group.

***

Dirk looked around. "The first thing we have to do is bury these poor souls. Gunny, can you see to getting a common grave dug?"

"Aye, aye Sir."

"JT, Tribec, Gorex and Dick, let's get rebreathers and long gloves on and get these people ready for burial.

Sam, MJ and Mary, I'd like the three of you to man the lasers on board the ships. Something tells me whoever did this is not very far away."

Susan was starting to walk toward the 205 when three Balaracian ships came in. Tribec saw the laser of the lead ship light up. He ran toward Susan and pulled her to the safety of an out-cropping of rocks. The ship fired. The ground where Susan had been, was dug up and burning. The three ships moved apart and slowly came closer. The lead ship started to land.

JT switched on his inter comm. "Scaner?"

"Here, Sir."

"Close up the ship. On my mark, take the ship to twenty miles up and orbit. 110 percent all the way. We have intruders here."

JT could see the elevator being brought up and the hatch shutting. He waited until the lead ship had almost landed. "Mark." The 202 shot straight up. The alien ship on the left fired. This shot also hit the ground where the 202 used to be.

John got into action and fired a ping at the lead ship. It suddenly did a nosedive into the ground. The ship on the right raised, but was a little to slow to get a shot off. Everyone ran for their ships. Dirk could see the lead ship try to right itself.

"John, hit that ship again."

John fired another ping, this time the ship didn't move. He had the lasers locked on the ship to their left and fired. The beam struck the alien ship on the starboard side, knocking it to the left, away from their ships.

Mary and Gorex were the first to get airborne. Mary went to 100 percent. The Balaracian ship didn't stand a chance. Mary fired, the laser struck the ship just behind the storage area and came out below the bridge. The ship shuddered and started to loose altitude. She followed it down, and watched it crash against the side of small hill. Gorex marked the spot on the grid chart. They waited to see if anyone had survived. They saw no movement. Mary pushed the throttle to 110 percent and did a roll back and headed toward the landing area.

The ship that had been struck by the laser shot from Oz was trying to get away. Mary pulled in behind it and tried to raise it on the inter-com, no answer. She moved to the side and fired a laser shot across its bow. It slowed and turned to land. Mary lowered the 204 and fired another shot. Warning the pilot, this is not the spot where I want you to land. The pilot got the message real quick. It turned back toward the landing site, with Mary directly behind. You make one false move and it'll be your last.

JT call the 202. "Scaner, return."

"Roger, Sir."

"204 to Oz"

"Oz here, go."

"Am returning with one captured ship."

"Roger, will mark landing area for captured ship, sending another ship to help guide ship in,"

"Roger, 204 out."

John contacted the 207. "Your vector to 204 is 187 degrees, 155 miles. Assist in guiding alien ship to landing area."

Dirk walked away from the immediate area and with a hand laser marked a circle on the ground.

"John can you read me?"

"Roger, Sir."

"Keep your pinger trained on the alien ship. If it makes one wrong move, nail it.

"Roger."

Gunny and JT went over to the lead Balaracian ship and went around to the air lock hatch. JT opened a panel on the side of the ship and push the lever, which would open the hatch. 'Whoosh', a blast of air came out of the ship.

"God, don't these people ever wash." Gunny said.

"I don't think so, Dad. The one Sam and I shot smelled just like this. Maybe it's their natural odor."

They enter the ship, weapons out. No one was moving. There was one Balaracian by the shuttle bay door. JT went to it.

"It's dead. There's blood coming from its ears and mouth. I think the second ping was to much for it."

Arriving at the bridge, they found two more, strapped in the pilot and navigators chairs. They were dead also.

"Let's get them outside and open all the hatches. Air this thing out." Gunny said.

They unstrapped the aliens and carried them outside and laid them on the ground. Gunny carried the last one out while JT opened the hatches. He started the ship up and set the landing struts out, righting it.

Gunny came back in with Sam and MJ and the four of them looked the ship over. They found more housing modules, along with ground moving equipment.

"Looks like they were planning to stay a while." MJ said.

"I don't think this is where they were planning to stay. There's nothing here. The ground is to dry and hard. Not enough rain. The only thing you could grow here would be rocks." Gunny said. "Did you notice the amount of instruments in the control room. Compared to an SS, these look like clip wing Piper Cubs. It's a wonder these things can even get off the ground."

They got the ship secured and left.

Mary and Dick were coming in with the other Balaracian ship.

JT looked around. "Where's Scaner with the 202?"

Sam called the bridge on Oz. "John have you heard from 202?"

"Roger, the sensors on 202 picked up a group of people and Dirk sent him over to investigate and report."

The Balaracian ship landed and the ramp was lowered. An Arian came out, with his hands raised.

"That's Korac." Triga said

Dirk looked at Triga, "Tell him to lay face down on the ground and put his hands and feet out."

She did. Korac stood there and then said something to her. Before anyone could move Triga took out her laser and fired. Korac dropped like a stone.

"That ought to teach him not to call me a lay." She looked at Dirk. "He was one of the senior pilots that forced me, when I was at the Academy. I should have killed him."

"Captain, we have a report from Scaner."

"Let's hear it."

"There is an encampment of humans at these coordinates, and there are no ships in the area."

"Roger, instruct him to return. Gunny, you and JT tie this one up and stow him somewhere. We'll get to him later."

Gunny looked over to JT. "I've got just the place for him. Get a couple of rebreathers"

JT came back and they put on the units and picked up Korac. They took him into the 'Ozzie Too' and placed him on the holding table in the capsule room. And then turned on the holding beam.

"Let him smell this for a while. He's the one who did it."

"Couldn't this be considered cruel and unusual punishment."

"I would think so, but like I said, he's the one who did this." They went back out side.

JT walked over to Dirk, "Captain, where do you want to bury these people?"

Dirk looked around. "There's a good spot, just below that outcropping of rocks."

JT walked over to the rest and told them to stand back a safe distance. "I'm going to dig a hole the easy way. Triga, let's take the 204 up and dig a hole."

"How are we going to do that?"

"With the laser. We'll blast a hole."

While JT and Triga were doing that, Kat and Clare went to the Oz and got fifteen mattress covers out of stores. These would serve as burial shrouds.

It took about ten minutes to blast a hole in the ground. Triga landed the 204 and shut her down. Everyone walked over to the hole the laser had made. It was about eight feet deep and at least twenty feet long by about seven feet wide.

Dirk studied the hole. Laser digging might be the thing of the future

The remains of the aliens were place in the shrouds, carried to the burial site and laid to rest. Dirk held a short service and the men set to work covering the grave.

***

The Ozzie Too was cleaned and fumigated. After the work was accomplished, all of the ships were made ready for flight. Neither of the SSs had fifteen-karat crystals in them and Ozzie Too was running on one crystal. Dirk called the crews over.

"We have got to get these ships over to the camp site Scaner found. Lieutenant Triga, you operate the Ozzie Too. Ensign Chambers take over the 208. DJ, you take the 206 and Susan you take the 201, Scaner will go with you. What I want is, each of the old pilots take a new one as a wingman. 208 your wingman to 202, 206 your wingman to the 205, and 201 your wingman to 207.

204 fly rear guard."

Aye, Aye, Skipper."

"We take off in pairs. 202 you're first and then this pair, this pair, the Ozzies, then the 204. Let's do it."

The small fleet went airborne. The 201 and 206 were a little shaky but soon settled out. Gunny and Dick had trained the young student pilots well. TF-101 flew the one thousand or so miles at twenty thousand feet and had a chance to look over the terrain. Once they had cleared a small mountain range they came upon a lush, green plain.

Animals grazing all over. Something like Great Plains of America would have looked like around 1750 AD.

"Oz to 202 and 208"

"202 here"

"208 here"

"Scout ahead and report."

"Click, click"

"208, go to 80 percent and spread." The two craft shot ahead and spread out a short distance, cameras on. Flying at that speed in took about twenty minutes to get to the location area.

"202, Bingo. I have the camp site in view, thirty miles, bearing 020 from me."

"Roger 208, let's go take a look."

"Oz this is 208, I see three pads large enough for the 'Ozzies' and eight smaller pads. We've spotted eight humans on the ground next to the buildings. There are eight large buildings and several smaller out buildings, over."

"Oz to 202 and 208, do not land, wait for fleet. Stand guard, out."

"Click, Click"

"Click, Click."

WATCH FOR THE CONTINUEING SAGA AT YOUR LOCAL BOOK STORE